SPECIAL MESSAGE TO READERS

THE ULVERSCROFT FOUNDATION
(registered UK charity number 264873)
was established in 1972 to provide funds for
research, diagnosis and treatment of eye diseases.
Examples of major projects funded by
the Ulverscroft Foundation are:-

- The Children's Eye Unit at Moorfields Eye Hospital, London
- The Ulverscroft Children's Eye Unit at Great Ormond Street Hospital for Sick Children
- Funding research into eye diseases and treatment at the Department of Ophthalmology, University of Leicester
- The Ulverscroft Vision Research Group, Institute of Child Health
- Twin operating theatres at the Western Ophthalmic Hospital, London
- The Chair of Ophthalmology at the Royal Australian College of Ophthalmologists

You can help further the work of the Foundation
by making a donation or leaving a legacy.
Every contribution is gratefully received. If you
would like to help support the Foundation or
require further information, please contact:

THE ULVERSCROFT FOUNDATION
The Green, Bradgate Road, Anstey
Leicester LE7 7FU, England
Tel: (0116) 236 4325

website: www.foundation.ulverscroft.com

Cecelia Ahern has sold 16 million copies of her books worldwide, capturing the hearts of readers in 46 countries. She wrote her debut novel, *PS, I Love You*, when she was twenty-one years old, and it became an international bestseller as well as a major motion picture. She is also the co-creator and producer of several TV series, including the award-winning ABC comedy series *Samantha Who?*.

You can discover more about the author at:
Website: www.cecelia-ahern.com
Twitter: @Cecelia_Ahern
Facebook:
www.facebook.com/CeceliaAhernofficial

HOW TO FALL IN LOVE

Adam Basil and Christine Rose are thrown together late one night, when Christine is crossing Ha'penny Bridge in Dublin. Adam is there, poised, threatening to jump. He is desperate — but Christine makes a crazy deal with him. His 35th birthday is looming and she bets him that before then, she can show him life is worth living. Despite her determination, Christine knows what a dangerous promise she's made. Against the ticking clock, the two of them embark on wild escapades, grand romantic gestures and some unlikely late-night outings. Slowly, Christine thinks Adam is starting to fall back in love with his life. But has she done enough to change his mind for good? And is that all that's starting to happen?

Books by Cecelia Ahern
Published by The House of Ulverscroft:

PS, I LOVE YOU

CECELIA AHERN

◆

HOW TO FALL IN LOVE

Complete and Unabridged

CHARNWOOD
Leicester

First published in Great Britain in 2013 by
HarperCollins*Publishers*
London

First Charnwood Edition
published 2014
by arrangement with
HarperCollins*Publishers*
London

The moral right of the author has been asserted

Copyright © 2013 by Cecelia Ahern
All rights reserved

This novel is entirely a work of fiction. The names,
characters and incidents portrayed in it are the
work of the author's imagination. Any resemblance
to actual persons, living or dead, events or localities
is entirely coincidental.

*A catalogue record for this book is available
from the British Library.*

ISBN 978–1–4448–2162–8

Published by
F. A. Thorpe (Publishing)
Anstey, Leicestershire

Set by Words & Graphics Ltd.
Anstey, Leicestershire
Printed and bound in Great Britain by
T. J. International Ltd., Padstow, Cornwall

This book is printed on acid-free paper

For David,
who taught me how to fall in love

1

How to Talk a Man Down

They say lightning never strikes twice. Untrue. Well, it's true that people say it; it's just untrue as a fact.

NASA-funded scientists discovered that cloud-to-ground lightning frequently strikes the ground in two or more places and that the chances of being struck are about forty-five per cent higher than what people assume. But what people mostly mean to say is that lightning never strikes the same location on more than one occasion, which is also untrue as a fact. Though the odds of being hit by lightning are one in three thousand, between 1942 and 1977 Roy Cleveland Sullivan, a Park Ranger in Virginia, was hit by lightning on seven different occasions. Roy survived all the lightning strikes, but he killed himself when he was seventy-one, shooting himself in the stomach over what was rumoured to be unrequited love. If people dispensed with the lightning metaphor and instead just said what they meant, it would be that *the same highly unlikely thing never happens to the same person twice*. Untrue. If the reasons behind Roy's death is true, heartbreak carries its own unique brand of sorrow and Roy would have known better than anyone that it was highly likely that this highly unlikely misfortune could

1

occur again. Which brings me to the point of my story; the first of my two highly unlikely events.

It was eleven p.m. on a freezing cold December night in Dublin and I found myself somewhere I had never been before. It is not a metaphor for my psychological state, though it would be apt; what I mean is that I literally had never geographically been to the area before. An ice-cold wind blew through the abandoned Southside housing development, causing an unearthly tune to play through broken windows and flapping scaffolding materials. There were gaping black holes where there should be windows, unfinished surfaces with menacing potholes and upturned flagstones, pipework-cluttered balconies and exit routes, wires and tubing that began randomly and ended nowhere, the place a stage set for tragedy. The sight alone, nothing to do with the minus-degree temperature, made me shudder. The estate should have been filled with sleeping families, lights out and curtains drawn; instead, the development was lifeless, evacuated by owners who had been left to live in ticking time-bombs with fire-safety concerns as long as the list of lies they were told by builders who failed to deliver on the promise of luxury living at boom-time prices.

I shouldn't have been there. I was trespassing, but that wasn't what should have concerned me; it was dangerous. To the conventional ordinary person it was unwelcoming, I should have turned around and gone back the way I came. I knew all these things and yet I ploughed on, debating with my gut. I went inside.

Forty-five minutes later I stood outside again, shivering, trembling and waiting for the gardaí as the 999 operator had instructed me to do. I saw the ambulance lights in the distance, which were quickly followed by the unmarked garda car. Out leapt Detective Maguire, unshaven, messy-haired, rugged if not haggard, whom I've since learned to be an emotionally hassled, pent-up jack-in-the-box ready to explode at any moment. Though his general appearance might have been a cool look for a member of a rock band, he was a forty-seven-year-old detective on duty, which took the stylish away from him and highlighted the seriousness of the situation I'd found myself in. After directing them to Simon's apartment, I returned outside to wait to relay my story.

I told Detective Maguire about Simon Conway, the thirty-six-year-old man I'd met inside the building who, along with fifty other families, had been evacuated from the estate for safety reasons. Simon had talked mostly about money, about the pressure of having to pay the mortgage on the apartment he wasn't allowed to live in, and the council, which had a case pending to stop paying for his replacement accommodation, and the fact that he had just lost his job. I relayed my conversation with Simon to Detective Maguire, what I'd said exactly already fuzzy, and I jumped between what I thought I'd said and what I realise I should have said.

You see, Simon Conway was holding a gun when I came across him. I think I was more surprised to see him than he was about my sudden appearance in his abandoned home. He seemed to assume I'd been sent there by the police to talk to him, and I didn't tell him that wasn't the case. I wanted him to think I'd an army of people in the next room while he held that black weapon in his hand, waving it around as he talked while I fought hard not to duck, dive and at times run from the room. While panic and fear welled inside me, I tried to coax him, soothe him into putting the gun down. We talked about his children, I did my best to show him a light in his darkness, and I managed to successfully talk Simon into putting the gun down on the kitchen counter so I could call the gardaí for help, which I did. When I hung up, something happened. My words, though innocent — and which I know now I should have left unsaid at that point — triggered something.

Simon looked at me, and I knew he wasn't seeing me. His face had changed. Alarm bells rang in my head but before I had a chance to say or do anything else, Simon picked up the gun and held it to his head. The gun went off.

2

How to Leave Your Husband
(Without Hurting Him)

Sometimes, when you see or experience something really real, it makes you want to stop pretending. You feel like an idiot, a charlatan. It makes you want to get away from everything that is fake, whether it is innocently and harmlessly so, or something more serious; like your marriage. This happened to me.

When a person finds themselves jealous of marriages that are ending, that person must know that theirs is in trouble. That's where I had found myself for the past few months in the unusual way when you can know something but not really know it at the same time. Once it had ended I realised that I'd always known the marriage wasn't right. When I was in the midst of it, I had felt moments of happiness and a general sense of hope. And while positivity is the seed of many a great thing, wishful thinking alone does not make a good foundation for marriage. But the event, the Simon Conway *experience*, as I was calling it, helped to open my eyes. I'd witnessed one of the most real things in my life and it made me want to stop pretending, it made me want to be real and for everything in my life to be true and honest.

My sister Brenda believed my marriage

5

break-up was due to a kind of post-traumatic stress disorder and pleaded with me to talk to someone about it. I informed her I was already talking to someone, the internal conversation had begun quite some time ago. And it had, in a way; Simon just hastened the eventual epiphany. This of course was not the response Brenda had in mind; she meant a conversation with someone professionally trained, not a drunken ramble over a bottle of wine in her kitchen at midnight, midweek.

My husband, Barry, had been understanding and supportive in my hour of need. He too believed that the sudden decision was a part of some ripple effect from the gun-blast. But when he realised — as I packed my belongings and left our home — that I was serious, he was quick to call me the most vile things. I didn't blame him, though I wasn't fat and had never been, and was intrigued to learn I was much fonder of his mother than he believed. I understood everyone's confusion and inability to believe me. It had a lot to do with how well I had hidden my unhappiness and it had everything to do with my timing.

On the night of the Simon Conway experience, after I'd realised the bloodcurdling scream had come from my own mouth, and after I'd called the police for the second time and statements had been taken for reports to be filed, after the Styrofoam cup of milky tea from the local EuroSpar, I'd driven home and done four things. First, I had a shower in an effort to cleanse myself of the scene; second, I thumbed my well-read copy of *How to Leave Your Husband (Without Hurting Him)*; third, I woke him with a coffee and slice of toast to tell him that our marriage was over; and fourth, when probed, I told him that I had witnessed a man shoot himself. In retrospect, Barry had more detailed questions about the shooting than about the end of our marriage.

His behaviour since then has surprised me, and my own astonishment equally shocked me, because I thought I was well-read on such matters. I had studied before this great big life test, I had read up on how we both would and could be feeling if I ever decided to end the marriage — just to prepare, to be aware, to figure out if it was the right decision. I've had friends whose marriages have ended, I've spent many late nights listening to both sides. Yet it never occurred to me that my husband would turn out to be the kind of man he became, that he would have a complete personality transplant, become as cold and vicious, as bitter and malicious as he has become. The apartment, which was ours, was now his; he would not let me step one foot inside it. The car which was ours was now his, he would not let me share it. And anything else that was ours, he was going to do everything in his power to keep. Even the things he didn't want. And that was a direct quote. If we'd had kids he would have kept them and never let me see them. He was specific about the coffee machine, possessive about the espresso cups, quite frantic about the toaster and had a rant about the kettle. I allowed him to flip out in the kitchen, as I did in the living room, the bedroom, and even when he followed me into the toilet to shout at me while I peed. I tried to remain as patient and as understanding as I possibly could. I was always a good listener, I could hear him out, what I wasn't so good at doing was explaining and I was surprised I needed to as much as he required. I was sure that deep down he felt the same about our marriage, but he was so hurt about it happening *to him* that he had forgotten how there were moments we both felt trapped in something that had been wrong from the beginning. But he was angry, and anger often deafens the ears to reality; his did, anyway, so I waited out the fits of rage and hoped that at some point we could talk about it honestly.

I knew that my reasons were right but I could barely live with the pain I felt in my heart over what I'd done to him. So I had that, and the fact I had failed to stop a man from shooting himself, weighing heavily on my shoulders. It had been months since I'd slept properly, now it felt as though I hadn't slept *at all* in weeks.

'Oscar,' I said to the client sitting in the armchair across from my desk. 'The bus driver does not want to kill you.'

'He does. He hates me. And you wouldn't know because you haven't seen him or the way that he looks at me.'

'And why do you think that the bus driver feels this way about you?'

He shrugged. 'As soon as the bus stops, he opens the doors then glares at me.'

'Does he say anything to you?'

'When I get on, nothing. When I don't, he kind of grumbles at me.'

'There are times when you *don't* get on?'

He rolled his eyes and looked at his fingers. 'Sometimes my seat isn't free.'

'Your *seat?* This is new. What seat?'

He sighed, knowing he'd been found out, and confessed. 'Look, everyone on the bus stares, okay? I'm the only one who gets on at that stop and they all look at me. So because they all stare I sit in the seat behind the driver. You know, the sideways one that faces the window? It's like a window seat, all tucked away from the rest of the bus.'

'You feel safe there.'

'It's perfect. I could sit in that seat all the way into the city. But sometimes there's this girl sitting there, this special needs girl, she listens to her iPod and sings Steps for the entire bus to hear. If she's there I can't get on and not just because special needs people make me nervous but because it's my seat, you know? And I can't see if she's on it until the bus stops. So I check the seat to see if it's free, then I get off if she's there. The bus driver hates me.'

'How long has this been going on?'

'I don't know, a few weeks?'

'Oscar, you know what this means. We're going to have to start this again.'

'Ah man.' He buried his face in his hands and slumped right down. 'But I was halfway into the city.'

'Be careful not to project your real anxiety

9

onto another future fear. Let's knock this on the head straight away. So, tomorrow you are going to get on the bus. You are going to sit *anywhere* there is a free seat on the bus and you are going to sit on it for one stop. Then you can get off and walk home. The next day, Wednesday, you will get on the bus, sitting *anywhere*, and you will stay on it for two stops and then walk home. On Thursday you will stay on for three stops, and on Friday for four stops, do you understand? You have to take it bit by bit, small steps and you will eventually get there.'

I wasn't sure who I was trying to convince. Him or me.

Oscar slowly lifted his face up. It had drained of all colour.

'You can do this,' I said gently.

'You make it sound so easy.'

'And it's not easy for you, I understand that. Work on the breathing techniques. Soon it won't be so difficult. You will be able to stay on the bus all the way into the city, and that feeling of fear will be replaced by euphoria. Your worst times will soon become your happiest because you will be overcoming huge challenges.'

He looked unsure.

'Trust me.'

'I do, but I just don't feel brave.'

'The brave man is not he who does not feel afraid, but he who conquers that fear.'

'One of your books?' He nodded at the packed shelves of self-help books in my office.

'Nelson Mandela.' I smiled.

'Pity you're in recruitment, you would make a

good psychologist,' he said, pulling himself up from the chair.

'Yeah, well, I'm doing this for both of us. If you can manage to sit on the bus for more than four stops it will broaden your job opportunities.' I tried to hide the tension from my voice. Oscar was a highly qualified whizz-kid scientist who I could easily get a job for — in fact I had, three times already — but due to his travel issues, his job opportunities were limited. I was trying to help him overcome his fears so I could finally place him in a job that he would show up to every day. He was afraid to learn how to drive and I couldn't stretch myself to becoming a driving instructor, but he had agreed to beat his public transport fear at least. I glanced at the clock over his shoulder. 'Okay, make an appointment for next week with Gemma, and I look forward to hearing about how you got on.'

As soon as the door closed behind him I dropped my smile and scoured the bookshelf for one of my 'How to . . . ' collections. Clients marvelled at the amount of books I kept, and I believed I alone kept my friend Amelia's small bookshop open. The books were my bibles, my go-to fix-it helpers when I was personally lost or needed solutions for troubled clients. I'd been dreaming of writing one for the past ten years but had never gotten any further than sitting at my desk and turning the computer on, ready, wired to tell my story, only to end up staring at the white screen and the flashing icon, the blankness before me mirroring my creative flow.

My sister Brenda said I was more interested in

the idea of writing a book than actually writing it, because if I really wanted to write, I just would, every day, by myself, for myself, whether it was a book or not. She said a writer felt compelled to write whether they had an idea or not, whether they had a computer or not, whether they had a pen and paper or not. Their desire wasn't determined by a specific pen brand or colour or whether their latte had enough sugar in it or not — things that were distractions and obstacles to my creative process whenever I sat down to write. Brenda often came out with pathetic insights but I feared that for once her observation of me might be true. I wanted to write, I just didn't know if I could and if I ever made a start I was afraid I'd discover that I couldn't. I'd slept with *How to Write a Successful Novel* by my bed for months but I hadn't opened the pages once, afraid that not being able to follow the tips would mean I could never write a book, so I hid it in the bedside locker instead, parking that particular dream until the time was right.

I finally found what I was looking for on the shelf. *Six Tips on How to Fire an Employee (With Pictures)*.

I'm not sure the pictures helped, but I'd had a go at standing in front of the bathroom mirror and trying to emulate the concerned look on the employer's face. I studied the notes I'd made on a Post-it inside the front page, unsure whether I was going to be able to do this. My company, Rose Recruitment, had been in operation for four years and was a small practice of four people, and our secretary Gemma helped us function. I didn't want to let her go, but due to increasing personal financial pressures I was having to consider it. I was reading my notes when there was a knock on the door, quickly followed by Gemma's entry.

'Gemma,' I squeaked, fumbling guiltily with the book in an effort to hide it from her. As I was stuffing it into an already crammed shelf, I lost my grip and sent it plummeting to the floor, where it landed at Gemma's feet.

Gemma giggled and bent down to pick up the book. Noting the title, she flushed. She looked at me, surprise, dread, confusion and hurt all passing on her face. I opened and closed my mouth, no words coming out, trying to remember which order the book had told me to break the news, the correct phrasing, the correct facial expressions, the tips, *clarity, empathy, not too emotional, communicate with candour or without candour?* But it took me too long and by then she already knew.

'Well, finally one of your stupid books worked,' Gemma said, her eyes filling as she dumped the book in my arms and turned, grabbed her bag and stormed out of the office.

Mortified, I couldn't help but be insulted by the emphasis on *finally*. I lived by these books. They worked.

★ ★ ★

'Maguire,' the unwelcoming voice barked down the phone.

13

'Detective Maguire, it's Christine Rose.' I put a finger in my free ear to block the sound of the ringing phone wailing through the wall from reception. Gemma still hadn't returned after storming out, and as I hadn't been able to bring everybody together to work out how to share Gemma's duties, my colleagues Peter and Paul were refusing to do the job of someone who had been unfairly dismissed. It was everyone against me, regardless of how many times I told them it had been a mistake. 'I didn't mean to fire her . . . today' was not a good defence.

It was quite simply a disastrous morning. But although it was obvious I needed to keep Gemma on — something I was sure Gemma was trying to prove — my bank balance disagreed. I still had to pay half the mortgage on the home Barry and I owned together, and from that month on I would have to fork out an extra six hundred euro to rent a one-bedroom apartment while I waited for us to sort it all out. Considering we'd have to sell an apartment that nobody wanted, for an eventual price that neither of us could really survive on, I imagined I would be digging into my savings for a very long time. And even in the event desperate times called for desperate measures, Barry had already waged a war on my jewellery collection, taking every piece he had ever given me and keeping it for himself. That was the voicemail I'd woken up to that morning.

'Yeah?' was Maguire's response, far from ecstatic to hear from me, though I was surprised he remembered my name.

14

'I've been calling you for two weeks. I've left you messages.'

'I got them all right, they clogged up my voicemail. There's no need to panic. You're not in any trouble.'

That knocked me off. It hadn't crossed my mind that I would be in any trouble. 'That's not why I was calling.'

'No?' he feigned surprise. 'Because you still haven't explained to me what you were doing in a deserted apartment block on private property at eleven o'clock at night.'

I was silent as I mulled this over. Almost everybody I knew had asked me the same thing, those who hadn't were clearly wondering about it, and I hadn't given anybody an answer. I needed to change the subject quickly before he tried to pin me down on it again.

'I had been calling to ask for further details on Simon Conway. I wanted to know the funeral arrangements. I couldn't find anything in the papers. But that was two weeks ago, so I've missed it.' I tried to keep the irritation out of my voice. I was calling him for more information, Simon had left an enormous hole in my life and endless questions in my head. I couldn't rest without knowing everything that had happened and had been said after that day, I wanted his family's details so I could tell them all the beautiful things he'd said about them, how he loved them so much and how his actions had nothing to do with them. I wanted to look them in the eye and tell them I had done all that I could. To ease their pain or ease my guilt? What was wrong with wanting both? I didn't want to sound so desperate as to ask Maguire those exact questions, and I knew he wouldn't tell me anyway, but I couldn't just draw a line under what I had experienced. I wanted, I needed *more*.

'Two things. Firstly, you shouldn't get so involved with any victim. I've been in this game a long time and — '

'Game? I watched a man *shoot himself in the head right before my very eyes*. This is not a *game* to me.' My voice cracked, which I took as a hint to stop.

There was silence. I cringed and covered my face. I'd blown it. I gathered myself and cleared my throat. 'Hello?'

I waited for a smart response, something cynical and cold, but it didn't come. Instead his voice was soft, the background wherever he was had gone quiet and I was worried everyone had stopped to listen to me.

'You know we have people in here to talk to after an event like this,' he said, gently for once. 'I told you that night. I gave you a card. Do you still have it?'

'I don't need to talk to anyone,' I said angrily.

'Sure.' He dropped the nice-guy act. 'Look, as I was saying before you interrupted me, there are no funeral details. There was no funeral. I don't know where you got your information but they've been telling you porkies.'

'What do you mean?'

'Porky pies, lies.'

'No, what do you mean, there was no funeral?'

16

He sounded exasperated at having to explain something that was glaringly obvious to him. 'He didn't die. Yet, anyway. He's in hospital. I'll find out where. I'll put a call through to them to let them know you're able to see him. He's in a coma though, won't be doing much talking.'

I froze, speechless.

There was a long silence.

'Is there anything else?' He was on the move again, I heard a door bang and then he was back to the room with the loud voices.

I struggled to formulate a single thought as I slowly sank into my armchair.

And sometimes when you witness a miracle it makes you believe that anything is possible.

3

How to Recognise a Miracle and What to Do When You Have

The room was still and quiet, the only sounds were the steady beeping of Simon's heart monitor and the whoosh of the ventilator as it assisted his breathing. Simon was the polar opposite of how I'd last seen him. Now he looked peaceful, the right side of his face and head bandaged, the left side serene and smooth as if nothing had happened. I chose to sit on his left side.

'I saw him shoot himself,' I whispered to Angela, the nurse on call. 'He held a gun up right here,' I gestured, 'And pulled the trigger. I saw his — everything — go everywhere . . . how did he survive?'

Angela smiled, a sad smile, not really a smile at all, just muscles working around her lips. 'A miracle?'

'What kind of a miracle is that?' I continued to whisper, not wanting Simon to hear me. 'I keep going over it, over and over in my head.' I'd been reading books about suicide and what I should have said, and they say that if you can get a person threatening suicide to think rationally, if they actually think about the realities of suicide and its aftermath, then they could, they *might* abort the decision. What they're looking for is a quick fix to end the emotional pain, not to end their lives, so if you can help them see another way to ease the pain then maybe you could help. 'I think, considering I had no experience, that I did okay, I think I really got through to him. I think he really responded to me. For a moment, anyway. I mean, he put the gun down. He let me call the guards. I just don't know what it was that sent him back into that head space.'

Angela frowned as though hearing or seeing something she didn't like. 'You know this isn't your fault, don't you?'

'Yeah, I know.' I shrugged it off.

She studied me, thoughtful, and I concentrated on the right wheel of the hospital bed, how it caused a black scuff mark when it was moved each time, lots of scuff marks back and forth, and I tried to count how many times it had been moved. Dozens, at least.

'You know there are people you can talk to about this kind of thing. It would be a good idea to get your concerns out.'

'Why does everyone keep saying that?' I laughed, trying to sound carefree but deep down feeling the anger burning my chest. I was tired of being analysed, tired of people treating me as though I was someone who needed to be handled. 'I'm *fine*.'

'I'll leave you with him for a while.' Angela stepped away, her white shoes silent on the floor as if she was floating.

Now that I had come, I didn't quite know what to do. I reached out for his hand but then stopped myself. If he was aware, perhaps he

19

would not want me to touch him, maybe he blamed me for what had happened. It had been my job to stop him and I hadn't. Perhaps he had wanted me to change his mind, he was willing me to say the right words but I'd failed him. I cleared my throat, looked around to make sure no one was listening and I leaned in closer to his left ear but not so close as to startle him.

'Hi, Simon,' I whispered.

I watched him for a reaction. Nothing.

'My name is Christine Rose, I'm the woman you spoke to on the night of . . . the incident. I hope you don't mind my sitting with you for a while.'

I listened for something, anything, and studied his face and hands for signs that he was upset by my presence. I didn't want to cause him any more pain. When all on the surface remained as it was, calm and still, I sat back in the chair and got comfortable. I wasn't waiting for him to wake up, I didn't have anything I wanted to say to him, I just liked being there, in the silence, by his side. Because when I was by his side I wouldn't be anywhere else, wondering about him.

At nine p.m., after visiting hours, I still hadn't been asked to leave. I guessed regular hours didn't count for someone in a condition such as Simon's. He was in a coma, on a life-support machine, and his condition wasn't improving. I spent the time thinking about my life and Simon's and how our coming together had irrevocably changed both of our lives. It had only been a few weeks since Simon's attempted suicide, but it had sent my life spiralling in another direction. I wondered if it was pure coincidence or if me being in that random place had been fate.

'What were you doing there?' Barry had asked me, confused, sleepy, sitting up in bed with his scrunched-up face, his tiny eyes enormous after he'd reached for his black-rimmed glasses on the bedside chest and put them on. I hadn't known how to answer him then; I wouldn't know how to answer him now. To say it out loud would be embarrassing, it would highlight how ludicrously lost I had found myself — the irony of that statement not lost on me.

Aside from what I was doing there, the fact I'd chosen to engage with a man with a gun in a deserted building was enough to cause me to question myself. I liked to help people but I wasn't sure it was just about that. I saw myself as a problem-solver and I applied that thinking to most aspects of life. If something couldn't be fixed, it could at least be changed, particularly behaviour. My belief system was born of having a father who was a fixer. It was in his nature to ask the problem and then set about fixing it as he did for his three girls growing up without their mother. Because he lacked Mum's instinct to know if things were right with us or not and he had no one else to discuss it with, he would question us, listen to the answer, then seek out the solution. It was his way and it was what he felt he could do for us. Left with three children under the age of ten, the youngest only four years of age, a father does what he can to protect his children.

I run my own recruitment agency, which sounds basic enough, only I prefer to think of myself as a match-maker, finding the right person for the right job. It's important to bring the right energy for the right company, and vice versa, what the company can do for a person. Sometimes it's just mathematics, an available job for an available person with the appropriate skills; other times, when I get to know the person, like Oscar, I really go beyond the call of duty when it comes to placing them. The people I deal with have different emotions about their goals, some because they've lost their jobs and are under great stress, others simply fancy a career change and are anxious but full of happy expectation, and then there are the ones who are stepping into the workplace for the first time, excited about new beginnings. Regardless, everyone's on a journey, and I'm in the middle of that. I've always felt the same responsibility for each of them — to help people find the right place in the world. And yet, using that philosophy, my words had landed Simon Conway in this room.

I didn't want to leave him alone, and returning to a borrowed flat with no television and nothing to do but stare at the four walls did not appeal to me. I had many friends who I could have stayed with, but as they were mutual friends of mine and Barry's, they were slow to offer, reluctant to get in the middle of the mess, to be seen to be taking sides, especially when it was me that was coming out looking like the bad one, the big bad wolf who'd broken Barry's heart. It was better for me not to put them through that stress. Brenda had invited me to come and stay with her, but I couldn't put up with my sister fretting about my supposed post-traumatic stress disorder. I needed to come and go as I pleased without any questions being asked, especially ones about my sanity. I wanted to feel free — that's why I'd left my marriage in the first place. The fact that I felt more at home in an intensive care unit than I did anywhere else said a lot.

* * *

So here was the thing I couldn't tell Detective Maguire, or Barry, or my dad and two sisters, or anybody, really. There was a specific place I was trying to find to make me feel better about myself. I learned this from a book: *How to Live in Your Happy Place*. The idea was to choose a place that made you feel uplifted. It could be somewhere you connected with a memory that enriched your soul or simply a place where you liked the light, or a place that made you feel content for a reason you couldn't recognise on a conscious level. Once you found that place, the book offered exercises to help you summon the same happy feeling you associated with that place absolutely any time and anywhere your heart desired, but it would only work if you had found the right place. I'd been looking. It's what I was doing on the building site the night I met Simon Conway. It wasn't the building site I was looking for, it was what used to be there before it became a building site. I had a happy memory there on that land.

It was a cricket match, Clontarf versus Saggart. I was five years old and Mum had died only a few months before and I remember it was a sunny day, the first after a long dark cold winter, and me and my sisters were there to watch Dad play. The entire cricket club was outside, I remember the smell of beer, and I can taste the saltiness on my lips from the packets of peanuts I was consuming one after another. Dad was bowling and it was close to the end of the match; I could see the intense look on his face, the look we'd been seeing every day for the past few weeks, the dark look with his eyes practically lost beneath his eyebrows. He went for his third bowl and the guy batting completely misjudged his swing and missed. The ball hit the wicket and the guy was out. Dad yelled so loudly and punched the air with such ferocity, everyone around us erupted in cheers. It frightened me at first, watching the mass hysteria, like they'd all caught some weird virus that I'd seen in a zombie movie and I was the only one who hadn't been affected, but then as I watched Dad's face I knew that it was okay. He was wearing the biggest smile, and I remember the looks on my sisters' faces. They weren't too bothered about cricket either — in fact they'd moaned the entire way over in the car because they were being taken away from playing with their friends on the road — but they were watching him celebrating, being lifted on to his team mates' shoulders, and they were smiling and I remember that was the moment I thought — we're going to be okay.

I went to the development to get that feeling again, but when I got there I saw a ghost estate and I met Simon.

★ ★ ★

When I left Simon at the hospital that night I continued on my quest to find places that uplifted me. I'd been doing it for about six weeks by that stage and I'd already been to my old primary school, a basketball court where I'd kissed a boy I believed was way out of my league, my college, my grandparents' house, the garden centre I used to go to with my grandparents, the local park, the tennis club where I spent my summers, and various other haunts that had been the location of good memories. I'd randomly dropped in on an old primary school friend's house and proceeded to have the most awkward conversation I've ever had, and immediately wished I hadn't bothered going. I had visited her because when I was passing I had a sudden memory: the hot warm sweet smell of baking in her kitchen. Every time I played there, her mother seemed to be baking. Twenty-four years on, the baking smell was gone, so was her mother, and in its place were my exhausted old friend's two children, who were using her as a climbing frame and wouldn't give us a second to talk, which was a blessing as we had nothing to say to one another anyway above the silent question on her lips: *Why the hell did you come here? We weren't even that close.* Assuming I was going through something, she was polite enough not to say it out loud.

For the first few weeks, not finding my place didn't bother me, the searching was a way of passing my time, but after three weeks my inability to find my place started to prey on my mind. Instead of re-energising me, it was in fact undoing the good memories that I had.

After that hospital visit, I was even more intent on finding a place. I needed a lift and knew that returning home to the magnolia-walled rental was not going to offer me any solace.

This was what I was doing the moment the highly unlikely event occurred for the second time in the same month to the same person.

4

How to Hold on for Dear Life

The streets of Dublin city were quiet on a Sunday night in December and it was bitterly cold as I made my way to the Ha'penny Bridge from Wellington Quay. Snow was threatened, but hadn't come yet. The Ha'penny Bridge, officially known as Liffey Bridge, the charming old foot-bridge with its cast-iron railings spans the river, connecting the north of the city to the south. It came to be known as the Ha'penny because that was the toll when it was constructed in 1816. One of the most recognisable sights of Dublin, it's especially pretty at night when the three decorative lamps are lit. I had chosen this place because as a part of my college degree, Business and Spanish, I had to live in Spain for one year. I don't remember how close we were as a family before Mum died, but I most certainly remember us tightening our bonds afterwards and then, as the years went on, it seemed unfathomable that any of us would ever leave the fold. Going into my college course I knew that the Erasmus placement was an inevitable, unavoidable reality and at that stage I felt the overwhelming desire to sever those bonds and stretch my wings. As soon as I got there I knew it was a mistake, I cried all the time, couldn't eat, couldn't sleep, could barely concentrate on my studies. It felt as though my heart had been ripped from my chest and left at home with my family. My dad wrote to me every day, witty musings of his and my sisters' daily life which attempted to lift my spirits but only fuelled the homesickness even more. But there was one postcard in particular that helped me snap out of the chronic homesickness. Or rather, the homesickness was still there, but I was able to function. That postcard had been of the Ha'penny Bridge, at night time, with the Dublin skyline lit up in the background and all the colourful lights reflecting in the Liffey below. I had been enchanted by the image, I'd looked at the pixellated people and I'd tried to give them names and stories, places they were going, places they were coming from, familiar names going to and from locations I knew. I pinned it to my wall when I slept and carried it around in my college journal during the day, I felt like it was a part of home with me at all times.

I wasn't stupid enough to think that this exact feeling would be replicated the moment I saw the bridge, because I saw the bridge almost every week. By this point I was well seasoned at searching for my happy place and knew it wouldn't be instant, but I was hoping I could stand there and at least recall the emotion, the experience, the feelings. It was night, the skyline was lit up in the background, and although the new buildings along the docks created a different image from my old postcard, the reflection of the lights in the dark river still seemed the same. It had all the right elements of the postcard.

Apart from one thing.

A lone man, dressed in black, clinging to the outside of the bridge while he looked down into the cold river that ran swift and treacherous beneath him.

On the steps of the Wellington Quay entrance a small crowd had gathered. They were standing looking at the man on the bridge. I joined them in their shock, wondering if that was how Roy Cleveland Sullivan had felt when he was struck by lightning for the second time: *Not again.*

Someone had called the police and they were discussing how long it would take them to arrive, and how they might not get there on time. They were all debating what to do. I couldn't help but see Simon's face before he pulled the trigger and then afterwards, in intensive care, replaying the way his face had changed in his apartment before he picked up the gun. Something had triggered that moment. Could it have been what I said to him? I couldn't remember the words I'd spoken; maybe it was my fault. I thought about his two little girls, waiting for their daddy to wake up, wondering why he wouldn't wake up like he always did. Then I looked at the man on the bridge and thought about the countless lives that would be impacted by his need to end his pain, his inability to see another way out.

Suddenly, adrenalin pumped through my body and there was no other decision that I could make. I had no choice: I had to save the man on the bridge.

This time, I would do it differently. Since Simon Conway I had read a few books, trying to figure out what I'd done wrong, how I could have talked him round. The first step would be to focus on the man, ignore the commotion around me. The three people beside me were starting to argue about what to do, and that wasn't going to help anyone. I put my foot on the step. I could do this, I told myself, feeling confident and in control.

The icy wind hit me like a slap across the face, telling me, 'Wake up! Be ready!' My ears were already aching from the cold and my nose was numb and starting to run. The tide was high in the Liffey, the water was black, murky, malevolent, uninviting. I detached myself from the people waiting expectantly behind me, and tried to forget that every word I said and every shaky breath I took could be carried on the breeze to the spectators' ears. My view of him grew clearer: a man in black, standing on the wrong side of the railings, his feet on the narrow ridge above the water, his hands clutching the balustrade. It was too late to go back now.

'Hello,' I called gently, not wanting to give him a fright and send him into the water. Despite trying to be heard above the breeze, I kept my voice calm and clear with an even tone and soft expression, remembering what I'd read: avoid sharp tones and maintain eye contact. 'Please don't be alarmed, I'm not going to touch you.'

He turned to look at me, then his eyes went straight back down to the river again, staring intently at the water. It was clear that I had barely penetrated the thoughts running through his mind; he was too lost in his head to notice.

30

'My name is Christine,' I said, taking slow, steady steps towards him. I stayed near the edge of the bridge, wanting to be able to see his face while I spoke.

'Don't come any closer!' he shouted, his voice revealing his panic.

I stopped, happy with the distance; he was an arm's length away. If I absolutely had to, I could grab him.

'Okay, okay, I'm staying here.'

He turned to see how far I was from him.

'Keep focus, I don't want you to fall.'

'Fall?' He looked up at me quickly and then down again, then back up at me and our eyes locked. He was in his thirties, chiselled jaw, his hair hidden beneath a black woollen hat. His blue eyes stared back at me, big and terrified, pupils so large they almost took over his eyes and I wondered was he on something or drunk. 'Are you for real?' he said. 'Do you think I care if I fall? Do you think I got here by accident?' He tried to zone me out again and concentrate on the river.

'What's your name?'

'Leave me alone,' he snapped, then added gently, 'Please.'

Even in distress, he was polite.

'I'm concerned. I can see you're distressed. I'm here to help you.'

'I don't need your help.' He blocked me out and focused on the water again. I watched his knuckles, wrapped around the iron, going from white to red as he tightened and loosened his grip. My heart hammered each time his grip

31

loosened and I dreaded them letting go completely. I didn't have much time.

'I'd like to talk to you.' I moved a tiny bit closer.

'Please go away. I want to be on my own. I didn't want any of this, I didn't want a scene, I just want to do this. On my own. I just . . . I didn't think it would take so long.' He swallowed again.

'Look, nobody is going to come near you unless I say so. So there's no panic, no rush, you don't need to do anything without thinking it through. We have a lot of time. All I ask is for you to talk to me.'

He was silent. More gentle questions led to no answers. I was ready to listen, ready to say all the right things, but my questions were being met by silence. On the other hand, he hadn't jumped yet, at least there was that.

'I'd like to know your name,' I said.

There was nothing from him.

I pictured Simon's face as he looked me in the eye and pulled the trigger. A wave of emotion rushed through me and I wanted to cry, I wanted to break down and cry. I wasn't able for this. Panic welled inside me. I was on the verge of giving up and returning to the small crowd of spectators to tell them I couldn't do it, that I didn't want to be responsible for another victim, when he spoke.

'Adam.'

'Okay,' I said, relieved he was engaging with me. I remembered a line in one of the books that said the person attempting suicide needed to be reminded that there were others thinking of him, loving him, whether he felt it or not, but I was afraid it would send him the opposite direction. What if he was here because of them or because he felt he was a burden on them? My mind raced as I tried to figure out what to do; there were so many rules, and all I wanted was to help.

'I want to help you, Adam,' I said finally.

'There's no point.'

'I'd like to hear what you have to say,' I told him, remaining positive. *Listen thoughtfully, don't say don't, don't say can't.* I ran through everything I'd read. I couldn't get it wrong. Not one single word.

'You can't talk me out of it.'

'Give me a chance to show you that even though it may feel like this is the only option, there are many more. Your mind is so tired now — let me help you down. Then we can look at the choices. They may be hard to see at the moment, but they do exist. For the time being though, let's get off the bridge, let me help you to safety.'

He didn't answer. Instead he looked up at me. I knew that look, that familiar look. Simon had worn that expression too. 'Sorry.' His fingers loosened on the iron bars, his body leaned forward, away from the railings.

'Adam!' I dashed forward, pushed my arms through the wide railings and wrapped them tight around his chest, pulling him back so hard that he slammed into the railings. My body was pressed so close to the railings that his back was tight against my front. I buried

33

my face in his woolly hat, squeezed my eyes shut and held on tight. I waited for him to pull away, wondered how I would keep my grip on him, knowing that I wouldn't be able to for long if he used his strength to resist me. I waited for a spectator to come running and take over, hoped that the gardaí were nearby so that the professionals could step in. I was out of my depth, what did I think I was doing? I squeezed my eyes shut, rested my head on the back of his head; he smelled of aftershave, clean, like he'd just taken a shower. He smelled alive, like someone who was on his way somewhere, not someone who had been planning to jump off a bridge. He felt strong and full of life too; I could barely wrap my arms around his chest he was so broad. I held on to him, determined never to let go.

'What are you doing?' he panted, his chest heaving up and down.

I finally looked up and checked on the crowd behind me. There was no sign of garda lights, no sign of anyone coming to help me. My legs were trembling as if it was me that was staring down at the depths of the Liffey's darkness.

'Don't do it,' I whispered, starting to cry. 'Please don't do it.'

He tried to turn around and see me, but I was directly behind and he couldn't see my face.

'Are you . . . are you crying?'

'Yes,' I sniffed. 'Please don't do it.'

'Jesus,' he tried again to turn and look at me.

I was crying harder now, sobbing uncontrolla-bly, my shoulders jumping up and down, my arms still wrapped around his chest, holding on for dear life.

'What the hell?' He moved some more, shuffled his feet along the edge of the ledge so he could turn his head and see my face.

Our eyes locked together.

'Are you . . . are you okay?' He softened a little, coming out of whatever trance-like state he had been in.

'No.' I tried to stop crying. I wanted to dry my nose, which was running like a tap, but I was afraid to let go of him.

'Do I know you?' he asked, confused, searching my face, wondering why I cared so much.

'No,' I said, sniffing again. I squeezed him tighter, hugging him like I hadn't hugged anyone for years, not since I was a child, not since my mother held me.

He was looking at me like I was crazy, like he was the sane one and I had lost it. We were practically nose-to-nose as he studied my face, as if looking for far more than what he could see.

The spell between us was broken when some idiot watching from the quays shouted 'Jump!' The man in black started trying to wriggle out of my grip with a renewed anger.

'Get your hands off me,' he said, struggling to shake me off.

'No.' I shook my head. 'Please, listen . . . ' I tried to compose myself before continuing: 'It's not what you think it's going to be in there,' I said, looking down and imagining how it would feel for him, staring into that darkness, wanting

35

to end it all; how bad things must be for him to want that. He was studying me intently again. 'You don't want to end your life, you want to end your pain, the pain you're feeling right now, the pain that I'm sure you wake up with and go to bed at night with. Maybe no one around you understands that, but I do, believe me.' I saw that his eyes were filling, I was getting through to him. 'But you don't want to end it all the time, do you? Just sometimes it passes through your mind, probably more often lately than before. It's like a habit, trying to think of different ways to end it all. But it passes, doesn't it?'

He looked at me carefully, taking every word in.

'It's a *moment*, that's all. And moments pass. If you hang in there, this moment will pass and you won't want to end your life. You probably think that no one cares, or that they'll get over you. Maybe you think they want you to do this. They don't. No one wants this for anyone. It might feel as if there are no options, but there are — you can come through this. Get down and let's talk about it. Whatever is going on, you can get through it. It's a moment, that's all,' I whispered, tears running down my cheeks.

I took a sidelong glance at him. He swallowed hard, he was looking down now. Thinking about it, weighing up his options. Live or die. Surreptitiously I scanned the bridge entrances on Bachelors Walk and Wellington Quay, still no gardaí, still no members of the public to help me. I was glad of that at this stage; I had managed to engage with him, I didn't want

36

anybody else to distract him, panic him, bring him back to that place again. I thought about what to say next, something that would make the time pass until professional help arrived, something positive that wouldn't trigger any anger in him. But in the end I didn't have to say anything because he spoke first.

'I read about a guy who jumped in the river last year. He was drunk and decided to go swimming, only he got stuck under a shopping trolley and the currents swept him away. He couldn't get out,' he said, his voice cracking with the emotion.

'And you liked the sound of that?'

'No. But then it will be over. After all that, it will be over.'

'Or it will be the beginning of a new kind of pain. As soon as you're in that water, no matter how much you want it, you'll panic. You'll fight it. You'll struggle to take in oxygen and your lungs will fill with water because, even though you think you don't want to live, your instinct will be to stay alive. It's *in you* to want to stay alive. As soon as the water is drawn into your larynx, another natural instinct is for you to swallow it. Water will fill your lungs, which will weigh down your body, and if you change your mind and decide you want to live and try to get to the surface, you won't be able to. And the thing is, there are so many people around you right now, they're ready to dive in and rescue you — and do you know what? You think it'll be too late, but it won't be. Even after you lose consciousness, the heart will carry on beating.

37

They can give you mouth-to-mouth and pump out the water and fill your lungs with air again. They could save you.'

His body was shaking and not just from the cold. I felt him go limp beneath my arms. 'I want it to end.' His voice shook as he spoke. 'It hurts.'

'What hurts?'

'Specifically? Living.' He laughed weakly. 'Waking up is the worst part of my day. Has been for a long time.'

'Why don't we talk about this somewhere else?' I said, concerned, as his body went rigid again. Maybe it wasn't a good idea to talk about his problems while he was hanging off the side of a bridge. 'I want to hear everything you have to say, so let's get down now.'

'It's too much.' He closed his eyes and spoke more to himself. 'I can't change things now. It's too late,' he said quietly, leaning his head back so that it rested by my cheek. We were oddly close for two strangers.

'It's never too late. Believe me, it's possible for your life to change. You can change it. I can help you,' I said, my voice little more than a whisper. There was no reason for me to project; his ear was right there, at the tip of my lips.

He looked me in the eyes and I couldn't look away, I felt locked in. He seemed so lost.

'And what happens if it doesn't work? If everything doesn't change like you say it will.'

'It will.'

'But if it doesn't?'

'I'm telling you it will.' *Get him off the bridge, Christine!*

He studied me, his jaw hardening as he mulled it over. 'And if it doesn't, I swear I'll do this again,' he threatened. 'Not here, but I'll find a way, because I'm not going back to that.'

I didn't want him dwelling on the negative, on whatever it was that had sent him here. 'Fine,' I said confidently, 'If your life doesn't change, it's your decision what you do. But I'm telling you that it can. I'll show you. You and me, we'll do it together, we'll see how wonderful life can be. I promise you.'

'It's a deal,' he near-whispered.

Dread immediately flooded my body. A deal? I hadn't intended on making a deal with him, but I wasn't going to discuss it now. I was tired. I just wanted him off the bridge. I wanted to be in bed, wrapped up, with all of this behind me.

'You need to let go of me so I can climb over,' he said.

'I'm not letting you go. No way,' I said sternly.

He half-laughed, a tiny one, but it was there. 'Look, I'm trying to get back on the bridge and now you won't let me.'

I took in the height of the bars he needed to climb, then the drop below. This was going to be dangerous. 'Let me call for help,' I said.

Slowly I removed one hand from his chest, not totally trusting that he was going to keep his word.

'I got here by myself, I can get back on the bridge by myself,' he said.

'I don't like the idea of this, let me ask someone to help.' But he ignored me and I watched him trying to turn around, his large feet on the narrow ledge. He moved his right hand to

39

a bar further away and shuffled his feet so that he could turn to face the bridge. My heart pounded as I watched, feeling helpless. I wanted to shout to the spectators to help, but shouting at that point would have given him a fright and sent him into the water. Suddenly the wind felt stronger, the air seemed colder and I was even more aware of the danger he was in after our brief respite. He angled his body to the right, twisting from his waist and preparing to swing his left foot over the water and turn to face the bars, but as he pivoted his weight on his right foot, it slipped off the narrow ledge. Somehow his left hand managed to grab the bar he had been reaching for just in time, leaving him hanging on with one arm. I heard the collective intake of breath from the spectators as I reached for his flailing right hand and clinging on tightly, used all my strength to pull him up. In that moment it was the fear in his eyes which terrified me the most, but on reflection it was that look that gave me strength, because the man who only moments ago had wanted to end his life was now fighting to live.

I helped pull him up, and he clung to the bars, eyes closed, taking deep breaths. I was still trying to compose myself when Detective Maguire came rushing towards us with a thunderous look on his face.

'He wants to get back on the bridge,' I said weakly.

'I can see that.' He pushed me aside and I had to look away while they manoeuvred Adam to safety. As soon as he landed on the bridge, we both sat down hard on the ground, all our energy spent.

Adam sat with his back pressed up against the railings, I sat opposite him on the other side, trying to stop my head from spinning. I tucked my head between my legs and took deep breaths.

'Are you okay?' he asked, concerned.

'Yeah.' I closed my eyes. 'Thanks,' I added.

'What for?'

'For not jumping.'

He grimaced, the exhaustion showing in his face and body. 'Always happy to oblige. Seemed like it meant more to you than to me.'

'Well, I appreciate it.' I gave him a shaky smile.

He raised his eyebrows. 'I'm sorry, I didn't catch your name.'

'Christine.'

'Adam.'

He reached across and held out his hand. I moved from the railings to reach and as I took his hand in mine he held on tightly and looked me in the eye.

'I look forward to you convincing me that this was a good idea, Christine. I think my birthday would be a good deadline.'

Deadline? I froze, my hand still wrapped in his. He'd said it softly, but it felt like a warning. Suddenly I felt faint, not to mention foolish, at the thought of the deal I'd agreed to. What had I done?

Despite wanting to take it all back, I nodded nervously. He shook my hand once, a firm single shake, in the centre of the bridge, and then he let go.

41

5

How to Take Your Relationship to the Next Level

'What the hell were you doing there?' Detective Maguire growled, pushing his face close to mine.

'Trying to help.'

'How do you know *him?*' Meaning: him *as well?*

'I don't.'

'So what happened here?'

'I was just walking by and saw that he was in trouble. We were concerned you wouldn't get here on time, so I thought I'd talk to him.'

'Because your talking did so well the first time,' he vented, then appeared to regret saying that. 'Seriously, Christine, do you expect me to believe that story? You were 'just walking by'? Twice in one month? Do you expect me to believe it was a coincidence? If you're playing at being some caped crusader — '

'I'm not. I was in the wrong place at the wrong time. I thought I could help.' Getting angry at my treatment, I added: 'And I did, didn't I? I got him back on the bridge.'

'Barely,' he fumed. He paced before me.

From afar I could see Adam watching me with concern. I gave him a weak smile.

'I don't think this is funny.'

'I'm not laughing.'

He studied me, trying to figure out what to do with me. 'You can tell me about this from start to finish at the station.'

'But I didn't do anything wrong!'

'You're not under arrest, Christine. I need to file a report.' He walked away, expecting me to follow him to the car.

'You can't take her too,' Adam protested. He looked and sounded exhausted.

'Don't you worry about what we're doing with her.' Maguire adopted a different, much softer voice for Adam's benefit, one I didn't know existed within him.

'Really, I'm fine,' Adam objected as Maguire started helping him to the car. 'It was a moment of madness. I'm fine now. I just want to go home.'

Maguire murmured supportive words but accompanied him to the car all the same, disregarding his wishes. While Adam was taken in one car, I was taken in another to Pearse Street station, where I was asked to tell my story again. It was obvious that Maguire wasn't entirely convinced that I was telling the truth. The fact is, I was holding back and he knew it. I couldn't bring myself to tell him what I was really doing on the bridge or at the housing development. And I couldn't tell it to the nice lady who came into the room after him, wanting to chat to me about my experience.

After an hour Detective Maguire told me I was free to leave.

'What about Adam?'

'Adam isn't your concern now.'

'But, where is he?'

'Being assessed by a psychologist.'

'So when can I see him?'

'Christine . . . ' he warned, trying to get rid of me.

'What?'

'What did I tell you about getting involved? There's a taxi outside. Go home. Get some sleep. Try to stay out of trouble.'

So I left the garda station. It was midnight on a Sunday and the cold went straight to my bones; the streets were empty of traffic, apart from the odd taxi. The all-seeing Trinity College stood dark and empty before me. I don't know how long I was standing there, trying to figure everything out, the shock finally sinking in, when the door behind me opened and I felt Maguire's presence before I heard him.

'You're still here.'

I didn't know what to say to that so I simply looked at him.

'He's been asking for you.'

My heart lifted.

'He'll be spending the night away. Can I give him your number?'

I nodded.

'Get in the taxi, Christine,' Maguire said, and threw me a look so threatening that I found myself hailing the nearest cab.

I went home.

Unsurprisingly I didn't sleep. I sat up, my coffee machine keeping me company as I watched my phone and wondered if Detective Maguire had given Adam the correct number.

44

When seven a.m. arrived and I heard cars on the road, I started to nod off. Fifteen minutes later my alarm clock woke me for work. Adam didn't call me all day, then at six p.m. when I was turning off my computer, my phone rang.

★ ★ ★

We arranged to meet at the Ha'penny Bridge, which seemed right at the time as it was our only link to one another, but once we were both there, twenty-four hours after the incident, it felt inappropriate. He wasn't on the bridge but standing beside it on Bachelors Walk, looking down at the water. I would have given anything to know what he was thinking.

'Adam.'

At the sound of my voice, he turned. He was wearing the same black duffle coat and black woollen hat from the previous night, his hands shoved deep into his pockets.

'Are you okay?' I asked.

'Yeah, sure.' He sounded shell-shocked. 'I'm fine.'

'Where did they take you last night?'

'A few questions at the station, then St John of Gods for a psychological assessment. I passed with flying colours,' he joked. 'Anyway I called you because I wanted to thank you, in person.' He shifted his weight from one foot to the other. 'So, thank you.'

'Okay. Well, you're welcome,' I replied, awkwardly, not knowing whether to shake his hand or give him a hug. All the signs indicated I

45

should leave him alone.

He nodded then and turned to cross the road to Lower Liffey Street. He wasn't looking where he was going and a car honked angrily as it narrowly missed running him over. He barely registered the sound and kept on walking.

'Adam!'

He turned around. 'Accident. Promise.'

I knew then that I would have to follow him. The hospital may have believed him, but there was no way I would leave him alone after what he'd been through. I pressed the pedestrian button for the lights to change but they were too slow; afraid I'd lose him, I waited for a gap in the traffic and ran across the road. Another car honked. I ran to get close to him and then slowed down, deciding I could make sure he was safe from afar. He turned right on to Middle Abbey Street and when he was around the corner and out of sight, I sprinted to catch up. When I rounded the corner, he was gone, as if he'd vanished into thin air. At that hour there were no businesses open for him to have disappeared into. I searched the deserted dark street ahead and cursed myself for losing him, wishing I'd at least gotten his phone number.

'Boo,' he said suddenly, deadpan as he stepped out of the shadows.

I jumped. 'Jesus, Adam. Are you trying to give me a heart attack?'

He smiled at me, amused. 'Stop pulling your *Cagney and Lacey* tricks on me.'

I felt my face redden in the dark. 'I wanted to

make sure you're okay. I didn't want to be in your face.'

'I told you, I'm fine.'

'I don't think that you are.'

He looked away, blinking repeatedly as his eyes started filling again. I could see them sparkling under the lamplight.

'I need to know that you're going to be okay. I can't just leave you. Are you going to get some help?' I asked.

'And how will all this amazing talking that people want to do with me fix anything? It won't change what's happening.'

'What *is* happening?'

He backed away.

'Okay, you don't have to tell me. But are you at least relieved? That you didn't jump?'

'Sure. It was a big mistake. I regret going to the bridge.'

I smiled. 'You see? That's good — steps forward already.'

'I should have gone up there,' he said, lifting his gaze to Liberty Hall, the sixteen-storey building which was the tallest in Dublin's city centre.

'When's your birthday?' I said, remembering our deal.

He actually laughed.

'Where are we going?' I asked, running to catch up with him as he strode along O'Connell Street. My feet and hands were numb, so I was hoping we hadn't far to go. He seemed to be walking aimlessly, without a destination in mind, which made me wonder whether death by

47

frostbite was to be his next suicide method.

'I'm staying in the Gresham Hotel.' He looked up at the Spire. 'Or I could have skydived and landed on that. It might have speared me right through the stomach. Or better yet, my heart.'

'Okay, I'm starting to understand your humour. And it's a bit sick.'

'Thankfully the hospital didn't think so.'

'How did you get out of there?'

'Charmed them with my boyish joy and wonder,' he said, still straight-faced.

'You lied to them,' I accused. Adam shrugged. 'Where do you live?'

He hesitated. 'These days? Tipperary.'

'And did you come to Dublin especially to . . . ?'

'Jump from the Ha'penny Bridge?' He looked at me, amused again. 'You Dubs are so arrogant. There are perfectly good bridges in the rest of the country, you know. No, I was here to see someone.' We reached the Gresham Hotel and Adam turned to me. 'Well, thank you. Again. For saving my life. Should I, I don't know, give you an awkward kiss or a hug or . . . I know — ' He held up his hand in the air and I rolled my eyes before giving him a high-five.

And then I really didn't know what to say next. Good luck? Enjoy your life?

He had no idea either, so the sarcastic comments continued to flow.

'I should give you a gold star,' he said. 'Or a badge.'

'I'd really prefer not to leave you right now.'

'My birthday is in two weeks. Not that much

can change in two weeks, but I appreciate you lying for me.'

'It's do-able,' I said, more confidently than I felt. Two weeks? I'd been hoping for an entire year away, but if that's what I had to work with, so be it. 'I'll use up my annual leave, then I can see you every day. It's definitely possible,' I said optimistically.

He gave me that same amused smile. 'I'd really rather be alone now.'

'So you can kill yourself.'

'Can you keep your voice down,' he hissed as a couple walked by and glanced suspiciously at us. 'Again, thank you,' he said, with less gusto. Then, leaving me on the pavement, he disappeared through the revolving doors. I watched him cross the lobby, then I followed him in. He was going to have a hard time shaking me off. He stepped into the elevator and, waiting until the last possible moment before the doors closed, I rushed forward and joined him. He looked at me blankly. Then he pressed the button.

We got out on the top floor and I followed him to the penthouse suite named the Grace Kelly Suite. As we entered the living room I could smell flowers. The door to the bedroom was open and I could see a bed sprinkled with rose petals, and a bottle of champagne sitting in a silver bucket at the end of the bed with two flutes criss-crossed. Adam glanced in at the bed, then away again as if the very sight of it offended him. He walked straight to the bureau and picked up a piece of paper.

I followed him. 'Is that your suicide note?'

He winced. 'Do you have to use that word?'

'What would you rather I say?'

' 'Goodbye, Adam, it was nice meeting you'?' He shrugged off his coat and threw it on the floor, then pulled off his hat and tossed it in the air. It narrowly avoided landing in the real fire which was smouldering in the marble fireplace. He collapsed on the couch, exhausted.

I was taken aback; I hadn't expected to see a head of thick blond hair under the woollen hat.

'What?' he asked, and I realised I was staring at his beauty.

Sitting down on the couch opposite him, I took off my coat and gloves and hoped the fire would thaw me out quickly. 'Can I read it?'

'No.' He moved it closer to his chest and folded it.

'Why don't you rip it up?'

'Because.' He placed it in his pocket. 'It's a memento. Of my trip to Dublin.'

'You're not very funny.'

'Another thing to add to my list of things I'm not good at.'

I looked around at the set-up and tried to figure him out. 'Were you expecting someone here tonight?'

'Of course. I always arrange champagne and roses for pretty ladies who talk me off bridges.'

It was wrong and I knew it was wrong, but I celebrated inside that he'd called me pretty. 'No, it must have been last night,' I said, watching him. Despite the jokes and self-assurance, he was fidgeting. I reckoned those jokes were the only thing stopping him collapsing in a heap right there and then.

He got up and made his way over to the TV unit, opening the cupboard below to reveal a mini-bar.

'I don't think alcohol is such a good idea.'

'I might be getting a soft drink.' He gave me a wounded look and I felt guilty. He retrieved a Jack Daniel's then threw me a cheeky look as he brought it back to the couch.

I didn't comment but noticed that as he poured it into the glass his hands were trembling. I sat and watched him for a while and then, unable to take it any longer, I got one for myself, only I mixed mine with a soft drink. I'd made a pact with a man who tried to kill himself, then followed him to his hotel room, so why not get drunk with him too? If there was such a thing as a rulebook on moral integrity and responsible citizenship I'd pretty much stamped all over it, so why not finish the job and throw it out the window? Besides, I was freezing to my bones and needed something to help thaw me out. I took a sip; it burned my throat all the way to my stomach and it felt good.

'My girlfriend,' he said out of nowhere, interrupting my thoughts.

'What about her?'

'That's who I was expecting. I came to Dublin to surprise her. She'd said that I hadn't been very attentive lately. Not present in her company, or whatever.' He rubbed his face roughly. 'She said we were in trouble. 'In danger', that was the expression she used.'

'So you came to Dublin to rescue your relationship,' I said, happy to finally be learning about him. 'What happened?'

'She was with another fella,' he said, jaw tightening again. 'In Milano's. She said she was going there with the girls. We live in an apartment there on the quays, only I've been in Tipperary a while . . . Anyway, she wasn't with the girls,' he said bitterly, staring at the contents of his glass.

'How do you know they weren't just friends?'

'Ah they were friends, all right. I introduced them. My best friend Sean. They were holding hands across the table. They didn't even see me walk in the restaurant. She wasn't expecting me to arrive, I was supposed to be in Tipperary still. I confronted them. They didn't deny it.' He shrugged.

'What did you do?'

'What could I do? I left the place looking like a complete eejit.'

'You didn't want to hit Sean?'

'Nah.' He sat back, defeated. 'I knew what I had to do.'

'Attempt suicide?'

'Will you stop using that word?'

I was silent.

'Anyway what good would hitting him have done? Made a scene? Made me look an even bigger gobshite?'

'It would have alleviated the tension.'

'So violence is good now?' He shook his head. 'If I had hit him, you would have asked why didn't I take a walk to cool down.'

52

'Boxing your so-called friend, who clearly deserved it, is better than suicide. It wins hands down every time.'

'Will you stop saying that word,' he said quietly. 'Jesus.'

'That's what you tried to do, Adam.'

'And I'll do it again if you don't keep your side of the deal,' he shouted.

His anger took me by surprise. He got up and made his way to the glass door leading out on to a balcony overlooking O'Connell Street and the rooftops of the Northside.

I was sure there was a lot more to Adam's story than wanting to end his life because his girlfriend was cheating on him. That was probably the trigger to an already troubled mind, but it didn't seem the right time to probe. He was tensing up again and we were both tired, we needed sleep.

Evidently he agreed. Keeping his back to me, he said, 'You can sleep in the bedroom, I'll take the couch.' When I didn't answer, he turned to face me. 'I assume you want to stay.'

'You don't mind?'

He thought about it. 'I think it might be a good idea.' Then he turned back to look out over the city.

There was so much I could say to him to sum up the day, give him positive words of encouragement. I'd read enough self-help books: pick-me-up phrases were a dime a dozen. But none of them seemed appropriate now. If I was going to help him out of this, I would have to figure out not just what to say but when to say it.

'Goodnight,' I said. I left the bedroom door ajar, not liking that he was in the room with access to the balcony. I watched him through the gap as he took off his jumper, revealing a tight T-shirt beneath. I couldn't help but look a little longer than necessary, trying to convince myself that I was doing it for his safety in case he suffocated himself with his own jumper. He sat down on the couch and put his feet up. He was too tall for the couch; he had to rest his feet on the arm of the couch, which made me feel guilty about taking the bed. I was about to say so when he spoke.

'Enjoying the show?' he asked, his eyes closed and his arms folded beneath his head.

Cheeks blazing, I rolled my eyes and moved away from the door. I sat on the four-poster bed, the glasses clinking beside me, the melted ice in the bucket tipping over and spilling on the bed. I placed it on the desk and I was reaching for a chocolate-coated strawberry when I noticed the notecard beside the display. It read, *For my beautiful Fiancée, Love Adam*. So he had come to Dublin to propose. Certain that I was only scratching the surface, I resolved to get my hands on that suicide note.

I had thought that the night I watched Simon Conway shoot himself, the night I left my husband, and every night since then had been the longest.

I was wrong.

6

How to Quiet Your Mind
and Get Some Sleep

I couldn't sleep. That wasn't unusual, I'd practically been an insomniac for the last four months, ever since it had occurred to me that I wanted my marriage to end. It wasn't a helpful thought. I had been searching for ways to find happiness, fulfilment, feelings of positivity, ways in which to rescue my marriage — not ways *out*. But as soon as I had the thought, *escape*, it wouldn't go away, especially at night when I didn't have anybody else's problems to distract me from my own. Usually I ended up following my nightstand read, *42 Tips on How to Beat Insomnia*, and as a result I'd tried soaking in warm baths, cleaning out my fridge, painting my nails, doing yoga — sometimes doing two of the three simultaneously — at all hours of the morning, in hope of finding respite. Other times I'd settle for simply reading the book until my eyes got too sore and had to close. I never seemed to drift away as the book declared I'd be able to do; there was no such thing as the lightless and feathery feeling of *drifting*. I was either awake frustrated and exhausted, or I was asleep frustrated and exhausted, and I'd yet to experience that pleasant glide from one world to the next.

Though I had realised I wanted my marriage to end I never thought about actually ending it. For a long time I spent my nights worrying how I was going to live with my unhappiness, until eventually it occurred to me that I didn't have to; the advice I gave to friends could actually apply to me. After that, I spent countless nights fantasising about a life with somebody else, somebody I truly loved, someone who truly loved me; we'd be one of those couples who seemed to have electricity sparking between them with every look and touch. Then I fantasised about me and just about every man I was attracted to, which became most men that were in any way kind to me. Including Leo Arnold — a client whose appointments I particularly enjoyed. Leo had become the subject of many of my fantasies, which caused me to become rosy-cheeked every time he stepped into my office.

Beneath it all, I recognise now, there was an underlying panic; panic that it was all too much for me to deal with, but now that I'd acknowledged it there was no making it go away. Each little problem between us was magnified till it became one more sign that we were doomed. Like when he finished before me in bed, again; when he slept with his socks on because his feet were always cold; and when he left his toenail clippings in a small bowl in the bathroom and never remembered to empty it in the bin. The way we barely kissed any more; those once-full kisses had been reduced to familiar pecks on the cheek. How bored I'd become with his stories, fed up with listening to him retell the same old rugby tales. If I were to judge my life in colours, which I'd learned to do from a book, our relationship had gone from a vibrant hue — at least, that's how it was for a while, when we were dating — to a dull, monotonous grey. I wasn't stupid enough to think that the flame would forever burn brightly in a marriage, but I did think there should be at least a flicker remaining after less than a year of married life. Looking back, I think I fell in love with being in love. And now my love affair with the dream was over.

That night as I lay awake in the penthouse of the Gresham Hotel, all my worries started to pile up. The worry of having left Barry; the money woes that followed; what people thought of me; the fear of never meeting anyone ever again and being lonely for the rest of my life; Simon Conway . . . And now Adam, whose surname I didn't know, who twenty-four hours ago had attempted to take his own life and was lying in the room next to mine on the couch beside a balcony with an impressive drop, beside a full mini-bar, and who was waiting for me to deliver on my promise of fixing his life before his thirty-fifth birthday in two weeks' time or else he'd attempt to kill himself again.

Feeling nauseous at the prospect, I got out of bed and checked on him again. The TV was muted and the colours flickered and changed and danced through the room. I could see his chest lifting up and down. There were a number of options available to me, according to *42 Tips*, to quiet my mind and get some sleep, but all I could manage while listening out for Adam was to drink camomile tea. I flicked the switch on the kettle for the fourth time.

'Jesus, do you never sleep?' he called.

'Sorry, am I disturbing you?'

'No, but the steam engine in there with you is.'

I pushed the door open. 'You want a cuppa? Oh. I see you have enough to drink.' Three small empty bottles of Jack Daniel's sat on the coffee table.

'I wouldn't say *enough*,' he said. 'You can't watch me twenty-four hours a day. Sooner or later you're going to have to sleep.' He finally opened his eyes and looked up at me. He didn't look remotely tired. Or drunk. Merely beautiful. Perfect.

I didn't want to tell him the real reason, or reasons, for my insomnia.

'I'd prefer it if I could sleep in here with you,' I said.

'Cosy. But it's a bit too soon after my break-up, so if you don't mind, I'll pass.'

I sat down on the couch anyway.

'I'm not going to jump off the balcony,' he said.

'But you've thought about it?'

'Of course. I've thought about the plethora of ways I could kill myself in this room. It's what I do. I could have set myself on fire.'

'There's a fire extinguisher, I'd have put you out.'

'I could have used my razor in the bathroom.'

'I hid it.'

'Drowned in the bath, or taken a bath with the hairdryer.'

'I'd watch you in the bath, and nobody can find hair-dryers in hotels.'

'I'd have used the kettle.'

'It can barely heat water, it couldn't electrocute a mouse. It's all noise and no action.'

He laughed lightly.

'And that cutlery can barely cut through an apple, never mind a vein,' I said.

He looked at the cutlery beside the fruit bowl. 'Thought I'd keep that one to myself.'

'You think about killing yourself a lot?' I tucked my legs up under me and snuggled into the corner of the couch.

He dropped the act. 'I can't seem to stop myself. You were right, what you said on the bridge: it's become like a really sick hobby.'

'I didn't quite say that. But you know there's probably nothing wrong with you thinking about it, as long as you don't act on it.'

'Thank you. At least you won't take my thoughts away from me.'

'Thinking about it comforts you, it's your crutch. I'm not going to take your crutch away, but it shouldn't be your only way of coping. Did you ever talk to anyone about it?'

'Yeah sure, it's the number one topic for speed-dating. What do you think?'

'Have you thought about therapy?'

'I've just had a night and day of it.'

'I think you could do with more than a night and day.'

'Therapy's not for me.'

'It's probably the way to go at the moment.'

'I thought *you* were the way to go.' He looked at me. 'Isn't that what you said? Stick with me and I'll show you how wonderful life can be?'

Again panic rose that he was placing all this trust in me.

'And I'll do that. I just wondered . . . ' I swallowed. 'Did your girlfriend know how you were feeling?'

'Maria? I don't know. She kept saying I'd changed. I was distracted. Withdrawn. I wasn't the same. But no, I never told her what I was thinking.'

'You've been depressed.'

'If that's what you call it. It doesn't help when you're trying your best to be jolly and someone keeps saying you're not the same, you're down, you're not exciting, you're not spontaneous. Jesus, I mean, what else could I do? I was trying to keep my own bloody head above water.' He sighed. 'She thought it was to do with my father. And the job.'

'It wasn't those things?'

'Ah, I don't know.'

'But they haven't helped?' I offered.

'No. They haven't.'

'So tell me about the job that's worrying you.'

'This feels like a therapy session, me lying here, you sitting there.' He stared up at the ceiling. 'I was given leave by my job to go and help run my father's company while he was sick. I hate it, but it was fine because it was temporary. Then Father got sicker, so I had to stay longer. It was hard to convince my job to extend the leave and now the doctor says Father's not getting any better. It's terminal. Then I found out last week that work are letting me go; they can't afford for me to spend any more time away.'

'So you lose your dad and your job. And your girlfriend. And your best friend,' I summarised for him. 'All in one week.'

'Why, thank you so much for saying that all out loud for me.'

'I have fourteen days to fix you, I don't have time for tip-toeing,' I said lightly.

'Actually, it's thirteen.'

'When your dad passes away, you're not expected to keep the position, are you?'

'That's the problem: it's a family business. My grandfather left the company to my father, next it falls to me, and so on and so on.'

The tension was building just talking about it. Realising I needed to tread carefully, I asked, 'Have you spoken to your father about not wanting the job?'

He laughed lightly, bitterly. 'You clearly don't know my family. It doesn't matter what I tell him; the job is mine whether I like it or not. My grandfather's will states that the company is my father's for life, then it falls to my father's children, and if I don't join the business, then it reverts to my uncle's son and his family inherit it.'

'Surely that saves you.'

He buried his head in his hands and rubbed his eyes with frustration. 'It screws me even more. Look, I appreciate you trying, but you don't understand the situation. It's too complicated for me to explain, but let's just say it involves years and years of family *shit* and I'm smack bang in the middle of it.'

His fingers were trembling. He rubbed them on his jeans, up and down, up and down. He probably wasn't even aware that he was doing it. Time to lift the mood.

'Tell me about your job, the job you love.'

He looked at me, a rare playful look in his eye. 'What do you think it is that I do?'

I studied him. 'A model?'

He swung his legs off the couch and sat up. It was so quick I thought he was going to dive on me; instead he looked at me in shock. 'Are you kidding?'

'You're not a model?'

'Why the hell would you say that?'

'Because . . . '

'Because what?'

He was flabbergasted. It was the first time I'd seen him so animated.

'Don't tell me no one has ever said that to you before?'

He shook his head. 'No. No way.'

'Oh. Even your girlfriend?'

'No!' He laughed quickly, and it was beautiful, a beautiful sound that I wanted to hear again. 'You're pulling my leg.' Then he laid down again, feet up, the smile and the laugh gone.

'I'm not. You happen to be the most handsome man I've ever seen and so I thought you might be a model,' I explained rationally. 'I wasn't making it up!'

He looked at me then, his face softer, a little embarrassed, as he tried to figure out whether I was joking. But I wasn't joking. If anything, I was mortified; I hadn't meant it to come out like that. I had meant to say he was handsome, but it came out wrong because it came out right.

'So what do you do?' I changed the subject, picking imaginary fluff from my jeans to avoid looking at him.

'You'll enjoy this.'

'Go on.'

'A stripogram. One of those Chippendales. Because I'm so handsome and all.'

I rolled my eyes and sat back.

'Ah, I'm only messing. I'm a helicopter pilot for the Irish Coast Guard.'

My mouth dropped.

'See, I told you you'd enjoy it.' He studied me.

'You rescue people,' I said.

'We have so much in common, you and I.'

There was no way Adam could go back to that job with him being in this frame of mind. I wouldn't let him, I couldn't let him, *they* wouldn't let him.

'You said the family company falls to your father's children after his death. Do you have any siblings?'

'I have an older sister. She's next in line, but she moved to Boston. She had to leg it over there when it came out that her husband had stolen millions from his friends in a Ponzi scheme. He was supposed to invest it for them but spent it instead. Took quite a bit from me too. Took a whole lot from my dad.'

63

'Your poor sister.'

'Lavinia? She was probably the brains behind it. It's not just that, there are other complications. The company should have passed to my uncle, who was the eldest brother, but he's a selfish prick and my grandfather knew he'd run the company into the ground if it was left to him, so instead it went to Father. As a result, the family was split between those who sympathised with Uncle Liam and those who took my father's side. So if I don't take over and it falls to my cousin . . . It's difficult to explain to someone who isn't part of the family. You can't know how hard it is to turn your back on something, even though you despise it, because there's loyalty involved.'

'I left my husband last week,' I blurted out. Just like that, I said it. My heart was hammering in my chest; it must have been the first time I'd said it to anyone, out loud. For so long I'd wanted to leave him, but couldn't because I wanted to be the loyal wife who followed through on my vows. I knew exactly the loyalty Adam was talking about.

He looked at me, surprised. For a moment he studied me, as if questioning whether my claim was authentic. 'What did he do?'

'He's an electrician, why?'

'No. Why did you leave him? What did he do wrong?'

I swallowed, examined my nails. 'He didn't do anything wrong really. He . . . I wasn't happy.'

He blew air out of his nose, unamused. 'So you find your own happiness at his expense.'

I knew he was thinking about his girlfriend.

'It's not a philosophy I like to preach.'

'But you practise it.'

'You can't know how hard it is to leave someone,' I echoed his earlier words.

'Touché.'

'You have to weigh up the risks,' I said. 'Together we would have both been miserable for the rest of our lives. He'll get over me. He'll get over me a lot quicker than he thinks.'

'And what if he doesn't?'

I didn't know how to respond. The thought had never occurred to me. I was sure Barry would get over me. He would have to.

Adam disappeared after that. He stayed in the room but vanished into his mind, no doubt pondering the future for him and his girlfriend. Getting over her wasn't an option; he wanted her back. And if his girlfriend felt for Adam the way I felt for Barry, they hadn't a hope in hell.

'So what do you do?' he asked, as if suddenly realising he knew nothing about the woman who was intent on saving his life.

'What do you think I do?' I played his game.

He didn't think for very long. 'Work in a charity shop?'

I had to laugh. 'That's random.' I looked down at my clothes, wondering if he thought my jeans, denim shirt and Converse trainers had come from a charity shop. They may have been casual but they were all brand new, and double denim was back in.

He smiled. 'I don't mean your clothes. It's more . . . you seem the caring type. Maybe a vet, or something to do with rescued animals?' He shrugged. 'Am I close?'

I cleared my throat. 'I'm in recruitment.'

His smile faded. His disappointment was palpable, his concern even more so. And he didn't try to cover it up.

In a few hours I would have twelve days left. And so far I had achieved nothing.

7

How to Build Friendships and Develop Trust

I would have sworn to anyone who'd listen that I hadn't slept all night, because I was sure I hadn't, but instead of the realisation that morning had finally come upon me, it was the sound of running water that forced me out of sleep mode. Confused that I'd been asleep, it took me a moment to remember where I was. I was wide-awake and immediately alert; I didn't do groggy. When I discovered the couch where Adam had been lying was empty I immediately jumped up, rushed into the bedroom, banging my knee on the coffee table and my elbow on the doorframe, not fully thinking things through, and barged into the bathroom where I was faced with a bare, very pert and muscular bottom which hadn't seen the sun for a long time. Adam twisted his upper body around, his blond curls were flattened and darkened and dripping down along his face. I couldn't stop staring.

'Don't worry, I'm alive,' he said, amused again.

I quickly backed out of the bathroom, closed the door suppressing an awkward giggle, and hurried to the guest toilet to make myself look presentable after a night in double denim. When I emerged from the living room, the water continued to fall in the bathroom. After ten minutes it was still falling. I paced the bedroom wondering what to do. Walking in on him once was a mistake, a second time would be plain creepy but I wasn't sure I could afford to be worried about my integrity when two nights ago he had attempted to kill himself, though apart from shrinking himself to death I wasn't sure he could harm himself in there. I had removed the glasses from the sink area so he couldn't hurt himself and I hadn't heard any mirrors smash. I was about to push the bathroom door open again when I heard the sound. It was quiet at first, then it sounded choked, so full of hurt, so deep and longing I let go of the handle and rested my head against the door, wanting so much to comfort him. Feeling helpless, I listened to his sobs.

Then I remembered the suicide note. If I didn't get my hands on it before he got out of the shower, I'd never see it. I looked around the room and saw his clothes discarded in the corner, his jeans strewn on top of his travel bag. I felt my way around each pocket and finally found the folded piece of paper. I opened it, hoping to gain more insight into the reasons of his attempted suicide, but instead found a series of scribbles, some crossed out, others under-lined and I quickly learned that it wasn't a suicide note at all; it was his proposal to Maria, practised over and over, rewritten until it was perfect.

A vibration from Adam's phone stole my attention away. It was beside the fresh clothes he'd laid out to wear that day. The phone stopped ringing and the screen revealed *seventeen missed calls.* It rang again. *Maria.* I made a quick decision, one that didn't involve much thinking through. I answered it.

I was mid-conversation with her when I realised the shower had stopped running, in fact I hadn't heard it in a while. I turned around, his phone still to my ear. Adam was standing at the bathroom door, as if he'd been there for a while, towel wrapped around his waist, his skin bone dry, anger on his face. I quickly made my excuses and ended the call. I spoke before he had the chance to attack me.

'You had seventeen missed calls on your phone, I thought it might be important so I answered. Also, if this is going to work between us, then I need total access to your life. No holds barred. No secrets.'

I stopped to make sure he understood. He didn't object.

'That was Maria. She was worried about you. She was afraid you'd hurt yourself after last night, or worse. She's been worried about you for a year now, extremely worried for nine months. She felt she wasn't getting through to you so she went to Sean for help, so they could figure out what to do. She fought how she felt for him, but she fell for Sean. They didn't want to hurt you. They've been together for six weeks. She didn't know how to tell you. She thought your behaviour was down to your sister leaving Ireland, then you having to leave your job, and your father being sick. She said every time she wanted to talk to you, something bad happened. She wanted to tell you about her and Sean, but then the news about your father's illness being terminal came. She said she'd arranged to meet with you last week to tell you finally, and instead you told her about being let go from your job. She wished you hadn't found out the way you did.'

I watched as he took all of this in. He was seething, the anger was bubbling beneath his skin but I could see the hurt too, he was really so fragile, so delicate, so heartbroken, a whisper away from breaking.

I continued, 'She seemed put out that I answered the phone, upset, almost angry with me that she didn't know who I was. She said in the six years you were together she thought she knew all of your friends. She was jealous.'

The anger seemed to lessen then, with thoughts of her jealousy of him and another woman like water over his burning rage.

I felt hesitant about adding the rest but took a gamble that I thought would pay off. 'She said she doesn't recognise you any more. That you used to be fun — funny and spontaneous. She said you've lost your spark.'

His eyes filled a little and he coughed and shook his head, macho man back.

'We're going to get you back to that way again, Adam, I promise. Who knows, maybe she'll recognise the man she fell in love with and she'll fall in love with him all over again. We'll rediscover your spark.'

I gave him space to think about that and

70

waited in the living room, nervously biting my nails. Twenty long minutes later he appeared in the doorway, fully dressed, eyes clear and hiding any proof of his despair.

'Breakfast?'

★ ★ ★

The dining-room buffet had quite an array of food to choose from and customers went back and forth several times to avail of the all-you-can-eat menu. We sat with our backs to the display with cups of black coffee and empty placemats.

'So you don't eat, you don't really sleep and we both like to rescue people. What else do we have in common?' Adam said.

I had lost my appetite three months ago, the same time I'd realised I was not happy in my marriage. As a result of losing my appetite, I'd lost a lot of weight, though I was working on it through my *How to Get Your Appetite Back One Bite at a Time* book.

'Broken relationships,' I offered.

'You left yours. I was left. Doesn't count.'

'Don't take my leaving my husband personally.'

'I can if I want.'

I sighed. 'So tell me about you. Maria said you'd lost your spark over a year ago, which was a comment that has really stayed with me.'

'Yeah, that has stayed with me too,' he interrupted, with false animation. 'I'm wondering if she'd realised that before or after she

71

fucked my best friend, or perhaps it was during. Now wouldn't that be a fine thing?'

I didn't respond to that, allowed him to have his moment. 'What were you like when your mother passed away? How did you behave?'

Maria had also revealed that detail over the phone, disclosing much of Adam's life and his problems as though I was a long and trusted friend who knew all of this information anyway. I'm sure she would have been far more careful with her words had she known the real situation, but she didn't, it wasn't her business, and so I'd let her talk; her rant an attempt to justify her actions and also a way for me to be enlightened on aspects of Adam's life that perhaps he wouldn't have shared with me himself.

'Why?'

'Because it's helpful to me.'

'Will it be helpful to me?'

'Your mother passed away, your sister moved away, your father is sick, your girlfriend has met someone else. I think that your girlfriend leaving you was the trigger. Perhaps you can't deal with people leaving. Perhaps you feel abandoned. You know, if you can recognise your triggers, it can help with being aware of those negative thoughts before you drop into the downward spiral. Maybe when someone leaves you now, you connect with how you felt when you were five years old.'

I was impressed with myself but I seemed to be the only one.

'I think you should stop playing therapist.'

'I think you should go and see a real one, but

for some reason you won't and I'm the best you've got.'

He was silenced by that. Whatever his reasons, that didn't seem to be an option. Still, I was hoping I'd get him there eventually.

Adam sighed and sat back in the chair, looking up at the chandelier as if it was that which had asked him the question. 'I was five years old, Lavinia was ten. Mum had cancer. It was all very sad for everyone, though I didn't really understand. I didn't feel sad, I only knew that it was. I didn't know she had cancer, or if I did I didn't know what it was. I just knew she was sick. There was a room downstairs in the house where she stayed that we weren't allowed to go into. It was for a few weeks or a few months, I can't really remember. It felt like for ever. We had to be very quiet around the door. Men would go in and out with their doctor's bags, ruffle my hair as they passed. Father would rarely go in. Then one day the door to that room was open. I went in; it had a bed in it that never used to be there before. The bed was empty but apart from that the room looked exactly the same as it used to. The doctor who used to tap me on the head told me my mother was gone. I asked him where, he said Heaven. So I knew she wasn't coming back. That's where my grandfather went one day and he never came back. I thought it must have been a fun place to go to never want to come back. We went to the funeral. Everybody was very sad. I stayed with my aunt for a few days. Then I was packed off to boarding school.' He spoke of it all devoid of emotion, totally disconnected as his defence mechanism kicked in to block out the overwhelming pain. I guessed for him to connect, to feel the pain, felt too much to bear. He seemed isolated and disengaged and I believed every word he said.

'Your father didn't discuss what was happening to your mother?'

'My father doesn't do emotion. After they told him he had weeks to live he asked for a fax machine to be put in his hospital room.'

'Was your sister communicative? Could you talk about it together, in order to understand?'

'She was sent to a boarding school in Kildare and we saw each other for a few days each holiday. The first summer we were back at the house from boarding school she set up a stall in town and sold my mother's shoes, bags, fur coats and jewellery and whatever else was of any value and made herself a fortune. Every single thing was sold and couldn't be bought back by the time anyone realised what she'd done a few weeks later. She'd spent most of the money already. She was practically a stranger to me and even more so after that. She's made of the same stuff my father is. She's more intelligent than me, it's just a pity she didn't put her brains to better use. She should be taking Father's place, not me.'

'Did you make good friends at boarding school?' I was hoping for some kind of circle where little Adam had love and friendship, I wanted a happy ending somewhere.

'That's where I met Sean.'

Which wasn't the happy ending I was hoping

for, as that trusted person had betrayed him. I couldn't help myself, I reached out and placed my hand over his. The movement made him stiffen and so I quickly removed it.

He folded his arms. 'So how about we drop all this mumbo jumbo talk and get straight to the problem?'

'This isn't mumbo jumbo. I think that your mother passing away when you were five years old is significant, it affects your past and current behaviour, your emotions, how you deal with things.' That's what the book said and I personally knew it to be true.

'Unless your mother died when you were five years old, then I think it's something you can't learn from a book. I'm grand, let's move on.'

'She did.'

'What?'

'My mum died when I was four.'

He looked at me, surprised. 'I'm so sorry.'

'Thanks.'

'So how did it affect you?' he asked gently.

'I think I'm not the one who wants to kill myself on my thirty-fifth birthday, so let's move on,' I snapped, wanting to get back to talking about him. I could tell from his surprised expression that I had sounded a lot angrier than I had intended. I composed myself. 'Sorry. What I meant was, if you don't want to talk, what do you want from me, Adam? How do you expect me to help you?'

He leaned forward, lowered his voice, jabbed his finger on the table to emphasise each point. 'It's my thirty-fifth birthday on Saturday week, I don't particularly want to have a party but for some reason that's what's being arranged for me by the family — and by family I do not mean my sister Lavinia, because the only way she can appear in Ireland without getting handcuffs slapped on her wrists is on Skype. I mean the company family. The party is in City Hall in Dublin, a big do, and I would rather not be there but I kind of have to be because the board have chosen that day to announce to everyone that I'm taking over the company while my father is alive, kind of like being given the seal of approval. That's twelve days away. Because he's so ill, they had a meeting last week to see if my birthday party could be moved forward. I told them it's not happening. Firstly, I don't want the job. I haven't worked out how to fix it yet, but I'll be announcing somebody else as the new head that night. And if I have to walk into that bloody room, I want Maria back, by my side, holding my hand the way it should be.' His voice cracked and he took a moment to compose himself. 'I thought about it and I understand. I changed. I wasn't there for her when she needed me, she was worried, she went to Sean and Sean took advantage of her. I went to Benidorm with him when we finished our Leaving Cert, and I've partied with him every weekend since I was thirteen — believe me, I know what he can be like with women. She doesn't.'

I opened my mouth to protest, but Adam lifted a finger in warning and continued.

'I'd also like to get my job at the coast guard back, and for everyone in my father's company who's worked there for the past one hundred years to get off my back because I was chosen to take Father's place instead of them. If I had my way, I'd rather any of them got the bloody job. Right now it doesn't look likely, but you're going to help with that. We need to undo my grandfather's wishes. Lavinia and I can't take over the company, but it must not fall to my cousin Nigel. That would be the end of the company. I have to work something out. If none of those things are fixed then I'll drown myself in a bloody stream if I have to, because I'm not living with anything other than that right there.' He jabbed the table with a butter knife to emphasise the final two words. He looked at me wide-eyed, wired, threatening, daring me to walk out, to give up on him.

It was tempting, to say the least. I stood up.

His expression turned to one of satisfaction; he'd managed to push another person away, leaving him free to get on with his plan to demolish himself.

'Okay!' I clapped my hands as if I was about to start a clear-up of the area. 'We've a lot to do if we're going to make this happen. Your apartment is out of bounds now, I assume, so you can stay with me. I need to go home and change, I need to get to the office to pick up some things and I need to get to a shop — I'll explain what for later. First, I have to get my car. Are you coming?'

He looked at me in surprise, at my not leaving him in the way he thought I would, then he grabbed his coat and followed me.

★ ★ ★

Once we were in the taxi my phone beeped.

'That's the third one in a row. You never check your messages. Not very encouraging for me for when I'm hanging off a bridge somewhere looking for a pep talk.'

'They're not messages, they're voicemails.'

'How do you know?'

I knew because it was eight a.m. And there was only one thing that happened as soon as it hit eight a.m.

'I just know.'

He studied me. 'You said no secrets, remember?'

I thought about it and out of guilt for having read his 'proposal', which was currently in my pocket, handed him my phone.

He dialled and listened to the messages. Ten minutes later he handed the phone back to me.

I looked at him for a reaction.

'That was your husband. But I think you already know that. He said he's keeping the goldfish and he's getting his solicitors to draw up paperwork to ensure you're legally never allowed to own a fish again. He thinks he might be able to prevent you entering a pet shop too. He's not sure about winning at funfairs but he'll personally be there to beat you and make sure you don't win.'

'Is that it?'

'In the second message he called you a bitch twenty-five times. I didn't count. He did. He said it was twenty-five times. He said you were a bitch

78

multiplied by twenty-five. Then he said it twenty-five times.'

I took the phone from him and sighed. Barry didn't seem to be cooling down at all. In fact he seemed to be getting worse, more frantic. Now it was the goldfish? He hated that goldfish. His niece had bought it for him for his birthday and the only reason she'd bought him a fish was because Barry's brother hated fish too so it was technically a gift for her, to be stored in our home for her to look at and feed when she visited. He could keep the damn fish.

'Actually,' Adam snatched the phone back from me with a mischievous look in his eye, 'I want to count, because wouldn't it be funny if he got it wrong?'

He listened to the voicemail again on speakerphone and each time Barry spat the word out viciously, with venom and bitterness and sadness dripping from every single letter, Adam counted on his hands with a big smile on his face. He ended the call looking disappointed.

'Nah. Twenty-five bitches.' He handed it back to me and looked out the window.

We were silent for a few minutes and my phone beeped again.

'And I thought I had problems,' he said.

8

How to Sincerely Apologise When You Realise You Have Hurt Someone

'So this is him?'

'Yes,' I whispered, sitting in the chair beside Simon Conway's bed.

'He can't hear you, you know.' Adam raised his voice above the norm. 'There's no need to whisper.'

'Shhh.' I was irritated by his disrespect, his obvious need to prove that he wasn't moved by what he saw. Well, I was moved and I wasn't afraid to admit it; I felt raw with emotion. Each time I looked at Simon I relived the moment he shot himself. I heard the sound, the bang that left my ears ringing. I ran through the words I'd said leading up to him putting his gun down on the kitchen counter. It had been going well, his resolve had weakened, we had been engaging perfectly. But then my euphoria had taken over and I'd lost all sense of what I said next — if I'd said anything at all. I squeezed my eyes shut and tried to remember.

'So am I supposed to feel something right now?' Adam interrupted my thoughts, loudly. 'Is this a message, a psycho-babble way of telling me how lucky I am that I'm here and he's there?' he challenged me.

I threw him a dagger look.

80

'Who are you?'

I jumped up from my chair at the sudden interruption by a woman in the room. She was mid to late thirties and held the hands of two little blonde girls who looked up at her with large blue wondering eyes. Jessica and Kate; I remembered Simon telling me about them. Jessica was sad her pet rabbit had died and Kate kept pretending she would see him when Jessica wasn't looking, to make her feel better. He had wondered if Kate would do the same thing about him when he was gone and I had told him he wouldn't have to wonder, wouldn't have to put them both through that if he stayed alive for them. The woman looked shattered. Simon's wife, Susan. My heart began to palpitate, the guilt of my involvement wracking my body. I tried to remember what Angela had said, what everybody had said: it wasn't my fault, I had only tried to help. It wasn't my fault.

'Hello.' I struggled with how to introduce myself. It may have been seconds of silence but it felt as though it stretched on for ever. Susan's face was not inviting, it was not warm and it was not reassuring. It did nothing to help my nervousness and worsened the sense of guilt I felt. I sensed Adam's eyes on me, his saviour, now floundering in my lesson in self-belief and inner strength.

I stepped forward and extended my hand, swallowed, heard the shake in my voice as I spoke. 'My name is Christine Rose. I was with your husband the night he . . . ' I glanced at the two little girls looking up at me wide-eyed.

' . . . the night of the incident. I'd just like to say that — '

'Get out,' Susan said quietly.

'I'm sorry?' I swallowed, my mouth suddenly dry. This had been my worst nightmare. I had lived this scene a thousand times in various ways and through the eyes of many people in my late-night/early-morning fears, but I didn't think it would actually come to fruition. I thought my fears were irrational; the only thing that had made them bearable was knowing they weren't real.

'You heard me,' she repeated, pulling her daughters further into the room so that the doorway was clear for me to leave.

I was frozen in place, this wasn't happening. It took Adam placing a hand on my shoulder and giving me a gentle shove to finally make me come to my senses. We didn't speak until we were both in the car and on the road. Adam opened his mouth to speak, but I got there first.

'I don't want to talk about that.' I struggled not to cry.

'Okay,' he said gently, then he looked like he was going to say more but he stopped himself and looked out the window.

I wish I'd known what it was.

★ ★ ★

I grew up in Clontarf, a coastal suburb of North Dublin. When I met Barry, I obligingly moved to Sandymount, his side of the city. We lived in his bachelor pad because he wanted to be close to his mother who disliked me because I was Church of Ireland although I didn't bother practising — I wasn't sure which bothered her most. After six months of dating, Barry proposed, probably because that's what all our peers were doing at the time, and I said yes because that's what all our peers were saying, and it seemed like the mature and grown-up thing to do at our age, and six months later I was married and living in a new apartment we had bought together in Sandymount with the party behind me and reality now and for ever stretching ahead of me. My business remained in Clontarf, a short DART journey away each morning. Barry had been unable to sell his bachelor pad and instead rented it; the rent paid the mortgage. It would solve a lot of our current problems if Barry moved back into the pad he had made such a song and dance about leaving, thereby allowing me to stay in our home, but no, he was claiming our apartment. He was claiming our car too, so I was currently driving a friend's car; Julie had emigrated to Toronto and still hadn't managed to shift the car, which had been for sale for a year. In return for the favour of driving it, I was also responsible for taking care of its sale, advertising it with a FOR SALE sign on the front and rear windows with my phone number, and as a result fielding phone calls, enquiries and test-drives. I was learning that people had a tendency to phone at random hours looking for the very same details as the car magazine advertisements already stated, as if they were expecting to hear a completely different answer.

My office was on Clontarf Road, on the first floor of a three-storey house which had been the home of my dad's three spinster aunts, Brenda, Adrienne and Christine, for whom me and my two sisters were named. Now the building was home to my dad and sisters' firm, which was called Rose and Daughters Solicitors because my dad was a feminist. My dad had held his practice there for thirty years, ever since his remaining aunt decided to move into a self-contained flat in the basement instead of looking after a large house by herself. As soon as my sisters were qualified, they joined the firm. I had been dreading the day I'd have to tell him I didn't want to work for the family firm, but he was more than understanding. In fact, he didn't want me to work with him.

'You're a thinker,' he said. 'We're doers. The girls are like me, we do. You're like your mother, you think. So go, think.'

Brenda took care of property law, Adrienne took care of family law and Dad liked to chase the accidents, because that's where he believed the money was. They took over the top floor, my office was on the first floor along with an accountant who had been there for twenty years and who hid a bottle of vodka in a drawer in his desk and thought nobody knew about it. It was obvious from the smell of the room and his breath, but mostly I knew because of Jacinta, the cleaner, who gave Dad all the gossip on each of the offices that paid rent. It wasn't a spoken agreement, but they had an understanding that the more information she supplied, the more Dad paid her. I frequently wondered what she told him about me.

The ground-floor businesses had changed so many times in the past few years I didn't know who was who when I passed them in the halls. Thanks to the recession, businesses were moving out as quickly as they moved in. The basement, which had been my great-aunt Christine's home in her final years, had gone from being an insurance company to a stockbrokers to a graphic design studio, and it was currently my home. From one Christine to another. My dad had grudgingly agreed to let it to me and furnish it for me; the day I'd arrived I'd found a single bed in the bedroom, a single chair in the kitchen and an armchair in the living room. I had to kit the rest out myself by raiding my sisters' houses. Brenda had found it hilarious to donate her son's Spider-Man duvet cover to me. She'd thought it would cheer me up, but it had only made me sadder about the state of my affairs. A duvet cover I could easily afford, so for the first few days I kept meaning to change it, only to keep forgetting until I got to the point where I didn't even notice it any more.

Next door was a bookshop, the Book Stand, also known as the Last Stand due to its stubborn inclination to stay open and current when every small bookshop for miles around had been forced to shut. It was run by my close friend Amelia, and I suspect that ordering books for me was the only thing keeping her in business, as the shop was almost always empty. The stock was low and most things you wanted had to be ordered, which meant it wasn't appealing to browsers. Amelia lived above the shop with her mother, who was in need of constant care as a result of a severe stroke. More often than not the bell ringing in the shop was not the sound of a new client coming through the front door but her mother upstairs, needing some attention. Still a child when her mother fell ill, Amelia had been caring for her ever since and she seemed to me to be in desperate need of a break, of some TLC. Like most carers, she needed someone to protect and care for her for a change. The bookshop seemed almost secondary to what Amelia spent her days doing, which was being at her mother's beck and call, devoting every thought and waking moment to her.

'Hi, sweetheart.' Amelia bounced up from her stool where she'd been reading to pass the time in the empty shop. She looked over my shoulder at Adam, who followed me in, and her pupils dilated at the sight of him.

'I thought you were waiting in the car,' I said.

'You forgot to leave the window open for me,' he said, poker-faced, looking around the shop.

'Amelia, this is Adam. Adam, this is Amelia. Adam is . . . a client.'

'Oh,' Amelia said, disappointed.

I knew what I wanted and headed straight for the self-help section. Adam wandered around the shop, seeming dazed, withdrawn, looking but not really seeing.

'He's gorgeous,' Amelia whispered.

'He's a client,' I whispered back.

'He's gorgeous.'

I laughed. 'Fred wouldn't like to hear you say that.'

She studied her fingernails and lifted her eyebrows. 'He's asked me to go to the Pearl for lunch.'

'The Pearl? That's very fancy.' I was confused by this, as Fred was not the spontaneous romantic type. Then it hit me. 'He's going to propose!'

Amelia couldn't keep a straight face any more, clearly thinking the same thing. 'I mean, he might not, he probably won't, but you know . . . '

I gasped. 'Oh my God, I'm so happy for you!' We hugged excitedly.

'It hasn't happened yet.' Amelia hit me. 'Stop jinxing me.'

'Can you put this on the tab?'

Amelia looked at my book selection. '*At last!* Christine, that's great,' she said, with relief.

I frowned. 'It's not for me. What do you mean?'

'Oh. Sorry. Nothing. No. It's . . . Nothing.' Her cheeks pinked and she changed the subject. 'Barry called me last night.'

'Oh?' Fear flooded my body.

'It was quite late. I think he'd had a few drinks.'

I nibbled on my nails.

Adam joined us. He was like a shark, sensing blood, he knew exactly when to be around me each time my life was being chipped away at.

'I'm sure it wasn't true, or maybe it was, but . . . but he shouldn't have said it to me anyway. Whatever you two talk about together really should be kept private, even if it is about me, so I'm not blaming you for what you said about me.' She looked hurt, her face contradicting everything she had said.

'Amelia, what did he say?'

She took a deep breath and went for it. 'He said that you think I'm a loser for living at home with my mother, that I need to get a life and move out. That I need to put her in a home and move in with Fred or else you wouldn't be surprised if he left me.'

'Oh my God.' I hid my face with my hands. 'I am so sorry he said that to you.'

'It's okay. I told him that I knew he was hurting but he was disgusting. I hope you don't mind.'

'No, that's fine, you're totally entitled to say what you like.' My face was red and I knew it, revealing my guilt. I couldn't deny that Barry and I had discussed those things, but how dare he tell Amelia. I wondered how many phone calls he'd made last night and how many truths he'd told to the people I loved, hurting them in order to hurt me.

Amelia waited for me to tell her it wasn't true.

'Look, I obviously didn't phrase it like *that*.'

She looked offended.

'I just worry that you're always looking out for other people and not for yourself. That it would be nice for you and Fred to live together, to have a life *together*.'

'But this is how it's been since I was twelve, Christine, you know that.' Amelia was becoming angry. 'I'm not going to ship her off to a home while I go live the life fandango.'

'I know, I know, but you haven't even been out of the country . . . ever. You've never taken a holiday. That's all I said — promise. I was worried about you.'

'You don't need to worry about me,' she said, lifting her chin. 'Fred is fine with the way things are. He understands.'

We were interrupted by the familiar sound of the bell. Amelia quickly excused herself to see to her mother. I left the shop with the book tucked in my bag, hidden away from Adam's eyes, feeling worse than ever.

'So now he's ringing your friends. That's smart,' Adam said. 'Your day keeps getting better and better.'

I put my chin up. 'Yes, but you know it's all about how you deal with it, Adam. Face it with positivity.'

He rolled his eyes. 'I have a problem with that. For example, I think your friend shouldn't be getting ahead of herself about her lunch today.'

'You were listening.'

'You were squealing.'

'He's taking her to the Pearl!'

'So?'

'Well, that's where people propose.'

'That's also where people eat lunch. She shouldn't get carried away before it happens. It might not happen.'

I sighed, feeling his energy draining me. 'You know, that's what we need to fix. You're a negative thinker. You keep thinking about all the bad things that *might* happen all the time. Eventually you begin to make them happen. Are you aware of the laws of attraction?' I thought about my run-in with Simon's wife, how I had replayed that scene over and over in my head until it had eventually happened. 'If you think life is crap, life will be crap.'

'Again, I don't think this is official therapist terminology.'

'So go see a real therapist.'

'No.'

We stepped inside and walked up the stairs to the first floor.

I stopped at the door to my office and struggled to get my key in. I tried another, then another, then another of the ten keys I had on the chain.

'What are you, a prison warden?'

I ignored him and tried the next key.

'Damn it. They've done it again. Come on.' I trudged up the stairs.

My sisters and my dad were sitting around the meeting table in their office when we entered. Dad was perfectly turned out in a pin-stripe suit, pink shirt and tie and handkerchief. His shoes were black and highly polished, there wasn't a hair out of place on his head, his fingernails were manicured and buffed so that there was a sheen from them. He was short and appeared more like a tailor than a solicitor.

'I knew it was because she'd met another guy,'

Brenda said, snapping her fingers as soon as she saw Adam. 'Jesus, Barry will die when he sees him. How's his baldy little head going to compete with that?' she referred to Adam's mop of blond curls.

'Hello, family,' I said. 'This is Adam — he's a *client*. Adam, this is my dad, Michael, and the two witches are Brenda and Adrienne.'

'Named after two of the witches who once lived here,' Adrienne told him, then looked at me and added: 'The third being Christine — so you are in fact one of us, no matter how much you try to flee.'

'They had purple hair and smoked a lot,' said Brenda, still scrutinising Adam.

'They never married,' Dad chipped in.

'Lesbians,' Adrienne said.

'Were not,' Brenda disagreed. 'Adrienne was a slut. She was proposed to five times.'

'By the same guy?' I asked.

'No. Different men,' Dad said. 'I think the third man went on to murder someone. But,' he frowned, 'I could be mistaking him for someone else.'

'Slut,' Brenda confirmed.

'She didn't sleep with them,' Dad said. 'Proposals were different in those days.'

'Lesbian,' Adrienne insisted.

I waited for them to finish. They played 'slut or lesbian' all the time with different people.

'You think everyone is a lesbian because you're one,' Dad said to Adrienne.

'I'm bisexual, Dad.'

'You've had five girlfriends and one boyfriend.

The man was an experiment. You're a lesbian. The sooner you realise that, the sooner you will be able to settle down and have a normal family,' he said.

'So how do you know Christine?' Brenda asked Adam. 'Take a seat.' She pulled out a chair.

Adam looked at me. I shrugged tiredly and then he sat.

He made a rapid assessment of my family and then said, 'She stopped me from jumping off the Ha'penny Bridge last night.'

'She's always been a killjoy,' Adrienne accused me.

'He wasn't jumping for fun,' I explained.

They all looked at him.

He fidgeted a little, unsure what to do with their stares in the light of that revelation. I'm sure he was wondering whether his timing was off, whether he should have mentioned it at all. But they were good at that, my family: drawing you in and making you feel that the important stuff wasn't really important at all. They decided what was.

Adrienne scrunched up her face. 'But the Ha'penny? It's not even that high.'

'What are you talking about?' Brenda asked her.

'That's hardly a drop at all. What is it, eight feet above the water?'

'He wasn't trying to kill himself with the drop, Adrienne,' Brenda said. 'I'd imagine he was trying to drown himself. Were you?'

They all looked at him.

He didn't know how to answer, his surprise

was so great. I was used to a range of reactions when I brought people home. Some of my friends couldn't cope with them; others dived right in and joined them; others, like Adam, were content to observe the unusual rhythm of their talk and humour, without taking offence, since it was clear that none was intended.

'I said I'd imagine you were trying to drown yourself?' Brenda spoke a little more loudly.

'He doesn't have water in his ears, Brenda,' Adrienne interrupted. 'She saved him, remember?'

They chuckled a little. Adam looked at me in surprise.

I mouthed, *sorry*, and he shook his head with a puzzled expression, as if there was no need for me to apologise.

'And well done, Christine,' Dad said, giving me the thumbs up. 'Good for you.'

'Thanks.'

'That probably makes you feel better about the last one, does it?'

Adam looked at me with a protective concerned expression.

'But the Liffey isn't that deep, is it?' Adrienne asked.

'Adrienne, you could drown face down in a puddle if you got stuck, or had broken your back or whatever,' Brenda explained.

Adrienne looked at Adam. 'Was your back broken?'

'No.'

She narrowed her eyes. 'Can you swim?'

'Yes.'

'Then I don't get it. It would be like Brenda eating ice cream all day to get skinny.' She turned to Brenda as an idea occurred to her: 'Which in fact, you do try to do.'

'Andrew, would you like to see my ad?' Dad asked.

'His name is Adam, and no he doesn't,' I said.

'I'm sure he can speak for himself.' Dad looked at him.

'Yeah, sure, why not?'

Dad left the table and went to his office.

'Dad's an ambulance-chaser,' Brenda explained.

'He does personal injury law,' I clarified. 'Makes more money than the two of them put together.'

'And spends it on pedicures,' Brenda said.

'And his back, sack and crack,' Adrienne said, and they both cackled.

'I heard that, and I only did it once,' Dad called, returning from the office with a video cassette in his hand. 'I was in India in extreme heat and it made the world of difference,' he explained calmly and we all winced at the image. 'Did you hurt yourself on the bridge, Andrew?'

'It's Adam, and no,' he replied politely.

'No rusty nails, sore neck, that kind of thing?'

'No.'

Dad looked disappointed. 'No matter. Now where can we watch this thing?'

'Our TV doesn't play cassettes. That's prehistoric.'

Again, he was disappointed. 'You know this ad

94

was before its time. I filmed it twenty years ago. Ireland wasn't ready for it. But now you see those guys on TV all the time. Especially in America. If you accidentally cut your big toe with the clippers they can get you money.' He shook his head in admiration. 'Do you have a VCR? You could go home to get it and bring it back.'

'He lives in Tipperary,' I explained.

'Why are you here?'

'Dad, aren't you listening?'

'He tried to jump off the Ha'penny Bridge,' Adrienne clarified.

'But there's great bridges in Tipperary. There's the old bridge in Carrick-on-Suir, Madam's Bridge in Fethard, that's a pretty one and there's the triple span railway viaduct over the River Suir — '

'Okay, thanks,' I interrupted.

'So, Adam . . . ' Brenda rested her chin on her hand and stared at him, ready to gossip. 'Did Christine tell you she left her husband?'

'Yes.'

'What do you think about that?'

'I think it was heartless of her. It doesn't sound like he did anything wrong,' he said, as though I wasn't standing right beside him.

'He didn't. I agree with you,' Brenda said.

'He was uninteresting though,' Dad said.

'Boring is not a divorceable offence,' Adrienne said. 'If that was the case Brenda would never have lasted with Bryan.'

'True,' Brenda conceded.

'Bryan isn't boring,' Dad defended his

95

son-in-law. 'He's an under-achiever. He's lazy. It's different.'

'Also true,' Brenda said.

'We have to go,' I said. 'I don't want to know who changed my locks, I just want the key to the new one.'

Brenda and Adrienne looked at Dad. He started laughing. 'Sorry I couldn't help it. She takes it so badly, it's *funny*. I'll get the key.' He stood and made his way back to the office again with the cassette in his hand.

'So I take it Gemma didn't come here looking for a key?' I asked. She was usually in before me, Peter and Paul in the mornings and I wasn't ready to face another day without her, not after the chaos in the office the previous week.

'We heard you fired her by dropping a *How to Fire Someone* book on her toe. That's not very cool, Christine.'

Adam looked at me, discontent on his face.

'It was an accident. Did she tell you that?'

'She was here on Friday looking for a job.'

'Tell me you didn't give her one!'

'We might.'

'You can't, she's mine.'

'You don't want her, but you don't want anyone else to have her. You're an abusive employer. I'm definitely hiring her,' Adrienne replied, an amused smile on her lips.

They loved to taunt me. They were all so *alike*. Their humour was and always had been unique and particular to them. I understood it but had never been amused by it. That made everything even more hilarious from their point of view,

96

which served to escalate their behaviour. It was as though they had a secret club and were doing everything they could not to keep it secret, hoping to welcome me in. But it was impossible for me. I was too different. Black sheep was an understatement; I was a completely different species.

'Gemma pre-empted my firing her. I was only thinking about it. I might have to make some cuts. The flat is costing me too much.' I glared at Dad as he dangled the key and I snatched it from him.

'I've never in all my years given a hand-out. You all have to pay your own way,' he said.

'There's such a thing as a helping hand.' I lost my temper a little.

'Well then, get back with your husband,' he said. 'There are worse things than marrying boring. Look at Brenda. Those kids are the best advertisement for superglue that I've ever seen.'

'Stay with me,' Brenda offered. 'We could always use some fresh blood.'

'No. I don't want to.'

'Why not?'

'You'd get on my nerves. And Bryan just, you know, *hovers*,' I admitted.

Adrienne and Dad started laughing. Adam looked amused even though he had no idea who Bryan was.

'That's true, he does hover,' Adrienne giggled. 'I'd never realised that before.'

'He's always like this — ' Dad leered over Adrienne's shoulder and made a face, and they both laughed. Adam laughed too.

'That's true,' Brenda agreed again.

'All I'm saying is, I'd appreciate it if the landlord would go a little more lightly on me,' I said.

'I've a mortgage to pay,' Dad said, abandoning his leering pose and sitting back down.

'This building's been paid for one hundred times over, and there was no one in that flat before me for a long time. The place reeks of damp, the toilet doesn't flush properly, and there's no furniture to speak of, so you're hardly missing out on a tenant by having me there.'

'Excuse me. I furnished it for you.'

'Putting a teaspoon in a drawer is not furnishing a flat,' I exaggerated.

'Beggars can't be choosers.'

'I'm not a beggar, I'm your daughter.'

'And you can't choose that, either.'

'That doesn't mean anything, Dad.'

He gave me a look to imply that it did mean something and I would have to figure it out.

'So what are you two doing?' Brenda asked Adam. 'Is she going to place you in a new job and send you on your way?'

Adam looked slightly amused by it all; his eyes had a glint of light in them. 'She has to convince me to like my life by my thirty-fifth birthday.'

They were all silent. They didn't need to ask what would happen if he didn't like his life by that deadline; it was implied.

'When's that?' Adrienne asked.

'Two weeks,' I said.

'Twelve days,' Adam corrected me.

'Are you having a party?' Brenda asked.

'Yes.' Adam appeared puzzled by the direction they were taking.

'Can we come?' Adrienne asked.

'You should get one of those cakes that looks like a cake but really it's cheese. Big circular cheeses, all layered up. They're very clever,' Dad said.

'Dad, you're obsessed with cheese cakes.'

'I think they're clever.'

'You look sad,' Brenda said, staring at Adam.

'That's because he is sad,' Adrienne said.

'I don't know if Christine is the right person for you,' Brenda said. 'JJ Recruitment is great.'

'Or I know an excellent therapist,' Adrienne offered. 'Which Christine is not,' she emphasised.

'If it's that man you're seeing, I wouldn't recommend him,' Dad told her.

'Hold on, are you questioning my skills?' I asked. 'Recruitment is more than simply finding someone a job. I help people all the time. I find out what people are looking for, then I take them from one place in their lives and bring them to another.' I tried to sell myself to Adam, without looking at him.

'Like a taxi driver,' Brenda said.

'No . . . it's more than that.' I tried not to let my frustration show because I knew they were only winding me up.

'Nobody's questioning your skills,' Brenda said.

'She means because you're sad too,' Adrienne clarified.

'Well, maybe they'll make each other happy,' Dad said, standing. 'Meeting's adjourned, let's get to work. Best of luck, Martin, and look into those cakes made with cheese. Very clever.' He flashed Adam a pearly white smile and made his way back to his office. There was the sudden sound of a police frequency.

'He's the best prospect you've ever brought home,' Brenda said quietly as Adam left the office ahead of me, shaking his head as if unsure of what he'd witnessed.

'Brenda, on Sunday night he tried to kill himself,' I hissed.

'Still. At least he had a life in him to kill. Barry barely had a pulse even on his best day.'

I followed Adam down the stairs.

'Oh, by the way,' Brenda screamed down the stairs, 'Barry called me late last night to tell me you PEE IN THE SHOWER!'

Adam and I froze at the top of the steps. He slowly turned to face me. I closed my eyes and took a deep breath. Then I marched down the stairs past him.

'I don't want to talk about that either,' I said loudly.

I heard him give a small laugh. That lovely sound I'd heard so little of.

When we got into my office, Gemma had left a message on my desk. She had taken one of my own books from the shelf: *How to Sincerely Apologise When You Realise You Have Hurt Someone*. I took it that Gemma was advising me to read it as opposed to offering any apologies herself.

As the morning drew on there was a flood of phone calls, texts and voicemails from friends and acquaintances who had spoken to or received communication from Barry the previous night. I realised then that perhaps I should start reading. It sounded as though I might have a few apologies to make.

9

How to Enjoy Your Life
in Thirty Simple Ways

The first thing I needed to do before sitting down with Adam was to cancel all of my appointments for the next two weeks. With no Gemma to help me with the logistics, I would have to delegate my work and meetings to my two colleagues Peter and Paul, who already weren't talking to me after Gemma's unfair dismissal. I sat down at Gemma's desk and got started. Cancelling Oscar took me the longest as I called him just as he had allowed the third bus to pass without getting on. I had to talk him through the entire experience of getting on the bus, sitting down and doing breathing techniques, then tell him a story to distract him, and then I had to supply him with my mobile number because he was so distressed that I would be out of the office for the next fortnight. But by the time I'd finished, I was able to bid farewell to an exhilarated man who felt like he could take on the world after accomplishing three bus stops. His next task was to walk home, which he would do with a spring in his step. As soon as I'd hung up, Adam shouted to me from my office.

'*Forty-two Tips on How to Think Positive Thoughts When Everything Is Going Wrong . . .*'

Another book title from my collection. '*Thirty-Five Ways to Think Positively . . .* ' He snorted derisively. 'These numbers intrigue me. Why so specific? Why forty-*two* and not forty? Why can't you round off your positive thoughts to the nearest ten?'

He moved along the shelf.

'*Five Ways to Show Love, Five Ways to Conserve Your Energy. Ten Ways to Conserve Energy.*' He laughed. 'Okay, I think I see how you do it. You file these in order of numbers, right? Do you say to yourself, 'Today I'm in the mood for a *long* route to conserving my energy,' or 'Today I'm feeling quite tired so I'm going to take the short cut to conserving energy'? Surely you would always go for *five* ways to conserve your energy, because wouldn't doing *ten* things when you had the option of five defeat the purpose? Do you think the person who wrote the five ways has a lot more or less energy than the person who wrote the ten ways? Because he has more methods, but he wrote a shorter book, which was probably less exhausting. They should meet up; maybe this guy could write a book called *How to Advise People How to Write How-to Books*. Six ways, twelve ways, thirty-nine ways, sixty-six ways — yes, we have a winner!' He held a book in the air. '*Sixty-six Ways to Solve Your Money Problems.* Sixty-six? I know just one: *go to work*,' he said to the book, and continued to browse.

'Some people can't work.'

'Of course. Stress is the new back problem.'

'You're not at work. In fact, I'm curious to

103

know where exactly they think you are.'

He ignored me. 'Is it like self-prescribed healing? You say, 'I need six ways to lose weight,' or 'This week I need twenty-one ways.' This week I'm a Nine Ways to Walk Up the Stairs kind of person.'

'That's not a book.'

'No, but it could be. You should write it. I'd like to know nine ways to get up a flight of stairs. The most obvious way is clearly never the one these people have in mind.'

Of course it was my ambition to write a book, but I wasn't about to share that with him, not when he had that opinion of self-help. I felt it was close to happening though. Only the previous week I thought about taking *How to Write a Successful Book* from the unpacked pile of boxes that contained my life in the flat downstairs. Barry hadn't been very supportive of my dream — not that that should have stopped me from doing what I wanted to do. I freely admit that in the past I had used his lack of support as an excuse because I was afraid of doing it, but things were different now and I had promised myself that I would try.

There were many themes going around in my head, but the working title was *How to Find the Job of Your Dreams*. So far I'd found thirteen variants of the same title in print and I'd read four of them and still felt I had more to add. The books I'd read seemed to focus on get-rich-quick schemes, whereas I always felt the end goal should be personal happiness. Brenda told me personal happiness didn't sell, that I should weave sex in the office into it, or at least dedicate a chapter to it; again, a family member's input into my personal ambitions proving infinitely unhelpful.

Adam meanwhile was still venting about the self-help collection.

'Is there a secret safe with a load of books for me? Maybe *One Hundred Ways Not to Kill Yourself?*'

Thinking he was hilarious, he plopped himself down in an armchair, which happened to be mine. Seeing as it had taken him so long to get there, I didn't object. I sat in the chair my clients usually sat in. I wasn't used to this angle of the room and I immediately felt discombobulated.

'You know you're not far off,' I said, beginning the session. 'I'm not going to give you one hundred ways not to kill yourself, but we are going to put together a crisis plan.'

'A what?'

I slid a book from the shelf behind me: *How to Cope with Suicidal Thoughts*. I flicked it open to the appropriate page. I'd read this back to back in the sleepless nights that followed the Simon Conway experience. 'It's basically a list of instructions you need to follow if you have a suicidal thought — of which you've admitted you've had lots. Since you already tried to act on it once, you might want to do it again.'

'I told you, I *will* want to do it again if nothing changes.'

'And until your birthday, you're mine,' I said, sternly. 'We have a deal. For the next twelve days I will do my very best to keep my side of the

105

deal. You will have to keep yours. Stay alive. That is your job. Follow the steps and you will stay alive. You may even start to feel closer to finding yourself again. That's how I can help you get Maria back.'

'Fine.'

'Okay. We'll get to the plan in a moment, it will take us a while to write up. First I'd like to talk. I need to get a real understanding of where you are in your life, how you're feeling.'

I left a silence. He looked left, then right, for the hidden camera.

'I'm feeling . . . suicidal.'

I knew he was being sarcastic, but I didn't laugh.

'Just so you know, suicidal is not a feeling. It's a state of being. Sadness is a feeling, loneliness is a feeling, anger is a feeling. Frustration is a feeling. Jealousy is a feeling. Suicidal is not a feeling. You can have suicidal *thoughts*, but a thought is merely that: a *thought*. Our thoughts are ever-changing, because we put them there. Once you grasp the difference between suicidal thoughts and your feelings, you will start to understand your emotions. You can separate your suicidal thoughts from your feelings. You will not think, Today I want to kill myself. You will think, Today I feel angry that my sister skipped the country and left me to run the business. Then you'll deal with your anger. Today I feel overwhelmed by the responsibility of my job — then you'll deal with feeling overwhelmed. I can help you learn how to get to the bottom of your suicidal thoughts, how to challenge these

106

thoughts and regain control. So, Adam, how are you feeling?'

He looked uncomfortable. He squirmed in his chair and looked around the room. Finally his gaze came to rest somewhere outside the window and he relaxed a little. After thinking about it for a few minutes he said, 'I'm feeling . . . pissed off.'

'Good. Why?'

'Because my girlfriend is shagging my best friend.'

Not quite what I was looking for, but I nodded at him to continue.

'I'm feeling . . . like an absolute idiot, for not knowing it was going on.' He leaned forward, elbows on his thighs, understanding that he was actually going to do this. He rubbed his face and sat up again. 'But I feel like I understand why she did it. The stuff you said this morning, about me being detached — she's right. I took my eye off the ball, I got distracted with all of this other stuff, it took over. I haven't been in a good place. But I can tell her that I've changed, and hopefully she'll change her mind.'

'When are you going to tell her that you've changed?'

'I don't know, today?'

'So you've changed overnight. All the feelings of being overwhelmed by work, of being abandoned by your sister, all that bitterness and anger at having to leave a job and life that you love to fulfil a family duty, all that disappointment with your life, with who you are as a person, all that feeling conflicted about your

107

father being terminally ill, feeling that you *no longer want to live* . . . All those feelings have just disappeared?'

He stared at the floor, his jaw tightening as he worked it over in his head. 'No. But it will change. You'll help me. You promised.'

'My help starts here, in this room. Things won't change unless *you* change you. So talk to me.'

We talked for two hours. When Adam appeared sufficiently drained, and my head was starting to pound with all the responsibilities he had resting on his shoulders, I decided to take a break. I knew the problems, now it was time to gain some perspective, to show him the joy of life. This was the bit I was nervous about. I wasn't good at it, I wasn't sure what to do or where to take him. Especially given that I wasn't exactly feeling the life and soul of the party myself at that moment.

'What now?' he asked. He looked tired.

'Um, hang on a moment.' I stepped outside my office; by this time Peter and Paul had arrived but they were still refusing to acknowledge my presence. I didn't care because I had other things on my mind. I took the new book I'd bought from Amelia, *Thirty Simple Ways to Enjoy Life*, the book Amelia had thought I was buying for me, and I recalled her remark: *At last!* Was I really that dull? I had tried to keep my troubles to myself, hadn't discussed my sadness with anyone. I thought I'd been covering it up so well.

I flicked through the first few pages.

1. Enjoy your meal, don't just eat. Taste it and appreciate its richness.

Food — seriously? But what else was I going to do with him? I stuffed the book back into my bag. 'Come on, let's go.'

'Where are we going?'

'To eat,' I said perkily.

I wasn't sure if Gemma would be back, but on the off chance, by way of explanation I placed a copy of *How to Share Your Financial Problems With People Who Depend on You* on her desk and hoped that she would understand.

⋆ ⋆ ⋆

The venue for item 1 on our list was Bay restaurant in Clontarf with views over Dublin Bay.

'So eating is fun?' Adam asked, his chin resting on his hand as if his head was too heavy for his neck. 'I thought it was something that was necessary for life.'

While he scanned listlessly through the menu, I took in the packed café. The place was brimming with people, the chat was loud, plates were piled high with colourful vibrant food, and the aromas wafting around the room probably had everyone's mouths watering, though they were making my stomach churn.

'Yes of course,' I lied. All I really wanted was to eat a green salad and have it over with, but I needed to set a good example for Adam. 'I'll have the braised lamb shank, with root

109

vegetables, harissa hummus and herb quinoa, please.' I forced a smile for the waitress while inwardly dreading the task of eating all that food.

'I'll just have a black coffee, thanks,' Adam said, shutting the menu.

'No, no!' I wagged a finger at him. I opened the menu and handed it back to him. 'Food. Fun. Eat.'

Adam looked lost as his tired eyes flicked across the menu.

'What do you suggest?' I asked the waitress.

'I really like the baked marinated salmon fillet on a bed of Mediterranean vegetable ratatouille and creamy mash.'

Adam looked as if he was going to vomit in his mouth.

'He'd love that, thank you.'

'No starters?' she asked.

'No,' we said in unison.

'So when did you lose your appetite?' I asked.

'I don't know, a couple of months ago. When did you lose yours?'

'I haven't.'

He raised his eyebrow.

'Alcohol and caffeine are not a good idea for someone who's depressed,' I said, trying to regain the upper hand and keep him in the spotlight.

'And what did you have for breakfast this morning?'

I thought about my black coffee at the hotel. 'Yes, but I'm not depressed.'

He snorted.

'*You're* depressed. You tried to kill yourself.

I'm just . . . a bit down.'

'A bit down.' He studied me. 'That's an understatement. Eeyore has nothing on you.'

I laughed despite myself. 'All I meant was, we should look at your diet, it will help you. That has a large part to do with depression. Clearly you're fit, I mean, you must work out a lot.' I felt my face get hot. 'I never see you eat, I don't know where you get the energy.'

'Would you like me to tell you in five ways or ten ways?'

'Just one please.'

'It's from when I'm stripping, you know? When I'm on stage, dancing with the boys.'

I laughed. 'I think you've got stripping and modelling completely mixed up.'

'Well, I don't know what goes on in your head,' he said with a smile.

The waitress placed two enormous plates of food in front of us. We both looked at it with dread.

'Is everything okay?' the waitress asked, noticing the reaction. 'Did I get the order right?'

'Yes, of course, this looks . . . delicious. Thank you.' I picked up my knife and fork, unsure where to begin.

'So when's the last time you went out to eat, Christine, since you think this is so much fun?' he asked, studying his plate and, like me, not knowing where to start.

'It's been a long time, but only because we were saving up for the wedding. Mmm, this is good. Is yours good?' *Don't just eat your food, taste it.* 'I don't know what this is — is it ginger?

It's really good, and I think I can taste lemon. Anyway, after the wedding we went away on honeymoon and then we had no money so we stayed in for most of the year or got the occasional take-away, which was fine because all our friends were in the same boat.'

'Fun,' he said sarcastically. 'How long were you married?'

'Eat. Is that nice? Is the mash creamy?'

'Yes, the mash is creamy,' he played along. 'And the carrots are carroty.'

'Nine months,' I ignored him.

'You left him after nine months? I've been with girlfriends I hated longer than that. You can't have tried very hard.'

'I tried very hard.' I looked down and played with my food.

'Eat. Is your lamb lamby?' he asked. 'So when did you know it wasn't right?' He took a forkful of salmon, chewed slowly and swallowed as if it was a giant pill.

I thought about it. Give the truth, or the answer I had given everyone else?

'No secrets,' he added.

'I had twinges of doubt for a while, but I knew it wasn't right, for sure, when I was walking down the aisle on my wedding day.' That was the truth.

He stopped eating, looked at me in surprise.

'Keep eating,' I said. 'I was crying my eyes out, walking towards him. Everybody still talks about it, they thought it was such a sweet moment. But my sisters knew. They weren't tears of joy.'

112

'Then why did you get married?'

'I panicked. I wanted to stop it but didn't have the courage. And I didn't want to hurt him. I couldn't see a way out; I was trapped, but it was a trap I'd got myself into. So I made myself go ahead with it.'

'You got married because you didn't want to hurt his feelings?'

'Which is why I couldn't stay married to him just because I didn't want to hurt his feelings.'

He pondered that, then nodded. 'That's a fair point.'

'If I'd stopped and thought about it at the time, really thought about it, then I would have seen another way out. A better way.'

'Like being on a bridge.'

'Exactly like that.' I pushed the food around on my plate. 'I loved him, you know, but I have a theory about love. I think that, however good it is, some love isn't meant to be for ever.'

He was quiet. We both took a few forkfuls of food. Eventually he dropped his cutlery on the plate.

'I surrender,' he said, hands in the air. 'I can't eat any more. Can I please stop now?'

'Sure.' I put my knife and fork down too, relieved. 'Jesus, I'm full,' I groaned, hands on my bloated belly, accidentally dropping my act. 'Imagine, people do this three times a day.'

We looked at each other and laughed.

'What's next?' He leaned forward, eyes shining.

'Er . . . ' I looked in my bag and pretended to root for a tissue. Surreptitiously I opened the book.

113

2. Go for a walk in the park. Don't just walk, take in your surroundings, remark on the beauty of the life around you.

'Let's go for a walk,' I said as if I'd that moment thought of it.

★   ★   ★

We were both ready to walk off the food we had forced ourselves to eat, so despite the extreme cold we made our way to St Anne's Park, the second largest municipal park in Dublin. Bundled up against the chill, we wandered around the walled garden, the red stables that held food markets during the weekends, the Herculanean temple by the duck pond — which I pulled him past quickly in case he felt compelled to jump in. The rose garden at this time of year was a disappointment and the wrong place to choose to sit on a bench and take a break. We looked out at the bleak cut-back branches with no colour whatsoever while the icy wind whipped our faces, and the cold bench permeated our coats and trousers straight to our bottoms. I used every opportunity and excuse I could to investigate his mind.

'Did you buy Maria flowers often?'

'Yeah, but not on Valentine's Day. I am absolutely not allowed to buy them on Valentine's Day. Too clichéd.'

'So what does she get?'

'Last year it was a grapefruit. The year before that a frog.'

114

'Hold on, we'll get back to the grapefruit. A frog?!'

'You know, so she could kiss it and get her Prince Charming.'

'Uck. That's pathetic.'

'Are you trying to build my confidence up or destroy me?'

'Sorry. I'm sure she loved the frog.'

'She did. We both loved Hulk. Until he escaped out the balcony window.' Then he smiled as if he'd thought of something funny.

'What is it?'

'Nah it's stupid . . . personal.'

The secret smile intrigued me; it was a look that revealed a side of him I hadn't seen before; a softer side, the romantic Adam.

'Come on, you have to tell me. No secrets, remember?'

'It's nothing. No big deal. We had a joke about me getting her a type of flower, that's all.'

'What kind of flower?'

'A water lily. She liked the painting, the Monet one?' He left it at that.

'There has to be more to the story than that.'

'Well, I decided to get her one. I wasn't allowed to get her flowers for Valentine's Day, but I thought this one would be an exception. I was in the park, saw them and thought of her. And so I went into the lake to get one.'

'In your clothes?'

'Yeah,' he laughed. 'It was deeper than I thought. It went up to my waist, but I had to keep going. The park officials practically chased me out.'

'I don't think you're supposed to steal water lilies.'

'Well, that's the thing — I didn't. I made a mistake. I got her the lily pad.' He started laughing. 'I was wondering why she thought they were so special.'

I started laughing. 'You eejit. What kind of person thinks a water lily is a lily pad?'

'Easy mistake to make, if you ask me. She liked it though. She used it in the apartment. She put a photo of us on it, with candles.'

'That was sweet.' I smiled. 'So you two are romantic then?'

'If you call it romantic.' He shrugged it off. 'We had fun. Have fun,' he corrected himself.

Oddly, I felt sad. Barry and I had no stories like that. I tried hard to think of one; not that I'd share it, but I wanted it for me, to remind myself of the fun. I couldn't think of anything. That kind of gesture never occurred to Barry nor had it to me, but I was getting a sense of Adam and Maria's relationship. It was spontaneous, fun, unique, *them*.

We got lost along the walkways, me doing my best to point things out, to make Adam feel and see all the life around us. I didn't know the names of anything and so I'd stop and read the signs, asking Adam to read the Latin names, which made us laugh when he got them horribly wrong.

'They sound like dinosaurs,' I said.

'They sound like diseases,' he said, shoving his hands in his pockets. 'Excuse me, Doctor, I have a touch of the prunus avium.'

116

'What's that?' I asked.

He checked the sign. 'The cherry tree, apparently. Imagine having a name like that.'

'Actually, what *is* your family name?'

His eyes lost a bit of the new regained light and I knew I'd touched a nerve. 'Basil,' he said.

'Ah. Like the chocolate.' I tried to keep his mood up.

'And the herb.'

'Yes, but the *chocolate*: 'With Basil, You Dazzle',' I said cheesily, quoting the company motto, which never quite worked if you pronounced it as the Americans did. So the joke motto was *With Bayzil, You Dayz-zle*. It was a much-loved Irish confectionery brand that had been around almost two hundred years, the very mention of Basil's instantly bringing smiles to every child and adult in the country. But not to Adam. Seeing the expression on his face, I added, 'Sorry, you've probably been hearing that all of your life.'

'I have. Which is the way out of here?' he asked, suddenly fed up with my company.

My phone rang.

'Amelia,' I read.

'Ah yes, the proposal that never happened,' he said, voice flat. He wandered off to give me privacy.

'Amelia,' I responded, my voice full of anticipation. I heard a sob down the phone. 'Amelia what's wrong?'

'You were right,' she cried.

'What?! How was I right?' My voice rang out. Adam stopped searching for the way out and

117

stared at me. He knew from my face what had happened and I knew exactly what was going through his mind: so much for positive thinking.

★ ★ ★

I ran all the way down Clontarf's promenade with the wind slapping my cheeks. I had to concentrate on my footing, darting and leaping and dodging patches of ice as if I were running an obstacle course all the way back to the bookshop. Somewhere behind me, Adam was slowly making his way back with my apartment key in his hand. I tried not to worry about him being by the sea by himself; I had given him strict instructions, rapidly run through the crisis plan one more time, and then started running. I needed to get to my friend.

Amelia was sitting in an armchair in the corner of the bookshop, her eyes red raw. On the other side of the shop a woman dressed in a Dracula outfit with a white face and blood dripping from her mouth was sitting in the story-hour chair and reading to a group of terrified three- to five-year-olds.

'They walked down the dark stairs into the basement. Flames of fire on the walls lit their way. Then before them, there they were — the coffins,' she said spookily.

One of the children let out a sob and ran to her mother. The mother gathered her belongings, threw the Dracula woman an angry glare and left the bookshop.

'Amelia, are you sure that story is appropriate?'

Amelia, who looked too comatose and blurry with tears to see past the end of her nose, seemed confused by the question. 'Elaine? Yeah, she's fine, I just hired her. Come on, let's talk.'

We left the bookshop and went upstairs to the apartment Amelia shared with her mother, Magda.

'I don't want my mother to know,' she said quietly, closing the kitchen door. 'She was convinced he was going to propose. I don't know how to tell her.' She started crying again.

'What happened?'

'He said he's got a job in Berlin and he really wants to move there because it's a great opportunity for him. He asked me to go with him, but he knows I can't go. I can't leave Mum, whatever about getting our own place. I definitely can't leave the country. What about the shop?'

I didn't think it was an appropriate time to remind her that the shop had been haemorrhaging money for the past ten years, unable to compete with the big book chains selling coffee, let alone online stores and e-readers. It was all I could do to stop Amelia spitting at people whenever she saw them reading from a tablet. She had done her best, introducing children's reading hours, author events and evening book clubs, but it was a losing battle. All for the sake of keeping her father's memory alive. The bookshop had been his pride and joy, not hers. It was him she loved, not the business. I had tried to point this out on various occasions, but Amelia wouldn't listen.

'Is moving your mother to Berlin an option?'

Amelia shook her head. 'Mum hates travelling. You know what she's like, she won't leave the country. There's no way she could live there!' She looked at me, horrified that I'd even suggested it. I could understand Fred's frustration. Amelia would never entertain the thought for a second.

'Come on. It doesn't mean it's over. Long-distance relationships work. You did it when he was in Berlin for six months, remember? It was hard, but it's do-able.'

'You see, that's the thing . . . ' She wiped her eyes. 'He met someone when he was there. I didn't tell you at the time, but we worked it out. I believed him when he said that it was over with her, but . . . Christine, he knows I'd never leave here. He knows that I'd never do that. The restaurant, the champagne, it was all a ridiculous charade to force me to be the one to end the relationship. He knew I'd say no, but at least this way he's not the bad guy. If he hasn't got back in touch with her already, he's planning to, I know he is.'

'You don't know that.'

'Have you ever not known something but known it at the same time?'

Her words struck me hard; I knew exactly what she was talking about. I had used the very same expression when thinking about my own feelings about my marriage.

'Oh God,' Amelia said, exhausted. Her head flopped down on her arms, resting on the table. 'What a day.'

'Tell me about it,' I whispered.

'What time is it?' Amelia looked up at the clock on the wall. 'That's unusual. Mum would usually have called for her dinner by now. I better check on her.' She rubbed her eyes. 'Do I look like I've been crying?'

Her eyes were red raw, matching her wild red hair.

'You look fine,' I lied. Her mother would know anyway.

As soon as she left the room, I checked my phone for messages from Adam. I'd given him the keys to my apartment and hoped he would be okay, but there was nothing in the apartment to offer him distraction, no television, no books. This was not a good thing. I quickly dialled his number.

'Christine! Call an ambulance!' Amelia shrieked from the next room. By her tone, I knew not to ask any questions. I cleared Adam's number and dialled 999.

Amelia had found Magda on the floor beside her bed. As soon as the ambulance crew got there, they pronounced her dead. She had suffered a major stroke. Amelia was an only child with no dependants and no one else to turn to, so I stayed with her throughout the ordeal, lending a shoulder to cry on and helping her make arrangements.

It was ten p.m. when I finally had the chance to look at my phone. I had six missed calls and a voicemail. It was from Clontarf garda station, asking me to call them about Adam Basil.

10

How to Make an Omelette
Without Breaking Eggs

'I'm here to see Adam Basil,' I said, bursting into Clontarf garda station. All the way there, my already cluttered mind had been further overloaded with what-ifs and awful, terrifying thoughts of what he might have done to himself. I couldn't even remember the journey.

The garda stared back at me through the hatch. 'Can I see some ID?'

I passed it through. 'Is he okay? Is he hurt?'

'If he was hurt, he'd be in hospital.'

'Of course, yes.' I hadn't thought of that and I relaxed. Then I tensed up again: 'Is he in trouble?'

'He's cooling down,' he said, exiting the office and disappearing from view.

I waited for ten minutes and finally the door to the waiting area opened and Adam stepped into the room. He looked a mess. I knew from the expression on his face that I would have to tread carefully. His eyes were dark. His shirt was crumpled as if he'd slept in it, though I knew he hadn't because his eyes were exhausted, and angry. If this was Adam after cooling down, I dreaded to think what he had been like a few hours before.

'You know it's not legal to lock me up for so

122

long,' he snarled at the garda. 'I know my rights.'

'I don't want to see you back here again, do you hear me?' The senior garda pointed a menacing finger at him.

'Are you okay?' I asked quietly.

He glared at me, then stormed past and out the door.

'We found him on a park bench, looking at the kids in the playground. The parents got anxious, suspicious, called us to go around. I went over to ask him some questions and he lost his head.'

'So you locked him up?'

'Speaking to a garda like that, he's lucky I didn't charge him. He needs to talk to someone, that lad. You should watch yourself,' he warned.

I followed Adam outside, expecting him to have disappeared. But there he was, standing by the car.

'I'm sorry I was gone all afternoon. Amelia was upset about breaking up with her boyfriend.'

He didn't seem too touched by her misfortune and I didn't blame him after what he'd been through that afternoon.

'I was about to call you and tell you I was on my way when she went upstairs to check on her mother and found she'd had a massive stroke. We called an ambulance but it was too late, she was dead. I couldn't just walk out on her after that.' Suddenly I was tired. So, so tired.

Adam's jaw softened. 'Sorry to hear that.'

We drove the short distance to the flat in silence and when we got inside he looked around the empty rooms, naked walls, my Spider-Man duvet.

'I'm sorry this is all there is,' I said, embarrassed. 'It's a rental. All my stuff is being held hostage.'

He dumped his bag on the ground. 'It's grand.'

'Adam, the crisis plan is there to help you. I know it might seem useless, but if you follow the steps, I'm sure you will find it helpful in future.'

'Helpful?' he shouted, giving me a fright. He pulled a rumpled piece of paper from his pocket and started to rip it up in a fury. I took a few steps away from him, suddenly aware that here was a total stranger with mental health issues that I had let into my home. How stupid had I been? He didn't notice me edging away.

'This thing was what got me into trouble. *Call someone on your emergency list whenever you have a suicidal thought*, it says. So I had one. First on my emergency list is you. I called you. You didn't answer. Second should be my girlfriend and third should be my best friend, but they're not on the bloody list. My mother's dead and my father's dying. They're not on the list. Failing that, *Do something that makes you happy whenever you have a suicidal thought*.' He clenched the remains of the note in his fist. 'Seeing as I'd already eaten my food and had my walk, what other happy thing could I possibly do today? Then I remembered the playground and heard the kids laughing and I thought, that's fucking happy, maybe they'll make me fucking happy. So I sat there for an hour, not feeling very fucking happy, and then this garda comes along and asks me if I'm some paedo! Of course I'm

124

going to have an attitude if he thinks I'm some sicko, gawking at kids. So you can take your fucking crisis plan and stuff it up your hole!' he yelled, throwing the tattered bits of paper in the air. 'Your friend's boyfriend left her, her mother died and you're not doing much better yourself. Thanks for showing me the beauty of life.'

'Okay . . . ' I faltered, trying not to be afraid of this man I didn't know while at the same time struggling to convince myself that I did know him, reminding myself that I'd seen glimpses of Adam being kind, showing his romantic side, being funny. Faced with this darkness and rage, it was hard to believe that other Adam existed. I looked at the door, trying not to let him see me. I could run. I could call the guards, I could tell them what had happened on the bridge, I could tell them he wanted to kill himself, I could end this all right now, because I had failed. I had made a mess of it all.

I took a deep breath in an effort to slow my heartbeat down. His shouting was making me so panicky, I couldn't think straight. At last there was silence. He was standing there, looking at me. I had to say something. Something understanding. Something that wouldn't trigger another outbreak of anger. I couldn't bear it if he hurt himself. Not here, not with me, not ever.

I swallowed and was surprised by how steady my voice was. 'I understand that you're feeling angry.'

'Of course I'm feeling fucking angry.' But he didn't sound as angry as he had before. He seemed to have calmed a little at my acknowledging it. That made me feel calmer; maybe I could do this after all. At least I could give it a try for a while longer. I didn't want to give up on him.

'I've got a remedy for that.' I side-stepped around him quickly, and went to the kitchen. I took six eggs from the fridge, and wrote on them with a black marker, noticing how my hand trembled. I wrote the names 'Basil', 'Sean', 'Maria', 'Dad', 'Lavinia' and 'Christine' on the eggs, then slid open the kitchen door leading to the long back garden.

'Come on,' I called to him.

He stared at me with dark eyes.

'Come on,' I said more firmly, trying not to be intimidated, trying to keep things moving. I was in control here, I needed him to listen to me. Reluctantly, he followed.

'I have six eggs here, with words representing things that are making you angry right now. Throw them. Throw them anywhere you want. As hard as you want. Crush them. Get rid of your anger.' I handed him the carton and indicated the open door.

'I'm tired of your *tasks*,' he spoke through his teeth.

'Fine.' I put the carton down on the counter and left the kitchen, going to my bedroom. Though I wanted very much to lock my door, I didn't like the message it would send him. Instead I sat on my Spider-Man duvet and stared at the magnolia wall, at the grid-shaped shadow the moon was casting through my window pane, and tried to think what I should do next. I had a huge task ahead of me and no idea how to proceed. Somehow I needed to make him see a therapist. I thought about ways I could get him to go. Maybe pretend we were going somewhere else and arrive at a practice? But if I did that, fooled him or tried to trick him in any way, I would lose his trust for good. Then he wouldn't even have me to help him, useless as I was.

For the first time since I'd agreed to this challenge, I was beginning to think I might not be able to deliver. Thoughts of him killing himself made me physically ill and I rushed to the toilet and locked the door. As I crouched in there, bent double, I heard him groan as if he was in pain, as if he'd been punched. Startled, I composed myself, splashed my face with water and hurried out. I stopped at the kitchen door. The light behind me spilled out into the black garden, which had been neglected since my green-fingered great-aunt Christine passed away. Now there was nothing but a long rectangular patch of grass, which hadn't been properly tended in at least a decade, and not at all in these winter months. I remembered how my great-aunt used to feed us strawberries plucked straight from the vines, edible flowers, wild garlic and mint, eating more for the token of it than the taste. I could picture her, picking gooseberries for her jam, her wide-brimmed straw hat shielding her face from the sun, her wrinkled skin drooping on her neck and chest, creasing and wobbling as she worked, and all the while her raspy voice breathless from emphysema

127

explained what she was doing. The garden was a long way from that now, yet the memory was there in a corner of my mind, the brightness of my youth on a sunny day when I felt warm and safe, contrasted with this cold dark night with fear and panic locked in my heart.

Out in the garden, Adam was looking down at the tray of eggs in his hand, choosing thoughtfully. He picked one up and gave it an almighty throw down the end of the garden. He let out a yell and it crashed against the end wall. Looking more motivated, he went back to the egg carton and picked another. He threw it, screaming as he released it into the air, watching as it smashed against the back wall. He repeated the process three more times. When he had finished, he stormed back into the house and slammed the bathroom door behind him. I ducked into the bedroom to give him space. The shower went on. I heard his angry sobs getting lost beneath the falling water.

I went outside to the carton. There was one egg left. I crouched down, picked up the egg and tears sprang to my eyes. The name on the remaining egg was 'Christine'.

★   ★   ★

I was in bed, propped up on pillows, tense and alert, unable to relax while he was in that mood, when he appeared in my bedroom doorway. Instinctively, I pulled the covers around me, fearing for my safety. Seeing my reaction, he winced, hurt by my fear of him.

'I'm sorry,' he said gently. 'I promise not to behave like that again. I know you're trying to help.'

I saw this was a different Adam from the one who'd raged at me earlier and I relaxed.

'I'll try harder,' I said.

'Ignore what I said. You're doing fine. Thank you.'

I smiled.

He returned the smile.

'Good night, Christine.'

'Good night, Adam.'

11

How to Disappear Completely
and Never Be Found

At four a.m., I had an epiphany. Adam had been right the night before: I needed to do better. He hadn't said it but he'd intimated it. I could see how vulnerable he was. I had to do better. Wide awake, my mind too wired now for sleep, I got up and threw on a tracksuit, then made my way as quietly as possible through the living room. The room was dark but Adam was sitting up, his troubled face illuminated by the glow of his laptop.

'I thought you were asleep.'

'I'm watching *Ferris Bueller's Day Off*.'

It was one of the things we had listed on his crisis plan as a distraction for when he dipped.

'Are you okay?' I tried to study his face but the computer screen didn't give off enough light to reveal his innermost thoughts.

'Where are you going?' He ignored my question.

'To my office. I'll be back in a few minutes — if that's okay?'

He nodded.

When I returned, his computer was over-turned on the floor, the cord from the charger was wrapped around his neck and he was hanging off the edge of the couch, his eyes closed and his tongue hanging out of his mouth.

'Very funny.' I kept walking, my arms overloaded with paper, pens, highlighters, and a whiteboard, which I set up in my bedroom.

Adam claimed he didn't want emotional help, insisting his needs were material, tangible physical ones. He wanted to get his job with the Irish Coast Guard back, he wanted his girlfriend back, he wanted his family *off* his back. I had assumed I could tackle this by helping him emotionally, but I had very little time. Perhaps what I needed to do was to treat his physical needs as I would his emotional. Emotionally he had his tools, he had his crisis plan. What was missing was a set of tools to cope with the physical needs, and I was going to give them to him.

Too curious to hold out any longer, Adam appeared at the door.

'What are you doing?'

I was making plans, charting things in a frenzy. Drawing grids, mood boards, highlighters, bubbles, all kinds of things were flying around on large white boards.

'How much coffee have you had?'

'Too much. But there's no point wasting time. Neither of us sleep anyway, so why not get started now? There are twelve days left,' I said, urgency in my voice. 'That's two hundred and eighty-eight hours. Most people sleep eight hours a night — not us, but people do. That gives us sixteen hours a day to do what we have to do, which leaves us with only one hundred and ninety-two hours. Not that much time. And it's four a.m. so officially we've eleven days left.'

I crossed out the figures and began feverishly working them out again. We had work to do in Dublin and pretty soon we would have to go to Tipperary to deal with the rest of Adam's problems.

'I think you're having a nervous breakdown,' he said, amused, arms folded as he watched me.

'No. I'm having an epiphany. You want my services full-on, one-on-one? That's what you're going to get.' I opened the wardrobe and pulled out a torch, checked to see if the batteries were working. I stuffed a bag with towels and a change of clothes. 'I'd suggest you get something warm on and bring a change of clothes because we're going out.'

'Out? It's freezing and it's four in the morning. Where are we going?'

'We, my friend, are going to win Maria back.'

He almost smiled. 'And how are we going to do that?'

I pushed by him in the doorway and he had no choice but to throw on his coat and follow me.

St Anne's Park is open all hours, though not the safest place to be at four-thirty in the morning. It had been the setting for attacks in the past and possibly a dead body or two had shown up there over the years. It wasn't particularly well lit after dark, which was a detail I had forgotten from my teenage drinking days.

'You're crazy,' he said, following as I lit the way with a torch. 'Don't you think it's a bit dangerous to be wandering around here?'

'Absolutely. But you're big, you'll protect me,'

132

I said, teeth chattering at the cold. The further we moved into the park, the more the caffeine hit wore off. The beer cans and fresh graffiti on display each morning were enough to tell me that we wouldn't be alone in the park, but with the countdown focusing my mind, there wasn't a second to lose. I did not want Adam's death on my conscience or I would never sleep again.

Even with the torch I could see only a few feet ahead of me and the sun wasn't due to rescue us for hours yet. But what I did have on my side was knowledge of the park. I grew up in that park and knew the five hundred acres like the back of my hand. But that was when it was bright; it had been at least fifteen years since I'd stumbled across the park in the dead of night, while out drinking with friends as a teenager.

Suddenly I stopped, pointed the torch left and right. Then I spun around, trying to get my bearings.

'Christine,' Adam said, warning in his voice.

I ignored him, trying to picture the place in full light. I took a few steps right. Then stopped, turned in the other direction.

'Jesus, don't tell me we're lost.'

I didn't say anything.

Adam shivered beside me. There were voices coming from the trees to our left. Then bottles clinked.

'This way,' I squeaked, heading away from the gang in the trees.

Adam was mumbling under his breath.

'Oh, what do you care, you want to die anyway,' I snapped.

133

'Yes, but on my own terms,' he protested. 'Death by skanky drunk is not what I was planning.'

'Beggars can't be choosers,' I found myself quoting Dad.

Thankfully we made it to the pond, and thankfully the lamps were on, to stop the likes of the gang in the trees from falling in.

'See?' I said, pleased with myself.

'I'd call that luck. An odd, fucked-up luck.'

'Well, don't just stand there — get the lily pad.' I stamped my feet and rubbed my gloved hands together. I felt his eyes on me.

'Excuse me?'

'Why else do you think I told you to bring a change of clothes?'

'It's minus four! I'm surprised that water hasn't iced over. I'll die of hypothermia.'

'If you weren't so choosy about your time of death, you'd make everything much easier. Well, if that's the way it has to be . . . ' I took off my coat and the chill ran straight to my bones.

'You're not going in there.'

'One of us has to, and you're clearly not willing.' I geared myself up, looked around the pond to find the right lily pad.

'But, Christine, think about the people who love you,' he said, mock-serious. 'They wouldn't want you to do this.'

I phased him out; I wasn't leaving the park without the lily pad. From the edge of the pond I scoured the lake for the nicest pad. Some were ripped, dirty-looking, and I wanted the greenest, most circular pad I could find, one that Maria

134

could use again to hold the things she treasured and loved, and hopefully Adam's photo frame would find itself upon it again. Maybe he'd throw his loose change on it when he came home from work before climbing into bed with Maria, or leave his watch on it while he took a shower, occasionally thinking about the crazy woman who helped him fish it out, that freezing cold night way back when he was having problems.

At last I located the one I wanted; it was rather inconveniently not the closest lily pad, but I could swim there quickly and back. It would be over in seconds. Ten seconds max. And it *was* a life-or-death scenario, which settled my internal wavering immediately. I wasn't sure how deep the water was, so I rooted around the trees for a branch or loose stick, and then put it in the water to test the depth.

'You're actually going to do this?'

The stick stopped halfway. It wasn't deep at all. Only a few feet. I could do this and I wouldn't have to swim, it was just a few steps away. The pond was murky, green and scummy, but I could do this. I rolled my tracksuit pants up, high above my knees.

'Oh my God,' Adam laughed, realising I was actually going through with it. 'Look, there's one right by the edge, I could reach that one.'

I looked at it. He could reach across and retrieve it with no problem.

'Do you think she'd look at that and think, Wow, he really loves me? It's disgusting, it's got something furry growing on it. Oh and look, it has a cigarette butt. I don't think that's the

135

message you want to send. No, we want that one.' I pointed to the furthest one out. 'The one untouched by the human hand.'

'You're going to freeze.'

'And then I'll dry. I'll get over it. As soon as I'm out, we're running to the car.'

I got into the water. It went far higher than I'd anticipated, way past my knees, soaking my tracksuit bottoms. I felt it rise all the way to my waist. The stick had lied, or had lodged itself on a rock. I gasped. I heard Adam laughing, but was too focused to admonish him. Now that I was in, there was nothing for it but to keep going. The floor felt soft and mushy beneath me; I dreaded to think of what was in there. Reeds and dead leaves clung to me as I pushed my way through the murky water. I wondered what diseases I could catch from it, but pushed on. As soon as I was an arm's length from the lily pad I reached for it and pulled it back with me. Five giant steps along the mushy floor and I was at the edge. Adam held his arm out and pulled me up. My tracksuit clung to my body and my clothes rained stinking pondwater. Squelching to my bag, I pulled out a towel, peeled my trousers and socks off, and quickly dried myself. Adam looked away, still laughing to himself, and I peeled my underwear off. I put my new tracksuit on, all the while gritting my teeth against the icy cold. With shaking hands I put my new socks and trainers on and changed my jumper for a warm fleece. He held my coat open for me, and I put my arms in and hugged myself. He plonked his woollen hat on my head and wrapped his arms around

136

my body in an effort to warm me. The last time we had been in that position was when we were on the bridge and my arms had been wrapped around Adam. Now Adam's arms were wrapped right around me. His chin rested on the top of my head and he rubbed my shoulders in an effort to keep me warm. My heart hammered at being so close to him. I wasn't sure if it was the return of the feeling I'd experienced on the bridge or if it was merely him, his closeness, his body pressed against mine, his scent overwhelming my senses.

'Are you okay?' he asked, close to my ear.

I was almost afraid to turn and look at him. I daren't speak in case my voice revealed the shakiness I felt. So I nodded, and in doing so rubbed against him even more. I wasn't sure if I imagined it, but I felt his arms wrap tighter around me.

We heard voices approaching; deep, male, not very friendly. The moment was over as suddenly as it had come. He let go of me quickly, picked up my bag and the lily pad that was lying on the ground.

'Come on,' he said, and we ran back the way we came.

Once in the car, Adam turned the heater on full blast in an effort to warm me up. He was concerned, my lips had apparently turned blue and I couldn't stop shivering.

'That was such a bad idea, Christine,' he said, his face all dark and frowning and concerned.

'I'm fine,' I insisted, holding my hands in front of the extractor fan. 'I just need a minute.'

'Let's go back to the flat,' he said. 'You can have a hot shower, and a coffee to warm up.'

'I know a twenty-four-hour garage that does crap coffee,' I managed through chattering teeth. 'We're not finished yet.'

'We can't give this to her now,' he said, looking at the dripping lily pad in the back seat. 'She'll still be in bed.'

'That's not where we're going.'

With a hot coffee inside me and another one waiting in the cup holder, I finally started to thaw.

'Why are we driving to Howth?'

'You'll see.'

Another recommendation in *How to Enjoy Life in Thirty Simple Ways*, after eating and walking, had been to watch a sunset or sunrise. I was hoping the light rising would help enlighten Adam. And if it worked for me too, then I wasn't going to complain. I drove up the coast road to Howth Summit and we were the only car in the car park. It was six-thirty a.m. and the sky was clear, the perfect setting for the sunrise over Dublin Bay.

We pushed our seats back, reached for our coffees, turned the radio on low and watched the sky. In the distance, pink was beginning to rise up from the sea.

'And . . . action,' Adam said. He opened a brown bag and held it out to me. I smelled sugar, my stomach churned and I shook my head.

He reached in and helped himself to a cinnamon roll. 'Look how cinnamony the

138

cinnamon is and how citric the lemon peel is,' he said. 'I am tasting my food and acknowledging it.' His voice became robotic. 'I am partaking in one of the many joys of life.'

'At least you're getting the hang of it.'

He bit into it and chewed, then he spat it back into the paper bag, dumped the rest of it in with it and scrunched the bag up. 'How do people eat that crap?'

I shrugged.

'Tell me something else funny that you did for Maria or that you did with her?'

'Why?'

'Because I need to know.' It was easy for me to say that, but truth be told, I couldn't stop thinking about the things he had done for her, the unusual gifts he got her. I longed to hear more.

'Uh.' He thought about it. 'She was a fan of *Where's Wally* — you know those books? So when I wanted to ask her out on our first date, I dressed up as him and kept appearing somewhere, everywhere she was. I wouldn't look at her. She'd be shopping and I'd walk through the shop without saying anything. I followed her around for the day, just appearing.'

I looked at him and my eyebrows shot up as far as they could go. Then I burst out laughing.

He beamed. 'She thought the same thankfully and said yes to going out with me.' Then his smile quickly faded.

'You'll get her back, Adam.'

'Yeah. I hope so.'

We were quiet as we watched the sky.

'If that lily pad doesn't get her back, I don't know what will,' he said seriously.

I burst out laughing. By the time I stopped the sky was bright.

'Right,' I said, putting the key in the ignition. 'Feel better?'

'Totally,' he said sarcastically. 'I no longer have the urge to kill myself.'

'Thought so.' I started up the engine and we drove home.

⋆　⋆　⋆

I was sitting on the only chair my dad had furnished the kitchen with, cleaning the lily pad first with a baby wipe and then buffing it to a shine with furniture polish. It was quite an impressive lily pad; it had a perfect ridge along the outside and I'd even tested the teapot and teacups on it for strength. I'd polished it up to perfection, and reasoned that the mild headache and cold I felt coming on was worth it. I was admiring my handiwork when at eight a.m. my phone started beeping. I battled with myself over whether to listen to the voicemail. I knew it was Barry, that it was more insults and hate, and I knew that I shouldn't listen but somehow I couldn't help it. I felt I at least owed it to him to listen, that ignoring his hurt would be yet another rejection.

Adam joined me in the kitchen. 'Is that him?'

I nodded.

'Why does he call at the same time every day?'

'Because that's when he's up and dressed.

Come eight a.m., he's at the kitchen table having a cup of tea and toast and a meltdown, checking his phone and thinking of ways to bring me down with him.'

I felt Adam watching me, but I didn't look at him, merely continued polishing the lily pad, the ridiculousness of the situation not lost on me. He was having a meltdown and I was polishing a lily pad that I'd stolen from a public park. Neither of us had gotten out of the break-up okay.

'Are you going to listen to them?'

I sighed and finally looked up at him. 'Probably.'

'To remind yourself why you left him?'

'No.' I decided to be honest. 'Because it's my punishment.'

He frowned.

'Because every horrible thing he tells me hurts me to my very core, and if that's my punishment for leaving him, then it makes me feel like I'm earning my freedom. So once again, I am a totally selfish individual who is using somebody else's pain as a way for me to feel better about myself.'

He looked at me, wide-eyed. 'Jesus. You don't half analyse shit. Can I listen?'

I put down the lily pad and nodded. I watched him as he sat on the counter and listened to Barry's message, his face constantly changing — eyebrows lifting and lowering, forehead creasing, mouth opening in delighted surprise — to display how entertaining he found Barry's insults, then he hung up, eager to report

141

back on what he'd heard.

'You'll love this one,' he laughed, eyes shining. The phone beeped in his hand. 'Hold on, he's left another one! This guy is unreal,' he chuckled, enjoying the entertainment snooping into my private life brought. 'Good man, Barry!' he teased. He dialled my voicemail again and listened. The smile froze, and the smile disappeared from his eyes.

My heart pounded.

Thirty seconds later he jumped down from the counter — not a long fall as his legs were so long — and handed me the phone. He wouldn't meet my gaze, then awkwardly began to leave the room.

'What did he say?'

'Ah, nothing interesting.'

'Adam! You were eager enough to tell me about the first message.'

'Ah that, yeah, okay, it was something stupid about your friend. Some girl called Julie who he says is a whore — no, wait: a slut. He used to see her out with different guys all the time. He met her in Leeson Street one night and she was with some guy who he knows was married.' Adam shrugged. 'He had some things to say about her choice of attire.'

'And that was funny to you?'

'Well, his delivery was quite exceptional.' He smiled a small smile. Then a sad smile.

I shook my head. Julie was one of my closest friends from college, the same Julie who had moved to Toronto and left her car with me to sell. Barry's attempts to hurt me continued.

142

'And what was the other message?'

He continued to walk away.

'Adam!'

'Nothing really. It didn't make sense. It was more of a tirade of angry . . . anger.' He stared at me, silent, then he left the room.

The way he looked at me, full of sympathy, pity . . . intrigue? I couldn't quite place it but it bothered me. I dialled into my voicemail.

'You have no new messages.'

'Adam, you deleted my messages!' I followed him into the living room.

'Did I? Sorry.' He concentrated on his computer.

'You did it on purpose.'

'Did I?'

'What did he say? Tell me.'

'I told you: your friend Julie is a slut. By the way, I think I should meet her; she sounds interesting,' he joked, trying to lighten the atmosphere.

'Tell me the second message,' I demanded.

'I can't remember.'

'Adam, they're my bloody messages, now tell me!' I shouted, standing in front of him.

My shouting did nothing to change him. I thought it might provoke him but it had the opposite effect, he softened, was sympathetic, which made me all the more angry.

'You don't want to know. Okay?' he said.

From the way he was studying me, it scared me to think what personal information Barry had revealed. It was obvious I wasn't going to get any information out of him, not then anyway, so

I left the room. I wanted to storm off, away from him, out of the apartment, just be alone to scream and shout or cry or rant with frustration at how my life had become so out of control, but I couldn't. I felt tied to him, as a mother did to her child, unable to leave him even if I wanted to in that moment. He was my responsibility, all the time, constantly, night and day. I needed to watch over him even if right at this moment, thanks to whatever Barry had said, he seemed to feel it was his job to protect me.

* * *

It didn't take me long to realise that Adam's moods were unpredictable. One moment he would be engaged in a conversation, sometimes leading it, other times merely tolerating it, and then all of a sudden he would be gone. Completely gone. He would retreat into his mind, with a look so lost, sometimes so angry, that I dreaded to think what he was thinking. This could happen mid-conversation, mid-sentence, even in the middle of his own sentence, and it could last for hours. He would close himself off completely. This was what happened after I shouted at him for deleting my voicemails. I watched him settling into another hour of being comatose on the couch, hating life, hating himself, hating everybody and everything around him, so I stepped in to remedy that.

'Right, let's go.' I threw his coat at him.

'I'm not going anywhere.'

'Yes, you are. You want to disappear?'

He looked at me, confused.

'You want to disappear,' I told him instead. 'You want to be lost. Fine. Let's get lost.'

* * *

Three-year-old Alicia was sitting on the front steps of her porch with a car seat beside her. Alicia was Brenda's youngest child and as part of my aunt duties, which I thoroughly enjoyed — with Alicia, mostly, as I couldn't quite connect with the boys who always wanted to tie me up and chant about spit-roasting me whenever I walked in the door — I took her out for a few hours every week. Our day-trips in this current form had started four months ago, probably about the same time that I started to think about leaving my marriage. I had been driving Alicia to a play centre where I could let her off her leash in a room built entirely of sponge and watch her bouncing from wall to wall and toppling down stairs into tubs of plastic balls, and then try to hide my horrified expression when she checked to see if I was watching. On the way to the play centre, Alicia announced at the traffic lights where we would usually take a right that instead she wanted me to take a left. In no hurry to see her being squished as she crawled between two padded, turning cylinders in the name of fun, and contemplative after my previous night's fantasy of me with another man, I had taken a left and then asked Alicia which way to go next. For an hour we drove around, taking turns at Alicia's command. We did this every week, always ending up in different places. It allowed me to think, it passed the time, and it allowed Alicia the novelty of exercising authority over a grown-up.

One of the pieces of advice in the *Simple Ways to Enjoy Life* manual was to *Spend time with kids*. It explained that surveys had shown the happiness caused by children was immense. Although I had read other studies that ranked it no higher than going food shopping. I suppose it depended on whether you liked kids or not. I was hoping this would be another way to get Adam to open his eyes to the beauty of life. And he wouldn't get arrested for watching this child.

'Hi, Alicia.' I gave her a hug.

'Hi, poo poo.'

'Why are you out here on your own?'

'Lee is doing a poo poo.'

Lee, her childminder, waved from the window with six-month-old Jayden in her arms. I took it as a sign I could take Alicia away.

I opened the passenger door, disturbing Adam, who was practically comatose.

'You can sit in the back seat beside Alicia. This is Adam, he's going to get lost with us.'

I wanted him to be able to engage in a conversation with her; in the front of the car she would be easy to ignore.

'Is he your one true love, poo poo?'

'No, poo poo, he's not.'

Alicia giggled.

I lifted the car seat and inserted it into the car, then helped Alicia in. Adam got in beside her, still disengaged and looking out the window. He took a break from his daydream to glance at the cute three-year-old being strapped in beside him. They both stared at each other; neither of them said anything.

'How was Montessori today?' I asked.

'Good, poo poo.'

'Are you going to say poo poo in every sentence?'

'Yes, wee wee.'

Adam looked confused but amused.

'Do you have any kids in your family?' I asked him.

'Yeah, Lavinia's. But they're pretentious little fuckers. Losing their house is probably the best thing that could have happened to them.'

'Nice,' I complimented him, sarcastically.

'Sorry.' Adam winced.

I watched them both in the rear-view mirror.

'So how old are you?' Adam asked Alicia.

Alicia held up four fingers.

'You're four.'

'She's three,' I said.

'And evidently a liar,' Adam accused her.

'Look my nose, woooo!' Alicia pretended her nose was growing.

'Where are we going?' Adam asked.

'Left,' Alicia said.

'She's three and she knows the directions?'

I smiled and indicated left. When I got to the end of the road, I looked at Alicia in the mirror.

'Right,' Alicia said.

I turned right.

'Seriously, you know the directions?' Adam turned to Alicia.

'Yep,' Alicia said.

'How? You're three.'

'I know all the directions. To everywhere. In the whole world. Want to go to poo poo street?' She threw her head back and cackled.

We took various turns, left, right, straight on, all on Alicia's instruction. Ten minutes passed.

'Okay, can I ask where exactly we're going?' Adam asked.

'Left,' Alicia said again.

'I know we're going left, but left to where?' he asked me.

'This is the way to get lost,' I said.

'So we just drive round and round, taking directions from a child?' he asked.

'Exactly. Then we try to find our way home.'

'For how long?'

'A few hours.'

'And you do this how often?'

'Usually on a Sunday. This is a special extra outing. It's better when the roads aren't busy. It's an interesting thing to do. The only rule is that the motorways are off limits. Once we ended up in the Dublin mountains, another time Malahide beach. When we arrive somewhere we like, we get out and take a look around. We discover new things every week. Sometimes we don't leave Clontarf and end up going in circles, but she never notices really.'

'Right,' Adam called out.

'That's the sea, poo poo,' Alicia laughed.

'Exactly,' Adam said, wanting out.

He was quiet for fifteen minutes as he disappeared into a mood.

'I want to have a go,' he said suddenly. 'Can I say the directions?'

'No!' Alicia snapped.

'Alicia,' I warned.

'Can I say the directions, please, poo poo?' Adam asked.

Alicia laughed. 'Okay.'

'All right.' Adam thought hard. 'Take a left at the lights.'

I studied him in the mirror. 'You can't take us to Maria's.'

'I'm not,' he snapped.

We took a left and drove for a few minutes. We eventually reached a wall, a complete dead-end.

'I swear this has never happened before,' I said, putting the car in reverse.

'Typical.' Adam folded his arms in a huff.

'Try again, poo poo,' Alicia said, feeling sorry for him.

'There's a small road down that way,' Adam said.

'That's a dirt track and we have no idea where it will take us.'

'It will lead somewhere.'

I took a left. My phone rang and I put it on speaker phone.

'Christine, it's me.'

'Oscar, hi.'

'I'm at the bus stop.'

'Good for you. How are you feeling?'

'Not too good. I can't believe you're taking two weeks off.'

'I'm sorry. But I'm always available on the phone.'

'I'd really like it if you were here in person.' His voice was shaking. 'Maybe you could meet me, maybe you could get on the bus with me?'

'Can't do that, Oscar. I'm sorry, you know I can't do that.'

'I know, I know, you say it's unprofessional,' he said sadly.

I'd go out of my way to help my clients, but I drew a line at physically getting on buses with Oscar. I looked at Adam in the mirror to see if he had heard and he smirked at my teachings versus our current scenario. 'You can do this, Oscar,' I insisted. 'Take deep breaths, allow your body to relax.' I was so distracted talking to Oscar that I was mindlessly driving down the country road, surrounded on both sides by green fields. It was a road I'd never been down before. Occasionally, when we came to a junction, I'd hear either Adam or Alicia shout a direction. Finally Oscar had made it four stops and was feeling jubilant; he hung up the phone, dancing all the way back to his house. Adam's phone, which was in the front of the car beside mine, started ringing. I could see it was Maria on the display screen. I answered it without Adam noticing and this time didn't bother with the loudspeaker.

'Oh, hi,' Maria said when she heard my voice. 'It's you again.'

'Hi there,' I replied, not wanting to say her name in case Adam grabbed the phone.

'Are you his messaging service now?' Maria asked, trying to joke but unable to hide the sharp edge in her voice.

I laughed lightly, pretending not to notice.

'Sure feels like it. How can I help you?'

'How can you *help* me? Well, I wanted to speak to Adam.' She was curt, crisp, her words clipped.

'I'm sorry, he's not able to come to the phone right now,' I said in a friendly tone, not giving her anything to be able to bark at me about. 'Can I take a message for him?'

'Well, did he get my last message from yesterday morning?'

'Of course he did. I told him straight away.'

'So why didn't he call me?'

We were approaching a crossroads.

'Left,' Adam said suddenly, breaking his chit-chat with Alicia.

'Right,' Alicia said.

'Go left,' Adam shouted.

Alicia was giggling and the two of them were screeching. Adam started blocking Alicia's mouth and she was yelling. Then he yelped because she had licked his hand. It was chaotic and I could barely hear Maria.

'You can't really blame him for not calling you back after what he discovered.' I said it gently, without blame, without judgement, a simple statement that put Maria in her place.

'Right. Yes. Is that him I hear?'

'Yes.'

'Left!' Adam shouted, blocking Alicia's mouth again so she couldn't scream directions.

Alicia howled with belly-aching laughter.

'Don't lick me again,' he warned playfully, then he withdrew his hand quickly, as if in pain. 'Uh! She bit me!'

151

Alicia barked, then panted.

'I'll tell him you called. He's in the middle of something, as you can hear.'

'Oh, okay . . .'

'Actually, where can he reach you today?' I asked. 'Will you be at home or at work?'

'I'll be at work until late. But it doesn't matter, he can get me on the mobile. Is he still . . . you know, angry with me? That's a stupid question, of course he is. *I* would be. Not that he ever . . . you know . . .'

I could barely hear the rest of what Maria said as the two lunatics behind me dissolved into more laughter.

'Who was that?' Adam asked when I came off the phone.

'Maria.'

'Maria?! Why did she call your phone?' He sat forward.

'It was your phone. No secrets, remember?'

'Why the hell didn't you tell me?'

'Because then you would have stopped laughing, and as far as she was concerned you were having a mighty fine time.'

Adam thought about that. 'But I want her to know that I miss her.'

'Trust me, Adam, she'd rather hear you laughing than crying. You being miserable will have her thinking she was right to go with Sean.'

'Okay.' He was quiet for a while and I thought I'd lost him. I checked Alicia to see if she was okay. She was taking her fingers for a walk along the window.

'Hey, this was an interesting idea,' he said,

152

which was as close to a positive remark as I'd heard from him.

'Good,' I said happily, then had to immediately put my foot on the brake as we approached some cars up ahead.

There was only room for one car on the road, but up ahead two cars had managed to squeeze alongside each other. One was facing us, the other heading in the opposite direction. Their doors were practically touching. Their windows were blacked out. By the time I realised that I shouldn't be staring, the car door opened and a scary-looking guy in a black leather jacket stepped out. He was tall and rather large and didn't look at all happy to see us. Neither did the other three men squished shoulder to shoulder in the back of the car who turned around to stare at us. The men in one car looked at the men in the car beside them. The men shook their heads and shrugged their shoulders rather nervously.

'Er, Adam,' I said nervously.

Adam didn't hear me, he was busy talking about poo poo with Alicia.

'Adam!' I said with more urgency and he looked up.

He lifted his eyes just in time to see the tall broad man walking towards us with a hurley stick in his hand.

'Reverse,' Adam said urgently. 'Christine, reverse — now.'

'No! Left!' Alicia yelled, giggling, thinking we were still playing the game.

'Christine!'

'I'm trying!' The clutch was grinding furiously,

153

I was in too much of a panic to find the right gear.

'Christine!' Adam shouted.

The large man took a step closer to the car, examined the screen, took in my mobile number displayed with the FOR SALE sign on the front of the car. Then he looked me in the eye and swung his bat back. I put my foot down on the accelerator and we went hurtling into reverse so fast that Adam was thrown back into his seat at full force. It didn't stop the large man from running after the car, swinging the stick. I kept an eye behind me, doing an okay job of reversing in a straight line, which then began to bend at almighty angles I hadn't noticed while on the phone.

'Shit, there's more of them!' Adam said, and I looked back out the front window to see three more men climb out of the car. 'Keep an eye on the road!' he yelled.

'Oh, shh — ' I began to curse, then remembered Alicia. 'Poo,' I said. 'Poo, poo, poo, poo,' I repeated over and over.

Alicia howled with laughter and joined in. 'Poo! Poo! Poo!'

'Go as fast as you can,' he said.

'I can't, it's bendy,' I said, bumping the car against another bush.

'I know, just concentrate. And go faster.'

'Are they following us?'

He didn't answer.

'Are they following us?'

I couldn't help it, I had to find out. I faced forward and saw the blacked-out windows

154

coming towards us. 'Oh my God.'

'Why are we going backwards?' Alicia asked, finally ending her laughter and sensing the panic in the car. Finally I had the opportunity to back up into a driveway, which I did rather quickly and expertly, and then took off, making a series of lefts and rights while Alicia called out directions to me, not noticing they weren't being followed. When we reached a large housing estate where there was life on the roads again, I slowed down, but continued to make a series of random right and left turns.

'Okay, I think you can stop now,' Adam said as I drove around a roundabout for the third time. 'They're not behind us.'

'Whoa, whoa, whoa, I'm dizzy,' Alicia sang.

'And I'm going to vomit,' Adam said.

I indicated and came off the roundabout. I dropped Alicia back at her house, where I did my best to explain to Brenda why Alicia was excitedly screaming 'Reverse!' and running backwards at top speed around the house and knocking into everything.

'So, Adam, do you find my sister's methods are helping you enjoy life?' Brenda sat at the table and pulled out a chair for him in her imitable style, which never gave people an opportunity to decline.

'So far we've eaten, walked in a park and gone for a drive with a kid.'

'I see. How was the food?'

'Actually, it gave me an upset stomach.'

'Interesting. And how was the park?'

'I got arrested.'

'You weren't arrested, they just put you in a cell to cool down,' I snapped, unhappy my therapy skills were being called into question.

'And the drive ended in interrupting a drugs sale,' Brenda finished for us.

We were silent. Then Brenda leaned her head back and laughed before changing the subject. 'Tell me, Adam, this party of yours, is it dressy?'

'Black tie.'

'Excellent. I saw the perfect dress in Pace. I might even get the shoes to match. Okay,' she stood up, 'I have to get Jayden's dinner ready. You two better scamoosh or I'll end up pureeing your asses.'

Adam looked at me with that amused expression that brought light into his eyes. This time I didn't care that it was on account of my mad family and my disastrous ways to enjoy life, I was just happy to see him alive.

It was only when we'd driven to the flat to collect the lily pad, and returned to the car after mere minutes inside the house, that we discovered the windshield of the car completely smashed in.

12

How to Solve a Problem Like Maria

Maria worked in Grand Canal Dock in a modern high-rise that looked like a chequered board from the outside. I was going to take care of the lily pad's delivery; Adam was sure Maria would personally come to reception to sign for it as long as she was told that it was from him. He was under strict instructions to remain outside, but in a place where he would be able to observe her reaction. Seeing as the building appeared to be built entirely of glass and steel, he had many possible vantage points; the tricky part was ensuring she wouldn't see him. I wanted the moment when Maria and Adam reunited to come when he was ready. He wasn't anywhere near ready yet.

I felt odd about meeting Maria. *The* Maria. The woman whose quite intimate details I knew and who I'd spoken to over the phone twice and who was the reason or one of the reasons that Adam, rather beautiful Adam, had ended up with his life hanging in the balance. As I walked across the marble floor with my heels tapping so that the long line of receptionists looked up to watch me, I realised I resented Maria. And what timing. I couldn't help but blame her for holding such power over a man she'd supposedly once loved while apparently oblivious to the effects of her rejection on him. When I thought of what he was going through right now to get her back, and her standing here with no idea, my blood boiled. Again, really not good timing, and inappropriate for me to become so protective of him when my role was supposed to be impartial, but I couldn't feel anything close to unbiased at that moment.

Rationally, I knew it wasn't Maria's fault. If Maria had been a friend confiding in me about Adam's behaviour, I probably would have supported her in leaving him once everything she'd tried to salvage the relationship had failed. But the woman bugged me despite all that. I knew I should really be telling Adam to move on, not to try to win her back. She was already with someone else, his friend; she'd moved on. Was a further rejection going to break him even more? Yes. It would kill him. I already knew that. I needed their relationship to work for Adam's life. Which brought me back to resenting Maria.

'I have a delivery for Maria Harty in Red Lips Productions,' I said to the receptionist.

'Who will I say it's from?'

'Adam Basil.'

I could see Adam outside, his woollen hat low, his duffle coat closed all the way up to his chin, his face was barely visible and what skin was exposed turning red raw from the cold. I would have to make sure I positioned myself so that Adam could see her reaction. I only hoped Maria wouldn't throw the lily pad on the floor and stamp all over it. I didn't think I'd reach him on time if he wanted to dive over the edge into the canal.

The elevator doors opened and a doll stepped out in skinny black jeans, biker boots, a T-shirt with a naked woman in a suggestive pose, jet-black hair which was rich and glossy and framed her doll-like chin, a severe fringe, big blue eyes, a perfect nose, and red, red lips. I wouldn't have thought she was Maria at all. I had pictured her as a corporate type, expecting a suit to appear, but as soon as I saw her, I knew. It was the red lips that gave her away and suddenly the company name made sense. I knew it was her and yet I couldn't call out to her as I watched her walk across the lobby to reception. I imagined she and Adam cut a very striking couple, turning heads wherever they went, and in that moment I resented Maria even more. Good old-fashioned female jealousy. I was annoyed with myself; I'd never fallen prey to that kind of thinking before. I wasn't the type. But then, I'd always been happy, settled in my life and now I wasn't, so anything, anybody secure sent my already wobbly confidence crashing down like a skittle.

The receptionist pointed over at me, and Maria took me in. In the days when they spoke to me, Peter and Paul greeted me as 'Casual Friday' in the mornings, because jeans were my staple wardrobe. And not just your regular jeans. I had them in almost every colour of the rainbow, as was the palette of the rest of my clothes. My wardrobe was one great kaleido-scope with the purpose of brightening up my day even when everything else in the world failed to comply. I'd gone from a muted wardrobe of blacks and beiges to this burst of colour in my mid-twenties. I always had on at least one item of colour after I'd read a book, *How to Enrich Our Soul Through the Clothes We Wear*, which taught me that our skin and soul took energy from the colours we wore, and wearing dark colours drained us. Our bodies craved colour the same way they needed sun, yet here was Maria, all in black and ultra-cool, as if she'd drifted out of an All Saints store, and there was me, like a packet of Skittles, my long, wavy, sandy-coloured hair beneath a stripy woollen hat that looked like I'd stolen it off the set of *Zingzillas*. My sandy 'beach' hair was carefully maintained and treated each week, tousled and teased into looking like it didn't care, like it didn't have a trouble in the world, but believe me it cared, it only pretended not to. My hair giggled and flirted, it blew in the breeze, whereas Maria's . . . that trendy bob with its strict fringe laughed in the face of danger, it *demanded* rebellion.

As soon as Maria spotted the lily pad in my arms, which wasn't difficult to see, her face broke into a beam. Relief flooded through me and I was afraid to turn around to see Adam's reaction in case I alerted Maria to his whereabouts. She clasped her hands to her mouth and started to laugh, trying not to attract too much attention to herself, though I guessed word would be around the office in no time that Maria Harty had received a delivery of a lily pad.

'Oh my God!' She wiped her wet eyes. They were tears of joy but also from the sudden memory of a person from another time. She

160

reached out to take the pad. 'This is probably the oddest delivery you've ever made.' She smiled at me. 'My goodness, I can't believe he did this. I thought he'd forgotten. It was a long, long time ago.' She held the lily pad in her arms. Suddenly embarrassed, she said, 'I'm sorry, you don't need people telling you their stories. I'm sure you've somewhere else to deliver to. Where do I sign?'

'Maria, I'm Christine, we spoke on the phone.'

'Christine . . . ' Her forehead crinkled then realisation set in. 'Oh. Christine. Is that your name? You've been answering Adam's phone?'

'That's me.'

'Oh.' Maria looked me up and down, sized me up in seconds. 'I didn't think that you were young. I mean, you sound much older on the phone.'

'Oh.' I felt all warm inside, loving the reaction, but knowing I shouldn't.

There was an awkward silence.

'He really got this for me?'

'He sure did. Dived into subzero temperatures. Got soaking wet. Blue lips and all,' I said, still feeling my head cold building.

Maria shook her head. 'He's crazy.'

'About you.'

'Is that what he's telling me? He still loves me?'

I nodded. 'He really does.' And for some reason my throat tightened. Unfortunate timing perhaps. I cleared my throat. 'I thought he should include flowers, but he insisted on those. I don't know if they mean anything to you.'

Maria looked down to the lily pad and it was

161

only then that she noticed the tiny lips wrapped in red foil. Adam had added them on at the last minute before I entered the building and suddenly everything was making sense to me. I now recognised them as the tiny chocolates that were scattered on the bed in the Gresham Hotel.

'Oh my,' Maria whispered, noticing them for the first time. She attempted to pick them up but couldn't hold the enormous lily pad with one hand.

I took it back from her so she could examine the tiny lips.

'I can't believe there were still some left. You know what they are?'

I shook my head.

'He made them for me the year we first met. Red lips are, well, kind of my trademark.' She started to open the foil and when she saw chocolate beneath she laughed. 'They're real!'

'Adam knows how to make chocolate?' I laughed, feeling doubtful. If Maria wanted to believe that then I shouldn't be placing doubt in her mind, but I couldn't help but question it.

'Well, not personally, obviously, but the company.' She carried on studying them. 'They were a prototype, they weren't supposed to ever see the light of day. I thought we'd eaten them all.'

'The company . . . ' I said, trying to figure it all out.

'He designed it for me, then he got the people at Basil's to make them. He put pralines, hazelnuts and almonds in it because he said I'm nutty.' She laughed, but her laugh caught in her

162

throat and her eyes filled. 'Shit, sorry.' She turned her back to reception and fanned her eyes to make them stop welling.

I was slightly in shock by this time but tried to play it cool. I could have asked Maria about Adam, learned more about him, but for some reason I didn't want Maria to find out that I didn't know; my insecurity since seeing her stopping me from doing my job properly.

'There's no need to be sorry. It's not easy remembering the good times. But he did want to remind you.'

She nodded. 'Tell him I remember.'

'He's still there, you know,' I said earnestly. 'He's as funny and spontaneous as you remember. Maybe not exactly like when you first met. Maybe that's impossible for anybody to be. But he makes me laugh all the time.'

Maria studied me closely. 'Does he?'

I felt my cheeks get hot. It was the woollen hat, must have been, going from extreme cold to stuffy office building heat and the head cold that I knew I was getting after being in the freezing cold pond. I wasn't going to take it off though, not with her and her poker-straight hair. Who knew what lurked beneath my hat?

'You really are looking after him, aren't you?'

'Well, yes.' I couldn't hold her gaze any more and so handed the lily pad over. 'I should let you get back to work now.'

'I hope he knows how lucky he is to have you.' Maria pushed it a little further.

I couldn't help my eyes filling a little. 'I'm only doing my job.' I flashed her a bright and breezy smile and tried hard for my response not to sound like a cheesy super-hero retort.

'And what job is that?'

'A friend,' I said, taking a few steps away. 'I'm a friend, that's all.'

I turned and left then, feeling my face blazing. I was thankful for the icy breeze that hit my cheeks as soon as I stepped outside. I kept walking, feeling Maria's eyes on me. I was glad to turn the corner as soon as I could, to escape the transparent surfaces and have solid brick between us. I stopped walking immediately and put my back to the wall, my eyes closed as I relived the conversation in a state of panic. What had come over me? Why had I reacted like that? Maria acted as if she knew something about my feelings that I didn't, she made me feel guilty and pathetic for momentarily feeling something I didn't feel, that I couldn't *possibly* feel. My aim here was to get them together, not to start having feelings for Adam. Impossible. Ridiculous.

'Hi,' I heard an excited voice say close to my ear and I jumped, startled.

'Jesus, Adam.'

'What's wrong? Are you crying?'

'No, I'm not crying,' I snapped. 'I think I'm getting a cold.' I rubbed my eyes.

'Well, I'm not surprised, swimming in ponds in the middle of the night. So, what did she say?' He was practically nose to nose with me he was so excited, so eager to hear the words.

'You saw her reaction.'

'Yes!' He fist-pumped the air. 'It was perfect. Just perfect. And was she crying? She looked like she was crying. You know, Maria never cries, that's really a big deal. You were talking for ages — what did she say?' He was hopping around, bouncing on his feet, searching my face for every little sign so he'd know exactly how it went.

I coldly cut out my emotions and told him the story, minus my own internal tormented thoughts. 'She asked if you were trying to tell her you still loved her. She said someone who jumps into subzero water to get a lily pad must really love someone. And I said that, yes, you did.'

'But I didn't do that.' Adam fixed me with those blue eyes which usually made my heart surge but right then made it ache. 'You did it for me.'

We held each other's gaze, then I looked away. 'That's not the point. The point is, she gets the point.' I started moving, I had to, I needed to get away.

'Christine? Where are you going?'

'Er . . . anywhere. I'm cold, I need to keep moving.'

'Okay, good idea. Did she like the chocolates?'

'She *loved* the chocolates, they're what made her cry. Hey, you made her *chocolates*? You're Adam Basil, as in 'With Basil, You Dazzle'?'

He rolled his eyes but was clearly ecstatic about the outcome. 'What did she say?'

'She almost made love to them, she was so happy to see them again. You made a woman chocolates? Jesus, Adam, you were good.'

'Were?'

'You know what I mean. You're getting there again.'

'They had praline, hazelnuts and almond in them, because she's nutty,' he said proudly.

'I know, she told me.'

'She did? What did she say?'

His eagerness was endearing so I rehashed the entire conversation, leaving out the part where Maria questioned me about my role in his life. I still hadn't made sense of that part yet.

'So you're Adam Basil of Basil's Chocolate.' I shook my head, still not believing it. 'You should have told me yesterday. You denied it.'

'I didn't deny it. As I recall, I said, 'Yes, and like the herb.''

'Oh. Well, when all this ends you'll have to make me my own chocolate, as a token of your appreciation.'

'Easy. Black coffee flavour.'

I rolled my eyes. 'Not very original.'

'Shaped as an espresso cup.' He tried hard to impress me.

'I hope you have a good creative team at Basil's.'

'Why? You wouldn't eat it anyway,' he laughed.

We were silent as we walked. I had to switch my brain off, I had a headache and it hurt to think, so I allowed him to lead me. I grabbed his hand as we approached Samuel Beckett Bridge; it was instinctive, I didn't want him to suddenly jump, even though I knew he was on a high after Maria's reaction. He didn't object. We held hands as we walked over the bridge, and when we were over it he didn't let go.

'Where do the company, Basil's, think you are?' I asked.

'Visiting my father. They said take all the time I need. I wonder if they'll accept the rest of my life.'

'I'm sure they'd be happy to hear that instead of the alternative.'

He looked at me sharply. 'They can't know.'

'That you tried to die by suicide?'

He dropped my hand. 'I told you not to use those words.'

'Adam, if they knew you were so miserable that you wanted to end your life, I'm sure that would be a big way out of the job.'

'That's not an option and you know it,' he said. 'It's not why I did it.'

We left a long silence.

'You should go see your dad.'

'Not today. Today is a good day,' he said, jubilant again about the Maria outcome. 'Where to now?'

'I'm a bit tired, Adam. I think I'll go home and have a rest.'

He looked disappointed, then concerned. 'Are you okay?'

'Yeah.' I nodded, needing to seem upbeat. 'I just need a catnap and I'll be fine.'

'I've arranged for Pat to collect us.'

'Who's Pat?'

'My father's driver.'

'Your father's driver?' I repeated.

'Well, Father's in hospital, he's not going to need him, and your car is out of action. So I called Pat. He's bored of waiting around anyway.'

Moments later, Pat rolled up in a two hundred

and fifty thousand euro brand-new Rolls-Royce. I knew little about cars, but while Barry displayed no real passion for anything in life he did know about cars and pointed out the good ones that 'gobshites' always seemed to be driving. In Barry's opinion, the Rolls-Royce was the car of choice for the biggest kind of gobshite. I greeted Pat the driver and sat into the car. It was deliciously warm after the freezing cold outside. Adam hadn't closed the door yet; he was staring at me, a thoughtful look on his face.

'What?' I asked.

'Rose petal,' he said simply.

'I love rose petal.'

'And the chocolate would be in the shape of a petal.'

'You're good,' I acknowledged. 'All the more reason for me to keep you alive.'

'You mean there's more than one reason?' he joked, and closed the door.

Yes, I thought to myself as I watched him make his way around the car.

13

How to Recognise and Appreciate the People in Your Life Today

I sat in the row behind Amelia at her mother's funeral. Apart from an aged uncle, her father's brother, who was out of his nursing home for the day, she was alone in the family front pew. Fred, who days before had asked her to move to Berlin with him, hadn't bothered to ask her a second time. In fact I had detected a panic within him when we spoke. His original proposal had been made in the sure knowledge that Amelia would say no because of her mother; now Magda had passed on and there was nothing to bind Amelia to the bookshop and Dublin, his terror was palpable. I was sure that Amelia was right about him having another woman waiting for him in Berlin. I caught his eye a few rows back and threw him the dirtiest look I could muster, all in the name of a friend. He lowered his eyes and when I felt satisfied he was sufficiently squirming I turned back to face the front, feeling like a dirty hypocrite and regretting it instantly. There had been no secret man waiting for me, that much was obvious, but I had walked out on Barry, ended our relationship for no real reason at all — well, no reason that anybody else could see. It was almost as if my unhappiness wasn't enough. If he didn't cheat on me, hit me or was unkind to me, nobody could seem to understand that my not loving him and being unhappy was enough of a reason. I wasn't perfect, but I tried my best, like most people, not to make mistakes. For an entire marriage to be a mistake was one of the most hurtful, not to mention embarrassing things that could have happened in my life. The thought of Barry possibly being in the church ended my wandering eyes.

Though Fred had hurt Amelia, how could I blame him when he had done the very thing that I had predicted in my private discussions with Barry? Amelia had been wedged in her rut of caring for her mother and devoting herself to a business her father had loved, a noble rut, granted, but one she had lodged herself in of her own free will. There was only so much of Amelia's standing still that Fred, or anyone in her life, could take.

Amelia's head was bowed, her curly red hair hiding her face. When she turned to me her tired green eyes were rimmed with red, the tip of her nose was red, raw from the tissues, the pain on her face clear. I smiled back supportively, then realised the entire church was quiet and the priest was looking at me.

'Oh.' I realised they were waiting for me. I stood and made my way to the altar.

Whether Adam liked it or not, I had insisted he come to the funeral and sit with me and my family. Despite his great mood after my meeting with Maria, I couldn't risk leaving him alone. We were taking great leaps forward, a little with Maria, a little with himself, but for

170

every leap there were a few steps back. I had banned him from reading newspapers and from watching the news. He needed to focus on the positive; the news did not. There were ways to keep in touch with reality without allowing yourself to be bombarded with information as outsiders saw fit. Yesterday, we had spent much of the day doing a jigsaw while I picked his brains in the most non-invasive way I could, then we played Monopoly, which meant I had to stop my questioning and concentrate to prevent Adam wiping the floor with me. It didn't work and I'd gone to bed in a bad mood. I knew these activities weren't going to save him, but they did help me learn more about him as it made it easier for him to talk to me. I think it also gave him a moment to think about his problems, process them while concentrating on something else at the same time, instead of bringing them to centre stage. This morning I'd listened to his muted sobs while he was in the shower and made plans for how to fix the rest of his problems. I believed that most things were possible if you put your mind to it, but I was also realistic; 'most' implied not everything. I couldn't afford to examine the odds in this case; there could only be one outcome.

I stood on the altar and placed my reading on the stand. Amelia had asked me to read and had left it to me to choose a piece I found appropriate. It was going to take an act of will for me to say these words; they had very special meaning to me and I had never read them aloud before, only to myself and rarely with dry eyes, but I couldn't think of a more appropriate time to read them. I smiled at Amelia, then looked over her shoulder, first at my family, then at Adam. I took a long shaky breath and directed my words at him.

'Where would we be without tomorrows? What we'd have instead are todays. And if that was the case, with you, I'd hope for the longest day for today. I'd fill today with you, doing everything I've ever loved. I'd laugh, I'd talk, I'd listen and learn, I'd love, I'd love, I'd love. I'd make every day today and spend them all with you, and I'd never worry about tomorrow, when I wouldn't be with you. And when that dreaded tomorrow comes for us, please know that I didn't want to leave you, or be left behind, that every single moment spent with you were the best times in my life.'

★ ★ ★

'Did you write that?' Adam asked me as we sat at the function after the funeral with cups of milky tea and a plate of ham sandwiches in front of us. Neither of us ate.

'No.'

We left a long silence and I waited for him to ask me who did write it, and I prepared what I was going to say, but he surprised me by not asking.

'I think I need to go see my dad,' Adam said suddenly.

It was enough for me.

172

Adam's father was staying at St Vincent's private hospital. He had gone in for a short procedure for his liver disease one month previously and he was still there. Mr Basil happened to be the rudest individual anybody could ever possibly meet but, despite the fact that without him life in the wards would be easier for everyone involved, they were still using the best of modern medicine to try to keep him alive. His room was not one anybody chose to enter, thanks to the fear of being abused, verbally for everyone, and physically for the young — or as he called them, 'ripe' — nurses. For the unripe ones, he resorted to other types of physical abuse, even throwing his urine at one nurse who'd interrupted his phone call. He would only permit a handful of the female nursing staff to look after him, and they had allowed him to think he actually had a choice in the matter. He wanted to be surrounded by women because he believed they were better at getting the job done on account of their ability to multi-task, their innate coldness and no-nonsense minds, but mostly because, as the perceived inferior sex, they felt the need and the desire to prove themselves more than men. Men's eyes wandered; he needed people who could concentrate on one thing at a time, and that thing was him. He wanted and needed to get better. He had a multi-billion international business to run and until they fixed him he would run it from the sparse room that had been transformed into Basil Confectionery's nerve centre.

As we followed the dinner lady, who pushed open the door to enter, I caught a glimpse of the old man and saw a full head of fine wispy grey curls and a long wispy grey beard, which extended only from the chin, not from the cheeks, and finished in a fine point as if it were an arrow pointing downward to the depths of hell. There was nothing soothing about this room, which he'd been sent to to heal. Instead there were three laptops, a fax machine, an iPad, more than enough BlackBerries and iPhones for the disintegrating figure in the bed and the two women in suits who huddled by his side. It wasn't a room that hinted at the possibility of goodbye to the world; it was a room that was alive, busy, ready to create; kicking and screaming and raging against the dying light. This was a room whose occupant wasn't finished with the world and would go down fighting if need be.

'I heard they were giving out Bartholomew tubs on the plane,' he snapped to the older woman. 'A little tub of ice cream for everyone, even in economy.'

'Yes, they've done a deal with Aer Lingus. For one year, I believe.'

'Why don't they have Basil's on the plane? It's ludicrous that Bartholomew would get there and not us. Who's responsible for this fuck-up? Is it you, Mary? Honestly, how many times do I have to tell you to keep your eye on the ball? You're so busy with those damn horses I'm beginning to

174

worry you've lost your ability to function.'

'Of course I spoke to Aer Lingus, Mr Basil, on many occasions, and have done so for years, but it is thought by them that Bartholomew are a more luxury brand, while we're a family brand. Ours are available — '

'Not ours, *mine*,' he interrupted.

She continued calmly as if he hadn't spoken: ' — to purchase from the inflight shopping, and I can tell you our exact revenue from this . . . ' She flicked through some papers.

'Out!' he suddenly yelled at the top of his lungs, and everyone jumped except the cool, calm Mary, who once again behaved as though she hadn't heard him. 'We're having a meeting, you should have called first.' How he'd seen us enter was beyond my comprehension, given we were trapped behind a trolley and I could barely see him.

'Come on,' Adam said, turning on his heel.

'Wait.' I reached out and grabbed his arm. I blocked the door and trapped him in the room. 'We're doing this today,' I whispered.

The dinner lady placed the tray on the table in front of Mr Basil.

'What is this? It looks like shit.'

The woman with the hairnet looked at him, bored, seemingly accustomed to the insults. 'It's shepherd's pie, Mr Basil.' She spoke in a thick Dublin accent, then changed her tone to a more sarcastic, superior one: 'Accompanied by a side salad of lettuce and baby tomatoes, accompanied by a slice of bread and butter. For dessert you have jelly and ice cream, followed by your enema

— so please do give Nurse Sue a call for that.' She smiled sweetly for a nanosecond then her original scowl returned.

'Shepherd's shit, more like, and that side salad looks like grass. Do I look like a horse to you, Mags?'

The dinner lady wasn't wearing a name badge. Despite the insults, she might have felt mildly complimented by the fact he knew her name. Unless her name was Jennifer.

'No, Mr Basil, you certainly don't look like a horse. You look like a skinny, angry old man who needs his dinner. Now eat up.'

'Yesterday's dinner looked like food and tasted like shit. Maybe this shit will actually taste like food.'

'And then hopefully today the enema will help you have a shit,' she said, picking up the tray from earlier and carrying it out of the room, head held high.

I thought I saw Mr Basil smile but the glimmer of possibility disappeared as quickly as it had come. His voice was gravelly, weak but authoritative. If he was this tough on his deathbed, I could only imagine what he had been like in the office. And as a father. I looked at Adam; his expression was unreadable. This visit was important, this was where I would have to appeal to Mr Basil's paternal instincts, to see how forcing Adam to take over the company was damaging his son's health. This was the basket in which I placed all of my eggs. Already I was concerned they'd decided to crush themselves on the way into the room.

'Actually, come back here,' the old man called. Mags halted.

'Not you, the pair of them.'

Mags patted my hand sympathetically as she passed and said gently, 'He's a right fucker.'

Adam and I approached the bed. No loving words were shared between father and son, not even a greeting of any kind.

'What do you have to do today?' Mr Basil barked. Adam looked confused.

'I heard you whispering: *We're doing this today*.' He mocked my previous whisper. 'Don't look so surprised, there's nothing wrong with my hearing. It's my liver that has me in here, and that's not even what's killing me. It's the cancer — and I think the fucking food will kill me before that does!' He pushed away his plate. 'I don't understand why they won't just let me out of here to die. I've got things to do.' He raised his voice again as a doctor entered to study his chart. There were two student doctors with her.

'It looks like you're doing plenty already,' the doctor said. 'The allowed number of guests per room is two.' She glared at us all as if we were responsible for causing the cancer to grow at such a rapid rate. 'I thought I told you to rest, Mr Basil.'

'And I thought I told you to fuck off,' he said.

There was a long uncomfortable silence and I suddenly felt the urge to laugh.

'You wait all day for a fucking doctor, then three of them come at once,' he said. 'To what do I owe the pleasure of your company? Is it the

177

thousands I'm paying you every day to ignore me?'

'Mr Basil, may I remind you to curb your tongue. If you're feeling more irritable than usual, perhaps we can take a look at your medication.'

He waved a pale thin hand dismissively, almost in surrender.

'A few minutes for you all and then I must insist on Mr Basil being alone,' she said firmly. 'We can talk then.' She turned and left with her merry men scuttling along behind her.

'I might see her again next week, whereupon she'll visit my bed and once again tell me diddly squat. Who are you?' he demanded, glaring at me.

Everyone turned their heads in my direction.

'I'm Christine Rose.' I held out my hand.

Mr Basil looked at it, lifted his hand, from which a tube protruded, and addressed Adam as he shook my hand limply: 'Does Maria know about her? I never took you for a two-timer, you always seemed such a pussy. Pussy-whipped. Rose — what kind of name is that?' He turned to me again.

'We think it's originally Rosenburg.'

He sized me up, then his eyes returned to Adam. 'I like Maria. I don't like many people, but I like her. And Mags, the dinner lady. Maria's smart. Once she gets her act together she'll go far. I don't think much of that shitty business — Red Lips. It sounds like porno.'

I couldn't help myself: I laughed, out loud.

Mr Basil appeared surprised, then continued,

watching me as he spoke. 'When she comes to her senses and stops making cartoons — '

'Animation — ' I interrupted, feeling I owed it to Maria after enjoying her annihilation a little too much.

'I don't give a shit what — then she'll do well. She'll be helpful to you when you're in charge, because God knows you couldn't organise a piss-up in a brewery.'

'Then why do you want him to take over the company?' I asked, and all heads swivelled to me.

Everyone, especially Mr Basil, seemed surprised, not that he'd dream of letting on. His authority must never be allowed to slip for a moment, no one else could be permitted to take the lead.

'Was that supposed to be a secret?' I muttered to Adam.

He shook his head, looking at me with wary eyes.

'What then?' I looked around, unsure what I'd done. The woman named Mary took a step back from the bed, the younger woman in grey followed suit.

'We'll leave you to it, Mr Basil. We'll be outside if you need us.'

He ignored her. Mary seemed to waver between leaving and staying.

'Tell me, how do you know my son?'

'We're friends,' Adam jumped in.

'Ah, he speaks!' his father said. 'Tell me, Adam, the office haven't seen you since Sunday. Apparently you were in Dublin to see me, but I'd have noticed if you'd come here and you didn't. If you're going to spend your time whoring around, then do it on — '

'He wasn't whoring — '

' — your own time. I don't like to be interrupted, thank you, Ms Rose.'

'There's an issue I'd like to discuss in private with you,' I said. 'Adam, you can leave too, if you like.'

Mr Basil looked at the two women by his bedside. They appeared anxious to get out of the room, and for that he was going to force them to stay. 'I trust Mary more than I trust myself. She's been with us since the day I took over forty years ago, and has known my son since he was in nappies, which was a phase that lasted longer than everyone hoped. Anything you have to say can be said in front of Mary. The other girl I'm not so sure of, but Mary thinks highly of her so I'm giving her a chance. Now cut the shit and tell me what you're here for.'

The younger woman beside Mary lowered her head, embarrassed. I pulled over a chair and sat down. *How to Break Sensitive News to a Dying Old Man*. This particular man didn't seem to deserve any sensitivity, given that he had none for anyone else. Well, if Adam wasn't going to speak to him directly, I was. I'd sort this out once and for all. I came from a world of honesty and forthrightness, I wasn't dramatic and certainly did not point out issues I had with people unless it was vital and unless it would improve the relationship, and I was grading Adam's situation as vital. If a person's behaviour has a negative effect on your life, you have to communicate with them, share the problem, discuss it, come to a conclusion. Communication is key in these situations, and clearly it was non-existent between this father and son. I sensed Adam was too afraid to stand up to his imposing father and so I would have to do it for him.

I spoke firmly and looked the old man directly in the eye. 'I'm aware that you're going to die very soon and you want Adam to take over the company so that control doesn't revert to your nephew. We're here to talk about that.'

Adam sighed and closed his eyes.

'Shut up,' Mr Basil snapped at him, even though he hadn't spoken. 'Mary, Patricia — outside, please.' He didn't even watch as they left, he kept his eyes on me.

I gave Adam a reassuring smile but he was unreadable, his jaw rigid.

Mr Basil looked at me as if I was the last person he wanted to have to talk to. 'Ms Rose, you have your facts wrong. I don't *want* Adam to take over the company. Lavinia is next in line, and was always intended to inherit. She's far more able for the job than he is, believe you me, but she's in Boston.'

'Yes, I hear she stole millions from her friends and family,' I said, putting him in his place. 'Here's the thing: Adam doesn't want the job.'

I left a long silence. He waited for more but nothing came. That was it, I was finished. He didn't deserve pandering and polite explanations.

181

'Do you think I didn't know that?' He looked from me to Adam. 'Is this supposed to be some elaborate reveal?'

I frowned. This wasn't going the way I planned.

Mr Basil started laughing, but even his laugh was joyless.

'His lack of interest in anything I do has made it patently obvious. He's been fannying around with helicopters since he could talk, and he's spent the last ten years messing around with the coast guard. I don't care if he doesn't want the job, I don't care if it makes him deeply unhappy. It does not change what must be. A Basil must be in charge of this company. A Basil always has and always will be in charge of this company. And it cannot be Nigel Basil — it must not be. Over my dead body.' He seemed unaware of the irony. 'My grandfather, my father and I have fought hard to keep this company in our hands through good times and bad since it was founded, and no bossy little bitch with too much mouth and too little understanding is going to change that.'

My mouth fell open. I heard another of my eggs crack under the pressure.

'Father, that's enough,' Adam said firmly. 'Don't speak to her like that. She's not trying to change anything, she's only telling you what she thinks you don't know. She wants to help.'

'And why are you communicating the message on my son's behalf?' He looked at Adam. 'Son, it's time you grew a set of balls. Don't let other people do your dirty work.' And then his tone turned nasty. Not comedy nasty as it had previously been, but bitter nasty, pure vitriol emanating from his eyes and mouth, which was twisted in a sneer. 'Did he tell you he doesn't receive a penny, no inheritance whatsoever, until he's done ten years with the company? Whether I'm dead or alive, he gets nothing. I think that might persuade him.'

Adam was staring at the wall, his face set.

'No, he didn't,' I said, now thoroughly riled by this vile old man. 'But I really don't think money is an issue for Adam. Mr Basil, if your company matters to you more than your own son's wellbeing, shouldn't you at least consider what is best for the company? I realise it's a family company and it's been there for generations; you've put your entire life into it, blood, sweat and tears — now you need to find someone who will go on doing that in your absence. The company will not flourish in Adam's hands because he's not driven by the same desire you are. If you really care about your legacy, find someone who will love it and nurture it as you have.'

He looked at me, his expression contemptuous, his eyes cold, then turned to Adam. I expected to hear spite but was surprised by his calm tone. 'Maria will help you, Adam. When there are decisions to be made that you don't know how to make, sound them out with her. Back when I started out, do you think a day went by that I didn't ask your mother her opinion? And you'll have Mary — she's my right-hand man. You think you'll have to do it alone? You won't.' He stopped, suddenly exhausted. 'You can't let Nigel step in, you know you can't.'

'Maybe Maria's too busy sleeping with Sean to help him out. Isn't that right?'

Startled, we all turned towards the doorway. A handsome young man looked back at us, the family resemblance obvious in his strong jaw and blue eyes. But his hair was dark instead of fair — and so was his soul. To me, he emanated bad vibes.

Amused, he raised an eyebrow at us, put his hands in his pockets and strolled over casually.

'Nigel,' Adam said curtly.

'Hello, Adam. Hello, Uncle Dick.'

I wish I could have felt for Mr Basil then. What could be worse than seeing someone you despise when you're ill in bed, wearing paisley pyjamas, powerless to defend yourself. And his name was Dick. But it was impossible to summon the pity.

'What the hell are you doing here?' Adam asked, not bothering to be polite and looking as though he wanted to hit him.

'I came to visit my uncle, but it turns out to be good timing — you and I never got to finish our meeting last week. You seemed to leave in rather a rush.'

'You two had a meeting?' Mr Basil looked as though he'd been stabbed in the heart.

'Adam came to me about my taking over Basil's. He quite liked the idea of the names *Bartholomew Basil* coming together — the greatest tribute to our grandfather, don't you think?' He smirked.

'You're a liar!' Adam's fury was evident. He trampled on my feet to get to his cousin, who he grabbed by the scruff of the neck and pushed all the way across the room till he slammed him hard against the wall. He wrapped his hand around Nigel's throat and held him there as his cousin struggled.

'Adam,' I warned, trying to hold back my panic.

'You're a bloody liar,' Adam said through gritted teeth. Nigel's veins were protruding from his forehead as he tried to pull Adam's hands away from his throat, but Adam was stronger. Instead, Nigel turned his effort to thrusting his fingers at Adam's nostrils, forcing his head back.

'Adam!' I jumped up. I tried to stop them but was afraid of getting too close when they were battling it out. I looked back at Mr Basil. His face was like thunder but he was ultimately an impotent old man in his sick bed — and he knew it. He started breathing very heavily.

'Mr Basil, are you okay?' I asked. I ran back to his side and pressed the call button for the nurse.

His eyes were watering.

'He wouldn't,' I said firmly. 'Adam wouldn't do that.'

He searched my face for signs of being misled.

'Of course, he wouldn't,' I said, beginning to panic and pressing the call button continuously. By the time security burst into the room, Adam and Nigel were scuffling on the ground. They immediately pulled Adam off Nigel and while they held him by the shoulders, with his arms trapped behind his back, Nigel swung his arm

185

and punched Adam hard, first across the jaw, then in the stomach.

Adam doubled over.

*   *   *

'I think your modelling days are over,' I joked weakly as I dabbed Adam's split lip once we were back at the flat.

He smiled and the blood started to spill all over again through his stretched cut.

'Ah, don't smile,' I said, dabbing at it again.

'No problem,' he sighed. He stood up suddenly, pushing me away, the aggression back in his body. 'I'm going for a shower.'

I opened my mouth to call out an apology. I had tried to do right and it had all gone horribly wrong. Our lunch at the restaurant had given him cramps, the walk in the park had led him to be locked in a garda cell, the random drive had led to a car chase, and my quest to tell his father the truth had led to him getting his face punched in.

Sorry.

But I didn't say anything. It didn't matter. I had said it in the car on the way home until I was blue in the face; I had tried to talk the entire episode into a positive experience, one about facing the truth and dealing with consequences, but I knew it was a hard sell. I'd misjudged the situation. I'd thought he had been too afraid to tell his father, but the fear was because he knew that his father was aware he wanted none of it but it made no difference. It had been naive of me, thinking I could hit upon an obvious way out of a situation Adam had spent years trying to extricate himself from. It was only after exploring every other possible escape route that he'd made his desperate decision on the Ha'penny Bridge. I should have known that, and the fact it hadn't occurred to me left me feeling awkward and embarrassed. He didn't want to hear my words any more. My words weren't fixing anything. My being sorry would change nothing.

⋆ ⋆ ⋆

At four a.m. I kicked the duvet covers off the bed in a fit of frustration and officially gave up on trying to sleep.

'Are you awake?' I called out to the dark.

'No,' he responded.

I smiled. 'I left a sheet for you on the coffee table. Pick it up.'

I heard him move across the room to retrieve the page I'd set out the night before.

'What the hell is this?'

'Read one.'

' "The best and most beautiful things in the world cannot be seen or even touched — they must be felt with the heart.' Helen Keller.' He was silent. Then he snorted.

' "It is during our darkest moments that we must focus to see the light.' Aristotle Onassis,' I called out, from memory, lying back down on the bed.

He paused and I wondered if he was going to

rip it up, or humour my attempt at lifting his spirit.

' 'Believe you can and you're halfway there.' Theodore Roosevelt,' I called out again, encouraging him to read another.

'Don't piss into the wind,' Adam called.

I frowned. 'That's not on the sheet.'

'Don't buy a telescope, just walk closer to what you want to see.'

I smiled.

'Never eat yellow snow. Don't smoke. Wear a bra. Never make eye contact while eating an ice pop.'

I was giggling in bed. Finally he was silent.

'Okay, I get the point: you think they're crap. But do you feel better?'

'Do you?'

I laughed. 'Yes, I do actually.'

'I do too,' he answered eventually, his voice soft and low.

I imagined he was smiling, at least I hoped he was; I could hear it in his voice.

'Goodnight, Adam.'

'Goodnight, Christine.'

I slept a little that night, but mostly I couldn't help thinking: eight days left.

14

How to Have Your Cake and Eat It

Detective Maguire sat across the table from me in an interrogation room in Pearse Street garda station. His eyes were bloodshot, with crinkled bags underneath as though he'd had a hard night partying the night before. Once again I knew this not to be true. He'd grudgingly agreed to see me, warning that for the time being he would merely listen to my story before deciding whether to refer me to his colleagues. I understood that to mean he was acting as a filter; if my complaint wasn't worth it, he didn't want to waste garda time. I felt my forehead prickle with sweat. The room was suffocating, with no windows and no ventilation. If I were a suspect I'd have been ready admit to anything, to get out of there. Thankfully, I'd insisted on the door being left open so I could keep an eye on Adam.

'Are you in the habit of picking up suicide victims?' Detective Maguire had asked when I arrived with Adam.

'I'm helping him with a job placement actually.' It wasn't a total lie.

I checked the door once again to make sure Adam was still there. He looked bored and tired but at least he was present.

'You always bring your work home with you?' he asked.

189

'You ever go home?' I snapped.

I realised too late that he'd been on the verge of opening up for once. My snapping immediately caused him to retreat to his shell; the force field went back up, and he shifted uncomfortably in his chair, clearly berating himself over his weakness in letting his mask slip.

My response left me feeling guilty; I realised I preferred dealing with the tough Maguire. I didn't want to relax and start sharing trade secrets with this man.

'So tell me again, you think a man wearing a black leather jacket and turtle-neck jumper, possibly an Eastern European, smashed your windscreen with a hurley stick because you possibly witnessed a drug sale between this man and a black car with tinted windows — of which you can remember no other details — on a country lane, for which you can't provide directions or a location because you were playing a game of getting lost. Have I got that right?' His tone was bored.

'My friend Julie's windscreen, not mine, but yes, the rest of that is correct.' It had taken me three days to make a report about the windscreen, partly because I was helping Amelia with her mother's funeral arrangements, partly because of my schedule with Adam but mostly because I was avoiding having to spend a single second in Detective Maguire's company, though in the end I knew he was the one who could help me.

'Why *possibly* Eastern European?'

'He had that look,' I said quietly, wishing I

190

hadn't mentioned that part at all. 'He was enormous, strong jaw, wide shoulders. But then he had a hurley stick, which made him look more Irish . . . ' I trailed off, my face reddening at the amusement on his face.

'So if he'd done a perfect somersault he'd have been Russian, and if he'd had a baseball bat that would have made him American? What if he'd come at you with a chopstick? Japanese or Chinese — what do you think?' He grinned, enjoying his joke.

I ignored him.

'Can anybody else corroborate your story?'

'Yes. Adam can.'

'The suicide man.'

'The attempted suicide victim, yes.'

'Any other witnesses who didn't just try to kill themselves five minutes ago?'

'He attempted suicide five days ago, and yes, my niece saw it all.'

'I'll need her details.'

I thought about it. 'Sure. Have you got a pen?'

He picked up his biro grudgingly, flicked open his notepad, which was blank despite my having spent the last ten minutes telling him what happened.

'Shoot.'

'Her name is Alicia Rose Talbot and you'll find her at the Cheeky Monkey Montessori, Vernon Avenue, Clontarf,' I said it slowly.

'She works there?'

'No, she attends it. She's three years old.'

'Are you fucking with me?' He slammed the pen down.

Adam peered into the room protectively.

'No, but I believe you are with me. I don't think you're taking this seriously,' I said.

'Look, I operate from the place that the most obvious answer is probably the truth. Your story about a Russian drug dealer with a hurley down a country lane has so many ifs and buts, I doubt it has any legs.'

'But it happened.'

'Maybe it did.'

'It *did*.'

He was silent.

'So what's the most obvious answer then?' I asked.

'I heard you left your husband.'

I swallowed, surprised it had taken this direction.

'The night of the shooting,' he prompted.

'What's *when* I left got to do with anything?'

He rubbed his stubbled jaw, red raw from too much shaving and not enough moisturising. Then he sat a moment, studying me, and I began to feel as if I were being interrogated.

'Did it have anything to do with the shooting?'

'No . . . yes . . . maybe,' I stammered, having realised I didn't want him to know. 'Why do you want to know that?'

'Because.' He shifted in his chair and started doodling on the pad. 'I've been in this job a long time and — take it from someone who has experience of these things — you shouldn't let what happens on the job affect what happens in your home life.'

I was surprised. I was about to snap back but

instead bit my tongue. It must have taken him a lot to say what he'd said to me.

'It wasn't because of what happened with Simon. But thanks. For the advice.'

He studied me for a while in silence, then parked the issue. 'Do you think your ex-husband has anything to do with the car being damaged?'

'No way.'

'How do you know?'

'Because he's not that type of person. He's not passionate like that. He doesn't even support a football team because he can't believe in anything that much. For his birthday one year his friends got him part of a fence for him to sit on — that's how devoid of opinion he is. Honestly, if you knew him you wouldn't be having this conversation. Let's move on.'

'How has he been taking you leaving him?'

'Jesus, Maguire, that has nothing to do with you,' I shouted, standing up.

'It may have something to do with your window,' he said calmly, remaining seated. 'A husband, recently left by his wife, humiliated, broken-hearted and angry, I'd imagine. He might have been your sweetpea when you were married, but you never know how much people can change. Like the flick of a switch. Has there been any threatening behaviour over the past few weeks?'

My non-answer was a good enough answer for him.

'But it's not even my car,' I protested. 'He knows that. Smashing it up would affect someone else, not me.'

'It's your friend Julie's, you told me. But you're driving it. And he's not exactly thinking rationally now. How does he feel about your friend Julie? Anything to say about her recently?'

I sighed, remembering the voicemail from a few days ago, and I looked out at Adam who was now clearly listening. He nodded at me to tell Maguire.

'Shit.' I rubbed my face tiredly. 'Then I'm not pressing charges. I'll pay for the damages myself.' I stood and paced the room.

'All the same, I'd like to pay him a visit.'

'Don't!' I stopped pacing. 'Seriously, he'll go ape-shit if he knows I told you.'

'Looks like he already went ape-shit. I'd like to make sure he doesn't do it again.'

'Please don't contact him.'

He sighed, then stood. 'What came first? The angry phone calls? Were they sad to begin with? Then abusive? Then he trashes your car.'

'Julie's car.'

'I don't give a shit whose car it is. The next thing on his list won't be sitting down to have milk and cookies with you.'

'But the Russian guy — '

'It's not the Russian guy. You have somebody at home with you?'

I didn't like the personal question and I wasn't exactly sure how to answer. I blushed, embarrassed to tell him Adam was staying with me. In the end I didn't have to say anything; I caught the look exchanged between Adam and Detective Maguire.

'Right.' Maguire seemed mildly satisfied that

194

I'd be safe. 'Think about it and let me know if you need me to drop him a visit.'

'Sorry to waste your time,' I said, mortified, as he left the room.

'Used to it by now, Rose,' he called down the hall.

★ ★ ★

'Shit,' I said, ending the call on my mobile. 'That was someone who wants to view the car. How quickly can you get a windshield fixed?' I unburied my head and then rooted through the empty cupboards for a telephone directory.

'Quickly. Don't worry about it,' Adam said, sitting on the counter swinging his legs and watching me. 'I know a guy who can do it, I'll give him a call.'

'That would be amazing. Thanks. How much will it cost?' I nibbled on my nails and awaited his response.

'Not that much. I'm sure your friend has insurance, I wouldn't worry about it.'

'There's no way in the world I'm going to tell Julie. I have to sort this out without her knowing. How much will it cost?'

'Christine, relax. It's a windshield, they get cracked all the time. A stone can bounce up from the road and crack it.'

'My ex-husband smashed it to a million pieces,' I said. 'It's not quite the same thing.'

'Takes the same amount of time to fix it, though. Do you think he did it?'

'I don't know. Detective Maguire seems quite

sure but I really can't see Barry doing it.'

He mulled that over for a moment, looked out the windows as if to make sure I was safe. I liked this protective side of him.

'I'll pay for the window,' he said suddenly.

'No way, absolutely no way. That's a stupid idea Adam,' I said angrily. 'That's not what I want, I wasn't trying to suggest that. I don't take hand-outs,' I said firmly.

He rolled his eyes. 'This isn't a hand-out. I owe you for your services anyway.'

'Adam, I'm not charging you for this. I'm not doing this for money. I'm trying to save your life. You *living* will be enough payment for me.' My eyes filled and I had to look away. I started looking for the directory in cupboards I'd already looked in, forgetting he said he'd call a friend. I was losing the plot.

'But you've cancelled all your appointments for two weeks. I'm costing you.'

'I don't think of it like that.'

'I know. Because you're kind. Now let someone be kind to you, because I believe you're going through a particularly shitty time, and I haven't seen anyone come to your aid once. I don't see anybody trying to help fix Little Miss Fix-It,' he said, watching me.

His comments took me by surprise and I momentarily forgot about the money. My family might be odd but I knew they were always there for me; Amelia was understandably quite distracted; Julie was in Toronto; and the others . . . Well, I had thought they were respectfully giving me space, but now, forced to think about

196

it, I realised perhaps they had taken sides. I pushed the thought out of my head and returned to money woes. Eventually I was going to have to talk to Barry about giving me back the money I'd lodged in our joint account. We'd set it up as our wedding and honeymoon savings account and we'd kept it open afterwards as the account from which we paid the mortgage, with me paying in larger amounts of money so that I wouldn't spend it. The message I had received from Barry that morning was that he had taken my money, my share of the mortgage payments and any extra I had lodged. I'd checked the account to see if he was telling the truth and the money was gone. It hadn't been a clever idea to get an ATM card for the account. He had withdrawn the whole lot.

'So anyway, this might make you feel better: I need your help on another matter,' Adam said, changing the subject. 'I need your help in getting a present for Maria.'

'Sure,' I said, feeling uncomfortable and confused over how my heart sank even further just at the thought of her. 'How about pink lipstick?'

His eyes narrowed, trying to figure out if it had been said with the malice that it sounded.

'No . . . ' he said slowly. 'That's not what I had in mind. You see, it's her birthday — '

'What?!' I snapped out of it. 'When is it her birthday?'

'Today. Why are you so angry?'

'And you're only telling me this now? Adam, this is a huge opportunity to win her over. We could have spent *days* planning this.'

'I'd been trying to think of a gift myself, but nothing seems good enough. There's the usual stuff — jewellery, diamonds, holidays — but we've done it all. It doesn't quite seem *enough* this time round. Besides I didn't think you'd let me see her anyway.'

He was right but I was still annoyed that he hadn't told me before now. 'What did you get her last year?'

'We went to Paris.' He looked at me and my resentment for Maria soared. 'But my heart wasn't in it. I wasn't feeling so great.'

'Why, what happened?'

'Nothing really. It was around the time my sister moved away. I had a lot on my mind. Maria thought it was because I was planning a proposal; it obviously didn't work out that way and . . . well, the trip was a bit of a disaster.'

His sister left. He saw people leaving as abandonment, I would have to be careful when we parted ways. The prospect made me feel sad.

'Are you okay?' he asked.

'Yeah, I'm thinking.' I went to my bedroom and picked up the book for inspiration. The next chapter was all about the benefits of learning to cook. I chucked the book across the room, not exactly happy with its solution to our dilemma. In fact, I was unimpressed by any of its solutions to date. Cooking as therapy? Cooking as a way to win Maria over? Unless he cooked Maria dinner . . . but how could that work?

'Adam, do you still have the keys to your apartment?' I called to him.

198

'Yes, why?' He appeared at the bedroom door. He always stopped right there, never crossing over the threshold into my private space. I appreciated that about him, always respecting the invisible boundaries, respecting my space.

I was thinking that maybe we could sneak Maria's birthday dinner into their apartment, but if Sean turned out to be there it would be a disaster and it would set Adam back after days of our hard work.

'I'd love to know where she'll be on her birthday. Is there any way you can find that out? Speak to her friends? Family? Without making a big deal, of course.'

'Our birthdays are in the same week, so *usually* we celebrate them together,' he said, annoyed. He took a deep breath to steady the anger. 'Her friends are taking her to Ely Brasserie in Grand Canal Dock.'

'How do you know this?'

He looked sheepish. 'I just know.'

'Adam,' I warned, 'I specifically told you not to talk to her.'

'And I didn't. I happened to hear a message on Sean's voicemail.'

'How could you *happen* to hear that?'

'Because Sean's an idiot who never remembers to change the pin code for his voicemail. I've been listening to his messages since Monday.'

I gasped. 'I didn't know you could do that.'

'So you obviously haven't changed your code.'

I made a mental note to do it immediately. 'It doesn't matter, you listen to my voicemails anyway.' I thought of the message he had heard and deleted. It was killing me to know what Barry had said, but I couldn't ask Adam any more than I had and in a way didn't want to hear the answer. I moved on. 'So what have the messages said?'

'He's worried Maria is a bit distant these days, ever since Sunday when I found out about them, but even more over the past few days. They've taken a break, or she's asked for space, to think.'

'About you,' I whispered.

Adam shrugged but there was light in his eyes.

'Yes, Adam!' I held my two hands up.

We high-fived and then he pulled me into a hug.

'Thank you,' he said into my ear, both arms wrapped tight around my waist.

His breath left goose bumps all over my body.

'No problem,' I said, wanting to stay there. I forced myself to pull away. 'Now let's get busy.'

'What are we doing?'

'You may have given her Paris last year but this year, my dear, you are going to bake her a birthday cake.'

★   ★   ★

Kitchen in the Castle was a unique cookery course operating from a kitchen in Howth Castle that dated all the way back to 1177. Always a popular venue for date nights and girls' nights out, this Friday evening was no different. The class was mainly made up of couples, of all ages, with one definite first date. There was also a group of three girls in their early twenties who seemed to get a case of the giggles as soon as Adam walked in.

'Christine! Yoohoo!' I heard a woman call my name. She was large and round, with a beaming smile on a pretty and girly face. I had no idea who this woman was.

'It's me! Elaine!'

I kept staring at her until finally it sunk in who she was. The last time I'd seen her she had been dressed as Dracula and reading a book to an audience of terrified children. In the last couple of days, since Amelia's mother had passed on, she'd been helping out in the bookshop.

'I'm here on a date,' she whispered so that her date beside her wouldn't hear. She failed miserably.

I reached out to shake his hand and was instantly sure that the man was gay.

'I met him at my 'How to Fall in Love' class.'

'Your *what* class?'

'Haven't you heard about it? Goodness, all the girls are going — lots of men too. Which is why I'm going,' she was still talking sotto voce. 'That's how I met Marvin.' She giggled and pointed at him proudly, then giggled again. This time she snorted and her eyes opened in shock and her hand flew to her nose to stop it from happening again. The twenty-somethings laughed together over what seemed to be a dirty joke or suggestive remark, or at least I imagined it was from the way they were watching Adam. One of them was moving closer to him. He smiled at her.

'And this is Adam,' I said loudly, placing a hand on his arm and tugging him closer to me. 'Adam, this is Elaine. She's been telling me about the 'How to Fall in Love' classes she attends.'

'Oh, it's fantastic! The course is run by Irma Livingstone — you know, the woman who writes the . . . ' Her voice dropped. ' . . . sex books. It's in the local church hall — '

'Appropriate,' interrupted Adam.

'Yes,' she continued, not realising what he'd said. 'And each week we learn tips on how to meet your equal and fall in love, and then we're encouraged to act out what we've learned with other members of the class.'

'So this is homework?' Adam said.

'No, it's a date,' she said quickly, defensively.

Marvin looked a little pained.

'You should come too.' She nudged me, but seemed unaware of her own strength and shoved me so hard that I flew into Adam, who steadied me again.

'Yeah, you should go too,' Adam said, fixing me with a playful smile.

'If I do, then you'll be coming with me,' I said, and his smile disappeared.

'I heard about what happened with your husband,' Elaine said in a low voice again. She looked at me pityingly. 'I met your husband, ex-husband, when I was going to work a few days ago. He told me what happened . . . and that he was giving you back your golf club. I'm glad it's been so amicable. It wasn't like that with me and Eamon — that's my ex-husband,' she

202

said, a shadow falling over her usually jolly disposition.

'My golf club?' I asked, confused. 'But I don't play golf.'

'Yes, you do,' Adam said. 'He left it on the windshield of your car, remember?'

'He . . . ohhhh. Right, yes.' So it had been him.

The cooking instructor welcomed us all to the class and we gathered around a main work bench, our names on stickers on our chests, to watch the display. The more serious couples took notes while Adam and I barely listened, and then it was our turn to start making our cakes. Adam folded his arms and looked at me. He was telling me he was there because he had to be, not because he wanted to be. I took the butter brush and began brushing the pan.

'So what did you learn today?' Adam asked Elaine.

'Today was about falling in love for the right reasons,' she said earnestly. 'And how to identify what those reasons are.'

'Wow. How much does this course cost?' he asked sarcastically.

Elaine wasn't stupid. She eyed him suspiciously, a little offended. 'One hundred and fifty euro for ten weeks. But Irma recommends two courses.'

'I bet she does.' He nodded seriously. 'Christine, are you sure that's right?'

'I've ended up paying everything I've ever owned for love, no point in asking me my opinion,' I said as I tried to sprinkle flour evenly over the butter in the dish.

'No, I meant the cake.' He smiled at me.

'Oh. She said the butter goes there so that the cake won't stick, and the flour is so the cake doesn't get greasy,' I said, getting frustrated as the flour stuck in uneven patterns to the tray and looked a claggy mess. I really was not enjoying myself. I didn't like cooking, baking even less so, and instead of Adam experiencing another 'joy' of life, I was doing it instead. It was rather joyless.

'Okay, time for you to do your bit now — make the batter,' I said, looking for a cloth to wipe my buttery hands on.

Adam was looking at me with an amused expression.

'What?' I snapped.

'Nothing. Just observing you enjoying life, that's all.' He returned his attention to Elaine. 'So what kinds of things did you learn about when she was teaching you how to fall in love for the right reasons?'

Turning her back on her date, Elaine filled us in on her class. 'Irma says that we think of falling in love as something magical and mysterious that happens to us and we have no control over it, which is why it's called 'falling'. But falling in love happens when a series of events occur with one person.'

She had Adam rapt.

'And, like anything in your life, if you want it to happen you have to make it happen. You can't sit on your couch at home and expect to fall in love. You have to be an active participant in the process. Irma teaches us the steps on how to be active in our quest to fall in love.'

'Like . . . '

'Like, narrow down what you want, be yourself, expand your social circle, be realistic about setbacks, laugh a lot, listen, be witty, tell some secrets, keep it fun. She teaches us about it in class and then we have practical work, exercises after class.'

'What kind of exercises?'

'Last week we had to go on a date and practise the listen technique, where you speak for twenty per cent of the time and listen for eighty per cent.'

'Listening's a technique now?' Adam asked, amused.

'You'd be amazed how many people don't do it,' she said. 'Well, I went on a date with someone from the class and it didn't go well. We were both trying to listen and nobody was doing any talking.'

Adam laughed.

'Chef! Are we concentrating?' the good-natured instructor called him out. A few heads turned and Adam tried to look busy.

'The next lesson is *secrets*,' Elaine whispered excitedly. 'We'll play a game of 'Never Have I Ever'. And then we'll ask questions like what's your most embarrassing moment, favourite childhood memory, greatest fear, any hidden talents, what things do you do only when you're all alone, what would your perfect day be? You know the kind of thing.'

'So that's your next class?' Adam asked,

looking at her date who was doing all the work so far, as was I for him.

She nodded enthusiastically.

Adam looked as if he was about to come out with a sarcastic remark, but he stopped himself. 'Good luck with that, Elaine.'

'Thank you. You too.' She smiled.

He looked at me, all red in the face from battling with the batter, and he smiled.

'She's going to find out a secret or two about Marvin, that's for sure,' I whispered. Adam chuckled.

'I didn't think you were listening,' he said.

'Twenty per cent listening. Eighty per cent trying to make batter.'

'I'll help.' He reached for an egg.

'Make sure you don't throw it at the wall,' I muttered.

Adam smiled and cracked an egg. 'You're witty.' Then he looked at me, thoughtful for a moment.

'What, have I got flour on my face?'

'No.'

'You have to separate them.' I pushed the bowl across to him.

'I don't know how to do that. You're separated, you can do it.'

'Ha ha,' I said, unimpressed. 'You keep getting funnier and funnier.'

'It's all this joyful living you're making me do.'

Elaine watched us, amused.

'You do three and I'll do three,' I said, and it was agreed.

Adam cracked the egg and moaned about the

206

feel of the white on his fingers. He put the broken yolk in one bowl, white and egg shells in the other. He was worse on the second, better on the third. I tried to fish the shells out of the white. Instead of putting the sugar into the egg yolk, I emptied it into the egg white. When I noticed what I'd done, I immediately started scooping it out and spooned it into the other bowl hoping the instructor wouldn't see. Adam sniggered. I poured vanilla and lemon extract in. Then I started to fluff the egg whites while Adam went into a daydream, no doubt thinking of his precious Maria. I couldn't help it, I dipped my chin into the fluffed egg whites, making a long thin beard, and turned to Adam. I put on the voice of his father, low and croaky.

'My son, you *must* take control of the company. You're a Basil, *Dazzle*!'

He looked at me in surprise then threw his head back and laughed, properly, louder than I had ever heard him before, such a joyous, free sound. The instructor stopped talking, the class turned around to stare at us. Adam apologised to everyone but couldn't quite manage to keep it together.

'Excuse me, I'll be back in a moment,' he said, and made his way down the quiet kitchen, laughing to himself, unable to stop, holding his stomach as if it was sore from laughing.

They all looked at me. The egg white dripped from my chin and I smiled at them all.

★　★　★

'Your cake is in the oven; it will take twenty minutes. Here,' I said, joining Adam outside. I handed him his coat, then revealed a glass of champagne. 'We have a ten-minute break and then we're icing.' I took a glug of the champagne.

He watched me, his eyes alight, and then he laughed again, another fit taking hold of him. It was a contagious laugh and soon I was joining in, though I was laughing at him laughing at . . . I wasn't sure exactly. After a while he stopped, then started again a little, then stopped.

'I haven't laughed this much in a long time,' he said, his breath travelling on the cold air.

'And it wasn't even that funny.'

He cracked up again. 'It was,' he managed to squeak.

'If I'd known putting egg whites on my chin would fix you, I'd have done it days ago,' I smiled.

'You.' He looked at me, his face alive, his eyes bright. 'You're a tonic. They should prescribe you for depression instead of pills.'

I was truly flattered by the compliment. It was the nicest thing he'd said to me and the closest I'd come to feeling I wasn't in the way of his life. Instead of saying something nice, I switched into therapist mode. 'Have you ever been on anti-depressants?'

He took a moment to think about it, reverting back to the client, the questioned one. 'Once. I went to a GP, told him how I was feeling, and he prescribed them. But it didn't quite help me in the way I wanted. I stopped taking them after a month or two.'

'Because they didn't deal with the root of the problem,' I said.

He looked at me and I could tell he was annoyed by my comment. He knew I was going to urge him to see a therapist again and so I held back.

'And cake-making is the perfect way to get to the root.' I smiled.

'Of course, because you know exactly what you're doing,' he said gently.

'Of course.'

We were silent for a while and I wondered whether this was the moment to admit that I felt way out of my depth, or whether him hinting at it was acknowledgement enough. As if sensing what was coming, he snapped out of his trance and broke the silence.

'Right, let's get icing.'

Before decorating our cakes, we first had to take them out of the oven. Ours was the only cake in the whole class to collapse in the middle. Almost magically, before our very eyes as soon as it hit the air, the centre collapsed in a little *poof*.

In turn, we collapsed into such hysterics that I almost wet myself and we were politely but swiftly asked to leave.

15

How to Reap What You Sow

En route to Maria's birthday celebration dinner in Dublin's city centre we stopped at a Spar to decorate her cake. We were still giddy, almost in a drunken state, laughing at every minor amusing thing that happened, both of us having been starved of such emotions for too long. Adam carried the heart-shaped sponge cake with the collapsed uncooked mushy centre and a burned ring on the outside.

'This is the ugliest cake I've ever seen,' Adam said, laughing.

'It needs a little face-lift, that's all,' I said, prowling the aisles. 'A-ha!' I picked up a can of spray cream and shook it.

'Hey!' the shopkeeper called out angrily. Adam immediately whipped out a wad of notes, and the shopkeeper silenced his protestations.

Adam held the cake while I sprayed. The first application was a disaster; I hadn't shaken the can enough and the cream exploded in a disappointing puff of air, spattering the cake and Adam's face and hair.

'I'd say that's twenty per cent on the cake, eighty per cent in my face.'

This sent me into stitches and it took a good few minutes before I could steady my hand enough to have another go. I was more successful with the second attempt and covered the top in spray cream. When I'd finished, Adam looked at it thoughtfully. Then he brought the cake over to the pick-a-mix and scooped up some milky teeth, then with a not-so-steady hand, he sprinkled them across the surface.

'What do you think?' He showed it to the shopkeeper.

The long-haired hippy was unimpressed. 'It's missing something,' he said.

I laughed. It was missing a lot of somethings.

'I'd add some crisps,' he said eventually.

'Crisps!' Adam held a finger in the air. 'That is a great idea.'

He directed me to open a packet of Hula Hoops, which I sprinkled over the top, and then I stepped back to survey my work.

'Perfect,' he said, studying it from all angles.

'It's the worst cake I've ever seen in my life,' I said.

'Exactly. It's perfect. She'll know I made it.'

Before we left, Adam stuck a football-shaped candle in the middle, with a happy, 'She hates football,' and we returned to the chauffeur-driven car.

★ ★ ★

We stood outside Ely Brasserie and watched Maria and her friends through the window as discreetly as we could without being seen by them or being asked to leave by staff. It was freezing outside, small flakes of snow were beginning to fall. My feet were numb, my lips

211

would barely move, my nose had long ago fallen off my face, or at least it felt like it had.

'Today I'm feeling . . . fucking freezing,' I said, and it earned a smile from Adam, our earlier hysteria having retreated for warmth. 'Do you know those girls?' I asked, barely able to move my lips to form the shape of my words.

Adam nodded. 'They're her closest friends.'

They were all pretty, fashionable women who turned plenty of heads but didn't seem to notice as they were locked in on each other, huddled together in the corner of the restaurant as they caught up on life, love and the universe. I couldn't take my eyes off Maria. Again the trademark red lips and the sleek black bob, and this time she was on trend in a stylish black leather dress. She was perfect. She chatted to each of her friends, seemed amusing, interesting and empathetic to whoever was talking. The only time I moved my eyes away from her was to watch Adam watching her, and it was clear she was having the same effect on him. She was hypnotic, the kind of woman most eyes would be drawn to. And she was nice. That was the killer. I resented her more than ever, but she was the perfect girl for a man like Adam. The two of them made a striking couple, their beauty equal and yet distinct, each of them quirky and unique. Adam couldn't tear his eyes from her, but he looked sad, as though losing her had taken away his soul, his everything.

I backed away a few steps and looked around, stamping my feet to get warm, anything to shake off this feeling of being an imposter or a gooseberry. What had gone so wrong in my life that I'd resorted to standing outside a restaurant and watching a beautiful woman living a life I was currently envying — and not only for the warmth? It was ridiculous and I felt like an idiot, a loser at the highest level. Suddenly I didn't want to be there any more.

'At last!' Adam said as the table was cleared for dessert.

I had delivered the cake into the restaurant. It hadn't been a difficult task, explaining to staff while trying to keep out of sight, that it was a surprise for the already seated birthday girl. The waitress had taken one look at the cake and laughed. Now we watched as four waiters began the procession to Maria's table. Adam crossed the road and approached the window to get a better view. Maria looked up in surprise, then glee as surrounding customers joined in the birthday song. I noticed some of her friends at the table throwing questioning glances at each other, trying to find out who had arranged the surprise. And then the cake was placed before Maria and she looked at it in confusion, the great big mess on the plate with cream, milky teeth and Hula Hoops that had turned soggy from the cream. For a moment she wore a neutral expression, as if politely maintaining a look of appreciation so as not to offend the unknown maker, then she made a wish and blew out the candle. She looked to the girls to see who had arranged such a thing. There were more shrugs and laughs, then she questioned the waiters to make sure they had the right table.

Adam watched them, anxiously, and I hoped that Maria would get that it was from him, so I wouldn't have to hold him back from running into the restaurant to explain it.

'Look, Maria, look at the teeth and Hula Hoops,' he urged her, quietly so that only I could hear.

'They have a significance?' I asked, surprised. I thought that he had randomly emptied packets on the top, I never sensed there was a reason to what he chose.

His eyes never left the window, but he'd heard me and he was answering in a distracted tone that made me feel I was in the way, that he'd rather not have bothered answering my question. 'On one of our first days out together she came to watch me play football. She was on the sidelines, the ball hit her face, chipped her front tooth. I bought her milky teeth so she could wear them on the way home, and I sucked her Hula Hoops until they were soft because her tooth was too sore to bite.'

Apparently reliving the story Adam was sharing, Maria looked up from the cake, understanding dawning on her face, and started laughing. She then calmed herself to tell the other girls. Although he couldn't hear, Adam laughed along with her. I by then had lost my sense of humour. I wanted to go home.

Then Maria stopped laughing and did a remarkable thing. She started crying. Immediately the six girls huddled around her and she was lost in a flurry of hugs and comforting words.

I looked at Adam. His eyes had filled too.

I turned to leave. At that moment I honestly didn't care if he stayed. I didn't think he'd even notice.

'Hey, Little Miss Fix-It,' he said softly, stopping me in my tracks.

He held up his two gloved hands. I high-fived him and his fingers bent to clasp mine. He looked down at me and I swallowed hard, my heart fluttering at being trapped under his gaze.

'You're a genius, do you know that?' he said softly.

'Well,' I looked away, 'we don't have her yet.'

Adam looked back into the restaurant. Maria was wiping her eyes with a napkin, she looked back to the cake and shook her head lightly and laughed.

Not yet. But we almost did.

I felt an odd kind of relief but it was tinged with sadness. I didn't have time to dwell on my feelings because Maria had put on her coat and was leaving the restaurant.

'Shit, did she see you?' I asked, detangling my fingers from his.

'She can't have,' he replied, mild panic in his voice.

We quickly walked away, moving as far from the restaurant as possible. When we were at a safe distance I turned and saw that Maria was standing outside the restaurant.

'She's having a cigarette,' I said, relieved.

'She doesn't smoke.'

We watched her. Her phone illuminated in her hand. Adam's phone started ringing. He quickly

215

silenced it but looked at the screen hungrily.

'Don't answer.'

'Why not?'

'Absence makes the heart grow fonder. You need her to really miss you and want you. Besides, you're still angry, I can sense it. You'll say the wrong thing and chase her away.'

'Like Barry?'

I turned from him.

'Did you want him to try to get you back?' he asked after a while.

I smiled sadly. We hadn't spoken much about Barry, not seriously. 'He didn't even try. I wouldn't have gone back, but it would have been nice if he'd tried. He never wanted anything enough. Not even me. I know that sounds ridiculous, seeing as I'm the one who left him.'

'Maybe he is trying. The voicemails. The phone calls . . . '

'This morning he told a mutual friend of ours who we spend New Year's Eve with that I despise going to her parties because I hate her cooking and listening to her intolerable children singing when they clearly have no talent and I can't wait to countdown the New Year so I can leave her house. She texted me, still very upset and angry about it. I'm disinvited from her parties for the foreseeable future.'

'Okay, so he's not trying to get you back.'

'No. He's bitter. Quite twisted at the moment. I don't think he's aiming for a reconciliation.'

'Tell your friend it's not true.'

I looked at him.

'Oh. It is true. So you do pee in the shower?' he teased.

I was thanking the darkness for hiding my scarlet face.

'Well, maybe not *everything* is true.'

'It's true!' He chuckled to himself.

'I had a mosquito bite, a really bad one. He walked in on me trying to . . . well, you know.'

'You pissed on your mosquito bite?' He started laughing.

'Sshh.' I punched his arm. 'Anyway, it didn't work,' I added and we both laughed.

His phone signalled a voicemail.

'That was a long one,' I said. 'Let me hear.'

'Adam, it's me.' Her voice was soft, gentle, it was clear how she was feeling, I didn't need to hear any more, but I listened all the same. 'I got your cake,' she laughed. 'It's the ugliest, most disgustingly thoughtful cake I've ever received. I'll never forget that day. That was the day we first kissed, with those teeth in our mouths,' she laughed. 'Thank you. You're crazy.' She laughed again. 'I missed that part of you, but . . . I feel like you're back. I'm so sorry I hurt you. I felt so . . . lost, I was worried. I didn't know what to do. Sean, he was . . . there and he cared and . . . he really cares about you too, you know. Don't hate him. Anyway, thank you. I'm calling to say thank you. I need to see you, call me — okay?'

Adam was grinning from ear to ear.

He lifted me up and spun me around in the air and I laughed so loudly in the dark cold empty

217

street that it drifted towards Maria outside the restaurant. But we needn't have worried; all she would have seen was a couple in the dark, having fun together, hiding in the shadows, quite possibly in love.

16

How to Organise and Simplify Your Life

When we returned to the flat, take-away bags in our hands, we saw the lights still on in Amelia's bookshop. It was ten p.m.

'That's bizarre,' I said. 'Here, you go on ahead.' I handed him the keys to the flat. 'Stay away from glass and electrics. I'm going to check if she's okay.'

He rolled his eyes. 'I'll come with you.'

Amelia opened the door as soon as we walked towards her, as though she had been standing there waiting for us. Her eyes were wide and urgent. I looked around. A table had been set up with wine, cheese and crackers, there were five empty bottles of wine on the table. The bookcases had been cleared from the centre of the shop and in their place were chairs, four rows of four, with a handful of people sitting before a podium where a woman was reading aloud from a book. Her hair was a beautiful long, flowing vibrant grey, and she was wearing a slinky black dress with a low neckline revealing a toned and rather oiled-up décolletage.

Elaine turned and waved at us excitedly before quickly turning back to face the speaker.

'Who is that?' I whispered.

'Irma Livingstone,' Amelia replied, rolling her eyes. 'I curse the day I ever said yes to Elaine.

Irma's her teacher at the 'How to Fall in Love' course, and Elaine thought it would be a wonderful idea to bring her here and ask her to read from her book. She's been reading for an hour.'

Amelia handed me the book. *How to Own Your Erogenous Zone*.

'Why? Who owns mine right now?' I asked, glancing over it unimpressed before Adam plucked it from my hands.

An old man in the front row had fallen asleep and was snoring loudly, a young bookish woman was scribbling copious notes, and one man seemed to be trying to hide a very large erection, unbeknown to Elaine, who was making eyes at him in the hope of getting a date.

Irma noticed Adam's presence. 'I was going to finish there, but I see we have company. Next I'll read chapter four: the pleasure of pleasuring yourself with your partner. I should warn you, this is quite an erotic passage — if you'll pardon the pun.' She smiled at Adam.

'Great,' Adam grinned at me. 'I love erotic passages. You girls go and talk. Toodle pips.'

I couldn't help but laugh as Irma's honey voice started to slowly, sensuously read her erotic passage.

Once we were in the quiet of Amelia's home above the shop we could talk. 'How are you?'

'I'm okay.' Amelia sat down, looking tired. 'It's quiet without her. Lonely.'

'I'm sorry I haven't been here for you.'

'You have. Besides, you have enough going on with Simon and Adam and Barry. And Adam,' she added with a little smile.

'Stop.' I shook my head, not able to go there.

'Barry sent me a nice text about Mum.'

'Well, that's good to hear, for a change.'

'How are things going with Adam?'

'Fine. Good. He's getting there, you know. Soon he'll be okay on his own. He won't need me any more so . . . It's great.' I heard the shake in my voice and how fake and ridiculous it sounded.

'Sure.' Amelia smiled. 'You're very good to help him.'

'Yeah, well, he's going through a tough time.'

'Uh-huh.' Amelia was biting her lip to stop smiling.

'Stop.' I shoved her gently. 'I'm trying to be serious here.'

'I know, I can see that.' Amelia laughed. Then her smile quickly turned to a frown.

'What's wrong?'

'I've been going through her things.' She stood up and retrieved papers from a kitchen drawer. 'And I found these.'

She handed me a bundle of papers. There was too much to take in, so I looked at her. 'Tell me what I'm looking at.'

'A storage unit. In Mum's name. She never told me anything about it, which is odd, because I took care of all her affairs. It was paid for by direct debit from an account I don't recognise.'

She showed me the number. I wasn't expecting to recognise it, but I did. It was the account my rent went to each month. Dad's company. Amelia missed my reaction and so I swallowed, waiting to see where this was leading.

'I wouldn't have known anything if I hadn't found this envelope with a key in it and details of the storage unit. It's from ten years ago. Look at the address on the envelope.'

The postal address was that of Rose and Daughters Solicitors.

'Do you know anything about it?'

'No,' I said. 'Definitely not.' Amelia's look told me she didn't believe me. 'Okay, not until two seconds ago when I saw the account number. Amelia, I promise you they never mentioned anything to me. They're handling your mum's will, aren't they?'

She nodded.

'Is there any mention of the contents of the storage unit in the will?'

'I don't know, I haven't been into your dad yet to hear it. But . . . I really thought I knew what was in Mum's will. We've talked about it.'

'Let's ask my dad.' I took out my phone. 'Simple, we'll solve this right now.'

'No.' Amelia took the phone from my hand. 'No. No quick fix-its right now.' Seeing my offended expression, she explained: 'What if your dad tells me I can't go in there?'

'He won't say that. Why would he? Her property is your property now.'

'What if I'm not supposed to know about it? As soon as we ask him, I'll be sealing my fate. I want to go and find out what's in there for myself.' I watched as her eyes clouded and she became lost in a thousand thoughts in her head.

222

'Why would she go to all this trouble for me not to see what's in there?'

★ ★ ★

The following day Amelia and Adam and I made our way down the corridor of 'Store-Age' a self-storage facility situated in a large retail park in Dublin. The doors on the units were luminous pink, as was the logo, to make it visible to traffic on the nearby motorway. It was enough to give me a headache, especially after a sleepless night spent trying to plot out Adam's future, but I reminded myself I was there to support my friend. In truth I was glad of the distraction provided by the unexpected turns Amelia's life was taking. Adam's mood had dipped again as his thoughts returned to a future spent in servitude at the family firm, and my idea of that morning — to present him with a gratitude journal in which he was to write each day, listing five things he appreciated, so that by the end of the week he would have thirty-five things, went down like a stone in a well. We'd turned to his crisis plan and he had opted to clean out my fridge rather than acknowledge what he appreciated about his life. It said a lot. Clearly, if I couldn't resolve the Basil Confectionery issue, the success with Maria would be in vain.

While mulling that over, I tried to keep the atmosphere light for Amelia.

'Maybe your mother was a secret agent and inside the storage unit is a collection of secret identities, wigs and passports, briefcases with concealed compartments,' I mused, continuing the game we'd been playing on the car journey over.

I looked at Adam, to hand it over to him.

'Your father had a large porn collection that he didn't want you to know about.'

Amelia winced.

'Your parents were into S&M and this is their secret lair,' I said.

'Nice,' Adam complimented me.

'Thanks.'

'Your parents embezzled millions and stored it here,' Adam said.

'I wish,' Amelia muttered.

'Your mother stole Shergar,' I said, and Adam cracked up.

Amelia stopped abruptly in front of a luminous pink door, and we walked into the back of her. She composed herself, glanced at me and then placed the key in the door, slowly turned it and pushed the door open, leaning as far away from the room as possible in case something leapt out at her. We were greeted with musty darkness.

Adam fumbled with the wall and switched the light on.

'Whoa.'

We stepped inside and looked around.

'Your mother was Imelda Marcos,' I said.

Each wall of the ten-by-ten-foot room was lined with shelving units crammed with shoe-boxes. Each shoebox was labelled with a year, starting from the bottom left-hand corner with

224

1954 and ending on the opposite wall with a box dated ten years ago.

'That's the year they married,' Amelia said, going to the box and opening it. Inside was a photograph of her parents on their wedding day, along with a dried flower from the bride's bouquet. There was a wedding invitation, the prayer manual from the ceremony, photos from their honeymoon, a train ticket, boat ticket, cinema stub from their first date, a receipt from the restaurant, a shoelace, a fully completed *Irish Times* crossword — all neatly filed away. Forget a memory box, it was a memory room.

'My God, they kept everything!' Amelia ran her fingers delicately along the row of shoeboxes, stopping at the final year. 'The year Dad died. He must have done all of this.' She swallowed hard, smiling at the thought of him curating this collection, then frowning, hurt by the fact they'd kept it from her.

She reached for another box at random and searched inside, then pulled out another and another. One by one she searched each box, exclaiming with delight as she found item after item representing a memory in their lives, and a memory in hers. Old school reports of hers, the ribbon she wore on the first day of school, her first tooth, a lock of hair from her first visit to the hairdresser, a letter she'd written to her father when she was eight years old apologising after they'd quarrelled. I began to wonder whether we should leave her alone in the room, sure she would want to spend endless hours poring through each box, reliving each year of her parents' married life and her life. But she needed someone to share her memories with and Adam was patient enough to stay alongside me so we could do that for her. Even he seemed touched by what he saw and I hoped it would be a good form of therapy for him to witness this love captured in a room.

She held up a photo of her parents in the Austrian mountains. 'That was at my uncle's holiday chalet,' she said, smiling as she studied the photo, running her fingers over their faces. 'They used to go there every year before I was born. I saw the photos and begged them to bring me, but Mum couldn't go.'

'She's been sick since you were a child?' Adam asked.

'Not at the beginning. She had her first stroke when I was twelve, but before that she was too afraid. She became very nervous about travel after she had me. I suppose it's a mother thing . . . '

She looked at us for confirmation, but neither of us could answer, having grown up without a mother.

'I had no idea they'd hung on to all this stuff.'

'I wonder why they kept it from you,' Adam said, more to himself than Amelia, too engrossed in browsing the shelves to register what he was saying.

It was the elephant in the room and he'd pointed at it and shouted. He realised that as soon as he'd said it and he quickly tried to cover his tracks. 'How amazing that they kept all of this.'

It was too late. Amelia had an odd expression on her face. He had reminded her that this room was a secret that they hadn't wanted to share with her. Why?

'Amelia?' I asked, concerned. 'Are you okay? What is it?'

As if snapping out of a trance, Amelia leapt into action and began scouring the shelves as though she knew what she was looking for and hadn't a second to lose. She ran her finger along the dates on the boxes.

'What are you looking for?' I asked. 'Can we help?'

'The year I was born,' she said, standing on tiptoes to read the dates on the upper shelves.

'Seventy-eight,' I told Adam. At six feet tall, he could reach more easily than we could.

'Got it,' he said, retrieving a dusty box.

He was just bringing it down to Amelia's level when she reached up and accidentally punched the box, sending it flying across the unit. The lid popped open and the contents cascaded through the air and scattered all over the floor. We got down on our hands and knees to retrieve as many bits as possible. Adam and I bumped heads.

'Ow,' I laughed and Adam reached out to rub my head.

'Sorry.' He winced, feeling my pain. He looked at me with those big blue icy eyes and I melted. I would gladly have stayed in that little room of love with him for ever. The thought excited me, gave me a glow; it was nice to have a crush again. It had been so long, and after

Barry I'd begun to worry that I'd never feel that way about anybody ever again, but there it was, alive inside of me, this ball of nerves and anxiety and excitement every time he looked at me. But then as soon as it happened, the reality of my situation hit me and it slithered away to the corner again.

'Are you okay?' he asked gently.

I nodded.

'Good,' he said with a small smile and I felt like I was buzzing from head to toe, just zinging.

I became paranoid then and realised Amelia, who was standing beside me, had gone very quiet. Assuming she was witnessing our moment, I looked up and saw tears rolling down her cheeks as she read a piece of paper in her hand. I sprang to my feet.

'Amelia, what's wrong?'

'My mother — ' She handed me the handwritten note. ' — was not my mother.'

My dear baby Amelia,

I'm sorry I am not able to care for you as I should. When you are older I hope you understand that this decision was made purely with love and nothing else. I trust you are in safe and loving arms with Magda and Len. I will think of you always.

Love and forever,
Your mummy

★ ★ ★

Back in Amelia's kitchen I was reading the note aloud to Amelia and Elaine. Amelia was pacing the floor, having moved from shock to grief, and now to an uncomfortable snappy anger, which made Elaine and I wary of what to say. Elaine was fingering the items in the shoebox: baby booties, a cardigan, a hat, a dress, a rattle, among other things.

'These were all handmade,' she said, interrupting Amelia's rant.

'So?' Amelia snapped. 'That's hardly the issue here.'

'Well, this is Kenmare lace.'

'Who cares what lace it is?' Amelia snapped again.

'It's just that it's not made by many people, not even now, so in the seventies there's only one place that would have made it.'

Amelia stopped pacing and looked at Elaine, realisation growing on her face.

'Now, now.' I had to stop the silliness. 'Let's not go there. I'm sure this could have been made by anyone in the world, Elaine. We mustn't go getting Amelia's hopes up about finding her parents.'

'Finding my parents?' Amelia whispered, stunned. It was as if the thought hadn't yet occurred to her. She had been so wrapped up in wondering why her adoptive parents had kept this from her and how they could have lied to her for so long, that she hadn't yet come round to thinking about the possibility of finding her real parents.

'All I'm saying is, this is Kenmare lace, made

229

with love and care. I know, because I started a lace-making class to meet men. Every single item in this box points to Kenmare. The lace is Kenmare lace and the sweaters are from Quills, which is Kenmare.'

'There's no way you could recognise the knitting is from Quills,' I said, in a rush to derail this ridiculous train of thought.

'The label is on it,' Elaine said, showing it to me. She looked up at Amelia. 'Amelia, I think your biological mother is in Kenmare.'

'Jesus.' I rubbed my face wearily. We were in for a long night.

★　★　★

Adam had gone back to my flat under strict instructions to complete the fifteen-hundred-piece jigsaw puzzle I'd bought for him. He had been unimpressed and unmotivated by the oil painting of a stormy sea puzzle that I'd been doing with him for an hour every day, so I'd purchased a topless babe on the beach jigsaw online, which had arrived that morning. I guessed he wouldn't be starting at the border for that puzzle.

I arrived back in the early hours of the morning, exhausted from going round in circles with Amelia. If Elaine hadn't been there it would have been easier to talk sense into her, but despite all my efforts, when I left late that night, Amelia was dead set on going to Kenmare.

'How is she?' Adam asked, bent over the coffee table with a piece in his hand. His forehead was furrowed, his lips pouted in concentration. It was sweet and it made me smile.

'What?' He looked up and caught me gazing at him.

'Nothing. You just answered my queries on whether you were a bum or a boob man.'

'Boob man all the way.' He had successfully completed one boob. As I had predicted, not one piece of the frame had been put together. 'This puzzle is much better than the last one, thank you.'

'I aim to please.' I got down on my knees and joined him in his quest.

I felt him watching me. He studied me for a bit and when I didn't meet his gaze he continued: 'I'm currently looking for a right nipple.'

We examined the glass table, our heads together. 'There.' I handed him a piece.

'That's not a nipple.'

'It is — it's a bit of the nipple and a bit of her armpit, and a bit of the sea. Look at the box: her nipple is hard and it's about to knock that surfer in the background right off his board. See, that's the board there.' I pointed at the piece.

'Oh yeah,' he laughed. 'You know, the way you talk, you turn me on like Irma.'

'Irma,' I snorted. 'I can't believe she asked for your number.'

'And I can't believe I gave her yours.'

'You what?' I shoved him. He shoved me back. It was all childish flirting and deliciously fun at the same time.

'So what's Amelia going to do?'

'She's a bit all over the place. It's a huge shock,

obviously. Though I wouldn't be surprised if I heard I was adopted. Might even be a bit glad.'

'Hear, hear,' he concurred.

'That's from her thong.' I handed him a piece. We sat in a comfortable silence.

'Amelia didn't seem all that shocked, considering,' he said suddenly. 'Did you notice the way she rushed to find the year she was born? She was frantic.'

'She said she hadn't a clue,' I protested, though deep down I agreed with Adam's instincts.

'And I say she knew. Sometimes you can know a thing even when you don't know,' he said, looking at me.

And there it was again. That sentence. I was looking at him in surprise.

'What's wrong?'

'Nothing.' I swallowed. 'Just . . . ' I changed the subject. 'Elaine is trying to convince Amelia that she needs to go to Kenmare to find her biological parents.'

'Elaine needs her head checked.'

I was silent.

He looked up at me. 'You do know it's a ridiculous idea, don't you?'

'I do. But Amelia wants to do it.'

'Of course she wants to do it. In the space of a week her entire world has toppled on her head. She's not thinking properly. She'd agree to go to the moon if someone suggested it.'

What he said hammered home. Not about Amelia, but about him. His world had almost ended on Sunday night, he wasn't thinking properly; he would do anything to make it right. I happened to be that anything. I swallowed hard, knowing that this experience was for him, not for me. I needed to extricate myself from the situation, I needed to stop *feeling* for him. I needed to get him out of Dublin, out of my life, and I needed to start fixing his life, laying the groundwork so that it would be comfortable enough to slip into, then I'd tuck him in and say goodnight and goodbye.

'I've never known Amelia to want to go anywhere in all the time we've been friends. She wouldn't go away for a weekend, or if she did it was under protest. She could never go anywhere, she's never even been out of the country. Her wanting to do this trip is a really big deal, regardless of whether she finds her biological parents or not. I told her I'd bring her to a private detective tomorrow to see if he can help.' I sighed. I was going to have to put Amelia to one side. 'Adam, we need to go to Tipperary. We need to fix things there. We've done what we can with Maria for now, it's time to leave Dublin for a few days. I'll have you back in time for your birthday, all set to announce that you're not taking over Basil's. You'll get your Maria back, your coast guard job back, Basil's will be rescued and I'll be out of your hair for ever.' I smiled tightly.

He didn't look too happy about it.

'Don't look so miserable. We've one more thing to do tomorrow before we leave Maria for a few days.'

I picked up the box beside the door; another

233

delivery that morning. Insomnia was good for some things. Online shopping.

'What's in that box?' He eyed it suspiciously.

'Maria said she wants to see you. Well, tomorrow, she is going to see you. A lot.' I opened the box and revealed its contents. 'Ta-da!'

His beautiful face lit up as he looked at me in amazement. 'Christine, I wish the world was filled with people like you, do you know that?' he laughed.

So fill your world with me! I shouted at him in my head.

17

How to Stand Out from the Crowd

The following morning the jigsaw had been abandoned. Eager for his next project, Adam was standing in the centre of Dublin wearing a white-and-red woolly hat with a red bobble, a black wig peeking out beneath it, round black glasses, a red-and-white striped jumper, his own blue jeans and a walking stick. One look at him kitted out as Where's Wally and I'd started laughing and hadn't been able to stop. Even dressed as Wally, he was beautiful.

Maria was going up the escalator in Marks and Spencer's when she saw, directly beside her but going down, a man who looked remarkably like Adam dressed as Where's Wally. He didn't look in her direction once, his head was held high and his eyes looked straight ahead. The expression on his face never changed, leading her to question whether it was an act carried out for her or merely a coincidence. But it was when she was putting broccoli into her basket and Where's Wally walked past her pushing an empty shopping trolley, disappearing round a corner as soon as she tried to follow him down the aisle, that she began to suspect it might be for her. When she was sitting on the fourth floor of Brown Thomas department store having a manicure and the same man walked by, weaving in and out of the clothes rails and eventually disappearing, she was sure it was him. Catching sight of him from the corner of her eye as she was buying flowers on Grafton Street confirmed it, and when she was buying a coffee in Butler's and he walked by the window before ducking out of view, she was laughing out loud. As she walked across the bridge in Stephen's Green, she was scanning the park for a sight of him. A flash of red caught her eye and she saw him on the path beneath the bridge. She watched him enter on one side, and she ran to the other side of the bridge to catch him exit. From that moment, every time she saw a flash of red she found herself stopping and staring, anticipation fluttering in her stomach that he would appear again.

'Adam!' she called from the bridge, but he didn't look up at her. Ignoring her, he stayed in character and continued his jovial Where's Wally jaunt, goofy and geeky with his funny walk, swinging his cane cheerily, his oversized ruck-sack on his back.

She roared with laughter. Passersby gave her strange looks, but she didn't care. If she'd been able to stretch her vision to see beyond the trees he disappeared behind, she would have stopped laughing. She would have seen the couple who'd been in the dark street near the restaurant the previous night, again breaking into laughter when he felt it was safe to abandon the Wally persona. Everywhere she saw that one man, she didn't see the woman behind him, with him, beside him, urging him on, supporting him. If

236

she had, she might have wondered then who the display was really for.

★ ★ ★

'Come on, you crazy man.' I pulled Adam's Wally hat off and threw it in his face. 'Let's get out of here, I'm hungry.'

'Hungry?' he asked in mock surprise. 'I can't believe it, we're healed.'

We sat together, me eating salad, but a little more elaborate than usual with walnuts in it, and he with his hot chicken dish. In no time at all we'd both cleared our plates.

I burped under my breath and Adam laughed. 'Look how far we've come,' he said.

He gave me a look that made my stomach flip. Then the knowledge of how this was to end made me lose my appetite all over again. Thankfully I was distracted by a phone call from Oscar, who needed to chat to me while he sat on the bus. Afterwards, reminded of my role at quite the perfect time, I got back to business.

'Today I'm feeling . . . ' I looked at him for more.

'Today I'm feeling . . . stuffed?'

'It's not a quiz, you know, you can't get the answer wrong.'

He thought about it. 'Today I'm feeling . . . happy. Restored. No not restored, renewed. Like I'm me, but a better version of me.' He looked at me intently. 'Does that make sense?'

I couldn't help it, I had to look away otherwise my eyes would reveal too much to him. Instead of meeting his gaze I focused on the salt and pepper canisters that I was idly pushing around the table. 'Good. I take it this is because you believe you have won Maria over again?'

He seemed confused by the question.

'What I'm asking is, are you ready to move on and get to the rest of business?'

He breathed in. 'That didn't go so well at the hospital.'

I had no answer for that. I started picking at my salad again. 'Why did you have a meeting with your cousin Nigel? He claimed that you talked about a merger.'

'I wanted to see him. I hadn't set eyes on him since we were twelve — can you believe that? The bad blood between Bartholomew's and Basil's was all between our fathers as far as I was concerned. My grandfather's will specifically states that if I don't take over the company, it falls to Nigel. I wanted to know what his intentions were, what he would do for the company.'

'You wanted a truce.'

'It didn't even occur to me that we needed a truce. Like I said, as far as I was concerned the quarrel was between our fathers, not us. I was looking for a way out, Christine. I wanted him to say he'd run the company exactly the way it should be run. Instead, he started talking about a merger, as if we were doing the deal right there and then.'

'And you told him no?'

'I listened. I mean, would it be so bad if Bartholomew and Basil united? It was my

238

grandfather's name so it would be fitting, and we'd leave all the bad blood behind us, start fresh. Merging the companies would help both brands. If there wasn't a rift, my father would agree in a heartbeat. But Nigel's just as bitter about the family firm as my uncle Liam. He wants to merge the two companies, then sell up. He said that way we could both get out of the business, spend the rest of our lives lying on a beach somewhere.'

Adam looked as if he wanted to punch a wall, the aggression was building up again. I put a hand on his arm for a moment.

'But selling up sounds as though it would solve a problem for you.'

'I don't want to run the business, but there's no way I want to be responsible for running it into the ground either. A lot of people are relying on me. I'd like to see Basil's end up in the right hands, so it stays a going concern. I owe my father and my grandfather that much at least.' He ran his fingers through his hair, exhausted by the whole affair.

'You think your sister would sell the company?'

'Lavinia would hold out ten years to qualify for her inheritance, then she'd sell it to the highest bidder, whoever that might be. But in order to do that, she'd have to come home, whereupon she'd be locked up — by me, if no one else, after what she did.'

'Adam,' I spoke gently. 'If you had jumped, if you *do* jump, where would that leave the business?'

'If I jumped, Christine, I wouldn't have to worry about this sorry mess any more, that's the bloody point.' He threw money on the table, stood up and left the restaurant.

★ ★ ★

I sat before my dad at his desk. He was staring at me blankly.

'Say that again?' he said.

'Which part?'

'The whole thing.'

'Dad, I've been talking for ten minutes!' I shrieked.

'And that's precisely my point, you. You were talking for too long, too boring, my mind wandered. And can you explain why we have eggs smashed all over our garden since Tuesday?'

I took a deep breath, closed my eyes and pinched the bridge of my nose for calm. 'It's part of his therapy.'

'But you are not a therapist.'

'I know that.' I felt defensive.

'So why isn't he seeing a therapist?'

'I've asked him to, but he won't.'

Dad was silent, all joking aside for once. 'You've taken on a lot here, Christine.'

'I know that. But with all due respect I haven't come here to be lectured on what I choose to do or not do with someone who needs help. Now, can we get back to the subject, please.'

'Yes, I'm wondering what that was again.'

'Dad, stop pulling her leg,' Brenda warned from the back of the office.

240

I turned around and saw both of my sisters had sneaked in unnoticed. 'Is nothing private in this family?'

'Of course not,' Adrienne said, moving into the room to sit at the desk with us. Brenda quickly joined.

'Christine, my darling pet lambykins,' Dad began, reaching out to hold my hands in his. 'You do know that, when I leave the company, and the universe, I do not expect you to suddenly be at the helm. Of the company, that is, not the universe.' He looked searchingly into my eyes. 'I'm concerned about you. You've always been the one who thinks, while your sisters and I do, but these past few weeks you've been getting caught up in an awful lot of doing and not so much thinking.'

I sighed. 'You've missed the point. I'm not talking about me. I know I don't have to take over the company.'

'She's talking about the suicide guy,' said Brenda, busy tucking into a packet of crisps.

'His name is Adam,' I snapped. 'Have a little respect.'

'Ooo-oooh,' the three of them said in unison.

'Have you kissed yet?' Dad asked.

'No,' I frowned. 'I helped him get back with his girlfriend. And next I'm going to sort out his job. I need help, what do you guys think? Can you help me? I don't understand the legal stuff.'

They all shrugged.

'You're useless!' I said, getting to my feet. 'I know people who go to their families for advice and they actually help.'

'That's in the Hollywood movies,' Dad said dismissively. 'You need to talk to a lawyer about this problem.'

'You are a lawyer.'

'No, a different lawyer.'

'One that cares?' Adrienne raised an eyebrow at him.

'I care,' he laughed. 'But you need one who isn't busy.' He stood up from his desk and carried a file to his immaculately kept filing cabinet. He came back with some papers. 'So he was on what's called force majeure leave. The Parental Leave Act 1998 as amended by the Parental Leave (Amendment) Act 2006 gives an employee a limited right to time off from work if they have a family crisis. It arises where, for urgent family reasons, the immediate presence of the employee is indispensable, owing to an injury to or illness of a close family member. The maximum amount of leave is three days in any twelve-month period or five days in a thirty-six-month period, and you are entitled to be paid.'

My heart sank. Adam had already taken two months off work. He had no legal leg to stand on to get his job back.

'If there's a dispute between your friend and his employer about force majeure leave, the issue can be referred using the complaint form which I've enclosed in the folder here.' He placed the document folder on the desk before me. 'Don't say I never give you anything. With regards to his grandfather's will, I can't offer you any legal advice because I haven't seen it. Get your hands on a copy and I will do my best to help him find

242

a way out. If that's the right thing.'

'What do you mean, 'If that's the right thing'? Of course it's the right thing,' I said, confused.

'What she needs to find is a therapist,' Dad told the others.

'She can always talk to us,' Brenda said. 'Remember that, Christine.'

'Not for me — he's talking about a therapist for Adam.'

'What about going to the cute therapist guy who was your client? The sex addict — Leo whatsisname,' Adrienne said.

'Leo Arnold, and he's not a sex addict,' I replied, a smile forming on my lips at Adrienne's attempt to cheer me up.

'Shame.'

'He was trying to quit smoking so I offered him some advice, that's all. And he was a client who I placed in a job, so going to him for a session would be unprofessional.'

'And living with a client for a week *is* professional?' Dad said.

'That's different.' To admit that Adam wasn't technically my client would open a whole other can of worms.

'It wouldn't be unprofessional if you sent Adam to see this guy,' Dad said.

'Adam won't see a therapist,' I repeated, frustrated.

'He won't help himself so he's making you do it all for him. Well, I'll tell you one thing, you can give him all the help in the world, but unless he learns to fend for himself, it'll be useless.'

We were all silent. It was surprisingly a valid point for Dad.

'On a different note, Barry thinks you're sleeping with Leo and that's why you left him. He called me last night to tell me,' said Adrienne.

I raged.

'He also said that you said the reason Brenda can't lose any baby weight is because it's not baby fat, it's greedy bitch fat,' Adrienne went on, eyeing Brenda as she sucked the potato-crisp salt from her fingers.

'I never said that,' I protested.

'No, but I wouldn't blame you if you had.'

'She has got a point,' Dad added, looking at Brenda.

Brenda raised her finger to the three of us and carried on eating.

'Have you bought a dress for the party yet? What are you wearing?' Adrienne asked.

'I'm concentrating more on keeping the birthday boy alive,' I replied, distracted by the news that Barry was obsessing over Leo Arnold. I was trying to figure out how he got the — correct — impression that I fancied the guy. I had never spoken about my clients with him.

'No point in him being alive if you look like shit,' Brenda said, and the three of them laughed.

'Brenda bought a lovely new pair of shoes,' Dad said. 'They're black peep-toe with the prettiest little pearls.'

Dad had a thing about women's shoes. He used to love bringing us shopping when we were growing up and had been known to surprise us with shoes for special occasions. He had good taste, too. In a way, he was a camp man trapped in a straight man's body; he loved women, loved their thinking, spent all of his working days with them, had spent his whole life sharing a house where he was outnumbered by women, including his aunts, and so had a great respect for them. He appreciated their behaviours and tendencies, their nuances, their need for chocolate at the time of the month that he knew by heart — a pre-requisite for raising three teenage girls single-handed — and tried his best to understand the continuously fluctuating hormones and need to discuss and analyse feelings and happenings.

'What makes you think you're going to the party?' I asked, surprised they were all getting prepared.

'He invited us when he was here, don't you remember?' Dad said. 'You don't think we're going to miss a bash like that?'

'It's hardly the bash of the year. He's only thirty-five.'

'No, but it's the night they'll announce that he's taking over Basil's from his father, which is a big deal, considering Dick Basil's been at the helm for over forty years. His father left it to him to run when he was only twenty-one. Imagine all that responsibility at such an age! Did you know Basil's exports its products to forty countries worldwide, a total of one hundred and ten million euro of Irish trade, and more than two hundred and fifty million euros' worth of chocolate produced in Ireland is exported every year. You better believe it's a big deal. They use all local ingredients, which is more important now than ever. I'm sure the Taoiseach will be there. He and Dick Basil are good friends. If he's not in town, most certainly the Minister for Foreign Affairs and Trade will be there, and possibly the Minister for Jobs, Enterprise and Innovation.' Dad clapped his hands. 'It will be a lot of folly on the night, and I shall look forward to it.'

I swallowed. 'Where did you hear all that?'

'*The Times*. Business page.' He lifted it up and showed it to me, then threw it back down on the table. 'Your boy is being handed a dynasty.'

'He doesn't want it,' I said quietly, panic for Adam beginning to swell in my stomach. 'That's why I'm taking care of him. If he has to take over the company, he'll kill himself. And he'll do it that night.'

They all looked at me in silence.

'Well then, you have six days to work on that,' Dad said, giving me a supportive smile. 'My darling baby daughter, I'm going to give you the best piece of advice I believe I've ever given you in your short life.'

I braced myself.

'I suggest you go find that sex addict.'

★ ★ ★

Leaving Adam in my dad's office with his laptop, with Dad under strict instructions not to make any inappropriate comments, I took myself off to

246

the waiting room of Leo Arnold, the client I had fantasised about most nights leading up to me leaving Barry. I never for a moment wanted any of these fantasies to come true, they were just that: fantasies, something to keep my mind occupied when reality felt too dark. I was sure he wasn't even my type; there was no actual attraction between us at all, I had created an entirely different Leo Arnold in my head, one that made appointments for late-night therapy sessions and, unable to contain himself a moment longer, dropped in on me when I was alone in the office, sometimes even when there was a client waiting outside. I felt my face flush at the thought of how ridiculous it all was, now that I was sitting in his waiting room, now that it was real life.

'Christine.' Leo suddenly appeared at the door. His secretary had of course told him I was waiting, but he still couldn't hide his surprise.

'Leo, I'm sorry I didn't make an appointment,' I said, my voice low so I wouldn't anger the others in the waiting room.

'No problem,' he said pleasantly, leading me to his office. 'I have a few minutes between appointments. I'm sorry it can't be longer, but I gather you said it was urgent.'

I sat before his desk, trying not to look around too much, though after imagining his office and the things we'd done there so many times in my mind it was hard not to want to know what the reality was. I glanced at the filing cabinet and thought of handcuffs. My face began to heat up and I knew I was turning puce.

'I'm guessing this is about your husband.' He cleared his throat. 'Barry.'

I looked at him in surprise. 'Actually, no.'

'You're here for a session?' he said, surprised.

'Why, what did you think I was here for?'

'Well, I thought it might be related to the um . . . phone call that I received.'

'From who?'

'From Barry. Isn't that your husband? He said he was your husband. Perhaps I've made a mistake?'

'Oh!' I said, realising, my face turning even more crimson. 'He called you?' I whispered, afraid to say the words aloud. The thought was too much for me to bear. How had Barry got his number? I thought back to the computer I'd left behind in the apartment. He must have got his hands on my contact list. There was no end to my cringing.

It was Leo's turn to go red. 'Er . . . yes, I assumed you knew. I wouldn't have said anything about it if I'd realised you didn't know . . . I'm sorry.'

'What did he say?' My voice was a little above a whisper.

'He believed that, um, we, that you and I were, um . . . well, I think the more polite way of putting it would be that he believed we were having an affair.'

I gasped. 'Oh my . . . Leo . . . I'm so sorry . . . I don't know how on earth he . . . ' I struggled to find the words.

'Well, that's more politely than he put it anyway.'

'I'm so sorry,' I said firmly, finding my voice, trying to remain professional. 'I have no idea how or why he would have come to that conclusion. He's going through a bit of a . . . I mean, we're going through a bit of a . . . ' *nightmare*, I finished, to myself.

'He said something about finding a heart around my name . . . ' Leo continued, his face as scarlet as mine.

'He said what?' My eyes sprung open wide. 'What on earth — I have no idea . . . ' I thought of the notepad I kept by the computer, the one I doodled on when working, I thought of the love hearts I always drew, sometimes stars, sometimes spirals, then remembered the one time, the one ridiculous childish moment where I'd put Leo's name in my bubble heart and thought it was funny, like I was back to being a schoolgirl again, like I had a choice who I could fancy, like it was a carefree, enjoyable thing instead of a betrayal. Trapped, trapped. I'd felt trapped and a name in a bubble heart had freed me for one moment, and now it had come back to haunt me. I cringed, I felt slightly sick, I wanted very much to get out of the office.

'He told my wife, actually,' he said, a little firmer now, his face no longer red, his anger coming through a bit more. 'I learned about it from her. She's pregnant. Six months. A most unwelcome time for her to hear that kind of thing.'

'He what?! Oh my lord, oh my goodness. Leo, once again, I'm so sorry, I . . . ' I kept shaking my head, looking around, wanting the floor to

249

swallow me whole. 'I hope she understands it isn't true? I mean, I could call her to explain, if you think that would — '

'No. I don't think that would help,' he said curtly, interrupting.

'Okay.' I nodded. 'I understand, believe me, I completely understand.' I looked around. I wanted to leave but I was quite paralysed.

'What did you come to see me about, if it wasn't that?'

'Oh, never mind.' I stood up, my face behind my hands, I was so mortified.

'Christine, please, it sounded important. And this meeting, you said it was urgent.'

I really wanted to leave. I wanted nothing more than to walk out of this office, never to see his face again, to find a way of deleting the memory, all knowledge of the conversation that had passed, but I couldn't. I owed it to Adam to help him the best way I could, and that meant swallowing my pride, my everything, and asking for help.

As I gave up the struggle, I felt a sudden freedom. 'It's not about me, actually. I'm here on behalf of a friend.'

'Of course,' he said, not sounding as though he believed me.

'No, really, it is about a friend, but that friend refuses to see a therapist and so I'm here on his behalf.'

'Of course,' he said in exactly the same tone, which was incredibly frustrating. If I'd told him it was about my pet monkey he probably would have replied in the same way.

So I told him the story of Adam and me, in the brief time we had, summarising Adam's attempt to end his life, my promise to help him, our journey together and the steps I'd taken him on in an effort to help him to enjoy life.

'Christine . . . ' Leo sat up in his large leather chair, looking concerned. 'This is rather troubling.'

'I know. Now you can understand why I'm here.'

'Of course your friend's situation is a concern, but it's more that what you have been doing with him, from a therapist's point of view, is incredibly damaging to him.'

I froze. 'Excuse me?'

'Where do I start?' He shook his head as if to clear it. 'Where did you learn these 'tips' on how to enjoy life?'

'From a book,' I said, my heart banging.

There was a flash of anger in his eyes and then he said sternly, 'This pop psychology is a menace. Christine, you have taken the power away from him.'

Seeing my confused look, he continued: 'You do not know better than him. You cannot help him by taking away his integrity. By trying to 'fix' his life, you are disempowering him, because intrinsically nothing will have changed, you'll simply have made him dependent upon you. Your pursuit of these quick-fix methods that you read in a book — '

'I've been trying to *help* him,' I said, angry.

'Indeed, I understand that,' he said gently, 'and as a friend I understand what you have tried

251

to do. But as a therapist — which I must point out is something that you are not — I have to say that you have not gone about this in the right way.'

'So I should have pushed him off the bridge?' I said angrily, standing up.

'Of course not. What I'm saying is, you must give him the power. You must let him have his own life in his own hands.'

'He tried to *take* his own life!'

'You're upset. I understand that you were trying to do the right thing, and that this is a particularly stressful time for *you* — '

'This isn't about *me*, Leo. It's about Adam. All I want to know is how do I make him better? Just tell me how to fix him!'

There was a long silence as he looked at me, then he smiled gently and said, 'Did you hear what you said, Christine?'

I had and I was trembling.

'You can't fix him. He needs to help himself. I suggest you confine yourself to being there for him, listening to him, supporting him. But whatever you do, stop trying to *fix* him before you go too far.'

I looked at him sadly.

'I hope that's of help to you. I'm sorry we didn't have more time today, but if your friend would like to make an appointment with me I would be more than willing to oblige. And if you feel it would help you to speak to somebody, I'll happily refer you to another therapist here I value highly.' Registering my confusion, he added, 'My wife would find my treating you . . . inappropriate.'

'Of course,' I whispered, cringing even more. 'Thank you so much for your time. And again, I'm so sorry.'

'On a personal note, if I may . . . ' he added, looking at me for permission to speak frankly.

I nodded.

'You are wonderful at what you do. I've recommended your recruitment agency to many clients around here who have fallen on hard times; I think they'd find your way of doing things enlightening, uplifting. You care about where you place people. And you went beyond the call of duty by trying to help me with my smoking habit. I have a pile of books I still need to read,' he said, smiling. I could smell the smoke from his jacket, but nonetheless I appreciated his gratitude. 'You're a fixer, Christine, but if you really want to help someone, to be a friend to them, sometimes you need to listen and let them do the work themselves. Be there for him. That's all.'

18

How to Make Absolutely Everything
Okay Again

I should have learned from my session with Leo
— stop meddling. In fact the message had come
through loud and clear, but I had set up this
meeting to solve Amelia's predicament before
meeting with Leo. I led the way up a staircase
over an Afro-Caribbean grocery on Camden
Street to the office of my cousin and private
detective, Bobby O'Brien. He was thirty-two
years old and hailed from County Donegal; after
joining the Gardaí, and being sent to a posh
Dublin suburb with not enough action, he had
decided to leave. Then, on my advice — after
continuously coming back to Rose Recruitment
having been fired from or having walked out of
the jobs I'd placed him in — he opted to set
himself up as the Lone Ranger and investigate
the juicy stuff all on his own.

Since I was unable to go with Amelia on a wild
goose chase to find her parents, I hoped Bobby
would point her in the right direction. The plan
was for me to introduce them and then leave; I
would put the power in Amelia's hands, I would
not take it away. Give others the power over their
own lives, give others the power over their own
lives. My new mantra.

Confronted with the door to Bobby's office,

254

Amelia froze at the top of the stairs. 'I can't do this.'

'That's absolutely fine,' I said, turning around and starting down the stairs again. 'Nobody will think any worse of you.'

'Hey,' Amelia said, stopping me. 'Aren't you going to try to change my mind?'

'No. I don't want to force you into anything you don't want to do, Amelia,' I announced, hoping Adam would get the message too. 'This is a difficult time for you and I appreciate that. This is your life and you're totally in control of it. You should make your own decisions, I don't want to influence you in any way or *project* my problems on to you, because thinking I can fix you *won't* fix me.'

Both Adam and Amelia narrowed their eyes at me suspiciously.

'What happened to her?' Amelia asked Adam.

'I think she hit her head,' he replied, poker-faced. 'Come on,' he said, encouraging Amelia to the office door. 'We're here now, let's do it.'

'But only if *she* wants to,' I insisted.

Adam rolled his eyes. Amelia stared at me, wide-eyed.

'You want to find your biological parents, don't you?' Adam asked.

She nodded.

'Then try this,' he said, taking control of the situation since I had pretty much flaked out on them. 'And if this doesn't work, try another route. Keep your options open. Be prepared for . . . you know . . . ' He looked around the grubby hall, the graffiti on the walls and tried not to breathe in the awful stench of fish, damp and sewerage that pervaded the old building. ' . . . anything.' He knocked on Bobby's door.

'Who's there?' Bobby replied, a certain urgency in his voice.

'It's Christine,' I called.

'Christine?' The surprise was more than evident. 'Do we have an appointment?'

'Er, no. I was hoping you can help. I have some friends with me.' Despite Adam's progress, his volatile mind and fragile state still left me afraid to leave him alone. Only that morning a car had cut across me, in the wrong lane to turn off a roundabout, and as soon as we pulled up beside it at the lights Adam had leapt out of the car and screamed at the terrified woman behind the wheel, who had three kids in the back seat. He had ignored my pleas to get back into the car and so it had taken the lights going green and the woman speeding away for dear life, almost in tears, for him to get back into the car, where he went quiet, cracking his knuckles over and over again. Afterwards it was an hour before he'd speak to me. He had acted as if coming with me on this trip was punishment, but it wasn't, I was simply afraid, always afraid to leave him alone in case anything else tipped him over the edge.

'What friends?' Bobby asked. There it was again, the slight fear, the distrust, as if he was up to divilment, or had been and didn't want to get caught. 'Look, if it's about your husband, I'm sorry I spoke to him that way, okay? We never got along — no surprises there — but he was way out of line calling me like that.'

I closed my eyes and counted to three at that revelation.

'Can you please open the door?' I asked impatiently.

There was the sound of locks and bolts being undone and then the door opened the slightest amount, a couple of inches, the chain visible. One blue eye peered out at us. It looked left and right, studied Adam and Amelia, then the hallway behind us. Apparently satisfied, he pulled the door to, slid the chain free and opened the door to usher us in.

'Sorry about that,' he said. 'Part of the job, you know. I have to be careful.' He closed the door behind us, slid the bolts and turned the key in the lock.

'Bobby O'Brien.' He smiled charmingly, and held out his hand first to Adam and then Amelia.

'You've met Amelia before,' I said. 'We're friends from school. She's at every family event.'

'Really?' He studied her. 'I'm sure I would have remembered a pretty woman like you.'

Amelia's cheeks pinked.

I rolled my eyes at his efforts to charm her. 'You stole her ice cream at my eighth birthday and threw it over the neighbour's wall.'

He thought about it. 'That was you?'

Amelia laughed. 'I look different when I'm not wailing that I hate boys.'

'Hasn't changed all that much,' Adam mumbled so only I could hear, and I threw him a look.

'How are you doing, Christine?' Bobby gave me a warm hug.

After he released me from his embrace he made his way to the window behind his desk. The vertical blinds were closed. He pulled the slats apart slightly and peeked out at the road below, then back at us.

'How can I help you?'

He was wearing a green T-shirt with 'Beer Heaven' written on it and ripped blue jeans. His hair was black and curly, falling down over his eyes, his skin was pale and his jaw stubbled. He always looked as if he was up to mischief, probably because he always was; never more so than now. I noticed Amelia was checking him out. I liked this, and fought the urge to meddle. Let them take control of this themselves, I told myself.

'Bobby, Amelia is the reason we're here. She recently discovered that her parents are not her biological parents. Amelia, would you like to take it from here? Show him what you found?'

While Amelia talked about the contents of the shoebox I looked out of the window to see what had been making Bobby so anxious. There was nobody there. I quickly closed the blinds and stepped away. Bobby noticed me and gave me a weak, nervous smile. I didn't want to know what he'd done.

'So basically you're saying that everything in this box, this collection of items that were left with you when you were passed on to your adopted mother, leads to Kenmare?' Bobby summed it up.

'I wouldn't say that,' Adam interrupted. 'The person who came up with that is extremely unbalanced.'

'Speak for yourself,' Amelia snapped, putting Adam in his place.

'So let's go to Kenmare,' Bobby said quickly, clapping his hands.

I narrowed my eyes at him suspiciously.

'You think it's a good idea?' Amelia asked, surprised. 'You think my friend is right?'

'I think your friend is a genius,' Bobby said. 'I mean, I would have recognised the lace at some stage myself, but she saw it straight away. I'd love to go to Killarney — '

'Kenmare,' I interrupted.

'Kenmare, excuse me.' He gave Amelia a charming smile. 'I'd love to go to Kenmare, ask a few questions. We'll find your parents in no time.'

I raised my eyebrows.

'I've had plenty of adoption cases,' he said, feeling the bad vibes Adam and I were giving out and selling himself a bit harder. 'Usually we go to the adoption authority and I assist people through that process. It can be a stressful business; it's not easy to think, to process everything,' he said, sincere now. 'We can get results that way too, but it's always good to follow any clues you can come up with yourself.'

'I already contacted the adoption authority,' Amelia said. 'I've downloaded paperwork from their website but,' she lowered her voice even though there was no one around to hear her, 'I'm not entirely sure this adoption was done

259

officially. There's no paperwork that I could find.'

'Yeah . . . ' Bobby fingered the note and looked deep in thought. 'I agree. So, what do you say?' He reached out his hand to Amelia, eager to close the deal, so he could flee from his nest.

'How much do you cost?' The cynical Adam interrupted their exchange.

'One hundred and fifty euro if I find them, plus my accommodation. Other expenses I'll cover myself. Deal?' He looked down at his hand, which was still extended.

Amelia seemed uncertain.

He dropped his hand.

'I can't promise miracles,' he said gently, 'but I've found parents and reunited families before. There's not much of a set-up here, but I'm good. I don't get paid until I solve the puzzle and I pay the rent every month. Just about.' He offered a cheeky smile.

'It's not you, Bobby,' Amelia said. 'It's the . . . situation. If I go ahead with this, well, then it's real.' She looked at me for help.

What was considered meddling? 'You should do what you feel is right,' I eventually said, then added, 'What have you got to lose? You haven't been on holiday for a long time. At the very least, you'll see another part of the country.'

Amelia smiled shyly. 'Okay.' She shook his hand.

Adam shook his head.

★ ★ ★

'I know this is crazy,' Amelia said, keeping her voice down as we walked back to the car. 'But I have to get out of Dublin, I have to get away from the shop. I need to get away. Get my head together. Everything has been turned upside down, I can barely think straight.'

'And you think the trip will help that?'

'No,' she laughed. 'But at least I'm going to have fun being wildly confused about it all. Bobby,' she smiled, 'he's an interesting one.'

I was only half-listening, trying at the same time to eavesdrop on the two men behind us.

'So how did you meet Christine?' Bobby asked.

'On a bridge.'

'Which bridge?'

'The Ha'penny.'

'That's romantic,' Bobby said, slapping Adam's back like they were buddies. Adam shoved his hands deeper into his pockets and waited for me to stop talking so we could finally get away.

I turned my attention back to Amelia.

'Thanks for humouring me,' she said.

'That's what friends are for. But can I ask a question? When we were in the storage room, you went straight to the box with the year you were born. You suspected, didn't you?'

'I always wondered. Sometimes I'd ask Mum and Dad questions about the pregnancy, about where I was born, and the answers they gave were all a bit too vague. Plus they never seemed to want to talk about it. I didn't want to make them uncomfortable or hurt them, so eventually

261

I stopped asking, I gave up on finding the answers. I had no idea what it was they were hiding. But I do know that Mum had four pregnancies before me and she lost every one of those babies. She said having me was a blessing from God. So I thought she was afraid of losing me the way she'd lost them, that's why she was so precious about me.'

'Your parents loved you so much.'

'I felt loved.' She smiled. 'So it's okay. It's not so much that I want to be reunited with my biological parents, I just . . . I want to know. And then I think I could walk away. It won't matter if they want nothing to do with me. I'm not sure yet if I want anything to do with them. All I want is to know the story. I feel like I deserve to know.'

'You do.' I thought about it. 'You're right, you know, if I was in your shoes and if I knew my mum was out there and I had a chance to find her, I'd do whatever it took. I'd do anything to get her back.'

'I know you would,' Amelia said, throwing a worried look at Adam before covering her concern with a smile that was too bright and too quick.

I swallowed hard.

★ ★ ★

'This is ridiculous,' Adam said from the door, watching me pack my bag.

Everything had seemed ridiculous to him all day. Pointless, a waste of time, ridiculous.

'What's ridiculous?' I asked, trying not to

sound as drained as I felt.

'Going to Tipperary.'

'How are you going to *not* take over the company if we don't go to the company to sort it out?'

'We can't sort it out, it's in my grandfather's will. There's no way of changing it. This trip will be a total waste of time.' His voice was hard.

I didn't know exactly how we were going to sort this out but where there was a will, there was a way and Adam had to face up to his responsibilities sooner or later. The prospect was making him tetchy, fidgety. He was moody again.

He left the room. 'So this is my last time here?' he said from the living area.

Then I got it. He had a problem with people leaving him, and him leaving too. I hurriedly followed his voice.

'You're moving on, Adam. This is a good thing.'

He nodded, not believing a word of it.

'Right now, I'm feeling . . . ' I prompted him.

He sighed. 'Right now I'm feeling . . . sentimental.'

I felt it too. Then his phone rang.

'It's Maria.' He handed it to me.

I stared at it, wanting to hang up straight away, but I thought of Leo's advice. 'Answer it,' I swallowed. 'Invite her to your party. If you want to.'

'Are you sure?' He looked uncertain.

'Of course.' I was confused by his reaction. 'Don't you want her to be there?'

The phone kept ringing.

'Yeah, only, you know . . . '

We stared at each other.

I wasn't sure what he was thinking, but I knew what I was thinking. *Don't answer it, don't fall in love with her, fall out of love with her. Love me.*

The phone stopped ringing, leaving a silent room. He didn't even look at the phone in his hand. He swallowed. He took a step towards me.

The phone rang again and he froze.

Then he answered it and walked out of the room.

★ ★ ★

While Adam was outside in the car with Pat, I tentatively made my way to Simon Conway's ward. I was on the lookout for his wife, his children or any member of his family who felt that taking a pop at me would alleviate their pain or bring Simon back to them. The only familiar face I saw — and I cowered away from her as soon as I saw her — was Angela, the nurse who had brought me to Simon's room the previous week, the night I'd met Adam. I froze when I saw her, but Angela smiled at me warmly.

'I'm not going to bite.' She smiled. 'Family only, but come on.' She led me along to the room. 'I heard about what happened the last time you were here. Sorry I wasn't on duty. I want you not to worry in the slightest about it. She was upset and needed someone to blame. You're not responsible.'

'I was there. I was the one who — '

'You're not responsible,' she said firmly. 'The girls said she felt awful about it after you left. She was so overcome with emotion they had to take the little ones out and calm her down.'

She didn't paint a pretty picture, but it did a little to relieve my stress.

'Did you speak to anyone yet?' Angela asked, and I knew she meant someone professional.

I hadn't forgotten the advice Leo had given me about Adam, but this was an entirely different problem. All the same, I'd been thinking about it and I'd finally figured out who exactly I needed to talk to.

I was left alone with Simon. The beeping and whooshing were the only sounds in the silence. I sat down beside him.

'Hi,' I whispered. 'It's me. Christine. Christine Rose, the woman who failed to save you from yourself. I'm wondering if someone should have saved you from me,' I said, eyes filling as the emotions I had been doing my best to suppress came flooding back to me all at once. 'I've been going over that night over and over again, trying to figure out what happened. I must have said something wrong. I can't remember. I was so relieved that you'd put that gun down. I'm sorry if whatever I said made you feel that you weren't important enough, that your life wasn't worth living. Because it is and you are. And if you're able to hear me, Simon, then you fight, fight for your life — if not for yourself then do it for your girls because they need you. There is so much of their life that they will need you for. I grew up without a mother, so I know what it's like to have the ghost of someone permanently in every moment in your life. You always wonder what would they think, what would they do if they were here, whether you're making them proud . . . '

I allowed a long silence where I let my tears flow, then I composed myself.

'Anyway, because of this guilt I feel about what I did to you, I've got myself in a whole lot of trouble. I met a man on a bridge and I have to help him see the beauty of life, convince him that life is worth living or else I'll lose him.' I wiped my streaming eyes. 'One of the things I have to do is help him win back his girlfriend. And if I don't get him back with his girlfriend he will kill himself. Those are the rules. It's only been a week but sometimes you know, you know? And this week I've learned some things.' I looked down at my fingers, realising it for sure, completely one hundred per cent.

I'd hoped to feel relief. Instead I had a pounding headache, a heavy heart, the whoosh of the ventilator and the beep of the heart monitor my only response. I wanted an encouraging nod, I wanted to hear that I was understood, that it was okay, that it wasn't my fault, that I would be able to work everything out. I needed to be given *tools*, where were my tools? I needed a good book that would fix everything; *How to Make Absolutely Everything Okay Again*, a simple step-by-step guide to mend hearts, clear consciences and make everybody forget.

Perhaps the realisation wasn't enough, the

silent admission wasn't enough; I needed to say it out loud. I looked up, fixed my eyes on Simon as though my words of heart-dripping honesty would be powerful enough to make him open his eyes.

'I'm in love with Adam.'

19

How to Pick Yourself Up
and Dust Yourself Off

'Everything okay?' the most beautiful man in my world asked me as I got into Dick Basil's chauffeur-driven car.

I nodded.

He frowned and studied my teary eyes. I had to look away.

'You've been crying.'

I sniffed and stared out the window.

'How's he doing?' he asked gently.

I could only shake my head, not trusting my voice.

'Did his wife say something to you again? Christine, you know you didn't deserve that. It was unfair.'

'Maria could treat me the very same way next week,' I said suddenly, not knowing that was going to come from my mouth, not really knowing it was on my mind.

Pat turned the radio on.

'Excuse me?'

'You heard me. Maria, your whole family, they'll blame me. They'll say I spent two weeks swanning about the place with you instead of getting you proper help. Do you ever think of what will happen to me if you go ahead with it?'

'They wouldn't blame you. I wouldn't let

them,' he said, getting upset at how I was being affected by this.

'You won't be here to protect me Adam, you won't be able to defend me. Everything will be my word against theirs. You don't know the mess that you'll leave behind,' I said angrily, barely able to get the words out. And by that I didn't only mean the situation, I meant myself.

Adam's phone rang and as soon as I saw the look on his face when he answered, I knew immediately. His dad had passed away.

★　★　★

Adam didn't want to see his father's body at the hospital, he didn't want to deviate from the plan of going to Tipperary, which of course was where we needed to go now anyway to make arrangements for the funeral. So we remained in the car as if nothing had happened, when of course everything had happened: he had lost his father and he was now officially the head of Basil's.

'Have you heard from your sister?' I asked. His phone had remained in his pocket where he'd put it after he received the call. He hadn't contacted anybody. I wondered if he was in shock.

'No.'

'You haven't checked your phone. Shouldn't you call her?'

'I'm sure she's been informed.'

'Will she come to the funeral?'

'I hope so.'

I was relieved by his positive response.

'And I hope the guards are waiting for her on the runway. In fact, maybe I'll call them and alert them myself.'

I wasn't so pleased then.

'Maybe this means the party won't go ahead,' I said quietly, feeling bad at trying to find a silver lining in the death of a loved one, but Adam was clearly in need of one.

'Are you joking? There's no way they'd cancel the party now — this is their big chance to prove that we're as strong and ready as ever.'

'Oh. Is there anything you'd like me to do?'

'No, thanks.'

He was silent as he gazed out of the window, grabbing every scene that passed, trying to hold on to being away from the dreaded place we were going to, trying to slow the car in its tracks. I wondered if he wanted me with him at all. Not that it would affect me being there; I was staying with him regardless, especially now, but it would be easier if I knew he wanted me there. I supposed not. He probably would have preferred to be alone with his thoughts, and it was his thoughts that scared me.

'Actually,' he said suddenly, 'will you read the reading from Amelia's mother's funeral?'

I was surprised. He hadn't commented on it much at the funeral, other than to ask me if I'd written it. I was deeply touched. That reading meant the world to me. I looked out of the window, blinked away tears.

We were driving down country lanes, the landscape was rich and green, vibrant, even on the icy morning. It was horse territory, plenty of trainers and stables with some of the best land for feeding their breeds, whether race horses or show horses, it was a big business in these parts — if they weren't making chocolates, that was. Pat wasn't taking too much care on the roads, he didn't pause before rounding sharp corners, took lefts and rights at roads that bore exact resemblance to the last turn we'd taken. I felt my nails digging into the leather seats.

I looked at Adam to see if he looked as nervous as I was. He was looking at me. I'd caught him.

He cleared his throat and looked away. 'I was . . . do you know you're missing an earring?'

'What?' I felt my earlobe. 'Shit.' I started searching my body for the earring, shaking my clothes roughly, hoping it would fall out. I had to find it. When I still didn't find it I got down on my hands and knees in the car.

'Careful, Christine,' Adam warned and I felt his hand on my head as I bumped it against the door as Pat rounded another corner sharply.

'It was my mother's,' I said, leaning over on his side and pushing away his feet to check the floor around him.

Adam winced, as though feeling my pain at losing it.

After finding nothing, I sat down, red-faced and flustered. I didn't want to talk to anyone for a while.

'Do you remember her?'

I rarely spoke about my mother; not a deliberate decision but because my mother had been in my life for such a short time that I had no references to her. I tried to summon her up now and then but had little to remember and therefore little to say.

'These earrings are one of the very few memories I have of her. I used to sit on the edge of the bath and watch her when she was getting dressed to go out. I loved watching her put on her make-up.' I closed my eyes. 'I can see her now, facing the mirror, her hair back off her shoulders in a clasp. She'd be wearing these earrings — she only ever wore these on special nights out.' I fingered my naked earlobe. 'It's funny the things we remember. I can see from the photographs that we did so much more together, I don't know why I remember that moment more than anything.'

I was silent for a while, then said, 'So to answer your question: no. It's a long way of saying no, I don't really remember her. I suppose that's why I wear these earrings every day. I hadn't figured that out until now. When people comment on my earrings, I know I can say, 'Thanks. They're my mother's.' It's a way to creep her into my conversations every day, somehow make her real and a part of my life. I feel like she's an *idea*, a bunch of other people's stories, a person who changes all the time in photographs, who looks different in each one, in different lights, different angles. I used to ask my sisters all the time when we'd look through the album: Is that the mum you remember? Or is *that* her? But they'd say no, then describe her in a way that no photograph captured. Even my

272

own image of her at her mirror is of the back of her head, her right ear, her chin. Sometimes I wish that she'd turn around in that memory so I can see her fully; sometimes I make her do that in my imagination. It probably sounds weird.'

'It's not weird at all,' Adam said gently.

'Do you remember your mother?'

'Bits and pieces. Small things. Problem was, I didn't have anybody to talk to about her. I think it helps your memory of a person, when people share stories, but my dad never talked about her.'

'Wasn't there anybody else to talk to?'

'We had a new nanny every summer; the gardener was the closest we had to a regular person about the house, and he wasn't allowed to talk to us.'

'Why not?'

'Dad's rules.'

We left a long silence.

'Your earring will turn up,' he said.

I hoped so.

'Maria said she'd come to my birthday party.'

I had forgotten to ask him. How had I forgotten that?

'Good. Great. That's . . . Adam that's really great.'

He looked at me. Big blue eyes searing into my soul. 'I'm glad you think it's really great.'

'I do. It's . . . ' I couldn't think of any other word other than *great* so I let the sentence die.

Finally the car slowed and I sat up, eager to catch a glimpse of the place where Adam had grown up. The plaques on the grand pillars announced 'Avalon Manor'. Pat heeded the speed limits here and crawled down the driveway, which went on for miles. The trees fell away to reveal a wide open green before an enormous period manor house.

'Wow.'

Adam looked unimpressed.

'You grew up here?'

'I grew up in boarding school. I spent holidays here.'

'It must have been incredibly exciting for a young boy, lots of places to explore. Look at that ruin.'

'I wasn't allowed to play in there. And it was lonely. Our nearest neighbours are a considerable distance away.' He must have heard the poor-little-rich-boy tone in his voice because he dropped it. 'That's the old ice-house. I always thought I'd renovate it and live there.'

'So you did want to live here,' I said.

'Once upon a time.' He looked away from me, out of his window.

The car pulled up before the sweeping steps that led to the enormous front door. The door opened and a woman with a warm face welcomed us. I recalled her from Adam's stories: Maureen, wife of Pat the driver. She had been housekeeper, or house manager as Adam called her, for thirty-five years, for as long as Adam had been alive. Though Adam never considered her as a maternal figure in his life — the nannies were employed to mind him, and Maureen, though warm, had children of her own, while her sole responsibility as an employee was the wellbeing of the house — I was sure Adam was

274

missing a trick. I was dubious as to how she could have turned a blind eye to the two motherless children under the same roof, and I felt sure that Adam was being obtuse if he believed that.

'Adam.' She embraced him warmly and he visibly stiffened. 'I'm sorry for your loss.'

'Thanks. This is Christine, she'll be staying for a few days.'

Maureen couldn't quite hide her surprise at the sight of a woman in Adam's company who wasn't Maria, but it was quickly masked by her welcome, though nothing could be done to hide the awkwardness which I know we both felt when it came to deciding the sleeping arrangements. The house had ten bedrooms and Maureen didn't know whether to lead me to one of them, or to Adam's room. She led the way tentatively, looking behind her now and then to try and catch Adam's eye for guidance, for a hint as to what to do, but as well as being laden with our bags, he was lost in his mind, his forehead furrowed as he tried to decode a cipher. I guessed that he'd left last week thinking he would be returning an engaged, soon-to-be-betrothed man and when that went suddenly pear-shaped he didn't intend to return at all. Now here he was, back in the place he seemed to detest so much.

I had been worried about our 'deal' all week, but that concern was nothing to what I felt now in Adam's company. He seemed detached, cold, even when I met his eye and smiled encouragingly. I imagined how Maria felt when she tried

275

to engage with him, reach out to him, be intimate with him and then was greeted by this withdrawal. I first thought of it as a shell of Adam, but then realised I was entirely wrong. He wasn't a shell, he was completely filled by someone else, possessed by an Adam who felt rage and loss and anger and resentment at the loss of control of his life. An Adam who was profoundly unhappy. He had lost his mother at a young age but in other ways his life had been sheltered. He didn't have to wonder about his next meal, schoolbooks, toys at Christmas, a home being taken from him. In his life, all of these things were taken for granted. And he'd taken it for granted that he was free to break away from his father's rule, plot his own destiny, with an older sister to step into the family business. Then all that had changed. Duty, the thing he had so avoided and celebrated avoiding successfully had strolled casually up behind him and tapped him on the shoulder and respectfully requested that he follow it this way. The party was over, the belief that he had control over his own fate, that he could build a different kind of life for himself, evaporated, melted before his very eyes like a house of wax.

He was at the end and he didn't like endings, he didn't like partings or goodbyes and he didn't like leaving. Change occurred on his terms when he was good and ready. It was the look in his eye, the tone of his voice, everything that made Adam Adam which had altered since we set foot in the house, and now that I thought about it, had begun to creep in since he'd hung up the phone

276

earlier. It gave me a sick feeling in my stomach, because I realised how utterly serious Adam was about leaving this world and I knew, if he attempted it again, this time he would get the job done, he would not stop until he was successful.

It was one thing to help someone who wanted to be helped, which I felt Adam was quite open to in Dublin. Here, in Tipperary, I felt he'd already closed the door and emotionally detached himself from me. He spent most of the day sleeping with the curtains drawn in an enormous room with an open fireplace and a couch area, which Adam insisted he would be sleeping on later, but for now he was in the bed and I was sitting, legs up on the window seat, in the bay window which looked out over Lough Derg. I listened to his breathing and watched the clock, all the while conscious that we were wasting time. Time, in this case, was not a healer; we needed to be talking, fixing and doing, I needed to be challenging and supporting him, but I couldn't do any of those things because he had retreated, detached and withdrawn himself, and I was scared.

I checked on Adam again; he was definitely asleep. His hands lay palms up behind him on the bed, his arms raised as though in surrender. His blond hair fell over one of his eyelids and I reached out to move it. He didn't wake and my finger remained on his soft skin a little longer. He hadn't shaved that morning and barely noticeable white-blond stubble glistened in the light. His lips were together, pouting that way he did when he concentrated. It made me smile.

Maureen appeared at the open door, and knocked gently to get my attention. I was startled and pulled back my hand as if caught doing something wrong. I wondered how long Maureen had been there. She smiled at me in a way that suggested she'd noticed my tenderness with Adam and, embarrassed, I made my way to the door.

'Sorry to disturb you, but I brought the extra blankets Adam asked for.'

They were for the couch, so I placed them there.

I could tell Maureen wanted to ask, but instead she said, 'And, well . . . ' She looked across at his sleeping body. ' . . . there was a phone call for Adam.'

'I don't think we should disturb him,' I said gently. 'You can tell him later. Or is it urgent?'

'It was Maria.'

'Oh.'

'She tried calling his mobile, but he's not answering. She wants to know if he wants her to come to the funeral. She said they had a few problems and she wasn't sure he'd want her here or not. She doesn't want to upset him.'

'Oh . . . ' I looked at Adam and tried to figure out what to do. The Adam in Dublin would have wanted her. This Adam needed her, but this wasn't the Adam Maria had fallen in love with and was falling for again. I was determined they should meet when he was back on form. Maria, seeing him like this, or being treated the way she had been previously, would send her running straight back into the arms of Sean. I would have

278

to talk about it later with him but I was sure he would agree with me. 'I think he would prefer her not to be here, but it's not because he's upset with her. Please let her know that.'

'Okay. I'll tell her,' Maureen said gently. She cast a quick look at Adam again, obviously wondering to herself: Should I trust this lady? Should I ask him myself?

It was when she was down the hall that I chased her, more comfortable speaking with her when Adam was out of earshot.

'Maureen . . . ' I wrung my hands together. 'We're not . . . together. Adam and I. He's not very well lately, he's having a few problems, personally.'

Maureen nodded, as if this she knew very well.

'He wouldn't appreciate me saying anything. I'm sure you know him better than me, but I'm trying to . . . help him. I have been trying to help him all week. I thought it was working. I don't know what he's usually like, but in the days following our initial meeting, he has seemed . . . lighter. This has set him back a bit. Though I know there's never a good time to lose someone . . . '

'You met Mr Basil?'

'Yes.'

'Well then, you'll understand when I say that, despite working for him for thirty-five years, we weren't exactly close.'

'The same could be said for his son.'

Maureen pursed her lips and nodded. 'I'm sure you won't take this any further, but Adam,' she lowered her voice, 'he has always been sensitive. He has always been hard on himself. He could never let go of things easily, even the smallest things. I tried to be there for him, but Adam preferred to deal with things alone, quietly, and Mr Basil . . . well, he was Mr Basil.'

'I understand. Thank you for the insight, and I assure you I won't repeat what you've said. I literally haven't taken my eyes off him for the week,' I explained.

'Most women can't.' She smiled and I blushed, tellingly.

'For reasons I can't explain, I can't let him out of my sight. Hence the bedroom situation, but I really need to go somewhere now and I wonder if you could keep an eye on him for me? I'm sure you have lots to do for tomorrow, but I'll only be an hour. If you wouldn't mind?'

I placed a chair outside the bedroom door for Maureen so that he wouldn't be freaked out to find her lounging on the couch at the end of his bed.

'Please ring me if he wakes, goes to the toilet, *anything*.' I cast a worried glance at Adam in bed, trying to decide whether to stay or go.

'It'll be fine.' Maureen placed a warm hand on my arm.

'Okay,' I said nervously.

'She was right,' Maureen said.

'Who was?'

'Maria. She asked me if Adam was here with a woman. Someone pretty who seemed to be taking care of him.'

'She did?'

'Yes.' Maureen nodded.

'What did you say?'

'I told her she would have to discuss Adam's business with Adam.'

I managed a weak smile. 'Thanks.'

★　★　★

I found Pat in the service kitchen, tucking into an egg sandwich. I was already dreading the drive in a confined space with him; speed and now an egg to top it off. I tried to politely wait until he'd finished, but knowing Adam was upstairs without me caused me to pace nervously.

'Fine,' Pat said, forcing the final half of the sandwich into his mouth, pushing back the chair, downing his cup of tea and standing up. He grabbed the car keys and headed to the car.

Mary Keegan, Dick Basil's right-hand 'man' lived twenty minutes away on an impressive patch of land. When I found no answer at the house, Pat pointed me in the direction of the stables and went back to the radio blaring sport in the overheated egg-fart-smelling car. He had been right about her whereabouts. I stood at the fence and watched the elegant woman on horseback as she jumped the obstacle course.

'That's Lady Meadows,' a voice said behind me, and I turned to see Mary. She was dressed for the occasion: wellington boots, a warm fleece with a padded waistcoat over it.

'I thought I was watching you.'

'Me? Certainly not!' she laughed. 'I wouldn't have enough time to be as good as that. I'm only

281

good for morning gallops and hunts. I do love hunts.'

'Lady Meadows is the horse or the woman?'

'The horse,' she laughed. 'The woman is Misty. She's a show jumper, competes professionally. Almost made the Olympics last time, but her horse Medicine Man broke his leg in training. Maybe next time.'

'You've a great set-up here. How many horses do you have?'

'Twelve. Not all of them are ours, but it helps with the fees. We're expanding though. She's even thinking about getting into breeding.'

'Is the dream for you to be here full-time?'

'Me? No. Why, have you been sent from Basil's to fire me?' She tried to make it appear she was joking, but it was clear from the fear in her eyes that she was worried.

'No, actually, quite the opposite.'

Mary looked intrigued.

We finished our conversation in what should have been the warmth of the bungalow, but with the door opening and closing as stable hands came and went there was little chance of any warmth remaining in the house. Mary kept her coat on and so did I, drinking as much hot tea as I could and warming my hands on the mug as I sat on an animal-hair-infested couch surrounded by three dogs; one sleeping, one with cabin fever as he wandered around the room sniffing at walls for a way out and another that sat in Mary's lap and watched me in a disconcerting manner without blinking for the entire conversation. Mary didn't seem to notice any of it, not the cold, nor the dog hair that I scooped from my mug. I wasn't sure if that was because she was so used to it all or because of my proposal.

She acted dubious but her interest was obvious. 'And you worked on this with Adam?'

'Yes.' I was only half-lying. 'He couldn't be here today because there's so much to arrange for the funeral.' I thought of him in his house, lying in the darkness with the bed covers over his head.

'And he's happy with this?' she asked, confused. 'With not having a day-to-day role in the company? With me making the decisions?'

'Absolutely. He'll be chairman of the board, so all decisions will have to be signed off by him, but I think it's the best way to move forward. Everyone I've spoken to is very sure that you could run the company in the way Mr Basil intends. You love the company.'

'It was the first place I worked after school.' She smiled. 'They used to be based in Dublin, but when they moved here it was great for the area. It *is* great. I spent the first year answering phones. Gradually moved my way up. But . . . ' She shook her head, confused.

'What's wrong?'

'Old Mr Basil wouldn't have wanted this. Mr Basil's family wouldn't want this. Lavinia would rather roll over and die than see me in her position. The Basils prefer to keep things in the family.' She didn't speak ill of anyone, she was too professional for that, but I could read between the lines and it tallied with what Adam

283

had said about feeling pressure from his family within the company over him getting the job and not them.

'As long as it's not his uncle's family involved,' I added.

'Well, of course,' she agreed. 'It won't go to Nigel, will it?' she asked, worried.

'That's the last thing Adam wants. And I don't think you have anything to worry about with Lavinia.'

'Are you sure Adam is happy with this?' she asked again, confused.

I stalled. 'Do you mind me asking, why are you unsure about this? I thought it was obvious Adam didn't want the job.'

'Oh, I sensed that, of course, but I thought it would be different when Mr Basil died. I thought he'd see it differently. It's hard to do your job when Mr Basil's breathing down your neck; he barely gives you a second to think and then he barks at you for not thinking. I thought that Adam would want to make it his own.' She shrugged. 'I thought his problem was with his father, not with the company. And he's proved he's good at it, the short time he's been there. He had some good ideas — and believe me, we could do with some fresh blood in there. It would be such a shame for him not to take the position. But, as you say, if this is what he wants . . . ' She looked at me as though she didn't believe me.

This confused me all over again.

My phone rang.

It was Maureen. 'He's awake.'

284

* * *

I didn't need to tell Pat to put the foot down, he was already driving over 100 mph on roads I would barely do sixty on. When I reached the house, I expected to find Adam outside or downstairs but instead I found him still in his bedroom, trying to talk a flushed-faced Maureen into letting him out.

'Slide the keys under the door, Maureen,' Adam said, the impatience in his voice clear.

'Uh. I'm not sure they fit,' she said nervously, then held her head in her hands in silent turmoil. She heard me on the staircase and looked up at me in relief. 'He had a shower and he was hungry so I brought him lunch and locked the door,' she whispered frantically. 'He kept saying he wanted to go for a walk.'

'Why didn't you let him?'

'You said not to let him out of my sight!'

'You could have followed him.'

She clamped her hands across her open mouth, not having thought of that. I felt my mouth twitch.

'He's very angry,' Maureen whispered.

'That's okay. He'll take it out on me.' I raised my voice. 'It's all right, Adam, I'm here, I'll help.'

I put the key in the lock and rattled it around as though I was having a difficult time. Adam kept pushing the handle up and down impatiently.

'Adam, stop! I'm trying to . . . ' Finally the key clicked in place and the door flew open. I was so surprised by the sudden force that I didn't have

285

time to move. Adam came bounding out, like a bull released, and my shoulder was the target as he bumped past, but he was too angry to stop and apologise and Maureen caught me as I flew back a few feet.

'Oh dear, my dear, are you okay?'

I didn't feel the burning until afterwards as I was more concerned about Adam running down the stairs, steam coming from his ears. I took off in pursuit.

'I want to be alone,' he said, power-walking out of the house and taking a left that led to a pathway along the lake.

His legs were so much longer than mine and I had to jog to keep up. A few quick steps, then a jog to catch up, a few quick steps and then another jog. Between a slight panic that he'd gone off the rails and the fact I was jogging I was a little out of breath already.

'You know I can't do that,' I said, running a bit, then walking, then running again to catch up.

'Not now, okay?'

I kept up with him, didn't want to say anything to annoy him. I remained at his side, silent but present. Not that he wouldn't be able to do anything just because I was there. He was strong, as the throbbing in my shoulder proved. Still, I persevered, I couldn't give up on him, I couldn't leave him alone, I couldn't —

'CHRISTINE!' he yelled in my face. 'GO AWAY.'

He'd stopped suddenly and it had taken me by surprise. He shouted so loudly it echoed around the lake, reverberated in my head, hurt my ears, made my heart bang in my chest. The flash of anger in his eyes, the single vein that throbbed in his forehead and the veins that protruded from his neck, his hands in fists, unintentionally threatening, made me catch my breath and hold it. I felt like a child who had been shouted at by an adult, that surprised, vulnerable, embarrassed feeling. And I felt alone, suddenly so very alone. He turned away from me and charged off and I collapsed, crouched over, hands flying to my knees as I gasped for breath, as I started to cry and for once didn't try to stop it.

I let him go.

20

How to Stand Up and Be Counted

I felt an odd sort of calm as I sat in the boathouse and looked out to Lough Derg. The edges of the lake had frozen over and ducks flew down, pecked at it and instantly soared to the sky as though it was too cold even for them, their hunger wasn't worth it. I sniffed again as my nose dripped, giving up on wiping it as it was completely numb, my eyes red and sore. I was sure my tears would have frozen had they not been flowing so swiftly. I didn't bother to wipe them, occasionally they would roll to my lip and I'd lick them, tasting the salt. It was an odd sort of feeling, waiting, feeling helpless to stop an act I had felt solely responsible for in waking and sleeping hours, and yet when it came to it I knew I wouldn't be able to stop. Not physically. My words were all I had, my thinking was all I had, but this time he didn't want to listen.

I heard footsteps behind me and my heart pounded. It was them, coming to tell me they'd found him. Possibly to arrest me — could they do that? Hadn't my failure aided and abetted him? I stared straight ahead, the lake dark and still, but cold, my breathing ragged in the silence. There was a break in the clouds and I looked up at the light and I had a sudden optimistic thought. The footsteps were slow, there was nothing panicked about them, nothing even threatening. They stopped behind me and then continued around the boathouse until Adam appeared beside me.

He sat down next to me. I held up a hand to stop him from coming any closer. I bit my lip to ward off a fresh bout of crying and, sensing I'd be unsuccessful, I turned my face away from him.

Adam cleared his throat but was quiet for a while longer. It was the right thing to do; sitting together, being in each other's company, was itself warming the chilly air between us.

'I'm sorry,' he said, and even after he'd taken so long to say it, it still felt sudden.

I didn't reply. I knew that I should but I didn't forgive him.

'Where did you go?'

'To let off some steam. Scared off a couple of hares and made a deer shit itself.'

I couldn't help it. A small giggle escaped.

'That's better,' he said, gentler. 'I hate seeing you cry.' He reached out and wiped a stray tear from my cheek. I closed my eyes and another one fell.

'Hey,' he said, sliding across the bench and putting his arm around me.

I decided not to speak, unable to control the lump in my throat. Instead I rested my head on his shoulder. He kissed the top of my head.

'I'm never myself when I'm here,' he said. 'I turn into this messy, angry . . . well you know.'

He left a silence. I didn't fill it. I was going to listen, not help him out.

'And you promised me you wouldn't tell anyone. That made me angry.'

'Tell anyone what?' I looked up at him.

'About you know, last Sunday.'

'I didn't tell anyone.'

He looked at me. 'Christine, don't lie, please don't lie. Not you. The rest of the world can lie to me, but not you.'

'I'm not.' I moved away from him. 'I wouldn't lie to you.' And as if to prove it, I said immediately, 'I told Maureen to tell Maria not to come to the funeral, I thought it would be best if she didn't see you like this.'

He tried to read my face. 'But that's not what I'm talking about.'

'I know. But it's the only thing I haven't told you. Plus the thing I'm about to tell you. But apart from those things I've kept my word. I would never tell anyone about how we met.'

'What are you about to tell me?' he frowned.

'I'll tell you after.'

'Tell me now.'

'Adam, who do you think I told?'

'Maureen,' he said, getting tense.

'I didn't tell her.'

'She locked me in the room.'

I winced. 'She panicked. I told her to keep an eye on you. That you were having personal problems, that — '

'Jesus Christine.' He didn't shout as loud as last time, I didn't think I'd ever hear that volume from anyone ever again, but the venom was there.

'That's not telling her, Adam.'

290

'It's telling her that there's something wrong.'

It was my turn to explode. 'Do you think there's a person who knows you who *doesn't* realise there's something wrong? Seriously, Adam, think about it. Do you honestly suppose nobody notices? That nobody cares? I had to go out and I was afraid to leave you. Maureen said she'd keep an eye on you. I didn't think she'd lock you up!'

Saying it sounded funny and even though I was angry, I smiled.

'It's not funny,' he said, surprised.

'I know it's not,' I agreed, the corners of my lips still twitching. 'Well, it is, a little.' Then my smile got bigger and wouldn't go away.

'I'm glad you think so,' he muttered, and looked away.

I waited for my nervous giggle to disappear.

'What's the thing you were going to tell me?'

'I went to see Mary today.'

'Mary Keegan?'

I nodded. 'I had a proposal for her. From you. Everyone's in agreement she's your dad's right-hand man, yes?'

He agreed.

'I wondered if it would work if you were chairman of the board, still in full control of the company — which meets the wishes of your grandfather legally — but Mary stepped in as managing director. That way she could run it while you maintain control by signing off on whatever it is that needs to be signed off. Then you could talk to your boss about getting your job back at the coast guard. You can be on

291

boards and have other jobs at the same time, can't you? I'm sure he'd be understanding.'

'So I'd be on the board of Basil's and keep my job.'

'Like Batman.'

He thought about it.

'Hey, don't go overboard with happiness.' I studied him, intrigued. I had solved his problems and yet there was still the battle there. He was wrestling with some inner turmoil. 'You agree it solves the problem?'

'Yeah, absolutely, thank you,' he said, distracted.

Usually, the more you keep pushing in the same direction and to no avail, the more it proves you're doing the wrong thing. I started to think perhaps I was pushing in the wrong direction. I'd spent a week trying to think how Adam could get away from the job he said he loathed but the solution still didn't fit.

'Let's play a game,' I butted into his thoughts.

'You and your games,' he groaned.

'What do you do when you're on your own and no one's looking? And don't be disgusting,' I said quickly, sensing by his look where he was going.

'Well then, nothing,' he said.

I laughed, happy he was back. 'I mean, do you talk to yourself? Sing in the shower? What?'

'Where is this going?'

'Just answer.'

'Will this save my life?'

'It will absolutely save your life.'

'Fine. Yes, I sing in the shower, that's it.'

And I knew he was lying. I cleared my throat. 'For example, when I'm bored, in a waiting room or whatever, I pick a colour and I try to find the number of things in the room with that colour and then I pick another colour and find a number of things in the room with that colour, and whichever colour has the most items in the room wins.'

He twisted around to face me. 'Why the hell would you do that?'

'Who knows?' I laughed. 'People think weird things all the time but never admit it. I also have a thing where I run my tongue along my teeth and I have to count each tooth as I do it. In car journeys, listening to people talk, you know?'

He gave me a weird look.

'Or I try to come up with ideas for my book.'

He looked interested. 'What book?'

'The book that I've always wanted to write. The book I shall some day write.' I got embarrassed and pulled my legs up, tucked them under my chin. 'Or I probably won't. It's just a silly dream I have.'

'That's not silly. You should do it. What would you write? Erotic fiction?'

I laughed. 'Like your friend, Irma? No . . . a self-help book. I don't know what exactly to write it about though.'

'You should do it,' he said encouragingly. 'You'd be great at it.'

I smiled, my cheeks pink, appreciating the encouragement I never got from Barry, and immediately I knew that I'd try it.

'I like to rhyme things,' he said suddenly.

'A-ha, do tell.' I turned my body to face him.

'Not small words,' he said shyly. 'I can't believe I'm telling you this. Maria doesn't even know this.'

Score one to me, I thought childishly.

'Not fat cat, but complicated words like . . . ' He looked around. ' . . . *deciduous* immediately says to me *fastidious*.'

'God, you're so weird.' I threw him a look.

'Hey!'

I laughed. 'I'm joking. That's cool.'

'That's not cool.'

'Hey, the secret mind is a very uncool place.'

'Is that the message?'

I looked out at the lake. 'What about 'Never Ever Have I Ever . . . '? My sisters and I used to play it while in the car on holidays.'

'You all must have near destroyed your dad.'

'I actually think we kept him alive. Okay, you start. Never ever have I ever . . . '

'You know, this sounds remarkably like one of Elaine's 'How to Fall in Love' techniques.'

'Well, maybe I do want you to fall in love.'

I felt his eyes searing into me.

'With life,' I clarified. 'I want you to love life. So go.' I nudged him.

'Okay, never ever have I ever . . . ' He thought about it for some time. ' . . . had a lollipop.'

'What?!' I exploded. 'Explain!'

He laughed. 'We were never allowed to have lollies as kids because they were dangerous. Every day we were told of the dangers: we'd choke, we'd break our teeth, we'd lose an eye or we'd cause someone else to lose an eye. And then finally we were told we could have them, but we had to sit down and eat or else we'd choke and die. I mean, why would any kid want that? So I never had one. It put me off for ever. I can't even stand to watch kids eat them.'

I laughed.

'Your turn.'

'Never ever . . . ' I knew what I wanted to say but wasn't sure whether to say it or not. I swallowed. 'Have I ever . . . been in love.'

He looked at me in surprise. 'But your husband?'

'I thought it was. But I'm beginning to think that it wasn't.'

'Why?'

We looked at each other and I silently said to him in my head, *Because it's nothing like this*, but instead I said, 'I don't know. Do you think that unrequited love is real love?'

'The answer is in the question, isn't it?' he said slowly.

'Yeah, but if it's not reciprocated, is the person experiencing the full, proper thing?'

He thought about it, he *really* thought about it and I waited for an answer that would represent all that thought, but he simply said, 'Yes.' He was obviously thinking about Maria, though I was sure Maria loved him dearly, despite her mistake with Sean.

'Christine, why are we talking about this?'

I really didn't know, I could barely remember how we got on to the topic. I had been trying to distract him and instead I'd ended up wandering into my own thoughts.

'I don't know.' I shivered. 'Let's go inside before we freeze.'

★ ★ ★

Since we were in Adam's territory I asked him to show me around. I wanted to get a feel for his life as a child and what his life would be if he moved back from Dublin, I wanted to know what it was that freaked him out so much that he became a different person down here. Adam took a car from the garage, which housed a selection of classic cars and sports cars in storage, and he drove us to the Basil's factory twenty minutes away, pointing out landmarks and sites associated with stories from his childhood.

'One of my ideas was to arrange tours of the factory. We could make money from it,' he said, thoughtful. 'I brought it to Dad, but he wasn't too keen.'

'What were your other ideas?' I asked. Mary had said he had some good ideas, which intrigued me. He'd given the impression he didn't care at all about the business, but being here had opened my eyes to the reality that he had cared, only his father had shut him down time and time again.

'An adventure park.'

'Seriously? Like Disney World?'

'Not that elaborate, but maybe a petting zoo, playgrounds, a restaurant, that kind of thing. It's being done elsewhere, I know that, and I thought it would be good for the area as a whole.'

'What did your dad say?'

His face darkened and he didn't respond. He indicated to pull into the factory and Mr Basil's — now Adam's — car space, but there was a car already there.

'What the hell?'

'Whose car is that?'

'I've absolutely no idea.'

He parked elsewhere and we made our way inside, Adam with a worried expression on his face as the weight of the world had once again landed on him and only him. I had a feeling I wasn't going to get my tour when I saw what was happening in the office. A meeting was in progress. An entire table filled with men in suits, no sign of Mary, and a strange woman in a trouser suit holding court. The woman looked out of the boardroom window, saw Adam and excused herself from the room. All the heads followed her, then turned back to each other to utter quiet words in ears before she returned.

'Ah, Adam, nice of you to join us.'

'Lavinia,' he said, shocked. 'What are you doing here?'

They didn't embrace, there was no warmth.

'A little birdy told me our daddy died. Hadn't you heard?'

He glared at her.

'I'm running the company, Adam, what do you think I'm doing?' she said firmly.

'You live in Boston. You can't run the company.'

'We're moving back. Maurice has agreed to face the music. He's co-operating with the gardaí, or at least he's going to. We've a few things to tie up first.' She smiled tightly but it didn't reach her eyes.

'You mean you talked him into taking the fall,' he accused.

She looked at me. 'Is this a new girl or has Maria finally changed her lipstick?'

He ignored the question. 'What do you think you're doing, Lavinia?'

'Everyone knows Daddy wanted me in charge, so I'm in charge. I'm merely obeying his wishes. God knows you wouldn't.'

'He was leaving that job to me.'

'Adam, let's not have one of your dramas. I'm back now and everything is going to be under control, so you can toddle off to Dublin and get on with your life. Everyone knows you don't want anything to do with the company.'

He looked at her coolly. 'That's where you're wrong.'

And I felt the direction shift, and in that moment everything clicked into place and I knew this time I was on course.

★   ★   ★

That night we lay in the same bedroom, me in the large bed, Adam on the couch at my feet. I was holding my breath while I listened to his breathing, which was solid and rhythmic. I listened and hoped; hoped that he would keep breathing for a long time, that his heart would keep pumping. It was as if I was relishing the sound of him living. It became so relaxing to me that I finally let go and breathed easily. I wasn't sure who fell asleep first, but the sound of his breathing near me carried me off delicately into a blissful sleep for the first time in a very long time.

21

How to Dig a Hole to the
Other Side of the World

'Our brother has gone to his place of rest in the peace of Christ. May the Lord now welcome him to the table of God's children in Heaven. With faith and hope in eternal life, let us assist him with our prayers.'

The congregation were standing at the Basil plot in Terryglass — Tír Dhá Ghlas, meaning the land of the two streams — at the north-eastern shore where the River Shannon entered Lough Derg. The world and its wife had turned out for Dick Basil's funeral; not because he was a popular man, no, they knew that wasn't true, but because of what he had brought to the community, to the communities, to the country. With a factory employing more than eight hundred people there were many families wondering and worrying about their jobs and their children's jobs now that Mr Basil had passed away. Hundreds of families survived on Basil pay cheques. He may have been a rude, arrogant man who took no prisoners and thought little of friendship, but he was a loyal man, a patriotic man who had been born and bred in North Tipperary. Though he travelled the world in his private jet, he always came home to the place he loved and did his best to help the

300

people and its villages and towns. In the midst of a recession, with rising industrial, labour and energy costs, he'd held strong to keep production in this place he loved when the cost-effective option would have been to move it overseas. Now the future of the factory was in jeopardy. Dick Basil had his own personal reasons for keeping the business close, and locals feared that whoever came after him wouldn't feel the same loyalty to the area, particularly if either of his children, Lavinia and Adam, who were standing by the graveside, both looking cold — and only one of them from the icy weather — took over. Two kids who had moved out of North Tipperary at the earliest opportunity; one who regularly graced the society pages hosting glamorous charity dos and lunches in designer dresses, the other out of public view, rescuing others in the Irish Coast Guard. One had a kindness, the other was selfish. They hoped for Adam but knew Lavinia was the business brain, though there had been accusations implicating her in a foul Ponzi scheme. Now it was rumoured her children had been enrolled in a nearby boarding school, adding fuel to the fire. And then there was their cousin Nigel, hiding among the black suits by the graveside, who since taking charge of Bartholomew's had closed down the Irish factory and moved production to China. Everyone hoped that if he got involved and the two companies merged, as rumour suggested, he wouldn't close down the Tipperary factory as well. They were keeping an eye on him. They watched everyone's faces, looking for signs of what was to come, until it was time for the congregation to bow their heads for the rite of committal. Change was ahead, they all knew it and were readying themselves. It was imminent and it was inevitable.

I felt awkward, standing between Lavinia and Adam at the graveside. Lavinia was wearing large black bug-eyed glasses and a severe black coat that looked like something from the Victorian era. Her blonde hair was perfectly coloured and coiffed, her forehead unnaturally wrinkle-free, her lips nicely plump and freshly injected. Her husband appeared significantly more aged than she. They were actually the same age, but recent problems and the looming threat of imprisonment had reduced him to a grey-haired, white-faced old man. The children stood beside him, ten and eight, their faces showing little sign of grief for their loving grandfather, because that man did not exist to them.

In the distance the cameras continued to snap. Click click click. Paparazzi and news photographers were competing for the best photo of the disgraced businessman who had returned to Ireland to bury his father-in-law. People like Lavinia frightened me. Cold, calculating, emotionally stunted, undefeatable, they were cockroaches skilled in survival, even if it meant destroying their adversaries in the process, even if those adversaries were their nearest and dearest. Their thinking was unnatural, their 'love' unnatural. Having seen her in action, I shared Adam's conviction that his sister was involved in the Ponzi scheme, yet somehow she had convinced her husband to fall on his sword and absolve her. It was a calculated move that had nothing to do with guilt and penance and everything to do with the legal block on Lavinia receiving her inheritance until she'd been working at the company for ten years.

I had read my piece as Adam had asked and when the Mass came to an end Lavinia had lifted her chin and looked down her nose at me.

'Lovely reading. Very moving,' she'd said with a smirk, as if the very idea of her being moved by anything other than a court order amused her.

The funeral, the whole day, was nothing other than awkward for me. I'd been rudely ignored by some while others had offered sympathies for a loss I couldn't feel. Old women with pinched, sympathetic faces had clasped my hands and squeezed them in an effort to convey their understanding of my pain, when the only pain I felt was in my fingers and knuckles as a result of their iron grip on me.

As the coffin was lowered into the ground I felt a shift in Adam's bodyweight, I felt his shoulder shake, his hand go to his face. I knew he'd want this moment to himself but I couldn't help it, I reached out and took his free hand in mine. He looked at me in surprise and I realised his eyes were completely dry. He was grinning from ear to ear, his hand trying to cover his smile. I looked at him in shock, my eyes widening, warning him to stop. People would see, cameras were pointed at him, but knowing this only made me want to laugh too. Laughing as his father's coffin was being lowered into the ground and earth was tossed on top had to be the number one most inappropriate moment, but that just made the laughter all the harder to suppress.

'What was that about?' I asked as soon as the crowd began dispersing and we were free to make our way through the well-wishers to the car. There was no limousine for the family; Lavinia and Adam had no intention of sharing a car. As chief mourner, Lavinia rode in the front car with Maurice and the children, while Pat, silent as usual, drove Adam and me in his dad's car, which was now nominally Adam's though Lavinia had announced her intention to challenge that.

'I'm sorry, it was just a thought that came into my head.' He smiled again, a laugh bubbling under the surface. 'I'm not going to pretend to be sad, Christine. I mean, I am genuinely sad that my father has passed away. It's a sad day, a sad thing, but I'm not going to mope around, acting like my world has fallen apart. And I'm not going to apologise for that. Believe it or not, you can be a fully functioning human being after the death of a loved one.'

I was surprised by this display of strength. 'So tell me what you found so funny as they lowered your father's body into the earth for eternity?'

He bit his lip, and shook his head, the smile forming on his face again. 'I was trying to remember him. I was trying to recall something moving, a moment we shared together. It's a big deal, seeing your father lowered into the ground,

I was trying to *feel* the loss, honour him . . . I thought having an appropriate memory would be fitting for the moment, respectful.' He laughed again. 'But all I could think about was the last time I spoke to him. The last time I saw him, you know, in the hospital.'

'Of course I remember. I was there.'

'But you weren't. After I was released by security and they took everyone out of the room, he and I spoke. I wanted to make sure he knew I hadn't done what Nigel accused me of. It was important to me that he knew that.'

I nodded.

He smiled. 'He didn't believe me. And he said . . . ' He started laughing again and I couldn't help but join in. 'He said, 'I don't like that bitch. Not at all. Not one bit.'' He could barely get the words out, he was laughing so hard. 'And then I left,' he squeaked, forcing the last words out.

I stopped laughing, not finding it funny any more. 'Who was he talking about?'

He managed to stop laughing for a split second to squeeze the word out, but then collapsed again into wheezy hysterics. 'You.'

It took me a while to see the funny side and the more I *didn't* laugh, the more he laughed, the more hysterical he became and the more contagious his laughter became to me. Pat had to drive around the estate for ten minutes so Adam could compose himself before joining the funeral-goers, and by that time his eyes were red raw from laughter and he looked like he'd been crying.

'I don't really get why it's so funny,' I said, wiping my eyes as we made our way up the steps to the mansion.

I could hear the rumble of polite reserved conversation inside. It seemed the whole of North Tipperary had turned out, and the Taoiseach's aide de camp was present; my dad had been right about the Basil family's connections.

Adam stopped on the stairs and gave me a look, a peculiar look that made my stomach go all funny. He looked as if he was going to say something but the door was pulled open wide and Maureen greeted us with a panicked look.

'Adam, there are gardaí in the drawing room.'

★ ★ ★

Adam said he'd called it the bad news room when he was growing up, and the name had stuck with him. The wood-panelled room had been the parlour of the original house, before the building was extended three thousand times in every direction. It was the room in which his mother had learned she had cancer, it was the room she'd died in, and while mourners gathered across the hall to mark Dick Basil's death, it was the room where Maurice Murphy, husband of Lavinia, was arrested by the guards before being led to a waiting patrol car and driven to the station for questioning, and it was where the family would subsequently learn that he was being charged with eleven counts of theft

306

and eighteen of deception for the sum of fifteen million euro. The remaining five million could not be taken into account as Mr Basil had refused to press charges and now was dead and buried, silenced for ever.

22

How to Solve Will and Inheritance
Disputes in Eight Easy Ways

'I don't understand why *she* has to be here,'
Lavinia said, neck tall and chin high as though
she had an invisible brace on which prevented
her from assuming the posture of a normal
human being.

I squirmed in the leather couch. I completely
agreed with Lavinia; why I was there was beyond
me too. It felt inappropriate to be present at such
a private affair — the reading of Dick Basil's will
— but Adam had insisted on me being there and
I had gone along with it even though I wasn't
sure why. For all I knew, he was worried he
might feel an uncontrollable urge to leap out the
window or cut himself with the letter opener or
do some damage with the eighteenth-century
poker in the fireplace if he didn't like what he
heard when the will was read. I still wasn't sure
what exactly he wanted to hear; I don't think he
was too sure either. All along I'd assumed that
the worst thing for Adam would be ending up as
CEO of Basil's, which was why I'd tried to figure
out ways to relieve him of that duty. But as soon
as Lavinia came into the picture, he suddenly
declared he wanted the job. Now he was on a
mission to ensure she had nothing to do with the
company. It was as if the minute she showed up

he realised he cared. It wasn't only duty, or a sense of rising to the occasion and doing what one must, it went deeper than that. Basil's was in his heart. It was a part of his make-up as much as his flesh and bones were. It had taken losing it for him to realise that.

'I should leave,' I whispered to Adam.

'You're staying,' he said firmly, not bothering to whisper. All heads turned to look at us.

We all sat fidgeting nervously: Adam and me on one brown leather couch, and on the other Lavinia and Maurice, whose lawyers had got him out on bail only an hour or so earlier. He appeared to be on the verge of a coronary; his eyes were red and raw, his face sagged with exhaustion, and his skin was dry and blotchy.

The reason everyone was nervous was because while Adam believed, and had been told, the job would go to him, now that the eldest child, Lavinia, was home she had prior claim. Plus there was no knowing what she might have done to secure her future while her father was on his death bed. So now Adam wanted the job and Lavinia wanted it more than ever.

Arthur May, the lawyer, cleared his throat. A seventy-year-old with long wavy grey hair, slicked with gel and tucked behind his ears, and a beard like a musketeer, he had attended the same boarding school as Dick Basil and was one of the few men that he'd trusted. There was a moment's silence while he looked around to ensure he had everyone's attention, then he began reading the will in a clear, crisp, authoritative voice that made it clear here was a man who was not to be argued with. When he reached the part where, in accordance with Richard Basil's wishes and in compliance with the last will and testament of the late Bartholomew Basil, Adam Richard Bartholomew Basil was to take control of Basil's and become its CEO, Lavinia jumped up out of the couch and screeched. No words in particular, just a banshee wail, as if she were a woman who'd been accused of witchery and tied to a burning stake.

'Impossible!' she spluttered, suddenly coherent again. 'Arthur, how could this be?' She turned and pointed an accusing finger at Adam. 'You tricked him! You tricked a dying old man.'

'No, Lavinia, that's what you tried to do,' Adam said coolly. He was utterly calm. I couldn't quite believe it; here he was, completely at peace with the decision and the role, when only a week or so earlier he had been threatening to jump off a bridge.

'This bitch had something to do with it!' She pointed her manicured nail at me. My heart hammered at suddenly being the centre of attention in another family's mess.

'Leave her out of it, Lavinia. It's got nothing to do with her.'

'You've always been the same, Adam — pussy-whipped by every woman you've ever been with. Barbara, Maria, and now this one. Well, I've seen your funny little bedroom arrangements and I can guess what's going on!' She narrowed her eyes at me and I recoiled. 'What, she won't sleep with you until you're married? She wants your money, Adam. *Our* money — and she's not

310

getting it. Don't think you can fool me, you little bitch.'

'Lavinia!' Adam exploded in that terrifying angry voice. He shot up from the couch as if he wanted to rip his sister's head off and eat it. Lavinia was immediately silenced. 'The reason Father left the company to me is because you *stole* five million from him. Remember?'

'Don't be so childish!' Tellingly, she looked away as she said this. 'He gave it to us to invest.'

'Oh, it's *us* now, is it? Pity Maurice has to face the music on his own, isn't it, Maurice?'

If Maurice had looked to be a broken man before, he seemed close to disintegration now.

'That's right, Lavinia,' Adam continued, 'Father gave the money to you to invest — in your villa in Nice, in the extension to your house, in all those fancy soirées you hosted to get your face in magazines and raise money for charities that I'm beginning to wonder even existed.'

'It wasn't like that,' Maurice said quietly, shaking his head and looking at the ground as if reading the words from the carpet. 'It wasn't like that at all.'

He'd probably been repeating the phrase continuously since the police took him in for questioning. He lifted his eyes to the lawyer, his voice still worryingly subdued. 'What about the children, Arthur? Did he include them?'

Arthur cleared his throat, put on his glasses, happy to get back to the point. 'Portia and Finn are to receive their inheritance of two hundred

311

and fifty thousand apiece on their eighteenth birthdays.'

Lavinia's ears pricked up. 'And what about me? His daughter?' She'd lost out on the big prize of running the company, but what was behind door number two? Perhaps she could save herself yet?

'He left you the holiday home in Kerry,' Arthur replied.

Even Adam was stunned. From the expression on his face he was veering between finding it amusing and feeling guilty for his sister who wanted and wanted so much that eventually she'd attracted her fears and lost everything.

'That house is a shit hole!' she shouted. 'A rat wouldn't holiday there, let alone live in the dump.'

Arthur looked at her as if he'd seen it all before and was tired of the histrionics.

'And what about this house?'

'It has been left to Adam,' he said.

'This is a fucking disgrace!' she spat. 'Granddad's will is perfectly clear: in the event of Dad's death, the company falls to *me*.'

'If I may explain . . . ' Arthur May took off his glasses slowly. 'Your grandfather stated that on your father's death the company should pass to the eldest sibling, which indeed is you, Lavinia. But there was a clause, of which you may not be aware, stating that if the eldest child were to be convicted of a felony or crime, or declared bankrupt, the company would pass to the next in line.'

Her mouth fell open.

312

'And I believe,' Arthur continued, giving her a long look with dancing blue eyes, which made me think he was rather enjoying this, 'that, leaving aside the recent criminal charges and whatever other actions may be pending, you have recently declared yourself bankrupt.'

'Jesus, Lavinia!' Maurice leapt to his feet, suddenly animated. 'You said that this would be okay. You said you had a plan. That it would work. I don't see it bloody working, do you?'

It was obvious from Lavinia's reaction that this was rare behaviour from him.

'Okay, darling,' she said in a calm, measured voice. 'I understand. I'm surprised too. Daddy gave me his word, but I think now he set me up. He told me to come home. Let's go somewhere to talk about this. *People can hear.*'

'I have spent the entire day, *the entire day* being harassed and interrogated over and over — '

'Okay, sweetheart,' she interrupted nervously.

'Do you know what they said I could get?'

'They're only trying to scare — '

'Ten years.' His voice trembled. 'The average sentence is ten years. TEN YEARS!' he yelled in her face, as if he didn't think she'd grasped the importance of what he was telling her.

'I know, dear.'

'For a crime I was not alone in — '

'Okay, darling, okay.' She smiled nervously, reaching for his arm in an effort to usher him out of the room. 'Clearly Daddy has tried to have his last laugh.' Her voice trembled then. 'But that's okay, I have a sense of humour too and I'll have

313

my last laugh. I'll contest this will,' she said, composure fully gathered.

'You don't have a leg to stand on,' Adam said. 'Give it up, Lavinia.'

I barely recognised the man I had seen trembling on the bridge, the man who had been silenced in his father's presence, who had retreated into his shell as soon as we'd driven through the gates of his home. Nor did Lavinia, evidently, because she was looking at him as if he had been possessed. But it didn't stop her getting in one last killer insult:

'You don't know the first thing about running a business. You fly helicopters, for Christ's sake. You are utterly inadequate and emotionally incapable of dealing with the pressures of running a business. You will ruin this company, Adam.' She tried to stare him down, but it didn't work. In the end she stormed out of the room with Maurice in tow, his energy spent now, shuffling along behind her like a shadow.

'I'm sorry about that, Arthur,' Adam said.

'Not to worry, old chap.' Arthur got to his feet and started packing up his briefcase. 'I quite enjoyed it,' he admitted, a mischievous glint twinkling in his eye.

Adam's phone rang. A concerned expression came over his face as he looked at the screen, and he excused himself and moved to the corner of the room to take the call.

Arthur leaned across to me and said quietly, 'I don't know what you're doing with this man, but keep doing it — I haven't seen Lavinia get a talking to like that in a very long time and I can't

314

recall this young man ever looking quite so self-assured. It rather suits him.'

I smiled, feeling proud of Adam and of how far he'd come, all in a little under two weeks. But at the same time he had a long road ahead of him — and I wasn't only thinking about Basil's and the pressures that would bring. The problems Adam had weren't the kind that would go away overnight, or even in two weeks. I could only hope he was in a better place now, with the tools to help himself. If not, I had failed.

'Arthur, it looks as though you're going to be busy for a while,' Adam said, coming off the phone. 'That was Nigel. It seems Lavinia had already done a deal with him to merge Bartholomew and Basil and sell the whole lot to Mr Moo.'

'The ice cream company?' Arthur asked, astonished.

Adam nodded. 'They were working on the fine print and were all set to announce it as soon as Lavinia got control.'

Arthur thought about it, then laughed. 'Your father certainly led her down the garden path. He took great delight in doing it, too.' Then he got serious. 'She acted without any authority whatsoever. Lavinia has no role in Basil, it won't stand up . . . unless, of course, you want it to?'

Adam shook his head.

Arthur smiled. 'Nigel is going to be one very angry boy.'

'I'm used to angry Basils.'

'You probably don't care to hear it, Adam, but your father would be proud of you. He wouldn't tell you, of course, he'd rather die first — which he has. But take it from me, kid, he'd be proud of you. He told me you didn't want the company, but — ' He held his hand up to stop Adam explaining. ' — I feel you should know that we worked hard over the last few months, drawing up this will. It was most definitely you he wanted at the helm.'

Adam nodded his gratitude. 'You'll miss him, Arthur. Friends for how long?'

'Sixty-five years.' Arthur smiled sadly, then he chuckled. 'Ah, who am I kidding? I'll be the only one who misses the old bastard.'

I looked at Adam, hands in the pockets of his smart suit, standing by the old fireplace in the mansion, a portrait of his grandfather above the mantelpiece, the resemblance startling. He was delicious. We locked eyes then and my heart began to hammer. My stomach flipped and whirled, I couldn't take my eyes off him and hoped he couldn't read how I was feeling.

'You asked me what I used to do here, when I was all alone as a boy.'

I nodded, happy he had spoken first, not trusting myself to say anything.

'It's noon.' He checked his watch. 'We have four more hours of light and then we can head back to Dublin. Okay with you?'

I nodded. The longer I had him to myself, the better.

★ ★ ★

In four hours, I got a taste of what his life had been like at Avalon Manor. We went out on the

316

near-freezing lake in the boat, we ate a picnic that Maureen had prepared for us: cucumber sandwiches and freshly squeezed orange juice, because that's what he used to have. Then we climbed in a golf buggy and he drove me around the two-thousand-acre estate. We went clay-pigeon shooting, had a go at archery, he showed me where he went fishing . . . But the longest time was spent sitting in the boatshed, wrapped in blankets, drinking hot whisky from flasks, watching the sun going down on the lake.

He sighed, a heavy weary sigh.

I looked at him.

'Am I going to be able to do this?'

My mind ran through a selection of words and phrases from my positive-thinking books, but in the end I stopped myself, settling instead on a simple, 'Yes.'

'Everything is possible with you, isn't it?'

'Most things are possible.' Then, more to myself. 'But not everything.'

'Like what?'

Like me and you.

23

How to Prepare Yourself for a Goodbye

Late afternoon darkness began to descend and after a magical few hours, feeling as if it was just the two of us alone in the world, I came back to earth with a thud. It was time to return to Dublin. Pat drove us and we travelled in a comfortable silence. There was the occasional attempt at chat, but each time we plummeted into silence again my stomach twisted with knots. The closer we got to Dublin, the nearer his birthday drew, and soon it would be time for us to say goodbye. An intense two weeks, over before we knew it. The most intense two weeks of my life, in fact, finished, just like that. Of course it was possible we'd be able to see each other again, but it would never be the same, it would never be as intimate, as intense. And I should have been happy. I should have been celebrating: when I met him, he wanted his life to end, and now he seemed to be on the right road to finding his way. If I cared about him, the last thing I should want was for him to need me the way he had back then.

Pat turned off the motorway and headed for the city centre.

'Where are we going?' I asked, sitting up.

'I booked a room in the Morrison Hotel,'

Adam explained. 'It's nearer City Hall. I thought it would be easier.'

I felt my chest tighten and a light panic setting in. We were separating, parting ways. Deep breaths. Deep breaths. In out, in out. Perhaps it was me who had the separation anxiety and not him.

'But our time's not up yet. We have one day left. Adam, if you think you're getting rid of me before this is done, you're wrong. I'm sleeping on your couch.'

He smiled. 'I'm fine.'

He looked fine.

'Well, maybe you are right now, at this moment, but we both know how quickly that can change. Besides, you have so much work to do on yourself. This is only the beginning, you know. And you really need to agree to see a therapist.'

'I agree,' he said simply. He looked amused.

'This isn't funny, Adam. Just because Maria is coming to the party doesn't mean anything for sure, not yet. I insist on staying with you until our deal is done.'

'I got us connecting rooms.' He smiled. 'And thanks for the reminder.'

I paused, embarrassed. 'Oh. I wasn't trying to panic you, I was only, you know, trying to *prepare* you for what might happen.' And again it struck me that I was the one who needed to be prepared.

When we arrived at the Morrison Hotel we were escorted straight up in the elevator to the top floor, where Adam had booked a two-bedroom penthouse suite.

'The view you requested, sir,' the concierge said proudly.

I walked to the floor-to-ceiling windows and peered out. Our room overlooked the River Liffey, and right below our window was the Ha'penny Bridge, shining gloriously, lit up on this dark evening with green uplighters and its three decorative lamps shining out over the water. I looked at Adam, alarm bells ringing in my head, but I tried not to react.

'Happy?' Adam asked.

'Our rooms aren't connecting,' I said cheekily.

'No,' he laughed. 'They seem to be separated by a dining area, a kitchen and a living room.' He looked at me, amused. 'I thought you'd like it.'

It was the most luxurious room I had ever been in, and I'd only ever been in two truly luxurious rooms, both courtesy of Adam.

'It's amazing.' I nodded. *Apart from the view*.

It was late by the time we got to the hotel and neither of us wanted to do anything other than order room service and watch TV on the enormous plasma, sitting on the enormous couch. I was more comfortable with Adam just sitting in and doing nothing than I had ever been with Barry. We were easy together. The icing on the cake was that I very much, very very much wanted to sleep with Adam. I'd had little desire to do so with Barry. I'd found his uncertainty sweet at first, but then as time went on it began to frustrate me; I wanted definite, manly, certain hands on my body and I was irritated by how unsatisfied I felt afterwards, with him panting beside me, breathless, while I hadn't even begun.

Of course in the beginning things had been different, but all too soon we became far too settled in our established routines and patterns. And we hadn't even been married one year. I couldn't imagine what we would have been like after thirty years.

Whereas Adam . . . being with Adam made me feel alive. Adam intoxicated me with dizzying effects. Despite the enormous couch, we sat close to each other in the middle. I was like a schoolgirl with a crush. I felt myself freeze and get all giddy. *He was close to me!* When our elbows brushed, I felt on fire. I couldn't concentrate on the movie. I was too happy, too light-headed, too sizzling and fizzling at that moment to be able to concentrate. I was also too aware of his proximity, his bare feet on the stool we both shared, his muscular body in tracksuit bottoms and T-shirt, reclining next to me, chilled out and oh so sexy at the same time.

I was afraid to move my eyes from the TV, afraid to look at him in case it was obvious, in case it showed, in case he realised the woman whom he trusted to help him out of the depths of his despair was secretly dreaming about pulling down his trousers and taking him right there on the couch. I peeked at him from the corner of my eye: he was staring at the TV, totally absorbed, his hand moving mechanically from the popcorn bowl to his mouth. I looked quickly, saw the popcorn fall between his plump lips. I swallowed. Took another sip of my drink.

'I'm going to have a shower,' he said suddenly, putting the bowl on the foot-rest. Then he left the room. The enormous couch seemed even more so now there was only me, and I felt like an idiot. I held my head in my hands, bounced my head repeatedly against my tucked-up knees and tried to remind myself that the man I was obsessing about had vowed to kill himself if he didn't get his girlfriend back by his birthday. His *girlfriend*. His birthday was tomorrow. The last thing he was thinking about was having sex with me.

I needed to get back into my role. I had seriously lost the plot. I put down the glass of champagne, feeling suddenly embarrassed, like I was the only girl at the party because the party was over and it had taken me until now to realise it. I straightened up, my cheeks blazing with the embarrassment of what I had been thinking, how selfish I had been — not to mention how dangerous it would have been, with Adam in his current state of mind.

Walking on tiptoe, I made my way to his bedroom and pressed my ear up against the door. I expected to hear the usual sobs, but all I could hear was the water falling in uneven patterns as his body moved around beneath the flow, sending it splashing in different directions. No tears. I smiled. He was ready. I needed Maria not to ruin it for him. I padded across the luxurious carpet to my bedroom, undressed for bed, and dialled Amelia's number. I had been so overwhelmed by my own life over the past few days I hadn't even thought to call her and see how she was doing. The phone rang and rang and finally a breathless Amelia picked up.

'What were you doing, a marathon?' I joked tiredly, trying to pep myself up for her.

'No, sorry I was, er . . . uh,' she giggled. 'Sorry. Are you okay? I mean, how are you?'

I frowned, listened closely to the background.

'Hello?' she asked again. I heard whispering.

'Who are you with?'

'Me?'

'Yes, you.' I smiled.

'Er . . . Bobby. You know. He's helping with the uh, search.'

I heard a snort in the background.

'Are you in Kenmare?'

'No. We abandoned that idea for now, we kind of got side-tracked with something else here, you see.' She giggled again. 'Christine, you *know* I can't talk right now.'

I laughed. 'Yeah, I'm getting that. I wanted to see if you're okay, that's all.'

Amelia's voice became clearer then. 'You know, the weird thing is, I am. I really, truly am.'

'Good.'

'How about you? I know tomorrow's the . . . birthday party. How is Adam? How's it all going?'

'Yeah, good,' I replied, and heard the tremble in my voice. 'I'll talk to you tomorrow. I'll let you get back to whatever you were doing.'

I hung up and held my head in my hands. When I looked up I saw Adam at the door, the door I always left open to listen out for him during the night. He was dripping wet, the towel wrapped low around his waist. Water dripped from his nose and chin as though he'd literally rushed from the shower without so much as a wipe down. He absent-mindedly wiped it away, pushed back his hair, smoothed it down with his two hands. As he did so, he further revealed his muscular body. I was staring unashamedly, feeling that his suddenly arriving at my door half-naked gave me licence.

I tried to think what to say. *Are you okay?* Or *Can I help you?* No, too shop-assistant-like. So I didn't say anything, I stood in my underwear, looking at him and being looked at. Then suddenly, very suddenly, for the first time in two weeks he stepped over the threshold, from his world into my world, and he was in my room and he was coming towards me, and my face was in his hands and he was looking down at me and the shower water from his hair was dripping on to my skin, his lips were on mine and he held me there, long and beautiful, a gentle brushing of his lips against mine for the longest time. I was afraid he was going to pull away then, that he'd decided this was all a mistake, but instead he parted my lips with his bottom lip and pushed his tongue inside my mouth. Finally believing he wasn't going away, I lifted my hands to his body and moved closer. I felt dizzy, everything rushing around inside me like a panicked messenger trying to share the news. I literally melted and came alive at the same time, a bizarre state of affairs. I led him to the bed, and as we lay down he ended our kiss and opened his eyes. He smiled at me, I smiled back and we continued.

We continued two more times.

While Adam was sleeping beneath me, his arms wrapped around my body, my head rising and falling on his chest, I felt contented and sleepy. Something about his heartbeat, his breathing, him *living*, had helped me to relax most nights that we shared the same room. It was one fix that my *How to Quiet Your Mind and Get Some Sleep* book had failed to mention: Fall in love with a beautiful man and listen to his heartbeat. He helped me to relax and I drifted off.

When I closed my eyes I was at the apartment complex with Detective Maguire, only this time the apartment complex was a rundown Avalon Manor, in Tipperary. There was yellow crime-scene tape around the building and Simon was on the roof. Detective Maguire was getting a ladder for me to climb, but I was protesting that I couldn't climb it because I was wearing a dress and it was windy. In the end though I climbed the ladder, my dress blowing up around my waist and everyone below me laughing. I had forgotten to put my underwear on because I had just had sex with Adam, which is what I told them. Maria was there and they all agreed I should be arrested for being so inappropriate. Everybody agreed, even Leo Arnold, who was standing beside Maria. Detective Maguire told them all that he would arrest me, but first I must save Simon. He began calling up to me on the ladder, negotiating a deal: if I saved Simon, he wouldn't arrest me. But he was laughing while he said it, jeering at me. Nevertheless I agreed and we made the pact. I climbed and climbed the ladder, not getting anywhere, everyone laughing beneath me as my skirt continued to billow out for all to see. Suddenly the ladder began to tilt backward, away from the house. I looked up and saw Simon on the edge of the roof; he was crying, looking at me with the exact look he'd had on his face that night. I could see the blame in his face, that if I didn't get to him he'd die. Maguire, Maria and Leo were roaring with laughter. The ladder was in limbo, hovering, going across to Simon and then changing its mind and moving backward again, and there was nothing I could do to stop it. Then Adam was there, mortified by me and my obvious failure, wishing he'd never met me. He was telling everybody this, and it was the last thing I heard before the ladder began to tilt back completely and I started plummeting backwards to the ground.

I woke up with a start. I looked at the clock and saw I'd only been asleep for twenty minutes.

'Okay?' Adam grumbled.

'Mmm.'

His arms were wrapped around me tightly, his chest rose and fell, and I drifted off again. I was back in the apartment block, the real one this time, only it was fully furnished and people were living there, every single apartment teeming with sounds of life, the way it was meant to be. Simon was standing before me with a banana in his hand, which he'd taken from the fruit bowl on the kitchen counter. He was telling me that it was a gun.

I started to speak, but I spoke too fast and my words blurred together, and didn't make any sense. Somehow he understood though. When I was finished my nonsensical talk, he put the gun down on the counter. I sighed with relief. I looked around for Detective Maguire, but there was no one there, so I waited for the gardaí to take over; I'd done the job, I was finished, I'd talked him down! But nobody came. Where was everybody? I was so relieved yet at the same time anxious, my heart was beating wildly in my chest. He was looking lost, exhausted from the experience. I knew I should say something, fill the silence.

'Now you can go home, Simon, home to your girls.'

I knew it was wrong as soon as I said it. The whole time he had been telling me that this apartment was his home, that they had tried to take him away from his home, and all he wanted to do was return with his family, to the home he'd saved for, the home he'd bought with his wife, the home he planned to live in with his children — their first home together as a family. The room suddenly emptied, became grey and unlived in, and I realised we *were* standing in his home. I had said the wrong thing. He looked up at me, and I knew instantly I'd made a mistake.

He picked up the banana, which had become a gun.

'This *is* my home.' He pulled the trigger.

★　★　★

I woke up, his words ringing in my ears. My heart was pounding in my chest, Adam was no longer beneath me, he was beside me in bed, the clock read four a.m. I sat up, hot and sticky from the dream, panic and dread twisting through my body at the memory of what had happened. I reached for the notepad beside the bed and wrote, *Had to go. Will explain. See you later.*

I pondered adding a X, but decided against it. I didn't want to come across as too attached, too presumptuous. By then I had wasted enough time and didn't have time to ponder it any more. I would be back before he woke up, hopefully. I got out of bed, threw on some clothes, and I was soon in reception waiting for a taxi. Twenty minutes later I was at the hospital.

I burst into the ward and, from the look on my face, security knew to let me through. Thankfully, Angela was on duty.

'Christine, what's wrong?'

'It was my fault,' I said, tears coming to my eyes.

'It's not your fault, I told you that.'

'I have to tell him. I remember now. I have to say sorry.' I tried to push past Angela, but she held me back.

'Now you're not going anywhere until you calm down, do you hear me?' Her voice was firm. A nurse stepped out from the station to see if everything was okay and, not wanting to make a scene, I immediately forced myself to calm down.

★ ★ ★

I sat at Simon's bedside, fidgeting. He had been taken off the life-support unit while I was in Tipperary, but he was still in intensive care. He was breathing unassisted though he still hadn't opened his eyes or fully regained consciousness. My fingers trembled as the words I uttered on the night of his shooting — which I'd forgotten, had somehow blocked out — came reverberating around my head, taunting me, blaming me, pointing the finger at me accusingly.

'Simon, I'm here to apologise. I've remembered what I said. You probably remembered all along and wanted to scream it at me, but now I know,' I sniffled. 'You had put the gun down. You let me call the guards. You looked different, relieved, and then I was so relieved, so happy to have prevented you from shooting yourself, but I didn't know what to do. It was probably only five seconds, but it felt so long. I was afraid you would pick up the gun again.' I squeezed my eyes shut, the tears rolled down my cheeks and I put myself back in the room from over a month ago. ' "Well done, Simon," ' I repeated. ' "The guards are on their way. They're going to bring you home, to your wife and girls.' And you suddenly looked different. It was because of what I'd said, wasn't it? *Home*. I said go *home*, but you'd spent the entire time telling me this was your home, the one you'd been forced to leave. I did listen to you, Simon, I completely understood, I . . . slipped up, at the end. I made a mistake and I'm sorry.'

I wanted to take his hand but felt any contact would be an intrusion. I wasn't a friend, I wasn't family, I was the woman who had failed to save him from himself.

'It would be wrong of me, selfish of me to suggest that there was a reason for you doing what you did, that any good at all could possibly have come from what you've done, but when I lost you I became so desperate to never make the same mistake again that I went beyond, have been going way beyond, in my efforts to save another man's life. And if I hadn't failed with you, then I may not have succeeded with him. I want you to know that.' I thought of Adam and the night we had shared together and I smiled briefly.

I sat with him in a long silence. Suddenly there was a loud beeping from a machine beside the bed. I froze at first and then jumped up. At the same time Angela came rushing into the room, and jumped into action.

'I was only talking to him,' I said, panicked. 'What did I do?'

'You didn't do anything,' she said quickly. She rushed to the door, fired a list of orders to another nurse on duty, then looked at me. 'You didn't do anything. Stop blaming yourself. I'm glad you were with him. Now go.'

The room became a flurry of activity and I left.

Simon Conway was pronounced dead that night.

24

How to Wallow in Your Despair in One Easy Way

I arrived back at the Morrison Hotel suite at five thirty a.m., exhausted and completely drained. I wanted to climb back into bed beside Adam's warm strong body, feel secure, have him recharge me with love and joy, belief and goodness again. This was what I'd expected to do, but when I walked into the suite, he was already up.

The sight of him made me smile and my heart lift, seeing him medicine enough for me, but then I saw the look on his face as I walked into the room and my smile disappeared. Warning bells rang. I knew regret when I saw it, I'd been looking at it in the mirror every day since I married Barry. I readied myself, steeled my heart, built up my wall around myself in preparation for the attack. The ice queen defences were engaged.

'You've been crying,' he said.

I looked at my reflection in the hall mirror and I was a mess. The clothes I'd thrown on were a mismatch, my hair hadn't been brushed, I wasn't wearing make-up, my nose was red, my skin blotchy. I didn't exactly look a sight to win him over. I was about to tell him about Simon when it began.

It began with a look and I knew, I knew it before he even said the words, immediately feeling like a piece of filth who had taken advantage of a sick man, and I wanted the moment to be over already so I could collect my bag and do the walk of shame back to Clontarf. Had I learned nothing from the Simon Conway experience? What had I done to Adam? He looked a mess; had I undone all the good work he had done on himself, made him confused and disgusted with himself, disoriented enough to send him straight back to the bridge beneath our window? How could I leave him now? In this state? Even when he asked me to leave?

'It's not . . . we shouldn't have . . . I shouldn't have . . . ' he tried to start it off. 'I take full responsibility,' he said finally. 'I'm sorry, Christine. I shouldn't have . . . come to you last night.'

'No, I should have known better,' I swallowed, my voice husky, sounding as if it'd had to travel a great distance. 'You have Maria, the big party, big day and exciting news to share with the world about your job, so don't worry.' I helped him say the words. 'Let's forget what happened. And please,' I placed a hand on my chest and my voice cracked, 'forgive me. I apologise from the bottom of my heart for being too . . . ' *Damaging? Needy? Selfishly looking after my own needs when I should have been thinking of his?* Where was I to start?

He looked sad.

'It was wrong.' I tried to keep my chin up, but how could I? I felt so awkward. 'Sorry,' I whispered, moving quickly to the bedroom. 'I don't want to leave you in case . . . '

'I'm fine,' he said. He was drained, exhausted, but I believed him. My being there wouldn't help anything now. I would have to risk leaving him alone.

'I'll see you later?' he asked. 'At the party?'

I froze. 'You still want me to come?'

'Of course.'

'Adam, you don't have to — '

'I want you to be there,' he said firmly, and I nodded, hoping now that Maria would complete the picture so that he wouldn't need my presence as he thought he might.

I did well to last until I'd arrived in my flat to break down in tears.

★   ★   ★

I hid in bed in the flat, ignored the phone, the door and the world while I covered my head with the duvet and wished I could take it all back. But the problem was, I couldn't even wish for that properly because last night had been so good, so incredible, something I had never experienced before, more than just good sex. Adam had been tender and loving, but I'd felt a connection, he'd been so confident and assured as if he knew it were the right thing. There was no hesitation, no tentative kisses or touches. And if at any stage I felt a tiny flutter of doubt, one look in his eyes, one kiss was enough to know that it was the right and most natural thing in the world. It wasn't like any one-night stand I'd ever had, it was

333

tender, we'd made love, like our history had made it really mean something and silent promises were being made for the future. Or else Adam was just that good and I was an absolute mug.

I had been ignoring my phone and door, but that wasn't to say anybody had bothered to call me. I knew this because I'd checked. I had the phone with me under the duvet and as I was consciously ignoring it I had to keep checking to see who it was I was ignoring. Nobody. But it was Saturday morning and most people were in bed or enjoying family time and weren't bothering to text. Not even Adam. It was the first time in two weeks that I wasn't with him and I missed him terribly, I felt a hole in my life.

The doorbell rang.

My heart lifted at the thought of Adam at the door, heart in his hands, or even better, his heart on a lily pad, offering it to me. But deep down I knew it would not be Adam at the door.

The doorbell rang again, which, when I thought about it, was unusual. Nobody knew I lived there, apart from family and close friends. Most of my friends were busy with their new young families or were hungover in bed. Unless it was Amelia. I knew she'd picked up on my sadness last night over the phone and I wouldn't have been surprised if she was there with two coffees in her hand, a bag full of cupcakes, ready to help lift me. She had been known to do it in the past. The doorbell rang again and, warming to the idea of coffee and sympathy, I threw off the covers, not caring how I looked, and dragged myself to the door. I pulled open the door, expecting to see my shoulder to cry on and instead was faced with Barry.

He looked more surprised to see me than I did him, despite the fact he'd rung the bell four times.

'I didn't think you'd be here,' he said, looking me up and down.

I wrapped my cardigan tighter around my body.

'Then why did you keep ringing the bell?'

'I don't know. I came all this way.' He shrugged. He looked me up and down again, clearly unimpressed with my appearance. 'You look terrible.'

'That's because I feel terrible.'

'Well, that's what you get,' he said childishly.

I rolled my eyes. 'What's in the box?'

'A few of your things.'

It looked more like a pathetic excuse to come over and harass me. Chargers from phones I'd long ago thrown out, headphones, empty CD cases.

'I knew you'd want this,' he said, clearing away the junk on the top and revealing my mother's jewellery box.

I immediately burst into tears, my hands flying to my face. He was taken aback, not knowing what to do. It had previously been his job to comfort me, it had been mine to let him, to *want* him to, but we stood there like two strangers — except two strangers would be kinder, as I cried and he watched me.

'Thank you,' I sniffed, trying to compose myself. I took the box from him and he stood there, uncomfortable, not knowing what to do with his fidgeting hands and no barrier for him to hide behind. He shoved his hands in his pockets.

'I also wanted to say — ' he began.

'No, Barry, please no,' I said weakly, 'because I honestly don't think I can take any more of what you have to say. I'm sorry, you know, I'm *really* sorry, sorrier than you can ever possibly imagine, that I hurt you. What I did was awful, but I couldn't *make* myself love you like you deserve to be loved. We weren't right for each other, Barry. I don't know how else to say sorry, I don't know what else I could have done. Stayed? And let us both be utterly miserable? Jesus . . . ' I wiped my stinging eyes roughly. 'I know I'm in the wrong here, Barry, I'm sorry. I'm sorry. Okay?'

He swallowed, was silent for a while and I braced myself for another of the most hurtful things he could think of to say to me. 'I wanted to say I was sorry,' he mumbled.

That took me by surprise.

'For what exactly?' I said, the anger rising, even though I was trying to suppress it. 'For smashing Julie's car? For cleaning out our joint account? Or for insulting my friends? Because I know I hurt you, Barry, but I didn't go and drag other people into it.'

He looked away. All the sorry seemed to have gone out of him. 'No, not for that,' he said angrily. 'I'm not sorry for any of that.'

336

I couldn't believe his cheek. He composed himself.

'I'm sorry for the voicemail. I shouldn't have said what I said. It was wrong.'

My heart hammered, he could only mean one voicemail, the one I hadn't heard, the one Adam had heard and deleted.

'Which one, Barry? There were an awful lot of them.'

He swallowed. 'The one about your mother, okay? I shouldn't have said it. I wanted to hurt you in the deepest way possible. I know that's your biggest fear so . . . '

He left a silence and I tried to figure it out. After an awkward pause I got it and realised I'd known it the entire time. Sometimes you can know something and not know it at the same time.

'You said I'd kill myself like Mum did,' I said, my voice trembling.

He had the decency to look ashamed. 'I wanted to hurt you.'

'Well, that would have done it,' I said sadly, thinking of Adam listening to the message. So he knew that my mother had killed herself, that in my deepest, darkest moments when everyone told me how alike me and my mother were I'd secretly worried we were too alike. A secret I'd shared with my husband and which had come back to haunt me even at a time when I knew I was not like my mother in that way. My mother had suffered from severe depression all of her life. She had been in and out of clinics and therapy since she was a teenager. Finally, unable

337

to beat the demons in her head, she had taken her life when I was four years old. She had been a thinker, a worrier, a poet. And of all the thoughts and poems she had written throughout her life as she tried to figure out her puzzling head there was one which I had clung to and made my own: the one I had read at the funerals of Amelia's mother and Adam's father.

I had always known, even as a child, how my mother had left the world. By the time I was a teenager, people were constantly telling me how like her I was, and it made me afraid. I came to dread the words, 'You are so like your mother.' Then, as I became an adult and learned about myself, I realised I was not my mother, that I could make different choices to the ones my mother had made.

'So . . . ' Barry said, backing away.

I didn't know what else to say. He walked up the steps to ground level and I started to close the door.

'You were right about us,' I heard him say suddenly. 'We weren't exciting or romantic, we never went anywhere very much and we probably never would. We didn't laugh like Julie and Jack, or travel the world like Sarah and Luke. We probably wouldn't have had four kids like Lucy and John.' He threw his hands up. 'I don't know, Christine, I liked how we were. I'm sorry you didn't.' His voice cracked and so he took a moment. I opened the door wider to see him.

'I've wished for the past month for you to be miserable, absolutely in the depths of hell. And now I see you like this — I can't feel that any more. You look worse than I do.' He shook his head. 'If you left me because you thought this would be an improvement, then we were worse off than I thought. I pity you.'

That set me off again. He took off down the road. I closed the door and returned to bed to hide from the world.

★ ★ ★

A few hours later and I still hadn't moved. I was hungry but I knew there was nothing to eat in the flat and I couldn't face going out to the shops, looking and feeling as I did.

My phone started ringing and I checked the screen to see who I was ignoring. Detective Maguire. I was definitely ignoring it. It stopped and then started again. I stared at the ceiling, my heart beating wildly. It only returned to a regular pace when the ringing stopped. I waited for the ringing to end and put it on silent.

The phone rang again.

'Leave a message,' I growled.

I got out of bed, feeling dizzy when I stood up. Then I thought about Adam and I panicked. Maybe he had done something. I dived for the phone and hit the button to return the last call.

'Maguire,' he barked.

'It's Christine. Is Adam okay?'

'Adam?'

'The man from the bridge.'

'Why, did you lose him?'

Kind of. But I sighed with relief that he wasn't hurt.

'Listen, I need you at Crumlin Hospital now. Can you come?'

'Crumlin?' I stalled. It was a children's hospital.

'Yes, Crumlin,' he snapped. 'Can you come? Now?'

'Why?'

'Because I'm asking you to.'

I was totally confused. 'I can't, I, er . . . I can't right now.' I searched for a lie but couldn't bring myself to do it. 'I'm not feeling good today.'

'Well, snap out of it, because there's someone here who feels a whole lot worse.'

'What is this about? I don't have to go any — '

'Jesus, Christine,' he said, and it came out almost a sob. 'I need you to get your ass down here.'

'Are you okay?'

'Just get here,' he said. 'Please.'

25

How to Ask for Help
Without Losing Face

Detective Maguire was waiting for me at the main entrance to the hospital. As soon as he saw me, he did what he had done every other time I'd met him and turned around and walked away. I took the cue to follow him. I jogged to catch up, and as I did I looked around for his partner. I didn't see him. In fact there was no other back-up whatsoever. I rounded the corner and found it devoid of Detective Maguire. A whistle had me running to the open elevator like the dog he seemed to think I was. I joined him and it was then I saw how awful he looked and my stomach churned, sensing the worst scenario ever. I gulped, trying to steady myself; I was not able for all of this, not so soon after losing Simon, after messing up so spectacularly with Adam, after having to deal with Barry. I needed a day alone, but nobody seemed willing to grant me that small favour. I needed to wallow; much could be achieved from wallowing. Perhaps that's what my book could be about. Christine Rose's *How to Wallow in Your Despair in Five Easy Ways*.

'You look terrible,' I said to him.

'You're not too perky yourself,' he said, without his usual malice. He was going through the motions, barely engaging. Something was most certainly wrong. More wrong than usual.

'Who am I going to see?' I asked.

'My daughter,' he said, his voice hollow, empty. 'She tried to kill herself.'

My mouth fell open and he stepped out of the elevator and rounded the corner. I had to snap out of my shock before the doors closed and the lift descended. I followed him.

'Uh, Detective, I'm very sorry to hear that, truly I am . . . ' I swallowed. 'But can I ask, why did you bring me here?'

'I want you to talk to her for me.'

'What? Wait!' I finally reached out and grabbed him by the arm and stopped him in his tracks. 'You want me to what?'

'Talk to her,' he said, revealing his bloodshot eyes. 'There's people here, but she won't talk to them. She won't say two words. I thought of you. Don't ask me why, I mean I don't know you, but you seem to have a way with this kind of thing and I'm too close to it, I can't . . . ' He shook his head, his eyes welling up.

'Detective — '

'Aidan,' he interrupted.

'Aidan,' I said softly, appreciating the gesture. 'I'm not able. I didn't help Simon Conway, and with Adam I . . . ' I didn't want to get into what had happened with Adam.

'You managed to get Simon to allow you to call us,' he said. 'That was good. You talked Adam Basil off the bridge, and he asked for you after that. I've seen you with him, in the station — he respects you. Plus I know what happened

342

with your mother,' he added.

I looked down. 'Oh.'

'You know about this. Just talk to her, please.'

I followed him through the ward, a series of corridors and confusing turns until finally he brought me into the ward. Of the twelve beds in the room, only one had curtains pulled around it completely.

I slowly drew back the curtain and came face to face with Maguire's wife, Judy, her eyes rimmed with red as she held the hand of the girl in the bed. I looked at the girl: thick auburn hair like her dad, honest crystal-blue eyes like her mother.

'Caroline,' I said gently. The girl's left wrist had been heavily bandaged and lay on the bed, her mother held her right hand tight.

'Who are you?' Judy asked, slowly getting to her feet but still not letting go of her daughter's hand.

'Aidan called me,' I said.

She nodded then and looked down at her daughter. I saw Detective Maguire's face crumble in the moment before he turned away and walked out of the ward, as if embarrassed by his display of emotion.

'Why don't you get some coffee?' I suggested to Judy. 'Caroline, is it okay if I sit with you for a while?'

Caroline looked at me uncertainly. Judy was still hanging on to her hand.

'I think maybe your mum could do with a break. I bet she's been here for a while.'

Caroline gave her a nod and I helped Judy let

go of her hand. As soon as she stepped away, I pulled the curtain across and sat down beside Caroline.

'My name is Christine. I know your dad.'

Caroline eyed me warily. 'Do you work here?'

'No.'

'So I don't have to talk to you.'

'No. You don't.'

She was silent as she mulled it over. 'They keep sending people to talk to me. Asking me why, why, why. They left a bunch of leaflets. They're disgusting. Insinuating disgusting things.'

'What kinds of things?'

'Like, did my dad touch me — stuff like that. I mean, they didn't say it in so many words, but I could tell they were wondering. Then they gave me all these leaflets. I've seen the shows.'

'I'm not going to ask you anything like that, believe me. I'm not a doctor, I'm not a therapist. I want to talk, that's all. It sounds like you've had a really hard time and I want to listen to you, without judgement.'

'Are you a garda?'

'No.'

The girl gave me a sidelong look, then played with the sheets on the bed with her good hand. The other remained limp and unmoving. 'So why did my dad ask you to come?'

'Because he knows that when I was young my mother killed herself.'

She looked at me then, gave me her full attention.

'She killed herself when I was four years old. So I understand what it's like, to live with

344

someone who felt the way you do.'

'Oh.' She looked down at her bandage. 'I'm sorry.'

'I understand why you don't want to talk to your parents. It's embarrassing, isn't it? My dad is still embarrassing and I'm thirty-three years old.'

Caroline smiled weakly.

'But that's why it's okay if you want to talk to me. I won't judge you, I won't tell you that you shouldn't have done this or done that, I'll just listen. Sometimes it helps to talk, to say things out loud. And if you don't know where to turn or who to talk to, you can ask me and I'll do whatever I can to help. There's always someone to turn to, Caroline. And we can keep it between the two of us — you won't have to worry about me telling anybody you don't want to know.'

Caroline's face crumpled and she started to cry. She tried to hide behind her good wrist, leaving the other one lying flat on the bed as if it had been forgotten, as if it had died in the attempt. Her shoulders shook as she was wracked with sobs.

'I didn't think there was anyone,' she admitted.

'Now you know,' I said gently, giving her a tissue. 'There is always someone to hear you and help you. Always.'

She wiped her eyes, composed herself, seemed to think about things.

'I slit my wrists,' she said. She lifted her hand up and showed me her bandage as if I hadn't noticed it already. 'I suppose you think I'm a

345

crazy person.' She studied me.

I shook my head.

'I went online and found out how to do it. I used my razor, but it was too difficult. It took me too long to break the skin. And it hurt. Nothing was happening to me, even though it was bleeding. I was lying there on the bed, waiting to die, but nothing happened. It just hurt. I had to go back online and see what I'd done wrong. Eventually I went downstairs to Mum to show her because I was scared.' She kept crying. 'Mum was screaming at me: *What did you do? What did you do?* And I swear I wanted to go upstairs and do it again so I could die and not have to see the way she looked at me. I felt like a freak. Dad won't stop asking me why. I've never seen him so angry. It's like he wants to kill me.'

'He doesn't want to kill you, Caroline. He's shocked and scared and all he wants to do is to protect you. Your parents want to make things better. They want to understand so that they can help.'

'They'll kill me.' She started sobbing again. 'Is that how you felt? Did you hate your mum?'

'No,' I said soothingly, tears coming to my eyes at the hazy memories of Dad coming home from the hospital, a fake jolly look in his eye as if they'd been on holiday, and Mum lying out on a deck chair in the back garden, fully clothed in the pouring rain because she wanted to 'feel something'. Even when she was in the room with me it felt like she wasn't there at all. I loved her, all I wanted was to sit with her, be with her. I would hold her hand and wonder if she even

346

noticed I was there. 'I never hated her, not for one minute.' I left a silence. 'Why was it so unbearable for you? What happened?'

'I can't tell them. Anyway, they'll find out soon enough. I'm surprised they don't know already. Every day I'd come home from school and I'd be waiting for them to realise. I was terrified. At school everyone knows, everyone's looking at me, laughing at me, saying stuff to me. Even my own friends. I had no one — no one who would help me, no one who'd talk to me. Not even Aisling . . . ' she trailed off, confusion and betrayal all over her face.

'Aisling's your friend?'

'Was. She was my best friend. Since we were five. She wouldn't even look at me. For a whole month. First it was everyone else and she was still my friend, but then it got worse: they started leaving things in my locker, gross things, they kept saying stuff on Facebook, spreading lies. Then they started dragging Aisling too, saying stuff about her too. She blamed me for what was happening and then she stopped being my friend. I mean, how could she?'

'Something happened that everyone found out about?' I guessed.

She nodded, tears streaming down her face.

'Online?'

She nodded again. Then she was surprised. 'Do you know?'

'No. You're not the first person it's happened to, Caroline. Were you . . . in a compromised position?'

'He told me it would just be for us,' she said,

347

her face crimson. 'And I believed him. And then a friend of mine texted me and said it was up on Facebook, and then everyone started ringing me. Some were laughing about it, some were really angry, calling me a whore and all sorts — people I thought were my friends. I went online to see it and I swear I was sick. *I* don't even want to see me doing that, never mind strangers. It was meant to be for a laugh, for us. I didn't think he would show anyone. I thought maybe a friend had taken his phone and done it, or it had been hacked, but . . . '

'What did he say?'

'He wouldn't talk to me, wouldn't even look at me. Then one day I got hold of him, told him how I felt about it, how I couldn't go on any more, and he just looked at me and laughed. He *laughed*. He couldn't understand why I was so upset. He said I should be happy. That loads of celebs have become famous because of it and now they're millionaires. I mean, we live in fucking Crumlin! How famous are we going to become? Where's our millions after that?' She started crying again.

'Were you and him having sex, Caroline?'

She was mortified by the question and it took her a while to tell me: she'd been giving him a blow-job, while they were at a house party one night, and they'd both had too much to drink. It was his idea to film it. He'd already started filming her before she had a chance to object, and when she saw the camera was on her she didn't want to stop, she didn't want to look like a 'wuss'.

'When did this happen?' I asked, anger rising in me. If I felt like this, I could imagine Detective Maguire's reaction. He'd make life hell for the boy with the camera phone, but after what he'd done that boy should consider himself lucky if Maguire at least let him live. I didn't envy Caroline, being a teenager nowadays; the landscape of issues such as trust and intimacy and sex had completely changed since I was her age, leaving boys and girls navigating a minefield.

'About two months ago, but he put the video up three weeks ago. I tried to ignore it. I tried to keep going to school, keep my head down, ignore them all, but I'm still getting text messages from people. Look.' She handed me her phone and I scrolled through the texts from her so-called friends, most of them so abhorrently evil I could barely believe what I was reading.

I understood why Caroline had felt she had nowhere to turn. Her friends had turned their backs on her; the guy she fancied had laughed at her, made a mockery of her; she was being taunted daily in the small world that was social networking — a world no one could escape, where lies flourished like bacteria before anyone had the chance to prove them wrong. And the poor girl was too embarrassed and too afraid to turn to her parents, afraid they'd 'kill' her. So she decided to do it to herself instead, end the embarrassment, the pain, the loneliness. A permanent solution to a temporary problem. This pain would not last for ever; she would bear the scars of the experience and she would remember it for the rest of her life, no doubt it would influence every decision she made from this moment on. But where pain was, healing could come; where loneliness was, new relationships could be formed; where rejection was, new love could be found. It was a moment. And moments changed. She would have to live through the moment to get to the next.

'Will you tell them?' she asked, her voice tiny, her body skinny and childish in the bed. 'Please?'

We parted ways, Caroline promising to keep in touch with me or with the numbers in the pamphlets the hospital had already given her if she ever needed somebody to talk to. I made my way out to the corridor where Judy was sitting semi-comatose on a plastic chair and where Detective Maguire was pacing like a caged animal.

'Tell us,' he barked as soon as I neared him.

'No,' I said firmly. 'I'm not going to tell you anything until you make a promise.'

He looked as if he was going to bite my head off.

'You will have to hold your temper. Caroline is so scared of your reaction — right now she's feeling isolated and fearful of being rejected by you. You want to help her, suspend your judgement and give her the support she needs from you.'

'Aidan.' Judy put her hand on his arm. 'Listen to her.'

'She already knows she's made a mistake; do not lecture her. Do not make her feel foolish. Not now, not while she's so vulnerable.'

Judy nodded her head emphatically, looking from me to her husband as if willing the understanding into him.

'She needs your unconditional love and support. She needs you to tell her you are not angry. You are not ashamed. You are not disgusted. You love her. You are there for her.'

He mumbled something that sounded like a threat.

'I'm serious, Aidan. You're not dealing with one of your criminals now. Caroline is your daughter. It's time you cut the intimidation, leave out the interrogation and the downright bull-headedness and *listen* to what she has to say.'

And then I told them what she had told me.

He listened this time. Judy's fingers turned white as she squeezed his arm while I spoke. She dug her nails into him when it seemed like he was going to bolt — either to his daughter's side or to find the boy who did this to her — but he stayed and I stayed with him till the red rage that I saw in his eyes left and was replaced by fatherly concern and a heart filled with love. Then I watched as he walked away from me, hand in hand with Judy, the two of them propping each other up as they approached their daughter.

Exhausted, I left the hospital to go home and prepare for Adam's birthday party. Despite his claim that he was in a good place now, Adam had barely begun on the road to healing himself. I was hoping Maria would show up and love him. If she didn't, I was afraid I could lose the man I loved for ever.

26

How to Find the Positive in a Catch-22

When I arrived at City Hall, late, Adam was standing at the main entrance greeting his guests. He was dazzling in his tuxedo and he took my breath away when I stepped out of the taxi. It was only when the taxi driver shouted at me to close the door because I was letting all the heat out that I realised I had frozen in place, transfixed by the sight.

Unlike my sisters, who had already arrived and had splashed out on new gowns for the black-tie event, I had gone against the grain of my multi-coloured wardrobe and settled for a gown that fitted my mood: my trusty full-length black dress, with a high neckline but a split up the thigh and backless. The split had raised somewhat as I'd climbed out of the taxi and now it ripped higher. As I tried to cover the bare thigh on display, I realised that Adam was no longer greeting guests but had turned to watch my-less-than graceful and entirely revealing entrance. I pulled my second leg out of the car, adjusted my faux-fur wrap and ascended the stairs, Adam's eyes on me the entire way. I felt every bit as naked and exposed as I had been on the ladder in my dream, even though I was wearing knickers this time. It was all I could do to mask my humiliation and heartbreak, let alone look him in the eye. So I didn't.

'You look beautiful,' he murmured.

He didn't do awkward very well. He was calm, solid, watchful, in control. This was the Adam of the past few days, the one I wasn't used to dealing with.

'Uh, thanks. I didn't have much time to get ready,' I said. 'Barry called around this morning, and someone else needed some help, and I don't know if you heard but Simon Conway, the guy who . . . you know, well, he passed away last night. That's where I was this morning when I left the room, so it's been one of those days.' Still feeling sorry for myself, my eyes filled and I looked away.

'Hold on, what?' he asked, concerned.

'Which part do you want me to repeat?'

'Simon died this morning?' His face immediately seemed to pale. 'That's why you left?'

I nodded. 'Well, I left because I remembered something that I had to tell him. But then I got there and he went into cardiac arrest.' I shuddered. It hadn't been a good day, it had begun with death, and I hoped it wouldn't end that way.

Adam seemed shaken by that news, relating to Simon and his woes far more than I would have expected.

'So is she here?'

He took a moment to register the subject change, my body language change, then dealt with it well, the way he could tell I wanted him to.

'No. Not yet.'

353

'Oh,' I said, surprised. 'I thought she'd be here at seven.'

'Me too,' he said, looking at the door again, anxiously.

It was eight p.m.

I had an intense feeling of relief, quickly followed by one of dread as my catch-22 situation once again kicked in. If it didn't work out with Maria then it wouldn't be my arms Adam fell into, it would most likely be the nearest bridge or the tallest building. I needed Maria to come and tell him she loved him or I wouldn't even be able to love him from afar. Suddenly, pining for him and *not* having him was vital, it was a treat, it was a bonus. It was the perspective I needed.

'Listen, Adam,' I pulled myself together and looked him in the eye, 'if she doesn't come tonight I need you to think of the crisis plan. I know we had a deal, but I want you to know I don't approve of it. I don't want you to . . . ' I swallowed, 'kill yourself. Think of all the things that we discussed. Remember the plan? You survived these past two weeks, didn't you? Use the tools I gave you. If for whatever reason anything goes wrong tonight — not that it will,' I said hurriedly, 'but if it does, remember what I taught you.'

'Happy birthday!' I heard a female voice behind me. Right when I should have felt jubilant, that defeated feeling came over me again.

Adam's eyes were still on me.

Maria joined us. 'Sorry, am I disturbing you?'

'No,' I said, blinking away my tears. 'I'm so glad you came,' I added, my words a whisper. 'He's all yours.'

★ ★ ★

'Is everything sorted?' Dad asked as I joined them.

All I could manage was a nod; I couldn't trust myself to speak as my eyes filled up with tears.

'Ooh, I knew it,' Brenda said sympathetically, wrapping her arms around me. 'You're in love with him, aren't you? Here.' She grabbed a champagne flute from a passing tray. 'Get drunk, it will numb the pain.'

I sipped the bubbles, wishing that were true.

'While we're on the subject of heartbreak,' Adrienne said, 'Graham and I broke up.'

She didn't quite get the same reaction from the family as I had.

'He didn't get the cakes made of cheese,' Dad said, disappointed. 'Why didn't he get the cakes made of cheese?'

I shrugged.

'But they're so clever,' he continued, confused.

'Not that anyone seems to care, there was something not quite right between us,' Adrienne added huffily.

'A penis, perhaps,' Dad said, and I couldn't help but giggle.

'Ah there she is, my baby girl!' He winked at me. 'Tell me, where is this dastardly girlfriend of his that you worked so hard to get him back

355

together with, so I can throw angry father stares in her direction.'

'Oh don't, Dad,' I sighed. 'They're perfect for each other, they're meant to be. I mean, the man was about to throw himself off a bridge if he couldn't get her back. How romantic is that?'

'Not romantic at all,' Adrienne said, still unhappy that her announcement had been overlooked.

'*Saving* him from jumping off a bridge is far more romantic,' Brenda said.

'You're lucky you saved him,' Dad said, then they all went quiet.

It had been almost thirty years since our mother had taken her life, since Dad had walked in to find her on the floor of their bathroom with the empty pill bottle beside her body. He had confessed to us that he hadn't tried to save her, a revelation we had been in various degrees of understanding about. Brenda understood, Adrienne saw his point of view but wished that he had called the ambulance services sooner, and I hadn't spoken to him for months. I had been nineteen and at college when he told me. Thinking I could save everyone or at least wanted to attempt to save everyone, I told him I would never forgive him. It had been hard on Dad at the time, because he had saved his wife six times already. He had given her CPR twice, pulled her out of a bath, done God knows what else, rushed her to hospital so many times he just didn't have it in him to keep trying, to persuade her to stay.

'You know what, Dad,' I said suddenly. 'I think

356

you did save her. She didn't want to be here.'

He was so moved by that he had to look away to compose himself.

'There she is,' I said, watching Maria enter the room ahead of Adam.

'Ooh, I won't know whether to shake his hand or lick his face,' Brenda said.

'Please shake his hand,' I said.

'Is that her? With the red lips?' Adrienne asked.

'You want to lick her face, don't you?' Dad said to her.

Adrienne giggled.

I sighed. 'I knew it. I told you she was beautiful.'

'In a Morticia Addams kind of way,' said Brenda.

Adam and Maria made their way into the room, Maria greeting people warmly, obviously familiar with most of the guests from her time with Adam. I downed my champagne and plucked the flute from Brenda's hands.

'Hey!' she protested, then gave up.

Then there was a tapping of a glass and everyone looked to a man on stage who was trying to hush the crowd.

He thanked a few illustrious guests for being there — the Minister for Trade, not the Taoiseach as Dad had been hoping for — and each time he named someone of importance Dad made an impressed face. He talked about the sad passing of Mr Richard Basil, who would be greatly missed — clearly he hadn't known him very well — and then announced Adam as

357

the new CEO of Basil Confectionery. There was a great cheer from the crowd and Adam moved towards the stage.

He climbed the steps and took his place, looking like a movie star.

'A friend of mine helped me word this speech tonight,' he said, looking out to the crowd. Maria smiled at him proudly from the wings and my throat tightened. 'I'm not the best at talking about how I'm feeling. Nights like this aren't always the easiest as it's overwhelming, but *I'm feeling* . . . honoured that you've all come here today. I've heard talk that it's a new beginning for Basil, but I'm hoping it's more of a continuation of its success, perhaps the beginning of new growth for the company. *I'm feeling* . . . uplifted and sustained by so many kind words so many people have had to say about my father, though it is clear, despite your good intentions, that you are all liars.'

That got a laugh from the crowd.

'My father was a lot of things, but mostly he was good at his job.'

Some nodding of heads. I spotted Arthur May, the solicitor, among the crowd.

'He put his heart and soul into the business. In fact I think he poured so much into the business that he had very little left for the rest of us.'

They laughed again.

'*I'm feeling* . . . proud that he has named me as his successor, that he felt me able for this role. I know that myself and the board and the wonderful Mary Keegan, our new MD, are united in our goals for the company. *I'm*

358

feeling . . . ready. My experience may be short and my task unfamiliar, but I have in my father and grandfather an example that I can follow with certainty and with confidence as I take on the traditions of Basil while at the same time looking to the future. And finally, I owe a great thank you to those who planned this evening and those it took to get me here.' His eyes rested on me. There was a considerable silence. He cleared his throat. 'Thank you from a full heart.'

As everyone broke into applause, I moved through the crowd, hurried, I couldn't get out of the room fast enough, I couldn't get enough air. I ran down a flight of stairs, grateful to find the toilets empty during the speeches, locked myself in a cubicle and burst into tears.

★　★　★

'Christine?'

It was Brenda's voice. I froze. The bathroom had filled up very quickly after the speeches had ended and there was a queue outside the cubicles. I was waiting for my puffy eyes to calm down before I risked opening the door to reveal a tear-stained face to anyone who might be out there. The problem was, I had been in there for so long I was a constant subject of debate for the queue outside.

'Christine?' Adrienne called. 'Christine, are you in here?'

'We think that one is out of order,' someone said.

Mortified, I took out my phone and started

furiously texting my sisters to leave me alone, but they began banging on the door, startling me and ending my frantic text.

'Christine, is Adam in there with you?' Adrienne asked, right outside the door.

'Adam?! Of course not!' I blurted out. I'd given myself away and I heard a woman in the queue say, 'It must have been the vol-au-vents.'

'He's missing,' Brenda said quickly. 'Did you hear that? They're bringing out the cake and no one can find him.'

'He's not with Maria, if that's what you're thinking,' Adrienne added.

That was exactly what I'd been thinking.

'We asked her where he was as she was leaving. She said she had no idea.' Adrienne lowered her voice and must have come closer to the door because it sounded right on top of her. 'They didn't get back together, Christine.' Her voice was low and urgent.

All of a sudden my pulse was throbbing in my ears and I could hear nothing else and couldn't wait to get out of there. I opened the door and suddenly didn't care about the twenty women staring at me or the fact no one would go into my cubicle after I'd been in there for so long. All I could see was Brenda and Adrienne's concerned faces — faces that never showed concern, not to their baby sister who was always far too concerned; instead they always maintained a breezy repartee that was meant to jolly me along just in case, God forbid, I *was* like Mum after all. But now they were looking at me, serious, concerned, panicked.

'Do you know where he is?' Brenda asked and I wracked my brain, searching, trawling through our conversation archive for a hint of where he could be.

'No, I don't know,' I stammered, trying to think straight. 'I can't believe Maria did that to him,' I said angrily. *Twice* now she'd broken his heart — couldn't she see how amazing he was?! 'I should have stayed with him, what was I thinking?'

'Okay, don't worry about that now, just focus on where he'd be. Think hard.'

I thought of the penthouse, the night we'd spent together, his last night. The view of the Ha'penny Bridge. I froze. He'd been planning it all along.

'She knows,' Adrienne said.

'Go, Christine,' Brenda urged me.

I lifted up the hem of my dress and I ran. Running in heels was no easy task, but a piece of glass in my bare foot wasn't an option either. Nor was jumping into the car with Pat, who was parked up outside. I needed to take a right on Parliament Street to get to the bridge, and that was a one-way street. Pat would only be bringing me away from the bridge to get closer to it. We didn't have time for that. I ran through the freezing temperatures, hanging on to my faux-fur shawl with one hand while holding my dress up with the other. I ran down Parliament Street and right on to Wellington Quay, attracting glances and comments from Saturday-night revellers. I saw the bridge in the distance but couldn't see anybody on it. I kept running, the cold burning my nostrils as I breathed it in, my chest burning as I gasped for air. As the bridge came nearer, I saw him. In exactly the same place we'd met two weeks previously, a figure in black, standing beneath the orange glow of the three lamps, the green uplighters casting him and the bridge in an eerie light. Despite my exhaustion, I dug deep within me for more energy and sprinted to the bridge. I ascended the steps.

'Adam!' I yelled, and he turned to face me, startled. 'Don't do this, please!'

He looked at me, concern, sadness, surprise on his face.

'I'm not going to touch you, I'm not going to come closer, okay?'

People kept walking across the bridge, unsure of what to do, stepping around Adam in a wide circle, afraid, as if he were a landmine.

I was crying. I had started some time during my sprint to the bridge and now I stood before him, a cold, shaky, out of breath, snivelling wreck.

He didn't say a word.

'I know things didn't work out with Maria . . . ' I tried to catch my breath. 'And I'm sorry about that, I'm so so sorry. I know you love her and I know you feel as though you have nothing now. That's not true. You have Basil's and there's a room full of people who are excited about that. And you have . . . ' I wracked my brain. ' . . . so so much. Your health, your friends . . . ' I gulped. 'And you have me.' I lifted my hands up, pathetically. 'I know I'm not what you want, but I'd be at the end of the phone any time. I swear I'd do anything to help you, to make you happy. Truth is,' I took a deep breath, '*I* need *you*. When we first met and I promised to show you the beauty of the world, I didn't know what the hell to do. I bought a book!' I laughed, pitifully. 'But you can't chase happiness. Joy happens spontaneously — it's not some generic, by-numbers formula that you follow. Only I didn't know that, I didn't know what to do. I think I'd stopped seeing the beauty of the world for a while, without even realising it. Being with you . . . you helped me to see how beautiful life is, how *fun* it is. You were my wonderfully bespoke original guide to happiness. You showed me that doing simple things are all you need as long as you're doing them with someone who *wants* to be with you. I was supposed to teach you and listen to you, but it was you who ended up showing me the way. And I know this isn't what you want to hear, but you helped me fall in love. Proper love. Not just with life.' I swallowed. 'But with you. I think I've always tried to play it safe. I've always tried to fix things for everyone around me and I've always been with people that are . . . safe.'

I thought of Barry and of our relationship. I had chosen somebody I'd known there'd be no drama with, no surprises, nothing that would break so I wouldn't have to fix it. I hadn't allowed myself to really fall in love. Not until I met Adam, who had brought nothing but drama and surprise every day I'd spent with him.

'I don't care if my love is requited or not, because being with you and the very *thought* of

363

you makes me happy. The point I'm trying to make is that you are loved because *I* love you, Adam. Please, don't do it. Please don't jump because *I* need *you*.'

Adam's eyes were filled with tears. A couple who had lingered to listen were standing holding hands and cooing, obviously missing the part that Adam was threatening to jump off the bridge.

I felt rather pathetic, spent after my revelations. I was drained and freezing cold. Pouring my heart out was all I could do to save him. So I waited, hoping, wishing, praying, that he would not only hear but *feel* my words, that they would somehow penetrate that part of his brain that was manipulating him into thinking none of it was worthwhile any more. I had failed with Simon, I could not, would not fail with Adam.

'Look at me,' he said.

I couldn't do it. I didn't want to hear his reasoning or his goodbye. I started crying even more.

'Look at him,' the woman urged and I looked up.

Adam had a smile on his face, and I was confused. This wasn't funny, why was he finding this funny? The couple were smiling too, as if there was a joke no one had let me in on. I felt like smacking them and saying, *You don't understand — a life is at stake here!*

'What side of the bridge am I on?' he said, smile still on his face.

'What?' I frowned, looking from him to the

364

couple. 'What are you talking about?' Was it metaphorical? Was it supposed to mean something? He was still grinning at me, completely calm, as though he was thinking rationally when I knew he wasn't. I thought back to when I first saw him on the bridge, he had been standing on the *other side*, his feet on the ledge, close to jumping off. I looked at him now, his feet on the concrete, not hanging over the edge, not clinging to the wrong side of the railings. He was standing on the bridge looking out at the view, which meant he hadn't been about to jump!

'Oh fuck,' I whispered.

'Come here,' he laughed, holding his arms out to me.

I clasped my hands to my head in utter embarrassment, cursing my sisters, cursing him, cursing myself. I had revealed my soul to him. I took steps backwards, mortified. 'Oh, shit, sorry, I thought that, my sisters said that, I assumed, wrongly that . . . '

He walked toward me, reached for me and stopped me from moving away. He was so tall he had to look down at me.

'I told Maria it wouldn't work with her and me.'

My mouth fell open. 'You what? What did you do that for?'

He seemed amused by me. 'Because I meant it. She hurt me, I don't want to go back there. I understand she wasn't treated how she should have been the past year, but I apologised for that. She admitted that she was moved by everything I had done to win her back, but what she was really nostalgic for was the old us, the way we were at the beginning. I suppose I was too. But I know now that we can't be that couple any more — too much has changed, life has moved on. We're over, there's no going back. I don't want to go backwards.'

I shivered, still in shock, and he pulled me close.

'Maria said to me, 'Is it because of that girl?' And I realised that was a big part of it.'

'What girl?' I asked, feeling like I was totally losing the plot.

Adam laughed.

'Adam, this is not funny. I have no idea what's going on. A minute ago I thought you were about to jump because you had no Maria, now you're telling me you weren't going to jump, and you don't want Maria because of some other girl that you never mentioned anything to me about. And I told you things,' I moaned, resting my head on his chest, mortified by what I'd said.

'Did you mean those things?' he asked softly.

'Of course I did.' I cringed. 'I wouldn't have said them if I didn't mean them. But, Adam, you have to understand why I said them. The circumstances — '

'You're the girl,' he interrupted my rambling. That stopped me. 'The girl Maria was talking about. I realised I don't love Maria. Whether I'm with her or not isn't going to determine whether I live or die. My problem was, I was unhappy with me. You made me like me again. You helped me live my life again. And whether I have you or not, it won't mean I'll jump, or end my life. I

366

need to be happy with me. All those things we did for Maria, I enjoyed them because I did them with you. I had fun with you. She may have been the reason, but you were the cause. While you were trying to make Maria fall in love with me, and make me fall in love with life, I fell in love with you.'

His hands were on my face, my stunned face. He laughed nervously. 'You can stop looking at me like that now.'

'Sorry,' I whispered.

'When I woke up this morning and you were gone, I thought that you had changed your mind,' he explained.

'No, I — '

'And then when you came back to the bedroom and you'd been crying, I thought you were going to tell me you'd regretted it.'

'No, I — '

'When you told me about Simon it made sense. I got it all wrong. I wanted to say it to you before you said it to me. I thought I'd make it easier on you.'

'You're an idiot,' I said gently, finally allowed to speak.

He smiled.

'Kiss,' the woman beside us said.

'I have conditions,' I announced, stopping him.

He pulled back.

'You know you still have a long way to go,' I said. 'I helped you in the best way that I could, and I'll continue to do that, but I'm clearly no therapist, Adam, I don't know how to help you when you become . . . that man.'

'I know,' he said, serious then. 'I came here to think about how far I've come. I'm not the same man that stood here two weeks ago, but I know I can be that person again if I don't get help, if I don't help myself. I feel like I've been given a chance to live — you helped me get that chance, and I'm going to grab it and try to make the best of it. I'm sure I'll mess up sometimes, but I actually feel for the first time in a long time that I want to try to enjoy my life. So yes, I'll start seeing someone about it. I don't want to get that low ever again.'

We locked eyes and smiled. He leaned toward me and we kissed. The man and woman cheered and then I heard their footsteps as they left us alone and made their way across the bridge.

★　★　★

Adam took off his tuxedo jacket and draped it around my shivering shoulders. My teeth were chattering, my toes ice-cold.

'I forgot to give you this.' He reached into his pocket and retrieved my mother's missing earring. 'Pat found it in the car this morning.'

'Thank you,' I whispered, filled with relief. I held the emerald stone in my hand tightly, feeling honoured that my mother had become part of one of the most outstanding moments of my life. I could feel her there with me.

'We can't leave the party,' I protested as Adam led me off the opposite side of the bridge.

'We already have.' He wrapped his arms

368

around me. 'It's my party, I can do what I like. And I'm taking the woman I love back to my hotel.'

I smiled. 'You know, I came up with an idea for my book,' I said coyly. I'd had the idea while I spent the day huddled under my duvet, crying over my life. Inspiration came from the most unusual places.

'You did? What is it?'

'It's called *How to Fall in Love*. It's going to be the story of how I met you.'

He smiled. 'You'll have to change our names.'

'I'll have to do more than that. I think there's a reason it's taken me ten years to start it. I was trying to write the wrong thing. I'm going to write it as fiction; that way no one will know it's true.'

'Except us,' he said, kissing my nose and taking my hand.

'Except us,' I agreed.

We walked hand-in-hand across the Ha'penny Bridge, safely to the other side.

27

How to Celebrate Your Achievements

I was positioned on Talbot Street with a 'Congratulations' banner in my hand, a party hat on my head and a party blower in my mouth. I was receiving some nasty glares from people passing, but I tried to ignore my embarrassment and concentrated on the people disembarking from the bus directly in front of me. Last off was Oscar, who looked rather shaky as he concentrated, head down, on making his way down the steps.

I blew the party blower and he looked up in surprise. His face broke into a smile and he laughed as I waved the banner in his face, attracting smiles from the crowd.

'You did it!' I shouted. 'You made it all the way into town!'

He grinned, embarrassed but proud.

'How do you feel?'

'Like . . . I'm *alive*!' he punched the air with his fist, as if he was going to burst.

'Good!' I laughed. 'And you remember this feeling Oscar, whenever you have a down day or a wobbly moment, remember how good it is to *feel alive*. Okay?'

He nodded enthusiastically, 'Absolutely, absolutely, I won't ever forget this.'

'Call Gemma and make an appointment for

Tuesday. We'll work on you getting a job, now that you can travel into the city.'

'Gemma's back? I like Gemma. But you know I always prefer Mondays. It helps me begin my week,' he said, concerned.

Gemma had agreed to come back after I'd posted her a *How to Tell Someone You've Changed Your Mind Without Appearing a Flip-Flopper*. The following day on my desk was *How to Deal with a Difficult Boss* and she was back at work the next morning. We had never discussed the incident.

'I'll be in Tipperary on Monday,' I said happily, looking forward to my next trip. I had given up on my quest to find my happy place after realising the book was a load of rubbish that succeeded only in making me feel worse about myself because I couldn't possibly live up to what it preached. I had brought it to read while sitting at the boathouse in Tipperary one day while Adam was at the office and it had frustrated me so much that I'd tossed it into the lake. Ironically, whenever I think of how I felt in that moment, it brings a smile to my face and an enormous feeling of freedom, a feeling I can summon up on demand.

On our way to get something to eat before Oscar went to catch the bus home again, my phone rang. It was Detective Maguire. I stopped walking, Oscar continued until he realised I was gone.

'Hey, what's wrong?' he called back to me.

I stared at the ringing phone, realising for the first time that I would probably always feel this

371

way about Adam for the foreseeable future, unsure of what his future held, always wondering if he was okay when I wasn't with him. I finally answered it, afraid of what I'd hear but more afraid of ignoring it.

'I'm calling on behalf of Caroline,' he barked. 'It's her sixteenth birthday next week. We're having a party on Friday. You'd swear she was going to the bloody Oscars the way she's going on. Anyway, she wanted you to come.' He cleared his throat and lessened the aggression in his tone. 'And I want you to come too.'

'Thank you, Aidan. I'll be there.'

Before he hung up he added, 'Oh, and bring that man from the bridge too, if you want. If, you know, he's in a good place at the moment.'

Yes, in this moment he was. Life is a series of moments and moments are always changing, just like thoughts, negative and positive. And though it may be human nature to dwell, like many natural things it's senseless, senseless to allow a single thought to inhabit a mind because thoughts are like guests or fair-weather friends. As soon as they arrive, they can leave, and even the ones that take a long time to emerge fully can disappear in an instant. Moments are precious; sometimes they linger and other times they're fleeting, and yet so much could be done in them; you could change a mind, you could save a life and you could even fall in love.

Acknowledgements

I would like to thank my editor Lynne Drew. *How to Fall in Love* is our tenth novel together: I can't quite believe it and I owe so much of my books' successes to you. Thank you for your understanding, patience, support, guidance and genuine excitement about what we're doing and what's to come. I appreciate the freedom given to me to create, and the brain-storming huddle when I need it too. Here's to another ten books! Thank you Thalia Suzuma for such calm and clever insight and for helping me shape the stories. I know, I know, I rush to the ending, always have and always will . . .

Thank you Louise Swannell, Martha Ashby, Elizabeth Dawson, Lucy Upton and Moira Reilly who I have almost daily dealings with, who are nothing less than amazing and make the not-writing-part-of-the-job so much easier and enjoyable.

I'd also like to say a special thank you to Victoria Barnsley, a woman with vision, who will be greatly missed at HarperCollins. Thank you for your wisdom, for your love of books, for your energy in keeping things different and fresh and for your support and belief in me. I wish you the best in the future.

Thank you family and friends for your support and for pretending to be interested when I excitedly announce that I have just thought of a new idea, and for listening to the new ideas, and for never asking what happened to the ideas that aren't realised in books, television or in films, but instead in my head and in notebooks which is equally as enjoyable for me. Thank you for knowing that all that stuff is important to me and for quickly forgetting it and then moving on to talk about proper life things. Thank you all for understanding me. Or pretending to.

Enormous thanks to Marianne Gunn O'Connor who bears the brunt of my constant ideas, emails, phone calls, stories, my 'what ifs' and my 'imagine ifs' and who helps turn my ideas into reality. Some people want things to happen, some people wish for things to happen, some people make things happen. You are one of those people who make it happen. Here's to ten more . . .

Thank you Vicki Satlow for the creative support, for always pushing the boundaries and helping me reach out to more readers across the world. Thanks to Pat Lynch, Mary Lavan and Anita Kissane. Thanks to Liam Murphy for holding parts of my brain together which don't usually go together.

With the subject matter being what it is, even more pressure was on to get it right and so I thank Allison Keating, at bWell Clinic, for your time and feedback on Christine and Adam's story which ultimately forced me to remould it to become a better story. Thanks to Maureen Black and Co. Solicitors for your help on the legal stuff of which I clearly don't have the brain for. To Fr. Michael McCullagh for the Rite of Commital. I took the information given from everybody who was so kind to advise me and then made it my own so if there are any mistakes in this novel, then they are entirely mine. I drew from *How I Stayed Alive When My Brain Was Trying to Kill Me: One Person's Guide to Suicide Prevention* by Susan Rose Blauner in order to understand my characters' journeys.

Thank you David, Robin and Sonny, my crazy little family who are my escapes from my escape world . . .

We do hope that you have enjoyed reading this large print book.

Did you know that all of our titles are available for purchase?

We publish a wide range of high quality large print books including:
Romances, Mysteries, Classics
General Fiction
Non Fiction and Westerns

Special interest titles available in large print are:
The Little Oxford Dictionary
Music Book
Song Book
Hymn Book
Service Book

Also available from us courtesy of Oxford University Press:
Young Readers' Dictionary
(large print edition)
Young Readers' Thesaurus
(large print edition)

For further information or a free brochure, please contact us at:
Ulverscroft Large Print Books Ltd.,
The Green, Bradgate Road, Anstey,
Leicester, LE7 7FU, England.
Tel: (00 44) 0116 236 4325
Fax: (00 44) 0116 234 0205